Katerina Diamond was born in Weston in the seventies, where her parents owned a fish and chip shop in the Greek community. She moved to Thessaloniki in Greece and attended Greek school where she learnt Greek in just 6 months. After her parents' divorce, they relocated to Devon. After working in her uncle's fish and chip shop as a teenager, she went (briefly) to university at Derby, where she met her husband and had two children. Katerina now lives on the East Kent coast with her husband and children. This is her first novel.

KATERINA DIAMOND

The Teacher

This novel is entirely a work of fiction.
The names, characters and incidents portrayed in it are
the work of the author's imagination. Any resemblance to
actual persons, living or dead, events or localities is
entirely coincidental.

AVON
A division of HarperCollins*Publishers*
1 London Bridge Street,
London SE1 9GF

www.harpercollins.co.uk

A Paperback Original 2016

1

A catalogue record for this book is
available from the British Library

ISBN-13: 978-0-00-826370-6

Set in Sabon LT Std by Palimpsest Book Production Limited,
Falkirk, Stirlingshire
Printed and bound in Great Britain by
Clays Ltd, St Ives

MIX
Paper from
responsible sources
FSC™ C007454

FSC™ is a non-profit international organisation established to promote
the responsible management of the world's forests. Products carrying the
FSC label are independently certified to assure consumers that they come
from forests that are managed to meet the social, economic and
ecological needs of present and future generations,
and other controlled sources.

Find out more about HarperCollins and the environment at
www.harpercollins.co.uk/green

Chapter 1

The Headmaster

Jeffrey Stone looked over the sea of despondent young faces as he gave assembly, occasionally glancing up at the steel frame of the atrium. At this time he had no idea that come the morning he would be discovered hanging from it by his neck.

The crisp white shirt collars and fresh faces stared forwards, past Jeffrey and into the space beyond; waiting for that bell. Everyone loved the idea of assembly until they were actually in it and were painfully reminded of the tedium. This ceremony was a strange limbo between work and rest; the calm before the storm. Jeffrey felt as though the clock was louder than his voice. With every tick and pause he expected the bell to ring, to rescue him from the apathetic gaze of both students and teachers. All feigning interest and failing; trying not to excavate their twitching noses. Jeffrey was always as relieved as they were when the end finally came, no longer forced to regurgitate anecdotes that no one wanted to hear, least of all himself.

The first clue to his forthcoming demise came when Jeffrey returned to his office and found the parcel on his desk. Tentatively he tore open the brown paper, as though something about the size and weight of the gift was familiar to him, from a time that he had tried to put out of his mind. Jeffrey's face paled as he stared at the contents of the package. It was an old German book. Of course he knew what it meant. It's not as if this was a bolt out of the blue but it had been twenty years since he had seen this book, twenty years since he had given it as a gift to someone; a ghost. The book was a surprise, but not the unspoken message its very arrival conveyed. It meant the end.

He put the book in the desk drawer, he would deal with it later. He picked up the wrapper and scanned it for information, he saw the handwriting, and the hairs on the back of his neck stood on end as it occurred to him the package had been hand-delivered. Why now? What was different about today? Not that today wasn't as good a day as any to die but over the years Jeffrey had presumed he had been forgotten. Got away with it, maybe. But now he knew that he had not.

He walked through the intricate wainscoted corridors for what he assumed would be the last time, running his fingers along the grain of the oak panels, the arabesque carvings almost worn down completely. Churchill School for Boys had been his home for so long. He wondered who would take his place. This building was centuries old, important to the history of the city of Exeter, one of a handful of gems that survived the Baedecker raids in 1942, Hitler's retaliation on Britain for bombing the towns of Lubeck and Rostock in Germany. It was a calculated attack by the Luftwaffe on the five most beautiful cities from a tourist-information book. During the raids a selection of the population hid in the underground tunnels built originally to bring fresh water into the medieval city. Now the city centre was a mish-mash of handsome old buildings either side of the road that ran straight through from east to west with large, ugly, square brick consolation structures squeezed in between them to hide the gaping holes where the shells had hit. Exeter was still littered with history but was an unforgettable testament to the atrocities that had befallen the country. But not this building, the school stood proud and alone, nestled among trees, a remnant of another time. The rich emerald ivy, always so thick and strong in the summer term, clung to the deep terracotta-red brick structure as though it were trying to pull it back into the ground, to reclaim it. This was one of the reasons he had so much love for the place. The traditional and exquisite among the ugly; the truth laid bare for all to see. This was his school, from the moment he had stepped through the gates as a student he was overwhelmed with a sense of belonging. Yes, Jeffrey could not imagine himself anywhere else.

'Mr Stone?'

Jeffrey turned around to see Avery Phillips walking towards him. Avery was the head boy. His gait displayed a confidence seldom found in the young academics at this school. Avery presented Jeffrey with an envelope.

'What's this?'

'It's the money from the fun run at the weekend, sir. We raised over five hundred pounds.'

'Marvellous, could you take it to the school secretary, though?'

'Yes, sir.' Avery turned about face and headed back down the hall.

'Actually, Avery, would you mind coming to my office for a moment, I have an errand for you.' Jeffrey stood to one side as Avery turned back and manoeuvred past him to take the pole position.

They walked briskly, Jeffrey trying to maintain focus on the back of Avery's head and not those beautiful broad shoulders, or further down. Many a wet Friday afternoon was spent watching Avery and his cohorts scrumming in the mud, wading through the thick gravy in their black shorts, clawing at each other with a carnal rage that plagued Jeffrey's dreams at night; he thought of these sixth formers and his chest would tighten with desire, and other parts besides.

Avery stood in front of the office door so that Jeffrey would have to lean in close to open the door before he could step inside, a wry smile on his face. Jeffrey often felt that Avery was a game player. As he lounged in the chair opposite Jeffrey's desk he sat in what seemed to be the most provocative position, slumped right back with his knees apart, his thighs pulling hard on the seams of his uniform. His head was tipped down and his eyes burrowed into Jeffrey's soul.

'I'll write you a pass, Avery. I need you to go off campus and deliver this note for me.'

'Yes, sir.' Avery's eyes were dancing and the curve of his mouth was somehow conspiratorial, like he knew this was to be their secret.

'It's of the utmost importance that no one knows about this, Avery, no matter what happens.'

'Of course, sir.' He leaned forwards, never breaking eye contact once.

Jeffrey scribbled HE HAS RETURNED on to a piece of paper and stuffed it inside an envelope, writing the name STEPHEN on the front. On a separate piece of paper he scribbled an address and handed both to Avery.

'Take it there, tell no one.' Jeffrey paused, waiting for Avery to leave but Avery held his gaze. 'Oh!' said Jeffrey, reaching into his pocket and pulling out a wad of notes. He handed them all over and the boy smiled. 'I can trust in your discretion?'

'Absolutely, sir.'

Jeffrey knew he could trust Avery because there was nothing he liked better than keeping secrets, Jeffrey had heard the tales of blackmail in the dorms, with compromising photos, exam cheats and even as much as him having dirt on the teachers – who was sleeping with who – to use as possible bribery material for better grades. Yes, Avery was a grade A student. If this hadn't been the end then Jeffrey would never have given the note to the boy, but it was and so no matter the consequences, he had done his part.

Jeffrey peered outside and watched from his office window as Avery left the school; leaving the sanctuary of the grounds. As Avery closed the gate behind him Jeffrey surveyed the area, looking across the empty courtyard at the more modest structure of the boarders' residence. He wondered for a fleeting moment how much time he had left. He should probably call his wife, but what would he say? He picked up the phone and stared at the keypad for a few seconds before dialling zero.

'Hold all my calls for the rest of the day, please, Elaine, I have some important paperwork to get through.' Jeffrey sat in his chair and looked out of the window at the boys running through the grounds; nothing had changed much over his employment at this school, the world outside was different now but here inside the walls of this tribute to a past long since forgotten there was still a gratifying feeling of tradition and ritual that had stood the test of time.

The school day progressed with the usual tedium – he worked through his papers, tied up as many loose ends as possible – but occasionally Jeffrey's mind wandered back to the curious book in his drawer. Jeffrey had always been so careful that no one knew about his proclivities, aware that it would be a career ender for him and he really did love his job, if people only knew how these boys made him feel. For almost thirty years Jeff had worked here, thirty years and no trouble as yet.

The wish to escape the grounds as soon as possible became evident about an hour before the final bell rang. The classrooms got noisier and during the final break of the day the corridors buzzed with the noise of the children who would ordinarily obey the stringent rules about the noise levels around the establishment. When the time finally came, silence overtook the main building as the boarders made their way back to the halls and the day students got on their buses and went home.

He pulled out the book and felt the outside; even the touch of it brought back memories like an old familiar friend. His heart thumped as he traced his fingers across the title of the book: *Das Geschenk*, The Gift. He opened the book and started to read, his German wasn't what it used to be but he knew this book well anyway. A firm believer in the old ways, Jeffrey had acquired this book for its historical relevance, for its insights into his 'condition' and how to change it. The book itself was out of print, rare and hard to find. Someone had gone to a lot of trouble to get this, and he knew who. It had been a companion to him when he had been searching for answers about himself, about why he was the way he was, why he needed to surround himself with pubescent boys, why even the smell of a woman left him feeling cold.

The half-light of the summer night pulled in and Jeffrey opened out his laptop, sure that he was now alone in the building; even the cleaners would be gone. He plugged in his mobile device, not wanting to use the school's network, and logged into a secure online photo storage website, furtively listening out for any noise in the school before entering his password. Folders and folders, each titled with a different year group, and within that a different name in alphabetical order: Jason, Marcus, Robert and so on. Jeffrey's favourites. He wasn't one of these idiots who kept the evidence on his

7

hard drive, he was smarter than that, and he paid good money for his security on the dark net. He clicked the first folder titled 'Daniel' but it would not open, asking for a secondary password – this was not supposed to happen. Panicking, Jeffrey tried to open the other files, but he couldn't. He wanted them gone, deleted, but he couldn't access them. No one knew about these photos, not even the boys themselves. Who could have found out, and how?

He found himself humming an old tune, he stopped but the music continued from somewhere else in the building, faint and familiar. His heart sank, his time had come. Mahler, dark at the best of times, rang out like a toll bell, the all too familiar melody signalling an end that had been written in the stars for decades now.

Jeffrey opened his office door and looked down the corridor, listening. The music was coming from the main assembly hall. He started walking and the music grew louder and more distorted with every step. He remembered the symphony well, today had been full of nostalgia for a time that maybe he shouldn't yearn to return to, a time when he caused so much pain.

This particular piece had the appropriate amount of thrill and dread for Jeffrey's purposes at that time, deliberately ironic that it should be the last thing he ever heard.

He opened the double glass doors and screwed his eyes shut at the volume of the music, the distortion cutting through him. On the elevated platform at the front of the vast room was a chair, hanging above it was a noose. To the left was a table, covered in a red velvet cloth, almost ceremonial in its appearance. On top of the table was a beautiful black wooden box. The music stopped but his ears continued to ring as they adjusted to the silence.

'Hello, old friend.' A man's voice, he didn't recognise it, but it had been so long.

'What do you want?'

'This is not about what I want. This is what must be done.'

'Why today, after all this time?' Jeffrey was afraid to turn around and look at his downfall.

'You don't know what today is? It's been eighteen years. Eighteen years since I saw exactly what kind of monster you are.' The voice was so slow, so completely resolute; it was not as he expected.

'If you think I'm going to hang myself, you've got another think coming.' Jeff looked up at the noose.

'I don't think, I know,' the man whispered with such resolve that Jeffrey understood he was not making a request.

'You'll have to force me and there will be evidence, they'll know it wasn't suicide,' Jeffrey's voice was panicked as he searched for a way out of this; feeling more pathetic with every word he uttered.

'One way or another, you die today. It just works out better for me if it looks like suicide, but I'm happy to do it the fun way.'

'You wouldn't!'

'I would! Make no mistake. I was there, remember? I saw what's inside you. I saw the sickness.'

'You wouldn't tell anyone. Who would believe you over me?'

'The pictures you took speak for themselves. The pictures you took of me back then, not to mention all the other boys since. I see you got rid of the hidden cameras in the changing rooms. Worried someone would figure out how much you like young boys?'

'How did you know about those?'

'I have been watching you. I put a key logger on your computer. That means I've been able to see every key stroke entered, every website, every password, every message you ever sent anywhere. I also put a VPN in. A private network so I have had access to your computer for several weeks now, not just access, but control.'

Jeffrey moved slowly towards the table, aware that the contents of the box could be almost anything, almost certain that it wouldn't be anything as merciful as a gun. He could feel the man was standing close behind him, almost close enough to touch, he thought about reaching forward to pick up the box and swinging it round hard, smashing the bastard's face in. But what if he was wrong? What if he wasn't that close? What would he do to him then? Jeffrey couldn't risk it.

'I never touched any of them!' Jeffrey whispered, aware of how disgustingly feeble he sounded.

'But it's only ever a matter of time when it comes to people like you, Jeffrey. You'll do it again, you won't be able to stop yourself. But even if you don't, you could have a heart attack right here at your desk and when they go through your drawers they'll find that flash drive. I have seen those pictures on those files. I've seen how you watch the boys. How long before you aren't just looking any more? People find those files and they draw their own conclusions.' The voice was so cold, so completely emotionless, not even mocking, nothing. 'Don't forget I saw first-hand how much you like to watch.'

Jeffrey drew in his breath as he felt a hand on the small of his back, slowly travelling upwards, gently sliding between the protruding bones of his shoulders. He imagined the hand on his bare skin as it reached the back of his neck, stroking tenderly, brushing through the sweaty tendrils of his dishevelled hair. His body stirred at the welcome touch of masculine fingers.

'Stop it!'

'I bet you imagined this a hundred times when I was younger, back when I was your type. You wouldn't have told me to stop then,' the man whispered in his ear. 'That's how you like them, isn't it, Mr Stone? Well I'm sorry I'm not that boy any more. I'm a man now.'

'What's in the box?' Jeffrey finally asked as he exhaled.

'Go on and have a look. I know how you like choices, so I'm giving you a choice.'

Jeffrey's hand hovered over the lid of the box. It was hand-carved and valuable, made from black ebony with an undecipherable image etched into the surface. His mouth dried as he opened it to reveal what was inside. It took every muscle he had to hold himself upright as he stared at the contents, feeling the blood drain from his face as the room began to spin.

'Do you know what that is?'

'Yes,' Jeffrey said, although he could no longer hear

his own voice over the sound of his heartbeat in his ears. He looked down at the pear-shaped metal device.

'It's beautiful, isn't it? Look how delicate the embossing is, the level of detail on those leaves,' the voice said, so close to his ear now he could feel the warm breath on his skin. 'Why don't you pick it up?'

'No.'

He felt the man's hand grip the back of his neck, he was strong. The man's body pressed against him in a way that both aroused and terrified Jeffrey. He caught the first glimpse of the man as his hand reached for the instrument in the box. It was big and strong, unfamiliar and yet there was something like déjà vu coursing through Jeffrey's memory.

'There really is something for everyone. I thought this was particularly appropriate for you. The Pear of Anguish. You know, back when these were invented, they believed the sentence had to fit the crime and the punishment should be carried out on the part of your body that had sinned.' He moved even closer to Jeffrey, his grip tightening and his voice lowering to a deep whisper. 'You're a liar and a sodomite . . . Where do you think I should put this?'

'Please . . .' Jeffrey offered futilely.

'Do you remember how these work?' He released Jeffrey and took a step away, taking the pear with him, beginning to pace. 'If I turn this screw at the end then the sides start to expand out, eventually making the circumference three times larger. Let's say, for example, I put it in your mouth. Of course, first I would have to get it past your teeth – that's likely to knock a couple of the front ones out. As it's expanding, of course, it will force most of the rest of them out of their sockets. Without anaesthetic I am sure you can imagine how painful that will be.'

'Stop . . .'

'Then your jaw will dislocate, which will most likely cause swelling in the back of your throat, not to mention how old this is, it's probably rife with bacteria. By the time your airway closes over you will be in so much pain I doubt you will even notice the lack of oxygen. It will be a slow death, hypoxia most likely, as one by one your major organs shut down. The flow of oxygen will be pitiful, but still enough to keep you alive and in agony for a good few minutes. In terms of pain, a minute may as well be for ever.'

'Enough!' Jeffrey shouted, his voice reverberating. He stared down at his clenched fists. They were white with fear.

'Of course, that's only if I put it in your mouth . . . You're not likely to die the other way, although I suspect you'll wish you had.'

'You'll get rid of the photos if I do this?' Jeffrey's heart was in his throat as he looked up at the noose, understanding that he had no choice, that this had always been the only possible end for him.

'You are getting the easy way out, Jeffrey, trust me. I promise I will destroy any evidence if you do this one thing for me. I would rather not draw too much attention to your death. You owe me this much.'

Jeffrey stood up on the chair, the feet sliding against the highly polished wooden floor. Once his neck was inside the noose all he needed was two seconds of insane courage and the decision would be out of his hands.

'I can't.' Jeffrey's voice broke and his eyes prickled with tears, warm, wet fluids ran down his leg on to the chair and floor.

'This will all be over in a few seconds, you can do it, I believe in you.' A little warmth from the cold voice? 'Isn't that what you used to say to me?'

Jeffrey filled his lungs with as much air as possible, as though that might help in some way. The chair wobbled a little and he grabbed hold of the rope; he just couldn't keep his balance. The man finally walked out from behind him and they stood face to face. The man pulled the black hood from his head and looked Jeffrey proudly in the eyes, this was the last thing Jeffrey would ever see. Jeffrey kicked the chair and his feet dropped, for a second he thought he might be able to touch the ground but his feet danced around desperately searching for some leverage and found just more air. The rope burned with each tug but he felt like he had no choice but to struggle, his body still grasping for life whether he wanted it to or not. Then came the darkness, and as his eyes blurred to a sliver, the smile.

Chapter 2

The Father

Adrian Miles' cheeks burned red under the heat of the sun. The sheets stuck to him as he turned over in his bed away from the open blinds. He remembered why he hadn't shut them as he saw the girl stirring next to him. She opened her eyes.

'Good morning.' She smiled. He was glad the sun was in her eyes and she couldn't see him searching his memory for her name. 'I had a great time last night.'

'Me too,' he lied. It was not that he didn't have a great time, he well might have, but the facts were a little blurry.

The phone rang and Adrian was grateful for the interruption.

'I'll just get dressed,' the woman said.

'Hello?' he said into the receiver, his eyes fixed on Hannah? Anna? As she got out of bed she walked across the room naked, sweeping her clothes up off the floor as she went. He couldn't entirely remember at what point over the course of last night he had managed to seal that particular deal. The situation was all too familiar to him. The absence of memory, the nameless semi-clad woman and the realisation that next time maybe he should just go to their place so that he wouldn't have to make nice in the morning. He could just disappear. Not the first time these thoughts had occurred to him, but at the time he was always too drunk to apply any kind of rationale.

'Adrian, I need you to take Tom today,' Andrea said on the other end of the line, her voice as cold and to the point as ever, she never called unless she absolutely had to.

'Hasn't he got school?'

'The school's shut, something's happened over there, sorry this isn't much notice but I need you to take him.'

'Can't he stay home on his own?' Adrian paused before continuing, unwilling to divulge any specific information about his personal life to his ex. He hated having to jump to her commands but ultimately knew he had no choice; not if he wanted to spend time with his son. 'I have to work later.'

'No, he can't, he's thirteen, Adrian, he can't be alone all day, just take him in with you and sit him in the corner, step up to the bloody plate, would you?'

'Hey, you are the one who made the rules and I'm just the one who follows them. I thought you understood how important today is for me . . .' He tried not to sound resentful – it didn't take much to make Andrea angry enough to refuse him access of any kind.

'Don't do it for me, do it for him.'

'Can I use your toothbrush?' the girl called from the bathroom doorway. Adrian cringed before nodding and waving her away, he could hear Andrea's scorn through the receiver. Even though she didn't want Adrian any more, and hadn't done for quite some time, she still managed to make him feel like he was betraying her in some way.

'Is someone there with you?'

'I'll be there in ten minutes.' Adrian hung up and sighed. He walked to the bathroom, the girl stood in her underwear brushing her teeth with his toothbrush. She shot him a foamy smile in the reflection of the mirror. He ignored the pangs of lust as his eyes travelled up and down her body. She spat into the sink and he sighed before saying, 'I have to go, let yourself out!'

Adrian scanned the floor for the cleanest pair of trousers he could find. He caught sight of himself in the full-length mirror. He had scratch marks across his chest and as he ran his fingers over his tired chin he noticed that his stubble was dangerously approaching beard territory. He should probably smarten up before returning to work, but it wasn't going to happen. These small acts of defiance made him feel like a little bit less of a bitch. He pulled yesterday's shirt over his head and grabbed his keys off the bedside table.

Adrian kept the car running and beeped the horn, he saw the neighbours' curtains twitching and decided to

17

beep again, making sure Andrea's neighbours knew that she hadn't always been the princess she was now, she had slummed it once at least. A ten-minute drive and yet it was like being in another world, just three digits on the postcode felt like entering another country, a cleaner, happier country. Not that the lower end of the city was a ghetto or anything. This regency-period neighbourhood stood high above Exeter city centre, past the prison and the red light district, near the University. All the front gardens were vibrant and blooming. The front doors all freshly painted and the lawns mown. Each house had a clear vista of the little people down below. It even seemed sunnier here. The light bounced off the grand white house. The sun was not diffused by the endless grey terraces that surrounded the tiny plot his modest home occupied on the wrong side of town. Tom walked towards the car with his shoulders hunched over, still uncomfortable in his ever-growing frame. He was just a kid, and yet he was only three years younger than Adrian was when he got Andrea pregnant, and now that Tom was an adolescent, Adrian couldn't help but compare himself to him. He reminded Adrian of himself, except Tom didn't have the same hang-ups. At least Adrian hoped he didn't. They say the first-born child always looks most like the father in order to help the bonding process but it hadn't helped much in Adrian's case, if anything it just made him a little sad.

Andrea was standing in the doorway scowling at Adrian, dressed in her power suit, anyone would think she was a lawyer or something, but no, she worked as a personal shopper in a high-end department store, hardly the end of the world if she took the day off. Adrian had fought long and hard for access to Tom and he could not say no to having him, because he knew she would use it against him, that's just who she was. She looked good though, she always had looked good and she probably always would. He reluctantly settled his eyes on the curves of her finely toned body. It was as though she had been sewn into her outfit. There wasn't a wrinkle or a pull in the perfectly tailored ensemble. Her thick black hair was pulled back into a silky bun and the brightness of the diamond studs in her ears flashed against her milk-chocolate skin. People often thought Andrea was Indian or Latin American due to her exotic skin tone but she was in fact half English and half Irish. Adrian looked at her full red lips and looked away before she caught him.

'I'll pick him up later on,' she said before switching tones. 'Love you, baby.'

'Bye, Mum.'

Tom got in and Adrian pulled away. The familiar awkward silence filled the car. Adrian would have liked to attribute this phenomenon to Tom being a teenager, but the truth was it had always been this way between them, every other weekend for the last seven years. Andrea had tried to shut him out completely, underestimating how motivated Adrian would be about this particular subject. He had fallen in love with Tom from the moment he had first seen him, he had tried his hardest to provide for Andrea but nothing he ever did was enough. Before Tom even turned two Andrea had remarried and she and her new partner had tried to block any kind of access for Adrian. He had finally managed to get regular visitation when Tom was six but by then the damage was already done. Tom and Adrian's relationship had been strained ever since.

'So how come your school's shut? Do you know?'

'Yeah, my mate Alex texted me,' Tom said excitedly. 'His dad's a teacher there. They found Mr Stone hanging in the atrium, killed himself, like right in the middle of it.'

'Is that a surprise?' Adrian didn't know much about the school Tom attended, Andrea had always maintained it was the best school in the area and so Tom would go there and that was that. She'd made a point of telling Adrian that his input on this matter wouldn't be needed and so he left all the school stuff to Andrea.

'Shyeah!' Tom looked at his dad like he was crazy. 'Apparently there's going to be some kind of inquiry.'

'No, I mean, did he seem depressed or suicidal or anything?'

'He was pretty miserable but then most of the teachers at that place are, they're all uptight, you know?'

'Still don't like it?'

'It's OK, bit poncey.'

'Well a lot of kids out there wouldn't mind going to that poncey school, Tom.' Even though Adrian himself felt exactly the same way about the school, and there was no way Tom would be going there if it weren't for his stepfather's money.

'I know,' Tom mumbled before slumping back in his seat.

Silence resumed and Adrian kicked himself for pulling out one of those parental lines, he didn't know how to deal with Tom really. His only reference was his own childhood and he knew that was not the norm, so he resorted to using variations on lines he had heard on cheesy sitcoms. To diffuse the silence he turned the radio on, he could feel Tom's disapproval at the folk jingle so he turned to another station. After a few minutes of fiddling with the buttons he gave up and turned it off as they pulled up outside his house.

The one thing Adrian did have right was his lounge. Tom would play it cool but he looked forward to spending time with his father's gaming set-up, if nothing else. Adrian spent most of his money on what most adults referred to as toys. Andrea had never asked for child support because after they broke up she fell into a relationship almost immediately with a much older, much wealthier entrepreneur. Every month since Tom had been born Adrian had used some of his wage to buy a toy for him, but not just any toy, collectable toys. *Star Wars*, *Star Trek*, DC or Marvel, anything that was highly sought after, it would all belong to Tom one day, when he was old enough to appreciate its worth. Every year Adrian would have to insure it all with detailed photographs and lists of everything he owned in case of a house fire, most of it was completely irreplaceable, but it was also incredibly valuable. His whole lounge was shelved from wall to ceiling with pristine boxes on every possible surface. Try explaining to a six-year-old that they aren't allowed to play with any of the cool stuff.

Tom sat in front of the large LED screen and turned it on, the surround-sound kicked in and the whole room came alive. Adrian knew the TV was too big for the room, but he also knew it would win him brownie points so he bought it anyway.

'Have you got "Zombie Flesh Hunters 2"?'

'That's an eighteen.'

'All my friends play it, they'll probably all be online today, I won't tell Mum, I promise.'

'Well, you've only got two hours before I have to go to work,' Adrian said.

'For fuck's sake!'

'Tom!' Adrian shouted, the loudness of his voice rang through him and he took a deep breath, his son stared at him wide eyed. He felt the ghost of his father standing behind him. He shook it off. 'Just watch your language, please, mate.'

'I'm not your mate,' Tom hissed.

Adrian opened the cupboard and tossed the game to Tom, seeing the hint of victory in Tom's hidden smile. Adrian left the room, he hated raising his voice, but even more than that he hated being played.

All traces of Adrian's house guest had gone from the bedroom, the only evidence she had been there was that the bed was made and Adrian's clothes were in the basket instead of on the floor. Even this small deed made him feel trapped. Fear of commitment was an understatement. In Adrian's case, it was a phobia. When Andrea had left him and taken his son he promised himself he would never put himself in that situation again, it was as though his heart had been ripped out. Whoever said it's better to have loved and lost clearly had no fucking idea what they were talking about. In

22

the bathroom Adrian looked in the mirror again. He checked his eyes weren't still bloodshot. As it had been six months since he had been allowed on the premises he probably shouldn't go back to work looking like a drunk, not after the way he had left – or been asked to leave. Last night he had needed the Dutch courage though and so he drank, he met a woman. It was the same old story, just a different night. He got in the shower; he could hear the blood-curdling screams and shotgun blasts through the floor as he washed away his hangover and whatever remained of his interlude.

Adrian stood outside the police station wishing he had never given up smoking. Taking a deep breath he walked through the glass doors with Tom in tow.

'Hey, Tommy.' Denise Ferguson beamed from behind the desk, obviously trying to avoid eye contact with Adrian. He suspected this would not be the last awkward encounter he would have today.

As Adrian pushed the second set of doors open he noticed the volume of the discussion change, along with the pace, everyone slowed down. He felt eyes on him so he kept his eyes on the floor and walked over to his desk.

'Detective Miles?' Adrian looked up. DCI Morris was standing in the doorway to his office. 'Come here, would you?'

Adrian motioned to Tom to wait there before walking into the DCI's office. Tom pulled out his phone and started messing around, headphones in to avoid being patronised by any of his dad's colleagues. Morris closed the door behind Adrian, who was glad to be out of that room for a moment. Morris had a warm smile on his face which made Adrian feel ill at ease.

'DCI Morris,' Adrian said.

'Take a seat, please, Adrian.'

Adrian sat in what felt like the naughty chair, you didn't get invited in here for just anything, a serious chat was at hand. DCI Morris didn't look a day older than the first time Adrian had met him almost twenty years ago. Of course, when Adrian met him he looked about sixty. It was the bald head; it's hard to age a man without any hair at all. Adrian realised this after taking a few witness statements in the early days – if there was a bald man involved you could pretty much forget a reliable description, witness accounts would span teenagers, pensioners and everything in between, depending on the visual capabilities of the witnesses themselves.

'Sir.'

'It's good to have you back, you've been missed.'

'Look, sir, about what happened—'

'As far as I am concerned, Adrian, it's over and done with now, things happen, they shouldn't but they do. The inquiry is over and I think six months is quite enough time to get yourself sorted. A "No further action" order is better than nothing. At least next time you will know to take a little more care when logging evidence.'

'There won't be a next time, sir.' Adrian cringed. 'And thank you for speaking to the commission on my behalf.'

'You did your time, we all make mistakes, I have had a few mishaps myself over the years.' Morris looked up as there was a gentle tap on the glass door. 'Ah, speaking of mistakes.' He took a deep breath and signalled to the woman standing outside the office. 'Come in!'

'DCI Morris? I'm Imogen Grey.'

'Yes, I know who you are. Perfect timing, come in and sit down, please, DS Grey.'

The scruffy brunette sat down next to Adrian and immediately started picking her thumbnails anxiously and biting her lip. She was wearing a shapeless sweat-shirt and baggy combat trousers. She crossed her legs away from Adrian without looking at him once.

'Sorry I'm late.'

'DS Grey, I would like you to meet DS Miles, you will be working together for the foreseeable.'

'Guv?' Adrian interrupted. Was she here to make sure he didn't mess up again?

'I know it's not ideal but Grey's just transferred up from Plymouth and I need someone I can trust to show her the ropes.'

'Babysit, you mean?' Grey scowled. Adrian realised he wasn't the one who was being monitored here; she was defensive and hostile about something. She was in the doghouse, too.

'Oh good, a couple of sulky teenagers, you two should get on like a house on fire.' Morris walked towards the door. 'I'll leave you alone to make your introductions.'

She didn't turn to look at Adrian. Instead she feigned interest in the standard-issue police posters. He knew what she was waiting for, she was waiting for him to speak first. It was a game, a manipulation. It was childish. He respected that.

'Well, you must have done something really fucked up to get stuck with me,' Adrian laughed and stood up. 'Come on, let's go and get your access codes sorted out.'

'Why? What did you do?' For the first time since she had entered the room she looked at him and he saw her face properly. Her freckled skin was peeling across her nose and cheeks, she spent a lot of time outside. Her hazel eyes were framed by the longest blackest eyelashes he had ever seen. Not a trace of make-up and he had no idea how old she was, her clothes suggested she was a fifteen-year-old boy.

'Lost some evidence, let a major local dealer walk. You know, a real career-defining moment.'

'Are you always this forthcoming?' Grey's face softened to reveal a cheeky smile. Adrian suspected that she was relieved that he was out of favour too.

'Definitely not. But if we're stuck together I would rather you heard it from me, Grey.'

'I guess that makes sense.' She smiled begrudgingly.

'So what did you do?' Adrian held the door open, instantly realising his mistake as she grabbed the door and signalled him out first.

'None of your business.' She winked, he almost thought she was going to slap his backside and, unless he was mistaken, the thought had crossed her mind too.

Chapter 3

The Taxidermist

She stared into the beady eyes of the dead cat, its lustrous fur still soft to the touch. As her finger brushed against the side of its hardened stomach she saw the dust erupting in tiny clouds. She put a yellow sticker on the animal, yellow means 'restore', this animal needed to be returned to its former glory, or as close an approximation as anything dead can have to something that was once alive. Abbey Lucas had worked in the Eden House Memorial Museum for five years now, she never ventured out on to any of the four main exhibition rooms, hardly spoke to any of the other staff and never dealt with the public, she just stayed here in the archive rooms. For the last five years she had been working her way through the thousands of stuffed animals, from kangaroo to platypus, from a common goat to this stunning example of evolution, the cheetah. She

27

wondered why no one ever bothered to stuff cows or sheep, maybe they were too boring to part with your money over. Although, Abbey had always thought cows were rather beautiful, with their big sad brown eyes.

Abbey walked down to the lobby, the porters were bustling. They were just reassembling the lobby after a week's closure in order to redecorate it. The whole building was undergoing refurbishment after a large sum of money was bequeathed to the museum when the former director died just a few months ago. They had been trying for the last fifteen years to get the funding to put the place back together. Only fourteen of the possible thirty-two exhibition rooms had been open to the public for quite some time, with most of the smaller ones on the second floor closed. The museum had been ravaged by an electrical fire around twenty years ago, bad wiring and a faulty circuit breaker had caused damage to at least a quarter of the building. As the owners had been unable to fix the place straight away, some of the rooms had been cordoned off or used as storage until they had enough money to go ahead with the refurb. The Neo-Gothic museum, built in the eighteenth century, housed various Celtic and Roman artefacts that had been discovered in the local area. It was also home to a huge menagerie of various animals, costumes and fossils. Fortunately the damage was predominantly cosmetic. The new colour on the walls was vermillion red, almost a bright orange. Abbey didn't think it belonged in a place like this, it was garish and distasteful. The red was a far cry from the drab Georgian grey that had been the colour in every single exhibit room since she had started here. Now each room had an accent colour, as per the interior designer's remit. Of course the most striking had to be the entrance. It was less of an accent colour and more of a full assault on the senses.

'Abbey!' Mr Lowestoft, the director, exclaimed with a winning smile. He was a gentle old man. Like a grandfather, with his round glasses, ruddy cheeks and novelty dickie bow, he always brought a warm feeling to her. It had been that way from the start. He had not only welcomed her but made her feel like this was her home. Every time he said hello it was as though he were greeting a beloved family member. Mr Lowestoft was one of the few people in the world who put her at ease.

'Mr Lowestoft, hello.' She smiled, a real smile full of genuine warmth, truly glad to see the old man. His presence in the museum had decreased since he had received the cancer diagnosis. A finished, fully functioning museum was to be his parting legacy.

'Ah, Abbey, I was hoping you would be here. What do you think? Do you like it?' He beamed, glowing with pride.

'It looks amazing.' She didn't have the heart to tell him anything different.

'I've been asked by the University if we would accommodate one of their PhD students for the foreseeable future while he writes his thesis on historic preservation, or something to that effect. I thought you would be the best person to deal with him.'

'Me?' She didn't know what else to say to that. She was used to working alone, she liked it that way.

'Oh, and I've got another surprise for you! Come and see!' He walked over to something large covered in a sheet, reluctantly she followed. She hated surprises. He pulled at the sheet and she was confronted with the grimacing mask of a samurai looking down on her from his lofty frame. His rigid leather body armour was polished to the point where she could see her reflection. 'I never understood why we keep this hidden upstairs. It's one of my favourite pieces.'

An evil grin was spread across the surface of the mask and a gaping black hole where the eyes should be. The demonic red horns that protruded from the helmet and towered above the face were razor sharp, menacing. She had forgotten just how vile the warrior's face was. It had been years since she had seen him, always walking the long way around to avoid ever walking in his path. The face had always seemed so inhuman and she could feel the black nothing staring into her. Involuntarily she found herself stepping backwards. She didn't want to have a panic attack; she had to get away from him.

'It looks perfect here.' She stepped back further, flustered, off balance.

'Are you all right, Abbey?'

'Yes, I'm fine. I just need to use the bathroom.'

Abbey rushed into the toilets reserved for the public and dabbed her face with cold water, trying to normalise the temperature of her skin. She could feel it burning. She really didn't like surprises.

Abbey emerged from the bathroom into the empty hallway. The silence of the museum magnified her solitude, the faint whisper of the atmospheric music in a distant corner of the museum at the edge of her hearing. She turned the corner and bumped straight into the security guard.

'Busy day?' Shane Corden was standing in her way. His bleached-blonde hair stuck to his glistening forehead.

'Yes.' She tried to manoeuvre around him but he side-stepped into her path again. He would play these games purely because he knew it disturbed her. 'Excuse me, I have to help get ready for the reopening. We've only got a couple of months. Don't you have somewhere to be?'

'Doesn't it bother you? Touching dead stuff all day?' He sucked on his bottom lip slowly and stared at her mouth.

'Not really.' She tried again to move around him but this time he just moved closer. She could smell cigarettes and alcohol on his breath as he stood almost toe to toe with her. It's just a game, he doesn't know anything, she repeated to herself over and over. She had to decide between looking him in the eyes or shifting her gaze and staring down at her feet. She wanted to do the latter but that's what he wanted too. So she would stare him down, hoping to God he couldn't see the darkness behind her eyes. She knew all he wanted was to make her feel uncomfortable. To exercise the tiny bit of power he had in this world over someone he knew he could get a reaction from. He liked to play this game with someone who was easily flustered.

His eyes dropped to her chest, hidden beneath the olive green blouse. She tried not to breathe hard as she didn't want to give him any more food for thought.

She could feel her lungs tightening and her mouth desperate to suck in more air. She would rather pass out than give him the satisfaction. Instead he backed away, eyes still fixed on her body.

'Have a good one then.' He smiled, his hand firmly on his baton, finger circling the tip. She slowly exhaled as invisibly as possible. He was such a creep, but at least he was honest about it. Before she had fully filled her lungs again he was gone. She scuttled back to her darkened corner of the museum. That was enough social interaction for one morning.

Abbey went to the museum canteen at noon, as always, to pick up her lunch, which she ate at the same table every day. Routine was everything, right down to the brown corduroy skirt she wore at the end of every week. It didn't take much to bring on her anxieties. Luckily this was not a popular or busy museum, if people were curious about anything these days they would just look it up on the internet, this suited Abbey just fine. Today she had a tuna sandwich; Friday was fish day at the museum, Mr Lowestoft insisted on this throwback to a more religious time, when people had values.

Abbey genuinely loved her job, she could not imagine doing anything else. She liked the familiarity of working with the same people every day, good people, and aside from Shane they were mostly sensible people. Abbey also liked that she got to spend most of her days alone, with only the dead for company.

'Is this seat taken?'

Abbey looked up at the stranger, her mouth full of

food, she chewed quickly to reply. The canteen was empty and she couldn't say it was taken. Did he just want the chair? Was he going to sit with her?

'No,' she finally managed.

He put his tray down opposite her and sat down, smiling. He took his coat off and hung it on the back of the chair, making himself comfortable. He was a young, slender man with black floppy hair. Although definitely older than her, she couldn't quite place his age. He looked eccentric, different. The most remarkable thing about him though were his eyes, they were cold and grey like cut glass, Abbey had to force herself not to stare.

'I'm Parker, Parker West.' He held his hand out to her over the table. She rubbed her palm on her skirt to remove any traces of tuna mayonnaise and then shook his hand.

'Hello.'

'You're Abigail Lucas?' He smiled again, she could not hide her surprise – how did he know her name?

'Who—'

'Oh, they didn't tell you? I'm going to be helping you with the archives. I have a masters in zoological archaeology and I'm working towards my PhD,' he said, almost embarrassed.

'Oh, yes, Mr Lowestoft did mention it. I didn't realise it would be today.'

She had already worked her way through Australasia and Southern America on her own, cataloguing every single animal, noting down its region and its place on the food chain. Up till now she alone had the power to decide the fate of these creatures. She could mark the animal for restoration or for destruction. Where possible she was to save the animals, although it felt so futile – so far she had condemned over two hundred animals to the incinerator, their final resting place. The worst cases were in the northeast corner of the building where there had been a leak in the roof that had gone unnoticed for far too long. She hadn't been able to save any of those, the mould and rot had set in so much that their deterioration had sealed the deal. She wasn't sure if she trusted a stranger with this responsibility.

'He just said you could probably do with a hand. This museum has a particularly quantitative supply of species and sub-species; it's a lot for one person to get through . . . in two months, is it?'

'I can manage it,' she said apologetically, internally scolding herself for apologising at the same time.

'Oh, no one said you can't. To be honest with you, I volunteered, no one is paying me. I'm writing a paper for my PhD, you see, well I won't bore you with the details of it but you would be doing me a huge favour if you would allow me to tag along, I might even be able to offer you my expertise with the identifications at least; you would obviously have to handle the actual restorations.'

'If you think . . .'

'The final decision is yours, my fate is in your hands.' He had a soft, pleading but mischievous look in his eyes, she wanted to smile at him, she wouldn't because that's not who she was. People, she knew, are rarely who they show themselves to be. There is always a lie, always a mask.

'Hello, Parker, you can call me Abbey,' she said after a pause. She would just have to deal with it.

'Nice to meet you, Abbey.' He half smiled. His anticipation was evident as he ploughed his way through his lunch, raring to go, eager to meet her dead little friends.

She thought of all the animals she had already worked through alone and decided maybe this wasn't the end of the world, it didn't mean that Mr Lowestoft didn't trust her, it just meant she could take her time and not worry so much about the self-imposed deadlines she had assigned. The hardest decision she had made on her own so far was on a small creature whose identification numbers had been ruined by water and damp, she did not recognise the animal and could not find it in any of the encyclopaedias. Maybe it was stored in the wrong part of the world, but there was no saving her – she knew the creature was a female, her teats were still enlarged from recent motherhood. Abbey wondered what had happened to this little beast. Her cheeks had been ravaged by termites but her black eyes were so calm. As Abbey had fingered the tiny bullet hole in the animal's chest, a spider had crawled out and she dropped the animal in shock, smashing what was left of her face. Abbey could not stop the tears as she placed the red sticker on the small animal, wondering if her children had befallen the same fate or if they had made it, at least for a little while. She wondered if they had got the chance to have children of their own; she liked to think they had.

When she took Parker through to the floor where all of the Asian cadavers were kept she saw how exhilarated he was, his eyes transfixed and wide, like a child on their first trip to a toy shop, not knowing where to start, unsure what to break first.

'Follow me.' She led him to the far end of the room, her voice echoed as did her footsteps when her shoes thumped against the polished wooden floors. The room itself was lit from a double row of green glass bricks slotted in above where the original windows had been, long since boarded up to accommodate the large metal shelving units that had been put in after the fire; metal didn't burn like wood. Everything in the room had taken on a hint of pale green as though it had been dipped in Chartreuse, a warm honey-green liquor. They could hear the music from the next room seeping in through the metal ventilation grates that sat above the oak skirting. It was the same music that had played every day since she had started. She didn't know what it was called but it was classical, sometimes the melody would run through her mind as she tried to sleep at night. She looked over at Parker, noticing him trying to take it all in, looking up and down, occasionally uttering an exclamation at something he had seen.

'So incredible,' he muttered. She got the impression he didn't mean to say that out loud. Usually when people learned what Abbey did they pulled a face and said something like 'Oh, that's nice' in the worst impression of a sincere voice they could muster, the idea of stuffing dead animals was completely repulsive to them, although they were entirely missing the point. Parker's response was a refreshing change, she was proud of her occupation; it was all she had.

'We basically operate on something similar to the Dewey decimal system, so the first two numbers correspond to a continent, then the next three numbers the species, followed by—'

'Yes, I know how it works.'

'OK, sorry.'

'No, I didn't mean to be rude, please, just ignore my . . . personality, sometimes I can be a bit . . . I'm sorry. Thanks for taking the time to explain it to me. Carry on.' He fumbled for words, this time she couldn't help but smile a little.

'You need to mark the animals down against the numbers on this register and then you need to mark whether they are to be kept or not. Anything that can be restored needs a yellow sticker and put a red one on the ones that are beyond saving.' She handed him the stickers.

'Nothing is beyond saving,' he said thoughtfully as he stared at the coloured sheets in his hand, his eyes looking through the paper and beyond. She studied his face for a moment, unable to look away. His skin was so pale and his hair so black against it. The gentle curls undermining his angular bone structure. He looked up quickly, drawing in his breath, as though for a moment he forgot he was not alone.

Abbey watched Parker working. Once he had begun to work he had not uttered a single word to her. She occasionally heard him mumbling to himself but essentially it was no different than working alone. The silence was not strained or awkward, it was just silence, something they were obviously both comfortable with. From time to time he would pull out a well-worn leather pocket book and scrawl something inside it, then put it back in his inside pocket. She wondered what he was writing, what was his paper about?

The day was drawing to a close, the natural light from the high-set windows changing to an orange glow as the sunset drew closer.

'Parker!' Abbey called for the fourth time, trying to snatch his attention as he scribbled furiously in his notepad, engrossed. He looked up, startled, almost scared, then his face softened into a smile as if he'd just awoken from a nightmare and pulled back into reality.

'What time is it?' He looked up at the windows, almost surprised at the warm dusk light that had crept up on them.

'It's seven p.m. now, I don't normally work this late but we did make a lot of progress, you have been a great help.'

'Yikes! Seven! I should get home.'

'Sorry, I should have thought, your wife must be worried.'

'Yes, Sally will be worried . . . and she will probably want feeding and some exercise.' He smirked at Abbey's confused and slightly embarrassed face. 'She's my dog.'

Abbey blushed, hoping to God he didn't think she was fishing for information, she wasn't, she wouldn't. Somehow she knew the thought never crossed his mind.

*　　*　　*

After Parker's departure, the museum was desolate. Abbey was just leaving when she walked past the front desk. The samurai was standing ever poised in his glass case by the entrance. The hairs on the back of her neck stood up on end as she allowed herself to properly look at him in this light. He was still, he couldn't hurt her or anybody else, but still she felt him staring, his hand on his katana.

'Still here?'

She spun round to see Shane right behind her, he was just wearing a white vest, the anthology of his life exposed in the form of tattoos. The ink consisted of tribal markings and thorny roses, a clichéd assortment. He flexed his muscles as he pulled his shirt on, she was unsure what he was trying to achieve, was he trying to frighten her? Even though she was alone she didn't feel scared of him.

'I'm just leaving now.' She moved towards the door.

'I saw you with that weird guy, the new one.' Shane smiled and moved in closer as he did up the buttons on his shirt. 'He's too good for you. You know that, don't you?'

Abbey put her hand on her bag; it wouldn't take much to just glide her fingers inside it. Her tools were in there along with her trusty scalpel. He wouldn't even feel the blade sink into his skin, the steel was so sharp it would only occur to him when he saw the blood and clutched at his throat, desperate to stop his life from ebbing away. She knew where to cut him so it would be quick, she knew her way around a scalpel. She wondered if the arterial spray would even show up on these hideous red walls. She moved her hand away and placed it on the handle to the external door.

'Don't forget to lock up,' she said as she slipped outside, her heart thumping. She looked down the museum steps to see Parker standing there, waiting. 'I thought you went home?'

'It occurred to me you were on your own in the museum with Shane, and I can see you don't care for him much.'

'How do you know that?' Abbey said as she walked down the steps towards him. She didn't like the idea that anyone knew what she might be thinking or feeling, that those things might be obvious in any way made her feel exposed.

'I just notice things like that,' he said quietly, before taking a deep breath. 'I thought maybe I could walk you home, it's almost dark.' He shuffled uncomfortably.

'What about your dog?' Abbey looked back up at the museum and saw Shane coming outside hurriedly, she saw his eyes searching until they met hers and brightened a little, before his gaze shifted a little and he saw Parker standing next to her. Shane's disappointment was evident as his lopsided sneer turned into a scowl.

'She will get over it, we have an understanding.' He smiled and followed Abbey, she turned to see Shane walk in the other direction as Parker remained oblivious to his presence.

For the next few weeks Abbey and Parker worked in silence. His enthusiasm for the task was unrelenting, every day he would be there early, ready and raring to go, working through lunch and at the end of the day he would wait for her outside and walk her home. He never bothered her with silly questions or idle small talk, for most of the time Parker was lost in his own world. At work he would often pull out his little black pocket book. Sometimes she would watch him and smile as he struggled to get the words on to the page fast enough in his excitement.

'So, why here? There are plenty of other museums that have big archives like this one, bigger even,' she finally broke the silence one day during what was supposed to be the lunch hour. She had taken to bringing her sandwiches into the dusty old store room, feeling guilty that he would be sitting in there alone if she went to the cafeteria.

'When I was a boy my parents brought me to this museum. I spent a lot of time in this place. I loved all the reconstructions of the Roman occupation and the artefacts and relics that were found in the local area, but they don't make you think like the animals do. I would sit and stare at the dioramas and feel completely lost in them. There used to be a bench opposite the African desert display where a lion had sunk its teeth into a buffalo. I would just imagine I was either the hunter or the prey, how it would feel to be one or the other, if it was even possible to understand being both.' He swallowed and closed his eyes, a thought he couldn't shake. He took a deep breath before starting again, a forced smile on his face. 'This is where it all started for me, this is where I decided what I wanted to do with my life, it was a bit of a eureka moment, so this place has always held a special place in my heart.' He spoke with a wistful tone to his voice. She could almost see his memories and his pleasure in revisiting them, then something else, fleeting sadness, a less pleasant memory, perhaps.

'I always wanted to be a vet, but I dropped out of uni and here I am.' She took a bite of her sandwich, unwilling to continue talking in case she said something she regretted.

His simplicity was magnetic to her, it had been years since anyone had fascinated her so much, he was almost like a child in his animated way of moving and speaking and yet, just like at that moment, occasionally she would see a melancholy about him, something she couldn't identify but something so precious that she just wanted to tell him it would all be OK. A lie, for sure, but she knew he needed comfort from something, she just didn't know what. He put her at ease and she trusted him, despite not knowing him for long. He was nothing like anyone she had ever met, although it had been a long time since she had met anyone new.

'What is it?' he asked, she realised she had been staring at him, she blushed and looked away.

'I'm sorry, I'm not used to working with people, I'm usually up here alone, and I didn't mean to stare.'

He didn't say anything, just smiled, a consoling smile. He didn't push the issue but it was too late, she felt her cheeks burning red.

The rest of the day passed without any conversation, without any incident, and Parker walked out at five o'clock exactly. She wondered if she offended him with her question, if his past was somewhere he didn't want to revisit. She really wasn't used to dealing with people, or, in particular, men. When she finally came to leave, Parker was there, leaning against the street lamp, brows furrowed, concentrating on the notebook in his hands. When he looked up and saw her, the tension left his face, melted away and was replaced with the most genuine smile. She felt special for a moment. It had been a long time since she felt that way. If she had to put a number on it she would say it had been five years. It was five years since she had left college, five years since she had to restart her life all over again.

Chapter 4

The Fresher

Then

The radio hummed softly, barely audible but just loud enough to quash any fear Abbey might have of being alone.

The street light shone through the window and lit up the room making it impossible to relax. Abbey wasn't much of a sleeper anyway, which was a shame because she had no social life.

She looked across the room at her roommate Dani's bed, it was empty and made; the curse of the pretty girl. Dani's bed was a deep purple and gold with saris draped from the ceiling. Even Danielle's vibrant posters were framed and hung in a precise manner, not like the dog-eared gig posters that hung on Abbey's side of the room.

Dani swung open the door and flopped on the bed,

a grin plastered across her face as she kicked off her heels.

'I've met the man I'm going to marry.'

Abbey sat up. When Abbey had first laid eyes on Danielle she had subconsciously tugged at her sweater, making sure it covered as much of her as possible. It was at that point that Abbey realised her role for the rest of the academic year – the weird one who bunked with the hot girl. What made things even worse was that Dani was just about the nicest person Abbey had ever met, probably because she had no insecurities and no reason to feel threatened by anyone really. They became good friends in no time.

'His name's Christian, he's just such a babe, I just met him over at Bar 42.'

'Christian Taylor?' Abbey knew who he was, of course she did, every girl on campus knew who he was.

'Mhm, he gave me his number, we're going out this week sometime,' Danielle squealed.

Christian was the boy at uni, THE boy, the one they all wanted, the trophy, the prize. He was the reason to wear a short skirt and the incentive to wear your hair up all pretty. He got in free to all the cool bars, the waitresses would slide him free drinks and the managers would turn a blind eye, knowing that where he went, the rest followed. Abbey was almost certain that Danielle had positioned herself in such a way that Christian could not help but notice her, she made sure they accidentally bumped into each other. Dani had just climbed up a few rungs on the social-status ladder.

When Abbey awoke the next morning Danielle was

in the shower. Abbey looked at the clock, she was late. She jumped out of bed and threw yesterday's clothes on, still in a pile at her bedside. Abbey was scrambling around the room that she shared with Danielle frantically searching for her left army boot.

'Hello.' Abbey spun around to see Christian in the doorway. She froze, and her heart was thumping. She had never seen a man quite as handsome as him before, he was twenty years old and his dark blond curls fell to his shoulders like a frame for his perfect face, he invoked a feeling of sexuality in Abbey that she hadn't felt before – pure desire. Her mouth watered just looking at him. His friend Jamie hovered behind him nervously, well aware that he paled in comparison, obviously torn between jealousy and hero worship.

'Hi,' Abbey finally managed to utter. 'Dani's in the shower.'

'And you must be Abbey.' He leaned forward and shook her hand, beaming a smile that made her knees weak. Even the people she considered her closest friends struggled to remember Abbey's name.

At that moment, Dani walked in with her perfectly tanned skin still glistening from the hot shower, her hair wet.

'Oh, hi, I didn't expect to see you so soon,' she giggled. Abbey was unfamiliar with this side of Danielle, she usually liked to dominate a situation but this time she was letting him be the man while she played at the ditsy blonde.

Jamie completely refused to even acknowledge Abbey's existence. Instead he stared at Danielle as though she were an untouchable goddess. Abbey was all too familiar with the type of boy Jamie was, he was ordinary looking, not ugly, but no one ever looked twice at him and he seemed crippled with insecurity and anger. He wanted the Danielles of this world not the Abbeys and he resented the idea that he was doomed to spend the rest of his life settling for, well, himself. To him the girl you had on your arm was a statement about who you were as a person, it didn't matter what they thought or did, it mattered what they looked like. He wanted other men to be jealous like he was jealous of Christian. It's a hard life being the best friend of an Adonis. Abbey knew this all too well, she was the Jamie in her friendship with Dani and she wanted nothing to do with him. She didn't want to be told that she couldn't have the Danis and the Christians if that's what she wanted.

The summer term was upon them and exam fever had hit hard. House parties were everywhere, it was the only way to get through the stress for the people who took their subjects seriously, for the slackers it was a perfect excuse to get wasted, everyone's a winner. Summer was a time of unity at the University – 'we are all in this together' – everyone sympathetic to everyone else's pressures and self-imposed expectations. It was a short semester and the campus was often deserted during that time. Abbey was dressed ridiculously inappropriately for such a warm day, stonewashed skinny jeans and a white crochet jumper, not a pretty white either, a white that's gone slightly grey in the wash. Her outfit did nothing for her rosy cheeks or her mousy hair, under all the clothes she had a better-than-average body, but you would never know it to look at her, her attire was more suited to a WI meeting.

'Abbey, wait up.' Christian was rushing towards her as she walked away from her room and she became aware of how ridiculous she must have looked, she wished there was a phone booth nearby so she could run in and out like a superhero, so that when he reached her she would be standing there in something pretty, something fashionable or attractive, but it wasn't going to happen.

'Hi,' she muttered, unsure what else to say, *I think I love you* seemed a little extreme given the circumstances.

'There's a party tonight at my place, Dani's coming, you should come too.' A personal invitation, she couldn't say no, she wanted to but she knew she wouldn't allow herself to, so better just to accept it now.

'Cool.' She struggled to get out anything meaningful, one-word sentences were as much as she could muster.

Abbey stared at herself in the mirror, she could be dressed in nothing but a bikini, her presence would still be dwarfed by the supernova that is Danielle. She hated herself for being jealous but just once she wanted to know how it felt to be desired, to be special.

'Wear this.' Dani flung a purple dress at Abbey. 'Trust me, it's my lucky dress.' Abbey felt the fine silk between her fingers and wondered how it would feel against her chunky thighs. She was the same dress size as Danielle but there is something about confidence that makes everything fit better. The purple dress was backless and shorter than anything Abbey would usually dare to wear.

'You don't think it will make me look like . . .'

'Like what?' Dani looked at her. Abbey was aware she should choose her next words carefully.

'I don't know, like I'm trying to be you? Single white female and all that.'

'Do you honestly give a shit what any of those people think?' Abbey loved how Dani referred to her friends as 'those people', it was part of what made Dani friends with everyone, she knew how to make you feel like you mattered, even if you really didn't. Abbey first saw Dani as one of those seemingly transparent people who were exactly the same on the inside as the outside, but the more time they spent together the more she realised Dani was a shrewd politician who liked to keep her options open, never upsetting anyone, never taking sides. It was probably a characteristic Abbey should pay attention to as she was always tipping her hand, showing all her cards and leaving herself open to attack.

Abbey slid the dress over her head conscious of the fact that this particular style of dress didn't allow for a bra, she felt her nipples press against the fabric, aware that with movement and friction she would not only be buoyant and full but leaving very little to the imagination.

'Jamie is totally going to lose his shit over you.' Dani beamed.

Jamie. Great. There's one thing Abbey knew for sure and that was that Jamie would never see her as anything more than a consolation prize. She was trying to ignore the hypocrisy of the fact that she wasn't interested in Jamie because he wasn't good enough, wasn't Christian.

Abbey still felt pangs of guilt as his name popped into her head. She wondered if Dani would still lend her the dress if she knew what Abbey was thinking, and she reckoned she would. Dani didn't worry about anyone stealing her man, least of all Abbey.

Chapter 5

The Businessman

Ian looked on nervously at the auditing team huddled together in the glass conference room, they were pointing out numbers to each other with puzzled faces as they clearly struggled to make sense of the accounts, this was their second week in the building and it wouldn't be long before they found the root of the problem, before they realised how bent Ian really was. Ian was good with numbers, really good, maybe a little too good as he believed in formulas, in a mathematical loophole for every situation, which is how he got into this mess in the first place. He was actually surprised how much he had gotten away with for so long. He had pushed the boundaries so many times and when no one noticed, he pushed more, until he was out of control.

He tried to read their lips, to see how close they were

to pinpointing the exact accounts that were faked. One of the men looked up and over to him, he nodded at Ian and then huddled protectively over his pile of papers. Ian's property business had been on the brink of failure for several years now. Ian spotted an opportunity and he took it. Although he was the owner of the company he still had shareholders to answer to and they weren't too fond of the company money being used to take risks, small or big. He took out loans against the business and gambled the money away on pretty much anything. Believing he had worked out a system with which to triple his investment and put it back before anyone noticed it was gone. He had a couple of successes but infinitely more failures, and so he borrowed money from friends and associates to make the loan repayments. If it had stopped there he might have been able to make his way out of this somehow, but of course he hadn't, because Ian was too clever for his own good.

'Mr Markham?' His six-months-pregnant secretary was standing next to him, resting a document box on her bump. He looked down at it, feeling the blood drain from his face.

'What is it, Emma?'

'I found this one in the back of Don's old office, he must have left it there by accident; do you want me to take it through to them?' Ian grabbed the box with a big smile.

'No, you go for your break now, you've done enough heavy lifting for one day. I'll take it.'

'Brilliant, thanks.' He watched her waddle off back to her station to get her nutrition shake. He could feel the panic rising in his throat as he walked towards the conference room. Instead of walking in, he entered the stairwell and made a break for the car park.

He clutched the box full of incriminating evidence and went down the stairs as fast as he could without falling. A year ago he had started a build in Malta, beach-front holiday properties, luxurious apartments with a place to dock your boat at the marina thrown in for good measure. A bargain at half the price, which is a ridiculous saying that he had never really understood, but it seemed to do the trick when he told people about it, he would show them the plans, the papers and the official artistic impressions of the stunning complex. He sold the apartments off plan and then the proceeds would go towards paying for the completion of the project, or that was the idea. The trouble was not only did Ian sell the apartments, he had already sold the land along with the planning permission, so he was basically selling something he didn't own any longer. Even with all the demands for answers, by the time they had waded through all the bureaucratic nonsense overseas it would be months before anyone would know what happened. Ian had funnelled that money through a ghost company and then used it to buy stock options, several bad decisions later and he was back to square minus twenty, owing a lot of people a hell of a lot of money.

He looked at the poster in the dingy car park. 'Say no to drugs' it said. It had been put up after a stint of muggings by crack addicts had taken place in the area. Ian would be a damn sight better off if he had a drug addiction – with Ian's problem he had lost a lot more money in a lot less time. A hundred on the dogs, then a grand on the horses, followed by ten thousand pounds worth of useless high-risk shares. It escalated quickly and beyond anything he had imagined. That's the problem when you can't admit you have a problem, you stop controlling it, it starts controlling you.

'Shit,' he muttered as he struggled with the box, trying to reach inside his jacket for the keys to his Aston. He dropped the box on the floor, its contents spilling out into a puddle, and he scooped it all back in again and unlocked the car door. Wedging the box in the passenger foot well and throwing his jacket on top to obscure it, he started the car and pulled away, checking constantly in the rear view mirror, making sure no one had seen him. It was lunch time, they wouldn't realise for a while and by then it would be too late. He drove out of the city to the safety of his converted barn house nestled in the bosom of the rolling Devonshire hills.

He felt a pang of regret as he drove towards the house – not for the money, he had taken it and he had spent it, he didn't regret that; part of him was a little relieved that it was all coming to an end, too. The regret he felt was for his wife, Debbie, they had lovingly restored the barn together, before all the money, before the job even, before everything. Debbie had been out shopping when her card for their joint account was declined, so she rang the bank to check why only to find the account was not only empty but in arrears. She had spoken to Ian about it and he had lied to her face, saying there must have been some mistake. The next day he put the money back, not his money, someone else's money. It had satisfied Debbie enough to not look into the matter any further, until a few months later when she accidentally opened some of Ian's post, talking about the re-mortgage agreement and how he was behind on the repayments and the house would be forfeit if he did not stump up the cash. She called the bank to find that he had borrowed everything against the house, their house, their home. A little more delving saw that their holiday home in the south of France was also gone, sold.

He pulled into the drive and saw the dining room furniture piled up in a bonfire heap on the lawn where Debbie had left it. She had taken everything else but left the table, the table that had been with them through thick and thin, the large piece of reclaimed oak that had been crafted to their specifications, now axed into pieces on their lawn, just kindling.

He looked behind him, feeling eyes on him, even though he knew that no one had followed him he felt his paranoia taking on a new extreme. He had been looking over his shoulder for a very long time now, his adrenaline was really pumping. He wondered what would happen to him when they eventually caught up to him. Now that Debbie was gone he was pretty sure no one would give a shit what happened to him, or maybe they would all line up to stick the knife in when they realised he had lost everything. He looked up at the magnificent house that he still adored and wondered how he had managed to screw everything up so royally. He was clever, right? Looking round at the land he owned, he realised that that would be taken too. The plantation would go, as would the small manmade forest that backed on to the field behind their property, which he and Debbie had bought for their dogs, dogs that she also took. If he hadn't lost everything she would be getting half of the house, half of the land. She could have it all for all he cared, it didn't mean anything without her. He hated to go inside the house now, even to sleep; it was cold and lonely, not just empty but hollow. Plus Debbie had taken all the beds.

He unloaded the box from the car and walked over to the large pile of hand-finished wood on his lawn that felt to him like a symbol of what he had become, once respected, now worthless. He looked at the dishevelled garden and thought of Debbie again as he poured liquid paraffin on to the debris. He would damage the lawn, the lawn that was a shadow of its former self, when she had left so had all the care, so had all the love. He tossed a match and watched the fire sweep through the years of memories that the table held. He remembered sitting at the table when they had no other furniture, discussing the house, how they were going to make it a home and the life they hoped to lead together. The flames licked higher and higher against the backdrop of the pale blue sky, the blue seeming dull in comparison to the intense orange flame of the bonfire, waves of heat pulsed from it into the ether.

Ian opened the box he'd brought with him and thumbed through the paperwork briefly, checking he had all the correct files. When he was sure, he threw the whole box on top of the flames, watching the fire engulf the box and its contents, immediately feeling his anxiety disappear. Even shredded documents could be reconstructed these days and with the amount of money he owed he was sure they would go to the effort of doing just that, yes, they would be thorough in their investigations. He reached into his pocket and pulled out the backup flash drive – his financial advisor had recommended he never keep anything 'hot' on his work hard drive, better to keep it separate. He never explained what he meant by 'hot' but considering his line of work Ian thought it was safe to assume that he was talking about financial irregularities and not hardcore pornography, although those rules can apply to both scenarios.

'Hello.'

Ian turned around to see a tall man leaning on the front gate. He was all in black with a hood pulled over his head, obscuring his face a little. He wasn't an auditor, that was for sure.

'What do you want?'

'You've got two minutes.' The man stood up straight and checked his watch. 'A hundred and eighteen seconds.'

'Two minutes until what? Who the fuck are you?'

'A hundred and twelve, a hundred and eleven.'

Ian was confused, then he looked down at the man's right hand and saw the crossbow.

'Are you fucking crazy?'

'A hundred and seven.' The man raised the crossbow and pointed it squarely at Ian's head, Ian's face dropped when he saw the weapon in a little more detail – there was a five-pointed tip on the arrows – he had seen this before; for the first time he really looked at the man's face.

'You?'

'A hundred and one.'

Ian didn't need to be told again, he ran, he wasn't a slim man, but he did go to the gym regularly and he was fitter than most men his age, so he was confident he could run fast enough, at least fast enough to make it to the woods where the trees might provide him with some kind of cover. He didn't want to look back, didn't want to see how close his pursuer was.

He climbed over the stocks into the densely wooded area, he knew the advantage was his inside the plantation, he knew all the potholes and burrows, all the nooks and crannies. Daring to check behind him, he saw the black figure walking through the field, in no hurry, just a solid march. Ian smiled to himself as he ran forward; he had enough time to use the path for a while before ducking into the more rough terrain. He made it about a hundred yards when he heard a snap, then a pain unlike anything he had ever known tore through him, he fell hard on the ground and screamed in agony. He looked at his legs and saw the large iron hunting trap clamped around his calf. Blood pouring from the wound, bone and sinew protruding, he sat up and tugged at the device, the silhouette of the man climbing the wooden stocks to get over the locked gate in his peripheral vision. He opened the trap just enough to slide his leg out, shrieking as the teeth dragged on his flesh, tearing it open.

Ian pulled himself to his feet again, tears streaming

down his face as he tried to run, putting everything he had into moving forward, knowing in his heart of hearts that he was done, but still trying. He heard the unmistakable sound of a crossbow being discharged, he knew that sound well and in the millisecond before it hit Ian sucked in a deep breath and closed his eyes, everything moving in slow motion as he waited for his life to end; instead he just felt his body jolt forward as the bolt entered his shoulder. The leaves rustled behind him and the last thing he saw before he passed out was a pair of black boots steadily approaching.

Ian woke with a start as ice cold water hit his face. The first thing that struck him was that his wrists hurt, he regained enough focus to see that he was strung up between two trees, off the manmade path that ran through the forest, way off.

'What do you want with me?'

'Really? You need me to explain this to you?'

'I'm not that person any more, I've changed,' Ian pleaded, words sticking in his throat – he was so thirsty.

'But I still am that person; you *made* me who I am, Ian . . . sorry . . . Mr Markham, sir.' Venom spitting as he said the name.

'Don't call me that.'

'Why not? You taught me so much, it's only fair I show the respect you're due.'

'What about the others?' Ian's head dropped and he saw that his shirt was ripped open, he looked further down still and saw the blood dripping swiftly from his injured leg. 'Why can't I feel my leg?'

'Time to be quiet now.' The man walked towards Ian

quickly and thrust a knife into the base of his stomach, Ian screamed as the knife was pulled across, but not from pain, he could feel everything but there was no pain. He watched the blood pumping out, then he felt the man's hand as it reached inside him, fingers moving, searching for something, he could feel it all, but still no pain.

'What the fuck have you done to me?!'

'I gave you an anaesthetic to help with the pain, a spinal injection. I don't want you passing out; you have to watch the show.' He pulled out a thin bloody tube from Ian's stomach, the lower intestine. 'Congratulations, it's a boy.'

That's when Ian saw the crank, he watched as the man attached his lower intestine to a hook and then walked over to a long metal pole that ran vertical parallel to him. He turned a wheel that was attached to the pole, which began to rotate slowly on some kind of mechanism, gathering up the line attached to the hook and wrapping it around the pole, followed by Ian's insides, covering the large metal stick like a candy floss. He stopped and picked up his crossbow, and started to walk away.

'You can't leave me here, the foxes will have me.'

'You better pray they finish you in less than eight hours, that's how long you have until the drugs wear off!'

'You're sick!' Ian shouted, but then emotion took him over and he began to cry, aware that the darkness was almost upon him. Suddenly a white-collar prison wasn't looking so bad. He knew if they came looking for him at the house they would find his reservations for the plane to go to South America and just assume that he had done a bunk, which was in fact precisely what he was planning on doing. No one would look for him and people rarely ventured into these woods, so the chance of someone happening by within the next hour or so was next to impossible. He watched as his only hope of survival disappeared into the forest. He was alone, all hope was gone.

Chapter 6

The Widow

'Come on, then, we're up.' Grey slammed a lukewarm cup of coffee on the desk in front of Adrian. She groaned and drank the contents of her own mug with a contorted grimace on her face. 'Some woman keeps calling about her husband, said he's gone missing and cleared out all her accounts.'

'And that's the reason I'm never getting married.'

'Sure it is.' Grey pulled Adrian's chair backwards so his feet slid off the desk on to the floor. 'Come on, I'll get you some real coffee on the way.'

'OK fine, goddamnit.' Adrian pulled himself out of his chair, his head still throbbing after the many shots he had downed the night before. 'You should probably drive.'

'I should definitely drive.' She snatched the keys from his hand.

Despite Adrian's first impression of DS Grey she was surprisingly motivated – scratch that, annoyingly motivated. Any case, regardless of whether it was some illegal fly-tipping or a serious violent assault, was awarded the exact same amount of professionalism and attention. They had worked together for three weeks now, settled into their respective roles within the relationship. Adrian let her boss him around and she let him be the butt of all her jokes, everyone was happy. This was the first female partner Adrian had ever had, he had worked with both DS Mike Daniels and DS Jonathan Fraser in the past, and he had never really been much of a team player. He knew that this time he had to play the game. He was under the microscope and he couldn't afford to make any more enemies. Besides, Grey was easy to work with, somehow they just fit.

In the unmarked police car Adrian put his shades on and rested his head against the window, a position he would soon regret. Grey drove as if she were in hot pursuit of a bank robber, pedal to the metal. You could get away with that kind of driving in the city but in this part of the Devonshire countryside you may as well just cut out the middle man and drive straight into a ditch.

'Jesus, don't they have country lanes in Plymouth?' Adrian felt something twang in his neck. 'You are giving me whiplash.'

'Quit being such a baby, Miley, you are fine.'

'What's your hurry? The only other case we have on at the moment is the lawnmower theft.'

'I want to clock off early today, I've got a date.'

'Seriously? I thought you were a . . . what's the word for a female with no privates, not a eunuch?'

'Please stop thinking about my junk, Miley.' She swerved into the driveway and they were confronted with a large art deco house.

'What a dump!' Adrian muttered.

'How the other half lives.'

On the luxurious cream velvet sofa the lady sniffed into her tissue, her eyes puffy and red.

'He calls me every day, well, he used to.'

'And he just stopped?' Adrian asked as Grey wandered around the room, fingers hovering above every surface. It was so clean and shiny, it looked like a show home, every item carefully placed and the only personal effects an alarming array of cat ornaments.

'Yes, he stopped. I haven't heard from him in well over a week.'

'But you're separated?'

'That's right.'

'Do you know anyone who would want to harm your husband?'

'Besides me, you mean?'

'It was a bad break-up?'

'It was and there's a long list of people who want to hurt Ian, he stole money, a lot of money from a lot of people. The auditors are still neck deep in the mess he left behind.'

'How much money are we talking?'

'Thousands? Millions? Who knows?'

Grey finally sat down next to Adrian and leaned back into the deep sofa until she was almost horizontal. He half expected her to put her feet on the coffee table, but instead she folded her arms and stared at Deborah Markham.

'You have to appreciate what this looks like,' Grey said.

'I know what it looks like, I'm not an imbecile, Officer.'

'So what is it you want us to do exactly?' Grey remained in her relaxed pose, looking more like a sullen adolescent than a police officer. She seemed to be unnerving the lady and Adrian could see the anger emerging from behind the tears.

'I want you to find the bastard! He's buggered off to bloody Rio or wherever and I am left to deal with the shit storm!'

'You don't think he's hurt then? This is purely about the money?' Adrian asked, he saw Grey smiling out of the corner of his eye.

'This is purely about nothing! I've lost everything! Why does he get to go away and pretend like nothing's wrong? I've had threatening phone calls and hate mail!' The tears had gone and Deborah Markham's face was alight with anger. 'He took so much from so many people. They see me here like this and think I've got their money or something!'

Grey sat forward and rested her elbows on her knees, she picked up a crystal cat, part of a set that was arranged carefully on the olive wood coffee table.

'Have you got their money?' Grey smiled as she ran her fingers across the prism-like cat ears.

'This house belongs to my aunt, she's letting me live here while I get back on my feet to save my dignity, it's the only thing he left me with.' She choked back the tears again.

'OK, Mrs Markham, we'll look into it.' Adrian interrupted before Grey could open her mouth again. He stood up but she remained seated, eyes fixed on Mrs Markham.

'Where's he been living?' she asked. Deborah Markham pulled out a set of keys from the handbag at her side.

'There's a converted barn on the road that leads to the estuary, the address is on the fob.'

Adrian took the fob and Grey put the cat down. He felt like he had just witnessed a hostage negotiation. The air was thick between them as they walked out to the car.

'What the hell was that?'

'She was full of it.' Grey smiled.

'She was distraught.'

'Distraught my eye, she's still got money, and plenty of it. Did you see the way she was groomed? Those are this season's clothes, new shoes – really expensive shoes – and you can't get that bag for less than a grand. I wouldn't be surprised if this disappearance isn't some kind of scam.' Adrian looked at her with surprise.

'How do you know about the clothes and stuff?'

'You think I don't know about fashion? What are you saying, Miley?' she said incredulously, a fake look of indignation on her face.

'Nothing, you just don't strike me as that kind of woman.'

'And what kind of woman do I strike you as?'

'I don't know, you dress like Tony Hawks,' he said, before adding, 'the multi-millionaire skateboarder, not the comedian.'

'What the hell does that mean?'

'Just drop it, it doesn't matter.'

'OK, let me ask you a question.' She sat forward.

'OK, shoot.' Adrian sighed, what had he done?

'What car do you drive?'

'You know what car I drive, I drive a Granada.'

'A Granada? Right, Jesus, Miley, they stopped making them like fifteen years ago.'

'She has sentimental value!'

'Whatever, I bet you know what a Mustang is, or a Ferrari, I bet you watch the lame car programmes on TV. I bet you think you know a lot about cars.'

'That's different.'

'I know a lot about clothes, specifically high-end, expensive clothing. You can tell a lot about a person by the way they dress.'

Adrian couldn't help but look her up and down, instantly regretting this decision as he saw that smile on her face again. He was beginning to understand that she only smiled like that when she had won some imaginary battle in her mind. Every time he saw that smile he would be reminded that she wasn't the scruffy slacker that she presented herself to be.

'The way I dress is a choice, calculated, Miley. I know what I'm doing.'

'You want everyone to think you're a dyke?'

'Maybe I am a dyke.'

'Pfft, please . . . I know you're not, I have seen you checking me out.'

'In your dreams!' She smiled and thumped him on the arm, a little flushed in the cheeks. 'Mostly I don't want people to think I am too competent. I don't want people to put their faith in me. I want them to think I am a washout and I want to prove them wrong.'

'It's very complicated in your head, isn't it, Grey?'

'I like it when people think they are superior to me, people let their guard down more when they don't feel threatened, they are easier to confuse.'

'That explains your amazing display of passive aggression back there.'

'Whatever gets the job done!'

'Is that why you got transferred out of Plymouth?' Adrian asked. It was a genuine question although the look her face assumed put paid to any notion Adrian may have had about them being comfortable with each other. She put her hands in the ten to two position and focused on the road ahead. The connection was lost. The conversation was over.

The barn was large and impressive. They walked up the gravelled driveway and knocked on the door, noting the incredible framing of pink sky around the house; it felt so completely secluded out there.

'Mr Markham?' Adrian called out.

Grey walked around the side of the house and disappeared from Adrian's view. Adrian tried every key on the bunch Deborah Markham had given them until he found the one that corresponded with the lock. He could tell from the absolute silence that they were alone here.

'Mr Markham? Ian Markham?' he called out again, just in case. The house was bare, stripped of furniture, a few lopsided pictures hung on the walls and a rug or two lay here and there.

'Looks like he's had some kind of bonfire out back.' Grey was standing in the doorway holding a document box. 'Left in a hurry, too, by the looks of it.'

Adrian took the box from Grey, a handful of papers remained in the bottom. Some tickets from various bookmakers, some shredded paper they could get the lab to reassemble, a couple of invitations to local fund-raising functions but nothing massively incriminating.

'Bag it all and we'll take it back to the station.'

'Check this out.' Grey pulled out a Visa bill, one of the recipients was listed as LHRBOOKINGS. 'LHR is the abbreviation for Heathrow, as in long-distance destinations, as in anywhere in the world non-extradition kind of thing. He's in the wind.'

'We'll take it back anyway, fuck it, you have anything better to do?'

They walked out of the barn house and looked again at the beautiful surroundings. No doubt the house would be repossessed and resold. The sun had muted in the afternoon sky and a cool breeze drifted through the air making the surrounding trees pulse as if they had their own heartbeat. The forest in the near distance looked like an underline for the beautiful orange sun.

Adrian breathed it all in before heading back into the city to deal with the Saturday-night binge drinking shift, part of his penance for messing his colleagues around before he got suspended. He wasn't proud of the fact that he had got people to lie for him, about his whereabouts, about how sober he was or wasn't, about a lot of things. He had so much to make up for and a lot of people to apologise to. He had promised to help Denise deal with the drunks on the desk on Saturday nights. He owed her a lot more than that but it was a start. Grey beeped the horn impatiently and he got in.

Chapter 7

The Outsider

Sally waited at the door wagging her tail, knowing her master was approaching; she knew him by his walk, by the sound of his breathing, by his smell. Parker walked in and was greeted with an extremely happy Labrador Retriever. Sally was his life companion, his best friend, the one who would never forsake him. Parker and Sally had met almost seven years earlier and it was love at first sight, they needed each other and they knew it.

His house was a true reflection of his character, books on every surface, a stack of black leather notepads teeming with words, a small brown sofa which was obviously Sally's favourite place to sit, judging by the layer of golden fluff on it. He fed Sally immediately, and as soon as she had finished her food he took her for a walk, walking past the museum that he had returned to this to town for. He saw Abbey leaving work and walked over to her.

'Abbey, this is my Sally.' Abbey turned and smiled at the dog, a big full smile, Parker had not seen that smile before, he felt just by looking at it that he was invading her privacy; it was not intended for him. Abbey knelt down and rubbed the dog's ears affectionately.

'She's lovely . . . Parker, I hope I didn't offend you earlier. I was worried when you rushed off.' She looked at him seriously while he racked his mind for what she could be referring to.

'Oh no, you didn't, I had to dash. I'm sorry but she barely forgave me for coming home late last night, I wouldn't want to be in trouble two nights on the trot. I thought I could make it home and back before you left.' He wasn't lying. He had explained earlier how Sally had been so unimpressed with his late arrival the night before she had left a present for him on the living room floor. 'I um . . . I wanted you to meet Sally.'

'I see. Well, then, I understand completely.' She beamed at him, the same smile she had used just moments before, he hoped she couldn't notice his cheeks flushing in this light.

'Can we walk you home?' Parker asked. Abbey took Sally's lead from him, her warm fingers brushing against his hands. He smiled back and put his hands in his pockets, walking behind them.

Parker wasn't good with people, he knew it, they knew it; unless you were two hundred years old and furry then there was little chance of him being able to connect with you on any level. Parker was deliberately aloof. He didn't like people to get too close, he didn't like the idea of anyone seeing beneath the veneer, the thin layer of personality that was between his mind and the rest of the world. This had been true for almost everyone he had ever met, but this girl, Abbey, was different.

Parker watched as Abbey kept her distance from him, head turned firmly away, he knew she didn't want to get close to him, she was just as happy as he was with prolonged silences – normally people feel the need to fill them with idle talk about God knows what. In some ways Parker was a little offended by her lack of interest in him, he was used to people wanting to understand him, which was funny because they never could, he made sure of that. Maybe there was something about dealing with the dead that made people like them bond, a kind of salute to a fellow enthusiast. But no, that wasn't it, she was different. He recognised the signs of a broken spirit immediately; the way she held herself told him more than any amount of words could. He didn't want to put her off, she had a sweetness about her. She wasn't like most of the girls he met, she was quiet, insular and guarded. He knew it wouldn't take much to push her away but he liked her for her shyness and he liked her instinct to be wary of people – he understood that feeling all too well.

Parker felt strange walking with Abbey. Again they did not talk, just walked, with her holding on to Sally's lead and Sally happily accepting her new controller as she bounded towards the river with her usual zeal. They crossed the Iron Bridge and headed towards the town, past the smattering of old pubs and tattoo shops that were long overdue for some cosmetic attention. This time it was Parker who felt the need to fill the silence as he searched his mind for a topic.

'Have you worked at the museum long?' Best to stick to talking about work.

'Five years,' she said, and that seemed to be the end of the conversation as she crossed the busy road and headed down South Street. He increased his pace to catch up with her.

'And you have no professional qualifications?' She looked at him with a raised eyebrow then turned and carried on walking. 'Sorry, I didn't mean that to sound rude, you really have done a great job, not that you need my approval or anything.' He should probably shut up now.

'Well it's not a well-funded museum, a friend of a friend got me the interview and I just convinced the director, Mr Lowestoft, that I knew what I was doing, they get to pay me a lot less than the going rate and I get to do the job I love. I know taxidermy isn't very fashionable any more but . . .' She turned back and smiled at him. He could tell she really did love the job, he had looked over the work she had done so far and been impressed.

Abbey stopped outside a dusty weather-beaten black door, she handed the leash back to Parker.

'Say thank you, Sally,' he said to his dog, who was still panting vigorously at Abbey.

'I would invite you in but I'm not allowed animals in the building.'

'I wouldn't call myself an animal!' Parker displayed his best mischievous smile in an effort to get her to reciprocate. She didn't. She just looked at her feet uncomfortably. She took her keys out and entered the building as he stood and watched.

'See you tomorrow,' he heard through the door, and breathed a sigh of relief. He looked down at Sally who was panting far too much considering they had barely walked three miles.

'Yeah, I like her too,' he said to Sally as he tugged at her lead, prompting her to carry on walking.

The next morning he found himself walking past Abbey's door on the way to work, it was not on his route but something compelled him to make it part of his course. He arrived at work before her and had to wait for her to arrive before he could get into the rooms they needed to work on today. Gemma, the girl on the front counter, was just settling into her seat for the day. 'Hey!' she proclaimed, a little louder than she needed to. He walked over.

'I'm Parker, I work in the archives.' He offered his hand. Gemma was one of those people who were friendly to everyone, an overabundance of chirpy goodwill seemed to flow from her every pore. He guessed that's why she was on the front desk.

'I wondered when you were finally going to introduce yourself to me. How are you getting on? Those rooms creep me out, all those dead things, ew.'

'At least they don't talk back.' He smiled awkwardly and she laughed louder and harder than his quip deserved. He noticed Shane watching him from across the room. When they thought no one was looking, he knew Gemma and Shane would sneak into the back rooms for some privacy. He could feel Shane's jealous eyes ablaze with anger.

'You getting on OK with Abbey?' she finally said when she calmed down, and he could tell she was asking even though she already knew the answer, and there was a hint of mocking in the way she said Abbey's name. He realised for once he wasn't the strangest person in the building.

The women who worked in the canteen could be heard gossiping almost non-stop when you were at their end of the building. Sometimes he caught the words but mostly it was the sound of inane exchanges, last night's soap operas, who was leaving 'the jungle', anything to make the time go by. Shane and Gemma would huddle together no matter what they were doing, either fighting or flirting, always in a whisper. Mr Lowestoft was occasionally seen roaming the halls looking at the progress and talking to the decorators who had somehow become invisible. Between the lady who gave the tours on the days they had school visits and the porters who moved the artefacts around silently when no one was looking, Parker realised he had never really seen anyone else talking to Abbey. The reason he got on so well with Abbey, if you could call it that, was because they were both the outcasts. In fact, for once, he thought it was possible he was the normal one.

'Yes, speak of the devil.' They both looked up as Abbey ambled through the large double doors. Parker smiled, more comfortable with Abbey's awkward stare than he had been with Gemma's overfamiliarity, he could sense Gemma sneering as he walked over and took Abbey's heavy bag before following her in silence through the unlit passageway to the area they needed to be in for today. As he walked beside her he watched her face. She was focused.

'If you start in that corner then I can get on with these guys today,' she said, he felt like she was fobbing him off.

'Can I ask you for a small favour?'

'OK.' She turned and faced him with a no-nonsense stance. Abbey was a no-nonsense girl, he wondered what she considered fun.

'It's a strange request, considering we've not known each other very long, but I need to ask you if you could look after Sally next weekend. I have a family thing to take care of and I don't like putting her in kennels. The address is on the key fob, you may as well take it now while I remember.' He handed her a key to his place. She just stared at his hand but he continued to hold the key out, unwavering. 'Just put some food in her bowl and take her for a walk, if you don't mind.'

'Oh . . .'

'I wouldn't ask but I don't know anyone else around here any more, and Sally really likes you . . . I like you . . . I mean, I trust you with Sally.' He felt stupid saying it, knowing also that now was not the right time to attempt one of his disingenuous smiles, he knew she could see through all of that. Abbey blushed again and took the key from him. Her hand brushed against his and he was surprised at how warm her skin was. She snatched it away self-consciously as he kept his eyes on her. Parker didn't feel the same need to be normal with her as he did with everyone else, he didn't feel the need for fake smiles and he didn't feel the need to speak when she was silent. He had noticed it more and more since they had first met; his ever decreasing need to be false with her. In fact, anything other than honesty was becoming hard. In all the scenarios he had imagined when he returned to this city, a genuine connection wasn't in one of them. He hadn't planned for this.

'We had better get on with it, they want this room cleared in a couple of weeks ready to redecorate it for the centenary celebrations,' she interrupted his thoughts.

She scuttled off to her corner of the room, stuffing his keys into her back pocket. He took that to mean she accepted his request.

Parker could make women fall for him, it was possibly because he was clever, women like that, but he was also good-looking in an awkward way. He had no interest in relationships. He was often more comfortable spending time with women because he was not the average man. Comfortable was maybe the wrong word, a little strong for the way anyone made him feel. The only time Parker couldn't get a woman to fall for him was when he actually liked the girl in question, not a situation that arose often. He had the gift of manipulation, something he had watched people around him possess as he had grown up. He had made a promise to himself, though, that he would only use it when he absolutely had to, he didn't want to become like the people who had influenced him the most. He had seen those people lie and lie again to get what they wanted, no matter who they hurt. No, he wouldn't indulge the part of him that wanted to deceive, manipulate and corrupt; he wanted to be better than that, he wanted to be good. He seemed to repel the women that fascinated him, maybe because he was trying to flirt, not something he was good at. He knew his ham-fisted attempts at light humour were never received in the spirit he intended them to be. The girls he had known before had all wanted to fix him and so he pushed them away, knowing full well that he was unfixable. Also he noticed something all the girls he liked had in common: they were good, too good for him. He always thought too much of them to inflict himself on them. That was his 'type', a girl he could never allow himself to be with. He put it down to his innate desperation to sabotage any chance for happiness he might be able to grab on to in the future. His past had been so dark, so unthinkably bleak that sometimes he thought he felt more comfortable in situations where there was absolutely no hope.

Chapter 8

The Host

Then

The door was already open when their cab pulled up to the house. A girl Abbey recognised was puking in the shrubbery of the house next door and she could see a couple of other people from her course fumbling with each other in the side alley, so undignified. Abbey imagined herself and Christian locked in the same embrace and suddenly it took on a whole new appeal.

She could feel the pit of her stomach humming with excitement as they walked in. The vibrations of the music thumped through her lower body and added to the rising anticipation. She scanned every corner of every room as they walked through. Everyone greeting Dani as they went by and she got sucked into conversation with some other girls, and Abbey continued through alone. For the first time she noticed eyes on her, not mocking or derisive but hungry and lustful. *So this is what it feels like.* It wasn't long before a drink was planted in Abbey's hand. She drank it with the confidence of someone who could handle alcohol far better than she could. Tonight was not the night to be Abbey, where was the fun in that? Tonight she was going to be better. *Stop holding yourself back and enjoy it!* She had always been well aware that her self-esteem issues were of her own creation. Being raised by a single father, she was never quite sure of the social etiquettes a girl should adhere to, just mostly guessing and copying had got her through this far.

She walked out into the garden to the sound of Katy Perry's 'Firework', fairy lights hung from the trees and willow fences, twinkling, magical. Her butterflies were worse than ever and as a small crowd parted she caught sight of Christian. She felt like she was in a movie. She took a deep breath and made her way towards him, praying he would see her before he saw Danielle. Jamie actually saw her first and whispered something to Christian who turned around. She could feel his eyes moving up and down her body as she pretended not to have seen them yet.

'Glad you could make it' He smiled as she approached and she saw something she hadn't ever seen before, excitement, lust. He had finally noticed her as a woman, she felt his gaze lingering on her breasts as she smiled at Jamie who seemed to be smiling back. It occurred to Abbey that she had never seen Jamie smile before and she was glad for that fact because it wasn't a comfortable smile, it was awkward and forced. She shook off the creepy feeling he gave her and turned her attention back to Christian, who was still trying to look like he wasn't checking her out. He was waiting for her to turn her back to him, she could feel it, he must have seen Dani in this dress before so he knew what to expect. Who knew a plunging backline could cause as much trouble as a low-cut top? She wickedly bit her lip as she walked to the punch bowl, feeling his eyes on her for the duration, her skin prickled and tingled at the idea of what he might be thinking about her right now. She thought about his lips on the small of her back and blushed to herself as she quickly necked another drink.

Four glasses of punch later and she was laughing freely. Why had she hidden in the background for all those years? The attention she was getting felt deserved. Tonight she was pretty. She could almost smell the hunger on the boys who were chatting to her, flattery in spades. Tonight everyone wanted what she had. Before long she was sitting on the sofa huddled between three boys from the cricket team, downing shots of tequila, she didn't much care for it but she was enjoying the party too much to suddenly be the sensible one again. Dani sat across from her, clearly happy with the reception her protégée was receiving.

'Come on, Abs, let's do it another way,' Dani called as she saw Abbey screw her face up at the offer of another tequila. The boys watched eagerly as Dani swept her hair to one side exposing her neck, she licked the palm of her hand and dragged it down leaving it glistening wet, and then she poured the salt on to herself. She was poised as though she were ready to be taken by a vampire. Abbey leaned over the table, only slightly concerned that her dress was far too short for this position and glad that she hadn't taken Dani's advice of wearing a thong. With one knee on the coffee table Abbey pressed her tongue against Dani's neck sweeping the salt away slowly. Dani poured the tequila straight into Abbey's mouth then grinned at her, exposing a lemon between her teeth, Abbey could feel the camera phones pointed at her as she placed her lips around the lemon in Dani's mouth, she sucked the juice and they continued to kiss over the table for the titillation of the hormonal boys. As Abbey pulled away she saw Christian watching them and suddenly felt a huge wave of betrayal, like she had somehow been unfaithful to him, even though he had Dani. Maybe she was mistaking his look, maybe it was intended for Dani but no, it was for her. The whoops and cheers only added to the cloud in her mind as the tequila mixed with the punch in her stomach. She had to get out of the room, away from all the noise.

Abbey staggered up the stairs, clinging to the railings and dragging her increasingly heavy legs to the bathroom, not entirely sure she would make it. She stumbled through the door and fell at the feet of the toilet, firmly gripping the basin as the contents of her stomach erupted from her mouth. Tequila tasted just as unpleasant on the way out as it did going in, only without the benefit of a citrus chaser it burned her throat. She felt a hand brushing the back of her neck as someone pulled her hair out of the firing line.

'It's OK. I've got you.' She was too queasy to be surprised to hear Christian's voice, but was grateful for the intervention. Well aware that this was probably the end of any future between them, she figured he was more concerned for his bathroom than he was about her. He helped her to her feet and passed her a towel.

'Thanks,' she barely managed to mutter through her embarrassment.

'Hey, it happens! Here, you can use my toothbrush if you want, I have another one anyway.'

There's something strangely intimate about letting someone watch you brush your teeth. She couldn't help feeling vulnerable and exposed, like this meant something. Abbey had never been good at reading signals but this felt so definite, the way he watched her, it wasn't the concerned look of a friend, it was something else, something far more significant.

Abbey lay down on Christian's bed, he had pointed her in the direction of his bedroom while he fetched her some water and paracetamol to relieve her throbbing head. He had no posters and a sparse minimalistic room, there was very little to indicate that anyone other than a methodical and organised person lived here. Abbey was surprised at the lack of personality the room displayed, she didn't know what she had imagined but it wasn't this impersonal and cold space. She must have dozed off. She awoke to find Christian sitting on the side of the bed holding a glass of water and pills, and she sat up and drank thirstily, washing down the tablets.

'Feel better?' Christian brushed the hair out of her eyes and smiled warmly at her, resting his hand on her shoulder.

'Sorry, I don't usually drink tequila.'

'It's good to see you let go . . . and you look amazing tonight.' His hand trailed down her back, fingers barely touching her skin. 'You're actually quite pretty.' He leaned forward and kissed her, mouth slightly parted, just enough for her to feel his hot, wet breath against her lips. What about Dani? she thought as she kissed him back. Was she still asleep? Was this a dream? Was he really kissing her? She held her eyes closed tight for fear that if she opened them his mistake would be realised and he would pull away, disgusted.

His hand was on her knee now, her instinct was to clamp her legs shut so that it could go no further but something inside her stopped that gut reaction, and as his hand travelled up past her thighs she just allowed it, despite every fibre of her being telling her to stop him. Dani would get over it, wouldn't she? Would she hate her? Blame her? Would she even find out?

Chapter 9

The Trick

Kevin Hart stared down at his wedding ring as he pulled at it, it was dull and scratched. The faded gold band had sunk between the swollen ridges of his fingers. He was much heavier now than when he had got married, years of wining and dining had taken their toll on his body, a fact he was able to ignore until he tried to remove the ring. It caught the hair between his knuckles as he dragged it over them and slipped it in his pocket. He reached for the whisky as the pink lights thumped against the back of his brain and washed down some of his migraine pills.

Kevin was a familiar old face among the fresh meat on offer. He would sit in his private booth at the end of the bar and peruse the drunken young men as they danced together on the floor in front of him, scanning the crowd for the stragglers, the ones who struck out and were feeling down on their luck. Don the barman was accustomed to Kevin's playbook, aware of Kevin's type. Occasionally, when a young desperado would slump against the bar, Don would glance over at Kevin and wait for the green light. Kevin didn't have what these young men had, he didn't have youth on his side, or even looks, but he had money and he had power; both far more valuable in this game.

Kevin watched as a shiny peacock dominated the floor, turning heads, each pose he struck designed to attract maximum attention and it worked as some of the men turned away from the less interesting ones, trying to catch his eye. A sweaty young buck wrestled his way out of the horde, defeated after losing his companion to the show; he shoved his way to the bar and ordered himself a drink. Don looked over to Kevin who was staring at the new prey eagerly, Kevin raised his little finger off the glass as he took a swig, and Don knew the score.

'Paid for by the gentleman in the VIP section,' Don said as he placed the drink on the bar, motioning towards Kevin. The young man instantly straightened up and puffed his chest out, knowing full well the booths were only ever occupied by the men with the moola. Kevin signalled to the empty seat beside him and his new friend wandered over.

'Martin,' the man held his hand out. Kevin ignored it; he didn't like to put them at ease. Martin was still curious enough to sit down even with a little bit of wind knocked out of his sails, the smile wiped from his face. Kevin wanted Martin to know he had no upper hand here; his youth and beauty were not enough to hold Kevin to ransom. Kevin wanted Martin to hang on his every word and he knew that in order for that to happen he would have to use those words sparingly.

'Would you like to earn some money?' Kevin eventually said.

'Oh, I'm not a pro . . . I mean, I'm not . . . I don't . . .' Martin sputtered.

'Relax.'

Kevin knew that everyone had a price, for everything. Years of business negotiations had taught him that you could get a person to sell you their first-born child if you knew what they really wanted. Martin was well dressed but the frays on the seams of his designer jeans and the bobbling on his high-end T-shirt had betrayed him. Martin yearned for a sugar daddy, that's why he had sat down in the first place, and at least temporarily, Kevin could be that person. Martin would be easily pleased.

'I'll pay you two thousand pounds to spend the weekend with me.' Kevin reached for the bottle of scotch and poured himself another, he could feel Martin's quandary as he held the bottle out to him, their eyes fixed on each other, searching for a clue about who the other man was. That was part of the fun for Kevin, part of the game; the mystery, anticipation and fear of the unknown. When Martin finally took the bottle from Kevin they both knew it wasn't the scotch he was accepting.

The key clicked in the door and Kevin pushed it open, allowing Martin to step inside the apartment first, it was dark but Kevin saw how Martin smiled to himself as his eyes adjusted to the light. The room was illuminated by the lights that bounced off of the imposingly decorated Gothic cathedral that directly faced it. The men he brought here always admired the sleek lines of the masculine furniture, the bay window overlooking the cathedral square and the smell, the smell of Egyptian cotton and stainless steel. Kevin knew that Martin would be impressed, this was a sought-after location and added to the image that he wanted to portray – that he had money, that he had power. This was Kevin's sanctuary, his home away from home, a place for him to be himself, to do the things he needed to do to feel sane. Kevin's wife, Mary, was used to his weekend absences, she liked the finer things in life and Kevin knew he was safe from her prying as long as the money kept coming in. They would not be disturbed.

'I'll pay you now.' Kevin threw a wad of fifties on the table in front of Martin, who looked up nervously before snatching up the notes and stuffing them into his back pocket.

'Nice place, real nice,' Martin said in his brash country accent as he stared at the family portrait that hung on Kevin's wall. The jovial face of the man in the portrait didn't match the man in front of Martin, he was younger and slimmer. In the picture were two teenagers, a lean, tall boy with an uncomfortable smile and a slightly younger girl in a pristine white dress. Kevin kept the picture there so that when his wife visited it just seemed like a home away from home, that way they could both keep up the pretence that nothing untoward was going on.

Open handed, Kevin slapped Martin across the face. Martin shot up and raised his hand to hit back. Kevin grabbed it and looked Martin in the eyes. In the instances when they reacted like that he wondered if they were genuinely surprised or if they were actually just play acting for him, he didn't really care either way. Some part of them must have guessed what he was paying for, or were they really that naive? He loved that look, the shock, the surprise, the indignation. Tears started to form in Martin's eyes as Kevin stared into him.

'I can always take the money back and you can just go,' he whispered. 'Or you can do what you're told and keep the money.'

It's one thing to refuse a lot of money; it's another thing to give it back after you have held it in your hands. This was a huge part of the turn on for Kevin, the part when they accepted, the part when they knew what was going to happen and still said yes, he lived for that very moment; acquiescence.

'What do you want me to do?' Martin pushed back the tears and lowered his hand.

'Take your clothes off.' Kevin took a step back and watched as Martin resentfully stripped down to just his underpants, he guessed this was Martin's lucky pair or something, bright and garish, labelled and fitted, probably expensive. 'All of them.'

As Martin stood there Kevin revelled in his discomfort, his firm golden silhouette framed by the backlight of the cathedral. Martin crossed his hands across his front, trying to keep a little of his modesty at least.

This made Kevin smile to himself. By the time Kevin was done with Martin his modesty would be the least of his worries.

The bedroom was darker than the lounge, just a bed sitting solemnly in the centre of the room. Martin stumbled forward and Kevin pushed him face first into the mattress. The floor felt strange to Kevin, something wasn't right about it but he dismissed the feeling as a side effect of the excitement. With one hand he undid his belt and ripped it from its position with ease before forming it into a loop and hooking it around Martin's neck as though he were a wayward dog, no chit chat, no foreplay. He spat into his hand and forced his fingers inside Martin, who stopped writhing when he realised the more he resisted the tighter the belt got. It had been months since Kevin had got to play this game, always too busy with work or family, mind-numbingly dull conference calls or his daughter's theatrical performances. Kevin savoured the image of Martin's body, its tiny contortions as he pushed harder, deeper.

Martin let out a yelp as Kevin yanked on the belt and pulled him upright, reaching around to feel his erection, even without Martin's cooperation Kevin knew how to exploit their bodies. He knew all the tricks.

'Stop it! It's too tight!' Martin rasped, making Kevin pull harder.

'Don't worry, I won't do any permanent damage,' he replied, wondering if Martin could tell he had a smile on his face.

If Kevin had been a more observant man he might have noticed that the strange feeling under his feet that he had dismissed earlier was not in fact his luxurious deep-pile carpet but a heavy-duty dust sheet; in fact if Kevin had been less impressed with his own magnificence and more astute to his surroundings he would have also noticed the shadowy figure standing in the corner of the room, but he wasn't; so he didn't.

As he ran his hands relentlessly up and down Martin's shaft he began to get hard himself, it was almost time to show Martin what he was really made of. Of course this was just the entree, the warm-up. Martin belonged to him for the next forty-eight hours, if he made it that long – they usually did, always thinking about the money. Kevin was no stranger to sadism, he had brought younger men back to this place for years. Like every good predator, Kevin made them agree to just enough to make sure they never told anyone, making sure they knew they could walk away whenever they wanted, they just had to give his money back. Occasionally if he really did go too far he might have to pay more after the fact. That's why he chose the men that he did, he knew which ones were desperate enough to go for it. Every two months he scheduled in time for this, coinciding with when he had to visit the field office in Exeter, telling his wife it was a regular audit. That seemed to be enough to satiate his appetite for the unpleasant.

Kevin suddenly felt a sharp pain at the nape of his neck, too acute to be a migraine. He struggled to keep a grip on the belt but his hand slipped down to his side, and as much as he wanted to he could not lift it again. Martin gasped and lurched forward. Kevin fell to his knees in an overwhelming fog of dizziness, he tried to think straight, he tried to talk, but the only sound he could hear in the place of words was a foamy gurgle. He reached up to his neck with his other hand and felt it, it was wet and warm. He tried to cough but a slow unrecognisable wheeze came out instead. He looked to Martin for answers but he was at the far end of the bed, staring at him, eyes wide in abject horror and knees huddled up to his chin.

'Get out of here.' A voice, another man's voice, not Martin's, came from behind him. He tried to turn his head to no avail. Martin scrambled to get off the bed as quickly as possible, ripping the belt from his neck. His face was twisted in anger with a trace of a smile, he swung the belt at Kevin, the buckle ripping into his cheek and he felt his teeth rattle inside his mouth. Kevin looked down and saw his shirt was saturated with red.

'You sick fuck!' Martin cried as he ran from the room, rubbing his neck.

Kevin had always wondered when his past would catch up to him and this was it. Through the haze he looked up and saw the man looking down at him. Was he one of the many young men he had brought here over the years, come back to exact his revenge? Kevin had always pushed the boundaries of what had been agreed beforehand, he found more pleasure in the resistance than the compliance and so he had half expected to run into one of them again. No, this man wasn't his type, but something about him was familiar. He saw the curved ceremonial knife in the man's hand and his body tensed involuntarily; the automatic response to fear as a surge of adrenaline caused his muscles to pull so tight that every hair follicle stood on end, giving him goosebumps. He watched the steel blade as it pierced the skin on his stomach, he felt his adrenaline surging even more as the man slowly dragged the knife upward by its hand-carved wooden handle and leaned towards him, his hot breath in Kevin's ear.

'I brought your knife back.'

Chapter 10

The Murder

The banging on the door woke Adrian up.

'Coming!' he groaned, before falling asleep again.

'Wake up, Miley,' Grey called through the letterbox.

Adrian rolled out of bed on to the floor with a thump, he arched his back and stretched out before standing up.

'I'm coming!' he shouted as he ran down the stairs in his underpants to open the door before Grey busted it down. He pulled the door open to have Grey thrust a coffee in his face.

'Get dressed, princess, we need to move.'

'What time is it?' Adrian noticed the street lamps still on even though it was clearly morning; must be early if they hadn't timed out yet.

'It's six-thirty a.m. but trust me, you're going to want to come right now.' She had an excited look on her face as she pushed past him into the lounge, knocking back the last of her own coffee.

Adrian noticed she was wearing the same clothes as the day before. It occurred to him that even though they had been working together a little over a month now, this was the first time she had been inside his house. He felt exposed, and not just because he was actually half naked.

'Did you even go to bed last night?'

'I'll sleep when I'm dead. I don't know about you, Miley, but I am getting pretty sick of being in the doghouse.'

'We just have to ride it out until they find another target.'

'Yeah, well, maybe you can wait that long but I'm fed up of getting all the crap.'

'So what do we do about it? I don't know how things worked down where you were before but we really just have to keep our heads down.'

'Sod that. I have been listening to the scanners, something big is going down.'

'Big how?'

'I don't know, it's all very hush-hush at the moment, but they called in the big forensic team and . . . I don't know . . . I just know it's a big deal.'

Adrian grabbed his black combats off the pile of clean washing on the sofa, he saw Grey doing her usual fingertip investigation of the room, she turned away from him as he got dressed and put her hands in her pockets.

'You've already seen me in my pants.'

'Nice place.'

'You being sarcastic?'

'These toys, yours or the kid's?'

'Still mine.' Adrian laced his boots up with one eye on Grey, hoping she didn't pick anything up or break it.

'You dressed? Let's go.'

Adrian got into Grey's black Mini. As she put the keys in the ignition the stereo started up, loud, progressive rock blasted through the speakers, the bass thumping through the tan leather seats. She slammed the car into first and pulled out so fast Adrian's head was firmly pressed against the backrest, he could only imagine what his neighbours were thinking.

They parked as near to the cathedral as they could, getting out on a cobbled road nearby. It was obvious to Adrian immediately that Grey had been right, something big was going down. In this town there weren't many problems that required more than two police cars at a time, except maybe on a Saturday night when they utilised the meat wagon. This was a five-car problem, add to that the three unmarked cars and the DCI's, Adrian's interest was piqued.

'What are you doing here?' Morris called across the other officers to Adrian. He was standing in a doorway to the side of a vintage gift shop; the city was littered with them. The street light shone directly on Morris' face, Adrian could see that he wasn't happy, in fact he was livid. Adrian looked up above Morris and saw the silhouettes of people bustling in the flat above. Police officers, crime techs and a few other people Adrian had never seen before.

'What's happened?'

'You need to go back to the station.' Morris walked towards him, pointing, just to drive the statement home.

'Hey, this is my free time, boss; I'm not even on shift for another four hours.'

'This does not concern you, Miles.'

Grey shot Adrian a curious sideways glance; she was obviously thinking the same thing that he was. Clearly a murder, that much went without saying. The DCI was angry not concerned, so Adrian knew that whoever was dead in that apartment did not mean anything to Adrian personally. So who the hell was it?

'Both of you get out of here now!' Morris ordered, his grey eyebrows knotted together even more aggressively than usual.

'OK, I'm going,' Adrian said, backing away. Morris turned and walked briskly towards the flat; he spun around to check Adrian was in fact leaving before disappearing back inside.

Adrian wandered back over to Grey.

'Something's going on.'

'Something to do with you, by the looks of it.' She was looking around suspiciously, eyebrows creased, focused.

'Me? I don't see how.'

'Check out the eyes, Miley, everyone's eyeballs are on you, like they are waiting for you to go nuts or something. Seriously, look at the body language.'

Adrian turned to look at the other officers on the scene and she was right, as his colleagues exited the apartment building they would see Adrian and look away, wary.

'I don't get it.'

'Come on.' Grey pulled out a cigarette and lit it, she wandered over to one of the uniformed officers who was leaning against his car on lookout. 'Hey, Jake.'

'Imogen.' He smiled, shifting the weight of his body on to his other foot and crossing his arms, classic defensive behaviour.

'Who's the stiff?' she asked

'Some businessman, I don't know.' He tried to look casual but it was evident he was trying not to look at them.

'What's it got to do with DS Miles?'

'Best leave it, don't get involved.'

'This is ridiculous, we are going to find out in about half an hour when it gets logged in the system!' Adrian's frustration was evident.

'You did not hear this from me.' Jake checked around to see if anyone was looking at them and then looked straight at Adrian. 'It's Kevin Hart, pretty fucking horrible in there too, he's been cut to shit.'

'Kevin Hart, as in the father of Ryan Hart?'

'One and the same.'

'Are you serious?' Adrian clenched his jaw and pulled the cigarette out of Grey's hand before nodding at Jake. 'Cheers mate.'

Adrian walked back over to the car and Grey followed him, he got in and waited for her to start driving. He dragged on the cigarette; the nicotine would have to do until he could get something stronger down him. She jumped in beside him.

'Going to tell me anytime soon who the dead guy is? I'm guessing the name means something to you?'

'You drive, I'll talk.'

'Where we going?'

'Ryan Hart is a dealer, remember I told you about the dealer I let get away, he brings in most of the meth for this area and pretty much controls the entire marijuana trade in the city.'

'Sounds like a useful guy to know.' She smiled as she pulled out.

'I had him, we busted a meth lab just outside the city and there was all kinds of evidence going on, we had some witnesses who were going to testify against him.'

'So this is the case that got you suspended?'

'There were documents, CD recordings of phone calls, rental agreements on the place, but they went missing. The witnesses pulled out or disappeared. I was drinking a lot. I don't know what happened but the case fell apart.' Adrian pulled another cigarette out of the packet lodged in Grey's ashtray. 'There was a gun . . .'

'Shit.'

'I still don't know how all that stuff went missing, but I was in charge of the investigation so I copped the heat. I kind of lost it for a while. Then Kevin Hart threatened to file a complaint against me for harassment of his son. I almost got fired for misconduct. Boss went to bat for me, really stuck his neck out. I would have been fired if it wasn't for him. He had no choice but to suspend me. Told me to get my head together.'

'Harsh. So do you think this has something to do with Ryan?'

'He was in bed with some pretty shady characters, so yeah, I wouldn't be surprised, I need to talk to—'

'Hold your horses, Miley, you probably shouldn't get involved in this!'

'We'll see.'

They pulled up outside a row of small terraced houses just offset from the main road, not two miles from where Kevin Hart's body had been found.

'You're going to get us both suspended.' She rolled her eyes at Adrian.

'I thought you were sick of the yard work?'

'Yeah, but this is different. Why did this guy get to you so much?'

Adrian paused, deliberating whether or not to say anything. He had to trust someone at some point, and if not Grey then who? He couldn't let himself withdraw again.

'Have you ever seen what meth does to a person? It's like watching someone decompose while they're still alive.' Adrian sucked in a deep breath and turned away before Grey noticed the glassiness of his eyes.

'Are you OK?' She put her hand on his.

'My dad was an addict of some kind or another for his whole life. Women, gambling, alcohol, you name it. But when he got into meth things got a million times worse. Ryan doesn't care if the people he's dealing to have families, he doesn't care if they are kids themselves. Getting people like Ryan Hart off the streets is one of the reasons I joined the force.'

'I'm sorry, that must have been hard.' Imogen looked over at the house then back at Adrian before nodding her permission.

'I promise I will be careful,' Adrian said as he got

out of the car. He leaned back through the window. 'I'm just going to take a look and see if anything's off.'

'All right,' Grey acquiesced. 'Just don't get me fired.'

'Look, I swear I'll be discreet. I won't talk to him, I promise.' He handed his half-finished cigarette to Grey and approached the house with caution, trying to see inside. The lights were off, no movement. He walked up the path to get a closer look. There was a gap in the front-room curtains, the sound of the gravel crushing underneath him. As he got nearer to the window, a dog started barking and howling inside the house, its massive body silhouetted in the Perspex of the front door. Adrian could see the door frame shaking as the dog became increasingly agitated.

'Shit!' Adrian muttered to himself as he tried to back his way out of the gate as stealthily as possible, Grey's car seemed so far away. It was too late, the door opened. Ryan Hart was standing there completely naked. He had the physique of a whippet, with only a thin layer of tattooed skin covering his lean muscular frame. There was an Alsatian sitting and panting by his side, waiting to be told what to do.

'And here I thought you didn't love me any more, Detective.' Ryan smiled a toothy grin. Between the smile, the dog and the homicidal naked man Adrian realised this was the most uncomfortable situation he had ever been in.

'Ryan. New dog?'

'Yeah, this is Spike. I don't believe you have met before. Is this an official visit, Officer? Only I'm pretty sure you aren't allowed within five hundred feet of me.'

'Where were you last night, Ryan?'

'With your mother.' Adrian watched as Ryan pulled open a drawer on the console table in the hall, he reached inside. Adrian's life flashed before his eyes as he imagined the double-barrelled shotgun pointing at his face. Ryan pulled out a business card and handed it to him. 'Look, whatever two-bit drug deal you think I may or may not have been involved in, I was at this guy's place, all night.'

'And he will verify that?' Adrian saw a police car turn into the far end of the street, he had to leave.

'Yeah, actually, him and about five other people, we had a poker tourney.'

'OK, thank you for your time.' Adrian tried to get back to Grey's car as casually as possible before the police car spotted him. Being seen with Ryan was all he needed. He did draw one important conclusion from his little interaction. Adrian knew Ryan. He had spent months following him, watching his every move, questioning him – the whole stalking deal – and the fact was Adrian knew when Ryan was lying. He knew his tell. Only this time he was pretty sure Ryan was telling the truth, and, furthermore, Ryan had no idea his father was dead.

Miles and Grey walked into the incident room to be confronted with a mass of red. A wall of photos of Kevin Hart's body, not even his body but his body parts.

'Gather round, folks,' Morris called out, and the chatter died down to a murmur, all eyes on him. 'Kevin Hart was killed and then apparently dismembered, not entirely in that order. The pathologist is having a little trouble pinpointing the time of death.'

'Why?'

'Because every single one of his major organs is missing.' Morris paused and sucked in a deep breath before continuing. 'It's looking like somewhere between six p.m. and basically this morning, but judging by how congealed the blood is it's been a fair few hours. Kevin Hart was last seen at six p.m. by a traffic warden who got blasted for trying to give him a ticket.'

'Does anyone look good for it?' Adrian asked.

'Miles, you come within a whisker of this case and I will ship you off to some remote Cornish fishing village where you will work out the rest of your career catching crab poachers.'

'Where are the organs, sir?'

'Absolutely no fucking clue, your guess is as good as mine. Some unis picked up Kevin's son Ryan, he's in holding.' Morris looked directly at Adrian in that moment, a warning. 'Daniels, I need you to get a statement from the wife, she's up in North Devon. My money's on the son, he's a real piece of work. Fraser, you can interview him. We have a bunch of violent crimes that trace back to him somehow.'

He looked directly at Adrian for the second time. 'Let's get this right, people! Don't let this fucker get away again!'

The incident room bustled as everyone returned to their stations. Grey sat on the edge of Adrian's desk and he could feel her staring at his furrowed brow.

'What now?' Grey asked as Adrian slumped back in

his seat, defeated, unsure what to do next. He knew more about Ryan Hart than anyone, but he also knew how much he had screwed things up last time. He was the reason Ryan was still out there. He wanted to get involved, he wanted to get him and put him away, but this is how it started last time, with the absolute certainty that he knew how to get Ryan off the streets. Followed by a dogged determination that practically drove him insane. He couldn't put himself or anyone else he cared about in that position again. As much as he hated to admit it, his help on this case would be more of a hindrance. He would have to bow to other people's instincts when it came to Ryan Hart, he had no perspective.

Chapter 11

The Mother

The Asia Room was done. It had taken them almost six weeks but they had done it, with time to spare. The room was an old disused ballroom that was being put back into use for the centenary celebrations. The next two weeks would be spent moving the animals that had been marked for restoration into one of the smaller storage rooms in order to make this room grand again, ready for a special dinner that would be attended by the mayor, the former directors and a few local minor celebrities in their respective fields, including several of the governors of the Churchill School for Boys.

Abbey was grateful for Parker's knowledge, it had made things go much faster. She liked working with him now, he was different. As time had gone on he had spent less and less time jotting things down in his pad and more time discussing the finds with Abbey. He was less guarded and she felt like they were friends. As they arranged the dioramas he would pick up a muskrat or a long-tailed weasel and go into great detail about the where and when, things she didn't know, like the habits and behaviours of the little creatures. He knew a lot about hunting rituals, he would get so lost in describing the animals in their natural habitat that she found it hard not to smile at him. He wouldn't see her smiling because he was hypnotised by an imaginary chase or lost in some faraway paradise.

Abbey and Parker stood side by side and watched as animals marked with red were tossed carelessly into large cardboard containers. Abbey found herself holding her breath, trying to keep back the tears that wanted to flow as she stared at the unceremonious end her friends were coming to. The disposal team were not careful, they did not respect the history at their finger-tips, they just mercilessly threw the creatures into the boxes, ready for incineration. As her hand rested help-lessly at her side, she felt Parker's fingers slide across her palm and gently hold on to her. She was grateful, even though she didn't acknowledge it, but she could feel that he understood in that moment. He squeezed her hand gently as a single tear rolled down her face. His fingers were so soft and smooth against her skin. Suddenly she remembered her little South American friend, the mother, the one she had not been able to identify. Still holding on to Parker she quickly ran across the museum to the room where she had left her, drag-ging a surprised Parker along with her. The men would be going there next, she had to know what she was,

Parker would know. They stopped to catch their breath. She saw Parker's confused expression but didn't have time to explain as she remembered that the stained-glass window had made it harder to see the identification number, which turned out to be too smudged to read anyway. She started to run again and found the aisle with the window at the end of it, they stopped and she let go of him as she saw her, carefully placed where Abbey had left her.

'What is she?' Abbey finally managed to say through her breathlessness.

Parker carefully took the creature from her and looked at her with the same affection Abbey had.

'She's a species of Lynx, I believe. It's hard to tell because she has no fur, which is their most distinctive feature. She's very young, too; they normally get much bigger than this. She's North American in origin, from Minnesota, I believe, or thereabouts. Did you know that the name Minnesota comes from the Sioux Indian language, it means sky-tinted water . . .'

Abbey's tears flowed freely as he described the beautiful surrounding to her. She was exhausted, not just with the job but with the work of being her, of being the Abbey she had been for the last five years. She felt the walls she had built crumble against her will. She wanted to be with Parker, to listen to him talk, to watch him, to not feel manipulated or used, to allow someone in.

Before she knew what she was doing she grabbed Parker by the collar and pulled him close, kissing him on the lips. He pulled back, surprised, and then his gaze softened into something so gentle, so completely sincere. His eyes moved from hers on to her lips, she held her breath for what seemed like an eternity as he moved in slowly, the multi-coloured light from the window bouncing off of his perfectly cut cheekbones. He kissed away the tear she could feel hovering on her lips, then the kiss turned deeper and unlike anything she had ever known, full of restraint and anticipation.

As Abbey held on to Parker she could not feel the weight of her memories any more. Parker had not tried to beguile her, he had not tried to put her at ease. She liked the way he was so eloquent and yet sometimes when he spoke to her about himself he tripped over his words, apologising for his most attractive feature. She could tell every word was calculated and thought out even when he had trouble saying them. She knew he wasn't being completely honest with her either, but she didn't mind. She recognised the lies for what they were, small mercies, to protect her from – what? From feeling uneasy? From a truth he didn't think she could handle? He was not smooth, he was not charming, he was awkward, aloof and somewhat naive. If Abbey could have she would suspend time for ever and exist outside of reality, outside of fear, outside of disappointment. She would freeze that exact moment and never move forward. She imagined the scene of her and Parker kissing in front of the stained-glass window, trapped inside a snow globe, where the pure beauty could be admired for ever.

What came next was always a let-down, maybe not immediately, but eventually there would be something, there always was. She had tried to get close to people, to men, since she left college, but the relationships never lasted. Men always wanted something Abbey was just not prepared to give. There would always be a part of Abbey still sitting on Christian's bed; she had never really left.

Parker finally pulled away. Abbey was breathless, dizzy. His eyes, for the first time she allowed herself to look into those eyes, so cold, so clear. She thought of the phrase he had used before, it so perfectly described them. Sky-tinted water. He had interlocked his fingers with hers; she could feel his heartbeat through his fingertips, thumping hard and fast.

'We're going to start on this lot now.' A voice broke the spell and she remembered where she was, the invisible magnet between them had been defused. She let go of his hands and resumed her position as overseer of the operation. When she turned back, Parker had gone.

Chapter 12

The Friend

Then

Christian's kisses were deeper and more passionate now. Abbey had opened her eyes and checked that in her drunken stupor she hadn't mistakenly started kissing someone else. He brushed his hand against her underpants and she thought about her beige tango knickers and suddenly wished she had worn the thong after all.

She heard the click on the door opening and jumped back, startled. Relief swept over her when she saw it wasn't Dani but Jamie. Then she blushed as she saw that Christian's hand was still between her legs. She put her hand on his wrist and tried to pull his hand away, but he resisted and kept it there, still gently stroking the top of her thigh. She looked up at Jamie, expecting him to leave the room when he realised his intrusion, but he stepped inside and closed the door behind him.

'Christian?' She pulled at Christian's hand again but still it wouldn't move.

'Don't worry about him.' Christian leaned in and kissed her harder than before, this time the butterflies in her stomach turned to big black moths, trapped and anxious.

'I should go.' She went to stand up but Christian's hand grabbed her shoulder firmly and Jamie moved closer, unbuttoning his shirt. At that moment she realised there was no way out of this room, not right now, she searched Christian's face for a sign that she was wrong, but there was nothing. She didn't recognise the face she was looking at.

'Dani will be wondering where I am.'

'She left already, said you should sleep it off.' Christian undid the clasp of her dress with ease. Over the course of the evening Abbey had imagined him doing it many times, but her fantasies never allowed for this particular scenario. She crossed her arms to cover herself but what had felt like the most courageous choice of clothing only hours before now felt like the worst decision she had ever made. Her focus shifted to the noise outside the room, laughter and music, a song she loved. She cherished the song for one last moment as she knew in the future it would forever be associated with this moment and the moments to follow. The moment she lost her faith in humanity, the moment she discovered the fragility of fantasy and the moment she understood the higher you put someone on a pedestal the further they have to fall.

Disappointment swept over her in waves, mostly disappointment in herself, in how naive she had been. She looked at the door, it looked so far away. Her body vibrated with dread as Jamie moved closer. Her mouth felt so dry and her breathing laboured as she tried not to panic, she didn't know why but she didn't want them to think of her as vulnerable. She had to keep it together. She wanted to leave but she couldn't. She wanted to get out. She had to get out. She closed her eyes and tried not to think about what was happening to her. Jamie sat on the other side of her and started to kiss her neck, his mouth felt cold and clammy. Her song played in the background, the romantic words twisted into a sinister threat as she slipped further and further away with every kiss, every touch. What would happen if she tried to leave? She really wanted to leave.

'I should go, I have a test to study for tomorrow.' Her voice felt so small and lost in the quiet room, the only other sound the heavy breathing and the muffled music through the door. 'Please . . . stop . . .'

No one was listening. Jamie pressed his mouth on to hers and pushed her back on to the bed. She tried to pull herself up but her shoulders were pinned from either side. Jamie moved and Christian's lips pressed against hers again, she could barely remember what she had felt like when he had kissed her for the first time just a little while ago. Everything had changed since then, the world had become such a different place in that short space of time. The only thing that she could think as the kissing turned to caressing and the caressing turned into something else entirely, was

113

stupid, stupid, stupid. She wondered if she screamed would anyone come. Not only that but screaming seemed like such a massive overreaction, as though she would be causing a fuss over nothing. Stupid. She closed her eyes and tried not to think about what was happening to her. She felt the pressure of a knee driving itself between her legs, which ached from being held so tightly together. She knew it was Christian, he wouldn't allow himself to come second to Jamie. There was an odd metallic taste in her mouth and she realised she had bitten into her pursed lips. She concentrated even harder on the music outside the room as he fumbled with his trousers and pulled hard at her underpants, ripping them loose. She held her breath as he pushed his way inside. Could he tell this was her first time? She braced herself as he ground against her until he let out a noise somewhere between a grunt and a groan before lowering his full weight on to her. She heard him panting into her ear and she felt sick again. She allowed herself to breathe. When he finally got up, she opened her eyes and saw Jamie undoing his flies and Christian slapping him on the back. It didn't hurt this time, she wasn't sure if this was because she had stopped feeling anything. Jamie was quicker, more frantic, she wished she had the guts to stare him in the face while he was doing it, but she just clamped her eyes shut again and waited for him to finish. She heard them talking but she couldn't make out the words, they swirled and jumbled in her head until they were nonsense. All the reasons this was her fault ran through her mind as they both used her body, a body she no longer felt connected to, as though it had separated from her mind and she was able to judge the one thing independently from the other.

When they were done and gone she lay on the bed alone for a while, unable to do much more than fasten the dress clasp around her neck and wipe herself clean with a T-shirt from his laundry basket. Christian's room, as cold as it had seemed when she first arrived, now looked clinical, sterile, hollow. The reason it had no character or personality was because Christian didn't have a soul. He had shown her his real face and it was grotesque.

She lay there sore, empty and heartbroken. Stupid. Just this afternoon she had wished for Christian's naked body to be pressed against hers but now it had happened she hated herself for ever liking him at all.

More immediately than that, she hated the fact that she would have to get home alone now, in this dress, it barely felt like a dress at all. She grabbed one of Christian's sweaters from a chair and tried to cover up just to get from this prison to her room, her sanctuary. Totally sober as she walked through the debris of the party, people still littered around and through the French doors, she saw Christian and Jamie laughing with one of Dani's friends.

'There you are!' She spun around to see Dani standing there with Christian's oversized jacket wrapped around her shoulders, a message to the rest of the boys at the party: hands off, she belonged to him. Abbey thought about the sweater she was wearing and wanted to rip it off, she didn't want to feel like his property, she didn't want people to think that of her.

'I thought you left,' Abbey managed to say after a moment of hesitation. In that moment she debated in her mind whether to break down or whether just to get the hell out of there.

'No, I was just about to come and get you. You were pretty out of it so I thought I would let you rest a bit.' She should go to a hospital and get a morning after pill, she should do something.

'I'm fine now, let's just go home.' Home. Home wasn't in her halls with Dani, home was with her dad. Oh my God, her dad, he would be so disappointed in her. She just wanted to curl up in her pink room and have him fetch her Horlicks and watch black and white movies together all day. Tomorrow was Sunday, she knew he would pick her up if she called, she desperately wanted to call. It was only an hour's drive. Would he know something was wrong if she called for no reason? Maybe she could pretend she needed to come home to do washing, yes, that was it; she would call in the morning.

Chapter 13

The Vicar

It was an unusually hot evening for August in Paris; the sticky heat was made even less bearable by the fact that wherever Reverend Stephen Collins tried to go, he was surrounded by hot and sweaty foreigners. He was working his way through the Pigalle district to get to the Hotel Shangri-La, the former home of the Bonaparte family that overlooked the Seine and the Eiffel tower, which was nothing like this run-down well-used part of town. He didn't usually venture this way, knowing full well that this was the epicentre of debauchery in the city of Paris, but today he had visited Sacré Coeur Basilica in Montmartre. The air was so thick he knew the storm was imminent, as did the amblers who rushed for cover as a crack of thunder ripped through the air, they crammed together under the awnings in front of the various seedy clubs as the raindrops began to fall.

This wasn't Stephen's first trip to Paris and it wouldn't be his last. When he had finally abandoned the school parish and renounced his faith in God he looked for something to reawaken his devotion to the church, but all he had found were yet more reasons to doubt the existence of God, himself being the most prevalent example he could think of. He would visit churches across Europe but quickly find himself in the wrong part of town, as if some instinct deep within him discovered these places without his knowledge. Within seconds the downpour was upon him, weighing him down, instantly wetting him through. The puddles on the uneven ground formed as though a tap were running into them. He dodged and jumped until he was on some sort of pavement.

Stephen's wife, Ellen, had died of cancer several years ago and the loneliness had been too much for him. He was unlikely to find anyone like her again, anyone who could deal with him, put up with his self-destructive streak. He had heard of places like this in the gentlemen's club he frequented back home, the men talked of the young beauties who were happy to give love and affection to an older man in exchange for a good meal and a few bob. When he had first visited Paris he had been shy, but these women knew how to put you at ease, they knew how to make you feel loved. He could walk into a bar and within seconds a girl a quarter of his age would be sitting and smiling at him, as if she had known him her whole life.

Tonight he was going to try somewhere new, it was too wet to make it to his usual haunt and a change was as good as a rest. He staggered away from the rain into a darkened club with a neon sign above the door and an arrow pointing inside.

'Hello sir.' An older Thai lady smiled perfect white teeth at him. He guessed she was the boss.

'Hello.'

'You want drink?'

'Yes, please.'

'You want girl?' Her face took on a devilish, knowing look as she stared into his eyes. Even though everyone in these places knew the score, Stephen couldn't help lowering his head and averting his eyes as he replied.

'Yes.'

'Sit, girl come.' She ushered him to a booth in the corner of the room, the place was quiet, the rain scaring off the potential marks.

No sooner had Stephen sat down than a girl appeared at his side, she was beautiful, her face full of kindness, no make-up, just natural beauty. He fell in love for the third time this week.

'Hello, Mr . . .' She spoke in a soft voice, barely audible above the music that was playing.

'Stephen.' He smiled.

'Hello, Mr Stephen, my name Lilly.' Stephen doubted very much that her name was Lilly; he knew the women were advised to Westernise their names for the customers.

'Nice to meet you, Lilly.' She scooched up next to him and placed her delicate hand on his. She sat nervously for a moment.

'You want come private room?'

'No,' Stephen said, almost offended. Not everything

was about sex, he just longed for companionship, the kind that's hard to come by for an old man like him, the kind where you don't have to answer any questions about who you are and where you come from, the kind you have to pay for. He had tried the British escorts back home but they had offered very little in the way of friendship, with their false eyelashes and fake tans. He liked the Thai girls because they behaved like women should behave, with respect and dignity, and the language barrier eliminated the threat of deep conversation. British women were just too brash.

'You come private room, I give sex to you.' Lilly smiled.

He wanted her to shut up. If he closed his eyes he could block out this awful place, he could block out the reason he was here, but he couldn't block out her voice. Her sweet sound was a painful reminder of his crippling loneliness and the fact that he was not only lonely but alone, totally and utterly alone.

'You want me dance?' she asked, a note of desperation in her voice. He could tell she was worried she wasn't pretty or good enough, worried he would send her back and ask for a different girl; he was thinking about it but he knew what the consequences would be for her if he did that. He couldn't do it. He saw the track marks on the inside of her elbows and realised that life was probably hard enough for Lilly already.

'No, it's OK, just sit with me.' He just wanted the warmth of her hand on his, the contact. He thought about his hotel room and how good it would feel to fall asleep next to someone again, how good it would feel to wake up next to someone; all the things you take for granted when you're married.

He wished he could go back and do things over, there was so much he would change; not just the way he had treated Ellen. He resigned himself to the fact that losing Ellen so many years ago had been punishment for the secret life he had led. People had come to him with their problems, searching for answers, and he had given them with resolve, with the certainty of someone who had all the answers, someone who believed in something bigger than himself. It had all been a lie though. He had feigned compassion and empathy, but behind closed doors he was a bitter lonely old man. Now he wanted someone to lie to him, to tell him that everything would work out, that there was a plan of some kind for him. Anything but this empty existence.

He looked over at Lilly, who was quiet and biting her lip, clearly unsure what to do with him if he didn't want to fuck her. He was jealous of her simplicity, of the knowledge she had of her role. Her role was to be an object of desire for lonely old travellers, but he didn't know what his role was any more. He hadn't worked since he stopped being a vicar, and had been living off his modest pension. Thankfully he had married money so hadn't needed to work after Ellen had passed. He had no friends and no family to speak of, except a nephew he had never met and probably never would. As far as Stephen knew he wasn't special to anyone, except maybe to Lilly in this moment. She hung on his every word, waiting to do his bidding, ready to fulfil her purpose.

Maybe she acted in the hope he would rescue her, would take her away from this place to a better life with him. But he was too damaged. Eventually he would hurt her like he had hurt Ellen, like he had hurt so many others. The kind of hurt that leaves physical marks. He wondered if his punishment was being alive, living with the memory of his past sins, always wishing for a second chance. But there are no second chances, not really. It was an unstoppable truth about Stephen, he was poison. That's why he stuck to these short intervals to his loneliness; he knew he deserved nothing better.

Lilly put her hand on his thigh, his body did not respond how it would have years ago, if anything the pressure of that expectation made him feel even limper. He reached into his pocket and pulled out a wad of money, sliding the notes into her hand under the bar, she put the money in her stocking and then proceeded to move her hand up his thigh. Part of him wanted her to carry on, but he had become superstitious since Ellen had died and he could just imagine her disapproving gaze looking upon him from the heavens. He didn't want to disappoint her in death as much as he had done in life. Sometimes his conscience won this fight, sometimes the beast inside him did. Tonight the desperate look in Lilly's eyes had made him reconsider, made him remember why he made these trips, or at least why he told himself he did.

'No, thank you, Lilly, I have to go now.' Lilly looked both hurt and grateful at the same time.

Stephen slid out of the booth and walked over to the madam at the pedestal by the door.

'She no good? I got young girl, I got virgin.'

'What? No . . . no, thank you.' He pulled out more cash and gave it to her, it shut her up and he walked out, disgusted with himself, he should have gone to his regular bar, the girls there at least pretended not to be so completely helpless, at least they shot up between their toes.

He placed his key card in the slot outside his hotel room door. He was on the third floor and was looking forward to staring out over the city and being as detached from the rest of the world as he felt. He clicked the door open and the lights were already on in his suite. The hairs on the back of his neck prickled, he felt his sixth sense kick into play, but he entered the room nonetheless.

He walked over to the seating area and saw a box on the table, gift wrapped with a bow on it. He sat heavily on the sofa, staring at the box in front of him, aware that his wet clothing was seeping into the luxurious white chenille. He wasn't afraid to open the box, he knew what was inside – he had seen a box like this before, he had given it to someone once. He remembered the excited look on their face and then the fear and acceptance that had come as soon as it had been opened.

'Are you still here?' Stephen said.

'Yes.' A man's voice came from behind him, it was deeper than he expected, older than he remembered, flat.

'I wondered if I would ever see you again.'

'You knew you would.' Still flat, unforgiving, controlled.

123

'Yes, I suppose I did. Are you going to kill me?' It was a stupid question and Stephen knew it.

'Open the box.'

Stephen looked inside the box and saw what he had expected to see – a collar, with a four-pronged metal bar attached to the front, two prongs at either end. It looked like a double-ended barbecue fork, one to stick in the neck, one in the chest. This was the exact collar, the exact box.

'I'm glad you got away, for what it's worth. I hoped you would be OK.'

'Does anything about this seem OK to you?' The voice cracked slightly, Stephen could hear the pain.

'No, I suppose not.' Stephen stood up slowly and removed his coat, throwing it on the sofa beside him. He stepped forward over to the window, looking out over the stunning illuminated city for one last time. He didn't focus on the shadowy reflection that approached him from behind, he was not scared, he wasn't going to run. 'Room service have strict instructions not to bother me for a couple of days.'

'I doubt it will take that long,' the man said as he pulled Stephen's hands behind his back and bound them together. He started to pull him towards the bedroom.

'Can I just stay in here? I know I have no right to ask you for anything but I would like to stand here, if this is going to be it.' He heard the man sigh and then he pulled Stephen over to the window and tethered him to a mahogany console table that was fixed to the wall. He wrapped the cord several times so the blood flow in his hands was restricted; they started to throb and Stephen thought of Lilly's gentle fingers.

Then came the collar. Stephen lifted his head as the man placed it around his neck and positioned the prongs between his chin and his chest; the pressure to keep the head up was exhausting, eventually when his head dropped the wounds would not be immediately fatal, but they prolonged the suffering and the pain was immense. It wouldn't take long though, not for Stephen, without his heart medication he doubted he would last the night and he was thankful for that. The heretics fork, that's what this was called, that's what would eventually kill him. He had to chuckle at the aptness of the name. From the corner of his eye he saw the man leave the room. This was it. He was truly alone now, and it was only a matter of time.

Chapter 14

The Break

It had been a week since a complacent Ryan had been questioned and released. Officers were stationed outside his house round the clock and Adrian was under the watchful eye of the rest of the force. Just in case he decided to do something stupid. Adrian had been asked to go through all of his old notes from his previous investigation into Ryan Hart to see if there was any indication that he was planning on killing his father. He could see by the thoroughness of his notes when he had started to lose it – half-finished reports, limited descriptions and vague comments as well as one-word scribbles in his notebook that probably made sense at the time of writing. He had been through the case before, it had been pulled apart to try and secure a case of harassment against Adrian and there was nothing, he knew it, Morris knew it. Adrian was well aware this was all just a way to keep him busy, keep him out of the way.

Adrian left work and walked a different route to usual. He didn't much fancy going home to be alone with his thoughts. He stumbled across a little pub, hidden away off the main streets, and it looked quiet so he walked in. He sat himself in the darkest corner he could find. It wasn't his local, it wasn't even a pub he had seen before. It was tiny and the clientele were obviously used to seeing the same faces night after night, but Adrian sat down nonetheless. He wanted to get drunk to the point where he couldn't remember his name. He remembered this feeling from the last time Ryan Hart had been the subject of their inquiries. The need to disappear, to stop thinking because things weren't adding up the way they were supposed to and he was so desperate to get Ryan off the streets. Something at the back of his mind was whispering to him, whispering what? He didn't know. But there was something he was forgetting, something he was missing. Something. Something.

He had just finished his fourth pint when he decided this wasn't enough of a distraction for him, he needed a little more tangibility, a little more human contact.

Adrian left the quiet pub and walked through the town, happy that he wasn't working tonight. Outside the pubs the smokers gathered in order to get their fix, he could really use a cigarette around about now. He watched the familiar sight of people much younger than him making all the mistakes he had made a hundred times over and then some. The urge to misbehave that was almost compulsory in the hot, sticky evenings. When you could practically taste the pheromones in the air, the smell of fresh sweat pushing all the right buttons; making all of these carnal encounters a little easier to engineer. The men plying the girls with alcohol just to get them to converse. The fake smiles and compliments when everyone just wanted the same thing, to find that one special person so they didn't have to go through this bullshit week in and week out. Adrian thought of how he had believed he had found that in Andrea, not realising that she had never felt the same. She knew she was destined for coffee mornings and designer shoes. Adrian was always a stepping stone, her rebellious phase before she settled down. He shook off the image of Andrea, it was no use thinking about her, she didn't care about him so he couldn't allow himself to care about her. And anyway, the Andrea he was in love with did not exist any more, she was a cold hard bitch these days and it was no act.

Back to the task at hand. Just outside of the very centre of town Adrian walked towards the prison and stopped at one of the many town houses that had been split into flats. The building itself was slightly dishevelled but still if you didn't look a couple of hundred metres to your left you would have no idea that it was in such close proximity to a category B prison holding just over five hundred men. He rang one of the buzzers.

'Hello,' a woman's voice came over the intercom.

'It's Adrian.' The buzzer sounded and Adrian pushed his way inside. The first door was open and Denise

Ferguson, the desk sergeant, was leaning against the frame, holding a large glass of wine. She looked at him apathetically.

'I wondered if I was ever going to see you again . . . here at least.'

'Were you expecting company?' He nodded to her short satin nightdress.

'I never know when to expect company,' she said with a pinch of bitterness, before opening the door wide and wandering inside herself, obviously waiting for Adrian to follow.

He sat on the sofa and watched her as she poured him a drink from the crystal decanter that occupied her white dresser. The whole room was white, or off white, or any other variation of white you can think of. She was either pretending to be angry or she actually was annoyed at him, to be honest he didn't care either way. He knew she probably didn't care either. The evenings always ended the same.

Denise had a short, almost masculine haircut, bright blue eyes and at work she always wore blood-red lipstick, but at home she was natural, he preferred her that way. Their relationship, if you could call it that, had started around two years ago. It was an informal arrangement. Strictly business. He hadn't had sex with her since before he had been suspended, usually they only got together after a particularly long day at work. They didn't flirt at work, in fact they barely acknowledged each other. No clandestine meetings or furtive glances. It wasn't because they had anything to hide, it just wasn't a big deal. It was convenient. The downside of course being that there was no passion, just a perfunctory fuck every few weeks.

Adrian walked over to where she was standing with her back to him. He came up behind her and took the drink she had poured him from her hand, pressing her against the dresser with his groin as he drank the neat scotch. He slammed it back down and trapped her hands underneath his, she arched her back and pushed back in all the right places. He kissed her neck and she moaned, letting go of whatever residual anger remained after being overlooked for so long. She tried to turn around but he kept his hands firmly on top of hers. The glasses on the dresser clinked and clattered as he continued to grind against her. Finally he released his grip, her hands were red from the pressure he had put them under. She turned to face him in the little space he had given her to move, brushing every surface of hers against him. Breathless she kissed him on the lips and he grabbed at her thighs, hoisting her up on to the side. She wrapped her legs around his waist and he kissed her back, deep and hard. He took her hands and held them behind her in one of his; his other hand on her throat, gently squeezing. This was her preference, and not his, but he was a pleaser, he liked to do what they liked, he was adaptable. She didn't like to mess around, her hand went straight to his belt and she undid it deftly. It wasn't long before he had picked her up again and thrown her on the white leather sofa. For all intents and purposes she was ready to go, clawing at his fly to get it open before this rare moment of urgency passed. Maybe it was because he hadn't been with her for months or maybe it was because he had had a particularly bad day, but it was over as quickly as it had started. The slightest amount of friction set him off, he didn't even have time to pull out.

'Sorry,' he said, disingenuously.

'I told you I'm on the pill.' She exhaled as he stood up.

'Yeah, well, I've heard that one before,' he said, a little less affably than he should have.

'Don't worry, Officer, I'm not the maternal type.' She pulled her nightdress down again and got up to get another glass of wine.

'I should go,' he said, half embarrassed but more concerned with the idea that she may want to 'talk'.

'Of course you should,' she huffed.

Adrian walked over to her and put his hand at the nape of her neck. He could feel the prickles of her short hair as she leaned into his palm like a cat who relished even the smallest bit of affection. He tilted her head towards him and kissed her again. He could taste the wine on her lips.

'I'm sorry,' he whispered.

He ran his hand down the front of her body slowly until he reached the top of her thigh. Sliding his hand between her legs slowly until she came closer. The viscous liquid he had left behind just moments before clung to his fingers as he moved them against her. Adrian kissed her neck and felt her exhale, making sure he was using just the right amount of pressure to cause those involuntary shudders. Steadying herself against the table she shook occasionally at his touch but he knew to wait, not to go too fast. He kissed the top of her shoulders and kept kissing in towards the collarbone until she squirmed. He pulled back and looked at her face, her eyes were closed and her brow furrowed, concentrating on the rhythmic movements of his fingertips. Faced with the sight of her breathless in front of him, his body responded. Her skin was aglow with a dewy perspiration. He pushed her up against the wall and kissed her hard before biting her neck gently at first then hard enough to draw tiny gasps from her lips. His body was close to hers now. He leaned against her to help her stay upright as his fingers worked with increasing vigour. She fought to keep her balance, digging her nails into his back as he pushed deeper until she finally wilted, loosening her grip and catching her breath at the same time. He waited a moment, revelling in the warmth of their connection, before pulling away slowly, giving her time to adjust to standing on her own again.

He went over to the sink and washed his hands, the connection broken again, the interaction finished.

'Why don't you stay . . .' she asked when she could speak again.

'I can't tonight. Maybe next time,' he said, not sure what else to say. Not wanting to be completely cold.

He felt like a shit but he left anyway, she could handle it, she knew the deal. This was just how it worked between them, the only way it could work. He had to battle out his demons alone before he subjected anyone else to them. He needed to get a handle on this case, it was time to stop fucking around.

*   *   *

It was Adrian's turn to buy the cigarettes – he had absolutely promised – and it wouldn't be long before Grey turned up. He left the house and looked up at the sky, it was white and there was a chill in the air despite it being late August. In weather like this the tower of St Thomas' church loomed over the compact terraces like an agent of doom. The white clouds rolled against the white sky in what felt like a stop-motion movie reel. Not the best day to have a hangover. Even though there wasn't a glimmer of sunlight it hurt to look up, it hurt to look anywhere. Adrian wished he had worn his shades.

He stumbled into Uncle Mac's, the corner shop at the end of his road. He stumbled because it was stacked floor to ceiling, with a small path carved out between all the products. It was a precarious task to move from one part of the shop to another without a mass of biscuits falling from the sky. He grabbed some milk and some bacon and headed over to the tiny counter. A young woman emerged from behind the giant chewing-gum racks that ran from the counter to the ceiling. She processed the items without looking up and put them into a blue carrier bag.

'Twenty of those as well, please.' Adrian pointed at the brand he knew Grey smoked.

'Twenty.' Her voice cracked as she copied him, he watched her lips as she silently mouthed the word over and over again. She put the cigarettes in the bag, too.

'I haven't seen you in here before, are you new?' He leaned down to get eye contact, she looked at him then looked away nervously.

133

'Yes, I'm new.' Her accent wasn't quite the same as Dimi's, the store owner.

'Are you a member of Dimi's family? He has a lot of family, huh?' Adrian smiled.

'Yes, family.' She kept her answers short.

Adrian pulled out his wallet to pay and he saw her eyes flash with fear as she saw his police badge. Dimi had told him before of the corruption of the police force in his home country. Adrian was embarrassed; he paid and closed his wallet quickly. He was ashamed that there were people in his position of power, albeit limited, who used it to manipulate and harm. If you can't trust the people who are meant to be looking out for you, then who can you?

'Keep the change.' He handed her a twenty-pound note. He liked Dimi but he was a penny pincher, always thrusting out-of-date products in Adrian's face at the counter. One time he wouldn't let him leave the shop until he had purchased a crate of cat food tins, and he didn't even have a cat. He was a persuasive old bugger all right. As Adrian walked out of the shop he heard the music blasting from Grey's car before he saw it. He rushed over and got in, the bacon would just have to sit on the back seat all day.

Adrian burst into DCI Morris' office. Morris was sitting at his desk staring down at the phone and rubbing his temples. He looked exasperated. The deep creases around his eyes were exaggerated by his frown.

'Sir, this is ridiculous. I know Ryan's history better than anyone else in this building and while you lot are all playing catch-up he's still out there living it large. He's making a fool out of us!'

Grey sauntered in behind Adrian, hanging back just enough to avoid being caught in the crossfire.

'Do you know who I just got off the phone with? The IPCC, Adrian. We're still hurting from your last run-in with Ryan Hart, we're lucky his lawyers didn't go for financial restitution. If we put you on the case too they will have your badge, maybe even mine! Can you imagine the newspapers if the Police Commission weigh in on this?'

'Let me worry about my badge, sir, there is no one who wants this bastard put away more than I do. I'll stay under the radar.'

DCI Morris stood up and leaned over his desk, staring Adrian straight in the eye.

'Miles, they want to send someone from the NCA down but I've promised them I can handle it. At this point, handling it means handling you as well, they made that very clear.'

DCI Morris sat back down in his chair. He wasn't shouting any more, that was a good sign.

'Just let us look over the files, sir, the new ones, too.' Grey stepped forward. 'What harm can that do?'

'Grey, you keep an eye on him, don't let him drag you down at the same time. All eyes are on us at the moment. I'm not stepping in for you next time, Miles.'

'Thank you, sir.' Adrian left the office and went to the incident room, grabbing Ryan and Kevin's files from the front desk.

'Stay away from Ryan Hart!' Morris shouting across

the room, everyone looked at Adrian, who was already thumbing through the reports.

Adrian's stomach lurched as he looked at the photographs of the crime scene. Everything about it was wrong. The room was immaculate, all apart from the bed where Kevin's body lay in several pieces, all re-arranged but still in the shape of a human being, if not in the correct order. The feet were on the wrong legs and the hands on opposite sides, too. There was something almost biblical about the scene, a sense of ceremony. A point to be made. As Adrian finished studying a picture he would hand it to Grey, whose face was in a constant state of grimace.

'Damn!' she muttered. 'Ryan had some real daddy issues.'

'It's too much. It's overkill.'

'You aren't wrong. This is the very definition of overkill.'

'I didn't get on with my dad either, but this?' Adrian took a deep breath and looked out the window, something was niggling at him. A memory?

'You don't think it was Ryan, do you?'

'I don't know, Ryan's a lowlife but I don't see him removing all of his dad's organs.'

'No?'

'He might make someone disappear, but to actually do that . . . this . . . it's . . .'

'You think someone else did it, as a message for him? Like a rival drug dealer type thing?'

'No love lost between Ryan and his father; there are plenty of other things that would upset him more. That dog, for a start. Some old duffer ran over his last dog then mysteriously ended up in critical condition over at Wonford Hospital. We could never prove it was him but it was, he told me as much. If you wanted to upset Ryan Hart, you would kill his dog not his dad.'

'Plus where are the organs?'

'Exactly!'

'I mean, removing them is weird, do you think it's some black market thing?'

'Kevin Hart was a fat old diabetic alcoholic; his organs were barely worth anything to him, let alone anyone else.'

'So why then?'

'I don't know, but I do know I need to speak to Ryan again.'

'Miley, are you trying to get me fired?' She smiled.

'We got him!' Daniels burst into the incident room holding aloft a photograph. 'CCTV got him down on the quay at 11:45, not at his mate's playing poker.'

'Go pick him up,' Morris said, clapping his hands together with a note of finality.

'The quay's a bit of a way from the vic's house,' Adrian said.

'You need to get back in the gym, son,' Daniels cackled. 'All that time off has made you soft. I can do that in ten minutes.'

'Yes, all right, Robocop, you are amazing but you're missing the point. This whole crime scene took a long time, it's meticulous and pristine. There were no prints, not even Hart's, so the whole place was cleaned. Even the blood doesn't tell us anything, he must have cut the body up in the bath or something because we are missing a good couple of litres. He would have had to get there, kill and dismember his father, clean up the crime scene, without leaving any forensics anywhere and then get back to the poker tourney well within an hour. No. Whoever did this took their sweet time about it.'

'The point is we've broken his alibi. If we keep digging into it we'll find out the rest, it's enough for a warrant to search his place at the very least,' Morris said rubbing his forehead, clearly frustrated with Adrian. 'Daniels, why are you still here? Go pick that bastard up!'

'Uniforms stationed outside his place just knocked on his door, sir, no answer. I think he's given them the slip,' Fraser said reluctantly.

'For fuck's sake!' DCI Morris snapped through his teeth.

'Let me talk to him, sir, when you find him,' Adrian offered, knowing full well he was pushing his luck.

'No, in fact, you can go home for the rest of the day. You too, Grey.'

'But, sir?' She threw her hands up in the air, ultimately knowing there was no point in arguing.

'You have got to stay out of this one. I don't want either of you here when we bring him in, we cannot let him get away with this one.'

'What did I do though, sir?' Grey asked.

'Grey, I'm sorry. Drive around, chase up on some old leads, do anything anywhere that isn't here. I want you both out of the way.'

Grey huffed and shot Adrian a look that would cut through glass. She walked out. He grabbed his jacket and car keys and followed. Adrian came out to see Grey leaning on his car smoking a cigarette, she offered him one, and he took it.

'This is bullshit.'

'I'm sorry.'

'Fuck sorry, tell me about Ryan.' She handed him her lighter.

'He's been in the system for ever, started out in some crappy chav gang and gradually moved himself into some kind of power position.'

'I thought his dad was loaded?'

'Yeah, but his parents kicked him out when he was about fourteen, kept getting pulled up for vandalism and criminal damage. The final straw was when he got done for selling rock at his posh private school, his parents ditched him, didn't want him to ruin their daughter's chances, his sister's. Said they didn't want his junkie friends hanging around her.'

'Any abuse?'

'No doubt. Kevin Hart's a big bull of a man, well, he was. He had a temper, I'm sure Ryan got his unfair share of it.'

'Sexual?'

'He had plenty of hospital reports from when he was a kid, cracked ribs, broken arm, you know, a lot of bike accidents, never a hint of anything else as far as I know.'

'Maybe Ryan just cracked.'

'And did that? Takes more than a couple of broken bones to turn you into the kind of person who would do something like that.' Adrian knew what it was to take a beating from your father – he had the scars to prove it, psychological and physical. He took a drag on the cigarette and turned away, trying to avoid eye contact with Grey. He had told her about his father's habit, but unless you ever cared about someone with a methamphetamine addiction you couldn't understand. There were no words to convey what it was like to come home from school at thirteen years old to find your father cutting into himself with a vegetable knife, trying to dig the imaginary beetles out from under his skin. Within a year the person you once loved and knew became something else, a demon of sorts, with a low rasping voice that said the most hurtful and obscene things. There was a difference between the high-functioning alcoholic he had grown up with and the man he watched slowly wane into nothing. The only saving grace was that his father managed to avoid arrest and so Adrian had the option of joining the police. He could feel Grey's eyes on him so he got in the car to avoid further scrutiny. 'You coming?'

'Where are we going?'

'I'll tell you when we get there.'

Chapter 15

The Monster

Parker had always known what he would do, he couldn't really remember if he had decided on his chosen career path or if it had decided on him, it had felt somewhat inevitable. He had been around museums his whole life. His father had been an archaeologist, his mother a photographer and so they travelled the world excavating sites and uncovering interesting artefacts. His parents had died in a car crash when he was ten and he had moved in with his grandfather. He hadn't lied to Abbey about that childhood visit to this museum, although maybe he hadn't quite been honest with her – that was something he did, told half-truths to spare people from the reality of his youth.

He sat in his kitchen eating his toast while Sally bounded around expectantly; she knew it was almost time for her walk. Sally had saved Parker's life and had been his companion for almost seven years now. It seemed stupid but she had given him purpose, a reason to stay alive, to keep fighting. The only child of an only child, Parker didn't have a loving extended family after his parents died. Without Sally he would have given up on himself. He needed that dependence, he needed that love, that feeling of being needed. Before Sally he had never known what it was to love. It had always been a mystery to Parker, the feeling of being bound to someone, putting someone else's wellbeing before your own. Before Sally, Parker had been full of hate, hate for himself, hate for his life and hate for the world. Sally had made him feel like he was worth loving. She had shown him that the world wasn't entirely hateful.

He grabbed her lead from the coat hook and smiled as her excitement went up a notch. It was beginning to rain a little outside; when they got home she would fill the house with that damp smell he found so distasteful.

He found himself standing outside Abbey's building as the light drizzle turned into a downpour, shielding his head with the morning paper. Increasingly he found himself walking Sally on this route. He wondered if he should buzz her flat, the kiss had meant something, hadn't it? He was unsure of which flat was hers. Compelled, he pressed a few buzzers but there was no response, it was very early on a Saturday morning, everyone was probably asleep. The rain got heavier with every passing moment and they needed shelter, he could hear Sally's unimpressed whimpers urging him to get them inside. His skin was freezing beneath his clothes. He stood back and looked up; trying to guess which window might be Abbey's. He walked to the alley by the side of the building and saw a fire escape attached to it; Sally followed him loyally up the stairs. They reached the second floor and Parker peered through the window; it was Abbey's lounge, she was asleep on the sofa. He watched her for a moment, had it not been for the rain and Sally's disapproving look he would have stood on the metal staircase and watched her for longer, but he felt guilty for even allowing himself this small indulgence. He knocked on the window and saw Abbey stir. She looked at her front door so he knocked again, finally she looked in his direction, at first she seemed scared until the state of him made it obvious he was no threat, not to mention poor wet Sally staring at her helplessly through the large window. She rushed over and opened it.

'What are you doing here?' she asked as she threw a large blanket over Sally before she had a chance to shake herself out all over the living room.

'Sorry! Underestimated the weather, totally didn't dress appropriately.' His long woollen coat was soaked right through, she took it from him and went to get a towel.

The rain started to thump against the window even harder and Parker was relieved they were now inside. It would have taken them at least half an hour to get back home.

Abbey gave Parker a towel, cold water dripped down his back from his hair. His clothes were stuck to him and he was starting to shiver. He threw his newspaper on the coffee table; it was wet through, barely worth keeping.

'I'll get you a dressing gown, you can put your clothes on the radiators, if you want I can switch the heating on for a bit.' He did want, the longer he stood inside with these sodden clothes on, the wetter he felt. Sally had already made herself at home, shaking and curling up on the ground, looking very sorry for herself indeed.

Parker started to undo his shirt, conscious that his skin was a shade paler than white, but so wet that he didn't care, the rainwater ran down his legs, he could feel his toes puckering from the moisture his socks had absorbed. He kicked off his shoes and bent down to remove his socks. Abbey returned with the dressing gown and he stood up quickly.

'Thank you, sorry about this, it was just drizzle when we left our place, I thought we might get away with it.' He had planned to walk past Abbey's place anyway, it was just dumb luck the weather had forced his hand and made him ring the doorbell and climb the fire escape.

'I'll make you a cup of tea.' Abbey's gaze was fixed on something behind him, a haunted look across her face. He grabbed the gown and when she had gone to the kitchen he looked to see what had spooked her. He saw the large mirror behind him. He was also shocked at the sight of his back, something he actively avoided looking at; it had been a long time.

The deep, ridged pink scars seemed more pronounced than he remembered, maybe due to the fact that his skin was so white in comparison. The long burrowed lines that stretched across his back in every direction had been no accident, there was no explaining it away as something small or trivial, they showed the malicious

144

intent that had driven them. He quickly put on the navy blue dressing gown before removing his trousers, grateful that Abbey was a sensible girl and his humiliation had not been added to by anything too feminine. He hung his clothes on the radiator and sat himself on the sofa, he tried to control his breathing, he could feel his heartbeat quicken and he was feeling guilty that he had come here at all. It was as though he had forgotten, or willed himself to forget. He'd thought for a moment that he was normal, like any other man; that's how she made him feel. Or maybe he had wanted her to see, perhaps deep down he was somehow thinking she might understand. That invisible string between them was pulling at his subconscious, making him do something different.

She held out a mug of tea when she returned and he concentrated hard on making sure his hand was not shaking when he lifted it to take the drink from her. She perched next to him on the sofa. He hoped to pull the conversation away from anything too personal.

Parker tried not to shiver, desperately focusing on the heat from the tea in his hands and not the fact that he was almost completely naked. He knew she was burning to ask him about his scars. He could almost see the unsaid words looming in the air in a thought cloud. He had come here for some reason, he could have turned around and gone home when the rain came down. He could have walked past her place. He could have done a million things to ensure that she didn't see what she had seen. Maybe a part of him had wanted to let her know that he understood whatever she was hiding from him; that he could see past the person she was pretending to be, and show her that there was more to him too. He wanted to make it easier for her; it was too late to pretend.

'They don't hurt, they just look bad. That's all.' He breathed out.

'Who did that to you?'

'It's not important, it was another life.'

'Can I see?' He was taken aback by the request, he could see she was a little taken aback by it herself. He stood up and took the robe off, his back facing her, completely naked, in her living room. Strangely he was more self-conscious about Sally seeing him like this, even though the dog was clearly more interested in the bowl of leftover bolognese Abbey had put in front of her. He stood so straight, almost like he was undergoing some kind of military inspection. Could she tell he had stood like this so many times before? He had been afraid to move, afraid of the punishment for disobedience. He kept his eyes fixed on the distance as he remembered the countless occasions when he had been instructed to stand to attention in his old life, remembering each lashing he had received, in a room so completely different to this one, devoid of any goodness. He relaxed his shoulders, stopping himself from conceding to his muscle memory, fighting against the dissociation that came with the stance.

The deep grooves in his back could not fully demonstrate the extent of the pain Parker had experienced, the full extent of the humiliation he had endured. He tried not to flinch as he felt her warm fingers on his back, knowing she meant him no harm. Her small hands began tracing their way across the lines that merged, crossed and blurred into one big monster, like a brand. She traced along the ripples on the surface of his skin where his torn flesh had clung to the instrument with each application, before it was ripped away only to be employed over and over again. He turned around, still aware of his nudity but wanting to look at her, to see the twisted look of horror on her face when she realised what sort of man he was. But there was no disgust, just sadness. She was crying, crying silent tears for him.

'Shhh, it's OK,' he comforted her. 'I'm OK.' He put his arms around her and he could feel her warm face against his cold skin, against his heart. Seeing his scars was not easy for anyone, he knew that. Of the handful of times anyone had seen them this was the first time he hadn't felt penitent. Instead he wanted to reassure Abbey that the worst was over; this moment wasn't about him. Abbey reached for his gown and helped him to put it back on. He fastened the tie and sat down. Abbey climbed on to the sofa next to him and pulled him close to her, stroking his hair. He had no answers for the questions he could tell she wanted to ask, not right now. It was true that his scars were no longer painful to touch but to talk about them was another matter entirely. The emotional damage ran through to his very foundation. He was nothing but damage, he was nothing but hurt.

'You don't have to tell me what happened,' Abbey whispered softly as her fingertips trailed through his hair. 'But if you ever want to, I'm here.'

147

Part of him wanted to get out now but Sally was snoring contented on the floor, her paws resting on Abbey's feet. He didn't want to leave the comfort and warmth of Abbey's embrace, he couldn't remember the last time he had been held like this. Probably not since his parents had been alive. The rain still pounded against the glass and Parker concentrated on the rhythm of the precipitation until his eyelids grew heavy. He allowed sleep to take him over, if only to escape the conversation he knew was surely inevitable now.

Chapter 16

The Confession

Then

Abbey's skin blistered with the heat of the shower, it was as hot as she could take without it physically scalding her, her scalp ached as the steaming droplets thumped against it. She wanted to burn away as many layers of skin as she could, she would peel them off if she had to. Her father would be there in less than an hour and this was her third shower since the night before. She wanted every trace of them gone before he arrived, she couldn't bear the idea of their smell on her. Her gums were red and sore, she had brushed and brushed her teeth, her tongue, her lips; knowing full well she would have to kiss her father on the cheek, if she didn't he would know, he would know what she had done with her mouth, what had been done to her body.

She stripped her bed and tossed her bedding into a black sack, she had no clothes to wash, only her knickers from the night before and she had thrown them in the bin. If she could have thrown herself away she would have, she felt completely disposable. How could she have been so stupid? Christian's words from the night before rang in her mind, 'you're actually quite pretty'. What had seemed like a compliment at the time took on a new meaning as she remembered his emphasis on the word 'actually'. Was he using the word to reassure her or was he expressing surprise at the fact he had never thought of her that way, even though she had imagined he had? The flirtations and interactions between them weren't what she had first thought them to be. Was he just figuring out how weak she was? Was he studying her to see how much he could get away with? No, she realised, he was building trust, building desire, making sure that when the situation arose she would feel too confused to cry out.

She sat on her bare divan as she waited for her father. She just wanted her dad to be there, wanted to be out of this room, out of this town, away. She couldn't imagine ever returning at this point, she didn't want to study, she didn't want to socialise, and she just wanted to be at home with her dad, like old times. Why did she have to go to university anyway? She could just get a job and work her way into a career, plenty of people did it. Her thoughts were interrupted by Dani, back from an early morning charity club meeting. She clocked Abbey's packed bag.

'I didn't know you were going to your fam's today!'

'I've just got to pick some stuff up from home.'

'That's a shame, me and Christian were going to see if you and Jamie wanted to come to the cinema, it's a cult movie marathon and it's only a quid to get in.'

'Can't. Sorry.'

'Hey, Mr Lucas!' Dani beamed.

Grateful to see her father's face peering round the door, Abbey shot up and grabbed her things. She didn't look behind her as she rushed out muttering a goodbye on her way.

In the car Abbey turned the radio up loud so she didn't have to converse with her dad, unsure of whether or not her voice would betray her. She felt shaky and the tears wanted to come, she hadn't cried yet but she had berated herself over and over again. A constant replay of the previous night's events circulated through her thoughts. She couldn't put her finger on what upset her the most. She couldn't confide in Dani because she had kissed Christian, she had wanted to so badly. She couldn't remember ever telling them to stop what they were doing. She must have done. Why hadn't she screamed the place down?

Lost in thought she didn't notice her father had stopped the car already, parked outside the house she had grown up in, a house she didn't want to taint by walking inside. But she still had a faint hope that all the good memories and precious moments would wash her clean, cleaner than any shower could. When the music stopped she snapped back to the present and she became aware of her father's gaze on her. Concern, love, protection, safety.

'Everything OK, pumpkin?' Pumpkin was what he had always called her, never by her name, not once that she could remember.

'Just a little hung-over.' Not a lie, but not the whole truth. Lying to him had always been impossible, he was too important to lie to. She had never really needed to lie before now but she wanted to protect him from the knowledge of what kind of girl she was. What kind of girl was she? She kissed her best friend's boyfriend, then what? What had actually happened? How could she want him so much one moment, then not at all the next? Her behaviour, her dress, the drinking, the flirting, she knew all of that would be under scrutiny; not what he did, he was the life and soul of the party. She knew no one would have a bad word to say about him. Was there even any point in telling anyone about it? No, there wasn't.

Be normal she told herself. Well, she had never felt normal anyway, always on the periphery of human behaviour but now so far beyond that, she could barely remember how to breathe, how to walk. Be normal, be normal, and repeat the mantra until it sinks in.

Exhausted from thinking, she walked in the house and flopped on the sofa in front of the TV, hoping to distract herself with mind-numbing sitcoms. She flicked through the channels but nothing was funny enough to be a distraction. Her father returned with a bucket of greasy fast food for Sunday lunch, cooking was never his thing and besides, this was exactly what she wanted. He always knew what she wanted, he knew her so well. She silently munched her way through four pieces of oily chicken, her dad smiled and chatted to her for the duration, and she just about managed to force a smile back.

'Your washing's dry so I can drop you back whenever you're ready.' His words echoed and bounced through her mind. Back? Could she go back? Maybe not just yet, just one night in her childhood four-poster bed before she faced that world. One night being a daughter again, safe with her protector, the only man she would ever trust again.

'I might stay tonight, if it's OK? I don't have any lessons tomorrow.' Her father's beaming smile warmed her heart. Of course she was welcome, always welcome here, this was home.

As she lay in the pink monstrosity that had been her bed growing up she was overcome with powerlessness, unsure of what she would do when she woke up in the morning. Something was on the tip of her tongue, she didn't know what it was but it needed to come out.

Sleep came easier than the previous night. When she woke up the next morning she almost forgot for a moment. Almost forgot what?

A breakfast of boiled egg and soldiers in her pink china egg cup was ready and waiting when she walked into the kitchen, with a steaming cup of strawberry tea. She had never been overly fond of the colour pink but as a single father who wanted to be the mother too, her dad always bought the girliest thing in the shop, scared that as a car mechanic he would never be able to fill both roles successfully – but not for lack of trying.

Her father sat opposite her opening his post, huffing at the bills and throwing the junk mail in the bin.

'Not hungry?' He nodded to her breakfast that remained untouched. She looked down at the plate, she wasn't hungry and she could still feel the undigested chicken in her stomach. She picked up a thin strip of toast and bit into it. It was cold, soggy and tough.

Her dad put the letters on the table and looked at her, she knew she had failed to fool him; he was worried. She tried to think of a lie to answer his next question, she could feel it coming, and she needed to be ready.

'What's the matter, pumpkin?'

'I was raped,' she blurted. As the words left her mouth she was instantly relieved, finally putting a name to what she was feeling, she hadn't allowed the word to form in her mind before now but it made sense, everything did.

'Oh my God, Abbey! Who? When?' And there it was, her name, she would never be pumpkin again.

'A party, Saturday, two of these guys that I know . . .' She was immediately wishing she could turn back the clock and take it back, rewind the last few minutes and become his daughter again, deal with this pain alone. He didn't deserve this, she felt horrible for doing this to him.

'Two . . .' The colour drained from his cheeks and his breathing laboured.

'It wasn't bad . . . I mean it was bad but it wasn't like . . . bad.' She scrambled for words that would spare him the mental images she knew he must be dealing with.

'Did they drug you? How could this happen?' The tears flew from her eyes before he could even finish the sentence.

'I was just a bit drunk, that's all, I didn't know . . . I didn't think.'

'I'm calling the police, those bastards won't get away with this!'

'God! Shut up! Shut up! Shut up!' She stormed upstairs and slammed her bedroom door shut; there was no going back now.

As she lay sobbing into her pillow she heard a crash downstairs. She could feel her father's anger through the floorboards, he had spent his whole life making sure she was safe, he'd taught her how to look after herself and as soon as he let her go this happened. She remembered how reluctant he was to let her go to university in the city and live in the halls of residence, but she had begged, promised she would be careful and now she wasn't sure he would ever trust her again.

She wanted to say sorry, wanted to hug him and comfort him, she knew this had always been his biggest fear as a father, that he couldn't protect her from every danger. That bad things happen to people was not a fact of life that her father found easy to accept. She couldn't fault him for his protective ways because the fact of the matter was maybe this never would have happened had she listened to her father. She would never have been allowed to go to that party, never have been allowed to wear that dress, she would have been too worried about disappointing him to get so drunk and she would have been home earlier. So many things would have been different if she had just taken heed and not filed his advice away as the ramblings of an overbearing parent. He knew best.

A gentle knock on the door of her room. She wanted to tell him to go away but she also wanted him with her, she didn't know anything any more. Why had she told him?

'I made you some Horlicks,' she heard through the door.

'Come in.' She sat up and wiped her face with her hands. He put the drink on her bed stand and sat at the far edge of the bed. She could see he had been crying. It was so strange, she had never seen him cry, ever. It broke her heart to think that she had caused him pain after everything her mother had put them through; they had always been a team. Her mother had chosen career over family when Abbey was small, but her dad had made it work. She wasn't sure they could come back from this.

'Do you want to talk about it? You don't have to, but if it helps I will listen.'

'It was Dani's boyfriend, I kissed him and then . . . things started to happen, his friend walked in on us and . . . stayed.'

'Did you make it clear to them, I mean, were they drunk? Was it all a big misunderstanding?'

'What are you saying? They held me down! I couldn't leave . . .' She swallowed hard and looked down at her hands, she was digging her nails into her skin to stop herself from screaming. 'You must hate me if that's what you think.'

He didn't speak right away, he just looked out the window; Abbey took his silence as confirmation of his disapproval.

'So you just let them . . .?' He stopped as he saw the hurt in her eyes, he couldn't finish that sentence. 'I'm sorry, poor choice of words. I don't know what to do here, Abbey . . . Do you want to call the police?'

'I wish I had never said anything.'

'We could go to the hospital, don't they say you should do that in this situation?'

'It's too late, I already showered a bunch of times. I'll get a morning after pill from the chemist's.' She found herself getting frustrated at the sound of his voice, of the doubt in his voice. With every question he asked she found herself wanting to yell at him that it wasn't her fault. Instead she just dug her nails into the back of her hand and stared straight ahead.

'I'm glad you told me.' She could tell he didn't believe the words he was saying but she was grateful for the lie.

'I just want to be alone, I'm tired.' Her father chewed on his lip and waited for her to speak again. She wanted words of comfort from him; she wanted him to tell her she never had to go back to that place again.

'I'll get your washing for you.'

Chapter 17

The Doctor

Dr Peter Vaughn washed his hands. The smell of mortician-grade sanitiser had permeated his skin. It smelled stronger and more unpleasant than the corpses that surrounded him. The silver slab in front of him contained the remains of Kevin Hart's body, the flesh already translucent with that silvery green sheen dead skin takes on, almost amphibian in appearance. It was hard to imagine that this white flabby shank of meat was part of a human body, but it was; it was a thigh.

Peter had known Kevin, he had specifically asked for this case, they wouldn't turn down the help of such a highly regarded pathologist; they couldn't. Peter and Kevin weren't friends as such, they hadn't spoken in years, but as he looked on Kevin's body all he could think of was the time they had shared, not just because when someone dies that's what you do. Even if you have only met a person once you are stuck with that memory, it becomes more significant than it ever had done before. In Peter's case there was not one memory but many. A custom they had shared together, a secret life, there was nothing indecent about their relationship but they had mutual experiences that could not be broadcast or divulged to anyone else. Ever. People just wouldn't understand. Even among their friends Kevin and Peter had been more in-tune with each other, which was possibly why Peter had distanced himself over the last eighteen years. He knew that Kevin still dabbled with the darkness. Peter had tried for the most part to play it straight, unwilling to jeopardise his career for a hedonistic urge that never dissipated, only grew. Peter had pushed the limits of self-indulgence in the past and he had come close to losing everything. Kevin enjoyed living on the edge, stepping over the boundaries. A part of Peter respected him for that, for following his desires and not becoming a slave to society. In Peter's mind Kevin was always laughing, a deep sinister laugh that couldn't be ignored, much like Kevin himself.

The door opened and Peter looked up, startled. He pulled away from the memory of the larger-than-life Kevin Hart and faced a man and a woman.

'Hello, Doctor, I'm DS Miles and this is my partner, DS Grey.' The man spoke, he was very direct, he looked straight into Peter's eyes. Peter wasn't used to dealing with the living.

Peter held his hand out to shake but the woman made a face at him and put her hands in her pockets. She was quite plain but that's all Peter could tell about her, her clothes were very casual and baggy, she dressed like someone much younger than he suspected she actually was. A big hoody and baggy corduroy flares with oversized trainers. She hoisted herself on to a vacant steel slab and crossed her legs as though she were at primary school.

'Is that Kevin Hart?' DS Grey asked.

'Of course, unless you know of any other dismembered corpses that have turned up recently?' Peter tried to make light of the situation.

Peter observed as DS Miles stared at the remains, lifting the sheet to look underneath. Between his silence and her juvenile demeanour Peter felt very uncomfortable.

'Not that I know of, no.'

'Well this is him, poor chap, really took a hammering.'

'There was a hammer?' she said. Peter looked over and saw the detective lie flat on the empty steel table, placing her arms by her sides and staring up at the spotlight.

'Um, no, there was no hammer. I just meant Hart junior was thorough.'

Peter had to be careful not to be defensive, he didn't want them to remember this meeting for all the wrong reasons. He had a role to play. He had to subvert the investigation, they were not allowed to get to the killer, because if they did then all the skeletons would be well and truly out of the cupboard.

'Cause of death?' DS Miles asked.

'Slice and dice,' DS Grey muttered, almost to herself. Her partner ignored her and looked Peter straight in the eyes again.

'It's hard to know without the organs but . . .'

'Yeah, what's with that?' Grey boomed as she swung her legs over the side of the table and jumped off. 'Why take the organs?'

'You will have to ask your suspect that.' His fuse was burning short with this woman, so he turned to the man instead. 'I read about the mix-up with the trial in the *Gazette*, DS Miles, I bet you're glad you'll finally get him for something.' Peter had to get away from the detective's stare, he felt it boring into him. He knew it was paranoia but he felt his collar tightening around his throat. What if they knew about the connection between himself and Kevin? He cursed himself for being the first to bring up the organs.

'Shame someone had to die first.' Miles was still staring.

'I'm sure that's not your fault, Officer.' Peter smiled and squeezed past DS Miles and stood the other side of the gurney.

'So, Doc, you ever see anything like this before?' DS Grey asked.

'Like this? God no. And thank goodness for that. Nasty business.'

'What kind of weapon are we looking for?'

'Well, several really, but the main perpetrator is a small knife, smooth, six inches long, max,' Peter lied, secure in the knowledge that they would have no idea he wasn't telling the truth. Any clues to the type of knife they were really looking for would narrow the field for their search considerably. Peter had been told that the detectives needed to be misled.

'Like a fish knife?' Miles asked.

'Well, no, nothing that sharp, the way the cuts are made, some brute strength was required. Most likely a man, I'd say, from the sheer energy required to dismember a human body in this way. Could be a strong woman at a push, perhaps. We're still running some tests against the weapons found at the suspect's house.'

'Lefty? Righty?' Grey asked, she was sitting on his desk now playing with his paperweight, which was a much-treasured human bone trapped in polished resin.

'Could you get down from there, please, miss?'

'Sure.' She hopped down, tossing the paperweight in the air before landing and catching it. Peter held his breath as one of his favourite possessions hovered just a few feet above the hard marble floor.

'Left-handed, from the angle of entry, the direction of the cut – the left hand has a naturally anti-clockwise predisposition.' Peter was annoyed now, this woman was very unsettling, it was like having an unsupervised child in the room.

'Something about this is really familiar to me, Doc, any ideas?' DS Miles interjected.

'No, I don't think I've ever seen anything like this before.' Peter spoke loudly over a clunking noise. He turned around only to see DS Grey opening and closing the pressure-locked drawers one by one and looking inside.

'Detective!' Was she messing with him? She shrugged and held her palms up before putting her hands in her pockets and leaning against the door, she was ready to leave. He felt his temper brimming at the surface. 'Please don't touch anything!'

'We'll get out of your way now, Doc, sorry for the inconvenience.' DS Miles flashed an angry look at his partner. Peter was relieved to see the whole scenario hadn't been orchestrated to elicit a response from him. They didn't know the connection; they weren't trying to break him. He waited for them to leave.

Peter's nerves were shot after the police visit and he needed to get rid of the sweat that had pooled around his collar. He pulled the sheet cover off the slab to reveal the rest of Kevin's body, namely his head. The years had not been kind to Kevin, although kinder than he had deserved, kinder than any of them deserved after what they had done to the boy; after what they had made the boy do. He wondered if years of looking at his own reflection and making excuses for the sins of the past had made him blind to the toll age had taken on him. The detective was right, of course, he had seen this before, although Miles didn't look old enough to remember the incident himself, but if he did any digging he would find it. He would find the story of the homeless boy that had been found in a disused warehouse on the outskirts of the city down by the river all those years ago. Back then no one cared about those throwaways, it was investigated for a short time before the interest and resources fizzled out, the lead detective on the case emigrated to Spain and that was the end of it; no one else cared. Peter remembered the case though, he remembered because he was there. He had seen the body back when he was a young up-and-coming doctor. He had seen the body before it was a body, he had known the boy, the boy they had killed.

Kevin Hart was a message for him, a message for all of them.

Peter pulled the sheet back over Kevin's face, he didn't need to examine the body any further, he had already written the report, and he had already been instructed on what to say. There was a plan. To the layman it looked as though he had done a thorough examination, with all the more obvious injuries noted down even though he had really only taken a cursory glance and made up most of the information. He made it look convincing though. He had of course recorded as few real facts as he could get away with. He didn't want the investigation to lead to the murderer because the murderer would inevitably, eventually lead back to him, and not just him either, there were others who had just as much to lose, maybe more. He slid Kevin Hart's body into the cold storage and left the morgue. Now he needed to disappear. Fast.

Peter lived alone. He'd never married. He opened the door to his house and rushed up the stairs. He grabbed what clothes he could from the dresser and threw them into a holdall, he could buy more clothes, he only needed the essentials; he didn't have time to worry about those other things. Peter zipped his bag and rushed down the stairs as quickly as he had ascended them.

As he put his hand on the front door handle to leave, the music started. The speaker system ran through his entire house and music was blaring from every room. Peter looked at the conservatory door, the control unit for the stereo was in there, and so was whoever had turned it on. Never had Mahler sounded as imposing as it did at that moment. Peter pulled at the front door handle but it did not budge, it was locked. Peter knew the only other way out was through the conservatory to the back door.

'Leave me alone!' he screamed, the music swallowing his words. Peter couldn't just stand there and wait to be murdered, he made a break for the other exit, he had seen what had been done to Kevin, and he wouldn't go down without a fight.

Chapter 18

The Cat

Adrian and Grey waded through old police files trying to find any cases similar to the murder of Kevin Hart. Adrian still couldn't shake the feeling he had seen something like that before. Something about the murder screamed ritual to him and not just common or garden patricide, something bigger.

Morris opened the door to his office with a big grin on his face.

'Pathologist's report confirms the knife we found in Ryan's flat was the knife used to kill his father.' He walked out into the centre of the incident room. 'Excellent work, boys! The most gruesome murder this side of London for decades and it's taken us less than a fortnight to nail the suspect. Daniels, I need you to set up a press conference, I've dodged as many calls as I can get away with. We'll make an announcement, keep everyone on high alert for Ryan Hart, get some photos out there; people like to put a face to a criminal, makes them feel safer. Now we just have to find the bastard. Any leads on where he is?'

'Excellent work, boys,' Grey said, quietly mimicking Morris for Adrian's ears only; he smiled.

'Let me question the sister, sir!' Adrian called out over the self-congratulatory hum that encompassed the room.

'No good. Daniels already interviewed her, she's got no idea; says she never wants to see her brother again.'

'I don't buy it, sir.'

'Look, whatever your beef with Ryan is, I will not have you harassing the rest of the Hart family, they are distressed enough already. We might make it through this without another media clusterfuck if you can just sit on your hands until we bring Ryan Hart in again. His sister doesn't know anything. No. You and Grey stay here and wait on the phones.'

'Sir?'

'You can help the guys by going through all Ryan's old case files again, see if there's anyone we missed before, any locations that jump out at you.'

'There isn't, we've looked. All his usual hangouts have been triple checked.' Grey's eyes rolled and she slumped back in her chair, Adrian could sense the reprimand about to fall.

'Look harder, Grey.' Morris stared her straight in the eye. 'A fresh pair of eyes might help. And for God's sake, neither of you speak to any reporters.'

Grey grunted and put her hand on the stack of files

of everyone who ever had been known to associate with Ryan Hart.

'I can find him!' Adrian implored.

'Then find him.' Morris leaned closer. 'From here! Let Daniels know if you find any solid leads and he can follow them through. Officially though, you two are off the clock. The last thing I need is you going off the bloody reservation again, Miles. We need this to be clean. You have history with Hart and his lawyers will use that against us if it ever gets to court. You know that.'

Adrian pulled his chair round next to Grey's and waited for the DCI to disappear back into his hole before picking a file off Grey's desk.

'You're right, Miley, there's no one in those files you didn't question, right down to his bloody primary school teachers, remind me never to piss you off.'

'I'm still not convinced it's Ryan.' Adrian sighed. 'And I really want it to be him!'

'Evidence doesn't lie.'

'Too much evidence, he's never been this careless before. The body is directly connected to him. He didn't get to where he is by being stupid. Everyone who spent more than five minutes with him knew he hated his father. I could buy it if Kevin Hart had just disappeared, but the way that happened, that wasn't Ryan's MO. He's never cut anyone up before. You don't think this is all a little convenient? We need to speak to that pathologist again.'

'We can't leave the building,' Grey whispered.

'You always play by the rules?'

'Lately, yes.'

'One of these days you're going to tell me what you did down there to get in the shit.' Adrian stood up and put his jacket on.

'I'm surprised you haven't googled me already. There were a few less than flattering reports speculating on the reason for my transfer. Needless to say, they made me look completely incompetent.'

'I figure you will tell me when you're ready.' He grabbed his car keys and looked over to the DCI's office, he was on the phone, turned away. 'I'll catch you later, Grey.'

Adrian walked towards his car, he thought she probably needed a wash at some point, the sunlight emphasised how neglected she had been. He remembered how he used to pay Tom a fiver to clean her with a bucket outside the house on summer days when he was younger. Washing the car together had always felt natural, unforced. Tom would let his guard down and talk about school or anything else that was on his mind, and Adrian would feel like they were connecting. It had been a long time since they had done that together. Adrian pulled out his phone and dialled Tom, it rang for a few moments, Adrian waited for the answer phone to kick in; he wasn't expecting him to answer anyway.

'Hi, Dad, what is it?' Tom answered, he was out of breath; walking fast from the sounds of it.

'I just wanted to know if you were coming over at all this weekend? I miss you. Be nice to see you before you go back to school.'

'I don't know, Mum and Dom are looking at booking a break in Lisbon, Dom's going to take me surfing.'

'Oh, OK. What about tonight? We can melee.' If all else fails, Adrian had the games console to fall back on.

'Maybe, I've got band practice now, I'm just about to get on the bus. I'll ask Mum and let you know.'

'Sure . . . listen, if you need a lift anywhere you know you can just ask?' Adrian said, but there was no response, he looked at the screen; call ended. He put the phone back in his pocket and got into his Granada.

As Adrian turned on the engine the car door opened and Grey got in.

'Sod it, let's do this.' She shrugged, scooping her hair up in a ponytail, ready for business. 'Called the hospital, Doc's not rostered on this afternoon. He lives over at East Hill.'

They knocked on the door of the large white stucco minimalist home. The car was parked in the driveway and music blared from inside the house. There was no answer at the door so Grey walked to the side and kicked open the gate.

'What are you doing? We don't have a warrant. You can't do that!'

'Now who's playing by the rules? In for a penny . . .' She smiled and disappeared from view.

'Hold up!' Adrian followed Grey to the side of the house, the window was open and the bin had been knocked over, Grey was pressed against the wall, chest heaving, moving in a slow sideways step, she had her stun gun ready. Adrian could also sense something was off. As the music reached a crescendo the hair on the back of his neck stood up. She pointed to what was obviously the doctor's cat walking towards them, its white paws a deep red, the fur around its mouth dreaded together and glistening with a burgundy gelatinous liquid. The white wall of the building came to an end within the next three feet and was followed by the glass windows of the conservatory; they would no longer have the safety of the house to hide behind. He knew whatever was in that glass room was going to be horrible.

Grey stopped. Adrian put his hand on her shoulder, she looked nervous, her breathing short and shallow, he wasn't sure if she was having some kind of panic attack, she looked so pale. He had not seen this side of her before. Until now he thought nothing fazed her. He nodded to indicate they should switch places. She let him.

Adrian took a deep breath before turning his head round the edge of the wall to see what was inside the conservatory, see if the coast was clear. He immediately recoiled and threw his head back against the wall unsure whether to gasp for air or throw up.

'You need to call for backup,' he managed to squeeze out between wheezes. 'He's dead.'

'What?'

He stepped out and turned to face the inside of the conservatory, the adrenaline still pumping through him as he looked at the scene again, somehow knowing the danger was gone.

The pathologist was strung up by his hands from the

central joist between the conservatory gables. He was naked, shoulders dislocated where his arms had been pulled behind him and hung. A mass of red blood pooled beneath him and a trail of what Adrian assumed were intestines ran from his open stomach to the floor and coiled in a pile at his feet.

'They're on their way.' Grey had her phone out, and by the unimpressed look on her face Adrian could tell she was speaking to Daniels. She came and stood next to Miles, her hand dropping to her side. 'Holy monkey.'

'I don't understand,' Adrian said, still focusing on the mess on the floor, anything rather than looking at the doctor's face. He saw the cat's paw prints leading in and out of the room, the body had clearly been there several hours.

'This is why I'm never getting a cat, those bastards will eat you alive if you fall asleep on the sofa,' Grey pondered out loud with a grimace on her face. 'I'm guessing Ryan thought he could get to the doc before the report came out or something.'

'That doesn't make any sense. What's he going to do? Kill the next pathologist too?'

'Maybe you don't know him as well as you think you do.'

'I lived and breathed this guy's case for a year, I know everything.'

'Files don't always tell the whole story.' Grey pulled out a cigarette and offered the carton to Adrian, he took one and she lit it for him before lighting her own.

'This is crazier than Kevin Hart's crime scene.'

'Maybe he's escalating, or having some kind of

psychotic break.' He could tell she was just throwing ideas out there, she was coming round to his way of thinking.

'I really thought I knew this guy, I don't get it.'

'What's to get? He's mental. I mean, I didn't like this doctor guy much at all, he gave me the serious creeps, but Jesus, no one deserves that.'

Adrian heard the police siren approaching and saw Daniels' unmarked car pull round the corner and into the drive. His phone beeped in his pocket, he took it out and looked at the message, it was Tom; he was at his place. He dragged on the cigarette one last time before stubbing it out and heading to the roadside to greet them. Daniels stepped out of the car.

'What the hell happened, then? Where's the body?' Daniels was annoyed.

'Out back in the conservatory, it's all kinds of fucked up,' Grey offered.

'What the hell are you doing here? I thought you were both benched?'

'We weren't looking for Ryan Hart here, I swear, we just came to discuss the findings with the doctor again. How come you got here so quickly?' Grey asked.

'Forensics are on their way.' Daniels looked at the cigarette in Grey's hand. 'I hope you haven't contaminated my crime scene. What happened to staying at the station?'

'Only thing we touched was the gate and the front door, didn't even go inside,' Grey snapped at Daniels, her disdain for Morris' lapdog was not something she particularly chose to hide.

'Like Grey said, we weren't looking for Hart here, obviously, just had a couple of questions for the doc, don't get your knickers in a twist.' Adrian walked over to the car and opened the door. 'I have to get going, I've got Tom tonight. I'll give you my statement in the morning.'

'Whatever!' Daniels said and wandered off round the side of the house.

'Give me a lift back to the station?' said Imogen. 'My car's there and I might look over those files again anyway.'

'We don't get overtime, you know?' Adrian got in.

Chapter 19

The Patient

Imogen stared at the clock; she had twenty-six minutes left. Twenty-six minutes of talking about herself. She was never comfortable doing that at the best of times, it was even harder when someone was taking notes. She would put long meaningful pauses in between her words in order to fill the space, so that fewer words had a chance to come out. The second hand was broken, she was sure, it was taking so damn long to go round.

'How is it working with your new partner?'

'OK, he's OK. A bit of a fuck-up, but I kind of like that.' She contemplated for a moment before surrendering a verdict, 'He's nice enough.'

'Nice enough? Better than your last partner?' her therapist asked. He was a much older man, Freudian in appearance, it felt more authentic that way. He foraged through the notes that had been sent through to him from her last therapist.

'A rabid goat would have been better than my last partner.' She smiled anxiously, instinctively she started picking at her fingernails, a nervous habit. She was deciding on whether to help him steer the questions to the juicy stuff instead of letting him root around in her file like a pig searching for apples in a trough, with no finesse.

'Is he still calling you?'

'I'm ex-directory, so he can't call my home. He already made me look crazy, maybe that's all he wanted. I think he's moved on.'

'Is he the reason you transferred?'

'I don't know what good that did. My boss is already putting me on the sidelines.' Her boss; she wondered if the old boys' network extended across the county and the reason she was on the bench had more to do with where she had come from than her current work. Was Morris bad? She knew her old boss was no angel, maybe that's just the way it was. Maybe she had been wrong about the nobility of the profession. She hadn't even been given the opportunity to prove herself here.

'Feeling like a fish out of water?'

'No. You know how the saying goes . . . wherever I lay my hat.' She had sixteen minutes left still, this was usually about the time the questions got really personal, it took a good forty-five minutes to settle into their respective roles of patient and doctor. She looked at her doctor in a different way, he was the same age as most of the victims they had uncovered so far. What if he was one of them? One of who? She still had no idea who could be perpetrating these heinous murders and the explanation was there, on the tip of her tongue, but maybe her mind wasn't allowing her to come to the conclusions that were practically begging to be discovered.

'How are you sleeping?'

'Sleeping? What's that?' She smiled.

'I will give you another prescription, if you think you need it.'

'It's OK, Doc, I am happy to just stay up all night, I'll start rattling if I take any more meds.' She didn't trust him.

'What about the panic attacks? Are they still occurring?'

'Not as much.' She felt like such a failure even talking about it so she tried to downplay it, as always, acting like it didn't bother her; but if it hadn't bothered her she never would have continued with the therapy after the mandated time period had expired.

'Why do you think that is?' he asked.

'Not knowing anyone actually helps with that.'

He scribbled in his pad.

'Do you trust your new partner?'

'I'm trying to, he hasn't given me a reason not to.'

'Did you tell him about the attack?'

'Not really, not yet.'

Dr Somner wrote something else in his notebook, she knew if she asked him he would tell her what it was but she decided it was better not to know. Coming to therapy had felt like the only option she had as she was crumbling under the weight of her own disquiet since the incident back home. But she was so resistant to it, always trying to avoid talking about the real issues. She would sit there and wonder how long she could drag out the formalities to give him less time to really get inside her head.

'What about work? I mean, the actual work. Are you coping with it?' he asked, peering over the top of his glasses.

She hated the word 'coping', it made it sound as though she were clinging on for dear life, at the brink of falling into an abyss of mental illness.

'Yes.'

'How do you feel you're getting on here?'

'It's a strange and horrible case and the pieces aren't quite clicking yet. But no, nothing about it is triggering me.' She hated that word too, the idea that within a fraction of a second she would lose all control and be thrust into insanity, without warning. Clinical words generally upset her; she didn't like the labels that came with the need to speak openly to a professional. PTSD was something soldiers got, wasn't it? She just wanted to get some things off her chest, not have it logged down on the record. She had asked him at the very beginning not to diagnose her. She didn't want a label. She tried to shake the idea that he was fishing for information. Paranoia was only a useful tool when you were in control of it.

'What about men? Have you been on a date with anyone since you left Plymouth?'

'That is beyond the scope of our meetings here, Doctor, I thought I made that clear.'

'How about your mother then, have you seen your mother this week?' He was writing again, she looked at the pen to see if she could discern the letters and words the movements were forming. She wanted to know what he was writing but she didn't want to give him the power he would get if she asked. So she stayed silent. It was all about who had the control. She realised that she had to work on allowing herself to be vulnerable, here of all places. She was working on it. He looked up from his pad and jolted her thoughts, pushing for a response. Therapy was mandatory after a serious attack if you wanted to return to service, followed by fortnightly follow-up sessions when you were actually doing your job. Making sure you could handle it. Even though she was worried any sign of weakness in her would be reported back and they would find some way of dismissing her she still elected to stay on after the window had expired.

'Yes, I go after work sometimes,' she conceded, not willing to admit how it was more often than that, that her life was that routine, that she had no life of her own. She didn't want him to know she drove to Plymouth almost every day, then he would ask her why her own life didn't matter, was she just avoiding it? She knew the answer to that and she didn't need him to tell her. She didn't need any of this.

'That's a fair distance from here.'

'I don't mind the drive, it clears my head.'

'And how is she?' He scribbled again.

Now there was a question. How is she? Was there even an answer to that question? There was only one possible answer, it was the answer she always gave to this question; it was a less offensive version of the truth.

'The same.'

Adrian arrived at home to find Tom sitting on the sofa playing some first-person shooter game, as usual. They grunted their hellos and Adrian sat and watched the video violence in a new light, unable to get the gruesome image of what he had seen earlier from his mind. These things happened to real people, they were probably happening right now, only minus the zombies.

'Rough day?'

'Pardon?' Adrian realised Tom was talking to him.

'You're a mess, you're all spaced out,' he said with a concerned look on his face.

'Thanks, I just had a bit of a crap day, that's all.'

'You're not going to lose it again, are you?' Tom looked away and stared at the screen again. 'I didn't tell Mum about it last time because I knew she would make me stop coming over and I like hanging out with you. I'm not a kid, you know.'

'You are a kid, and that's OK, there's nothing wrong with that.' Adrian tousled Tom's hair, not sure how else to put him at ease. 'I don't want you to have to be grown up and deal with things like . . . like you had to deal with before . . . with me. It should never have happened and I'm sorry.'

'It wasn't that bad, you don't need to keep saying sorry for it. I've seen Mum drunk before plenty of times. She drinks when . . . "he's" away on business.'

'I know, but . . . I was pretty tanked up that night.

You being there was kind of the wake-up call I needed, though.'

'So what happened? Today, I mean . . . why was it so hard?'

'I saw something really horrible that I wish I hadn't. I don't really want to talk about it to be honest, mate, but thanks for asking.' He pulled a half-hearted smile.

'It's OK.' Tom shrugged and carried on playing the game.

'I'm just going to grab a shower, when I come back down we'll play a campaign together.' Adrian stood up and went upstairs to get clean.

Under the steaming hot water Adrian could feel Peter's entrails all over him, he hadn't even touched the body but for the first time he had seen what a person looked like turned inside out with such malice, something he could never un-see. It was messy and chaotic, not like the dispassionate post mortems he had attended in the past. He pulled fresh jeans on after his shower and made his way downstairs, it would be takeaway pizza again tonight. As he descended the stairs he could hear Tom's laughter, he spent all day with those kids at school and yet the first thing he did when he got in was meet up with them online. He went into the kitchen and made himself an extra-strong coffee, he wanted something stronger but he didn't like Tom to see him drinking. He would wait until Tom was in bed before cracking open the scotch.

As Adrian approached the lounge he heard another laugh, a deeper laugh, a man.

He knew that laugh.

He pushed the door open a crack and his heart contracted. Ryan Hart was sitting next to Tom on the sofa. In his hands was a controller. They were playing and laughing.

'Tom, go to your room,' Adrian said as calmly as he could manage, his heart in his throat, the image of the doctor's guts still fresh in his mind.

'Come on, let us finish the game, I'm not done killing him!' Ryan laughed and winked at Adrian.

'I'll give you twenty quid if you go right now, Tom.' Adrian pulled the note out of his pocket, Tom shot up and grabbed the money before rushing up the stairs. Adrian hated to bribe Tom but he wanted him gone without the battle of wills that usually ensued when he told him to turn the machine off.

'Detective.' Ryan smiled and said, 'Fancy a match?'

'Give me one good reason why I shouldn't pick up that phone right now and call this in?'

'I need your help.'

'Mine?'

'I'm in deep shit, Detective.' Ryan smiled nervously.

'You're right about that, why are you here?'

'I didn't know where else to go. This is going to make you laugh,' Ryan laughed, 'you're the only person I can trust.'

'After what you've done? You think I'm going to help you?' Adrian couldn't believe his ears.

'You honestly believe I did that to my father? And now this pathologist guy? I saw the news, they are saying that I'm the suspect for that, too! Come on!'

'Why come to me? I despise you, categorically, and

182

it's on the record. Have you forgotten I tried to put you away? I almost lost my job trying to put you behind bars.' Adrian walked to the windows and looked up and down the road before pulling the blinds.

'Yes, you did, and that's why I know you're not bent, I know I can trust you.'

'What are you talking about?'

'You never wondered how I slipped through your fingers before? You had me bang to rights, Detective.'

'I made some mistakes.' Adrian remembered the sleepless nights fixated on every single detail of Ryan's life, the drinking and the pills; the downward spiral and the descent into obsession, compulsion. Adrian hated the way people like Ryan seemed to just get away with infecting others, pushing their poison. Those were the people that made Adrian wish the law was a little less restricted, that gut instinct would be enough, that proof was just a formality. He had known Ryan was bad news for a long time. Their paths had crossed on a handful of occasions over the years, but no matter what happened, he walked. Either someone else would take the fall for him or witnesses would disappear and every charge resulted in 'no further action' being taken. It wasn't long before he became more of a key player and therefore extra careful. Adrian wanted him off the streets, having a teenage son made Adrian even more determined to keep scum like Ryan out of his city.

When Adrian had lost the evidence, he was drunk. He had spent the night before in his car with a bottle of scotch outside Ryan's house, he could barely remember any details about that day. Adrian was grateful to be taken off the case in the end because he was a mess and he had let everyone down. In his pursuit of Ryan he had turned into the kind of person he hated the most. His father. When they finally suspended him, the world stopped spinning. He hadn't only lost evidence, he had lost his mind, too.

'Are you sure?' Ryan had traded the menacing smirk that usually adorned his face and instead had taken on a less defensive expression.

The coffee wasn't cutting it any more so Adrian went to the drinks cabinet and poured them both a drink. He was struggling to understand what Ryan was saying. Was he trying to pull another fast one? He handed a glass to Ryan before settling the bottle on the coffee table for ease of access.

'I'm listening.'

'I know you think I'm this big badass who kills anyone who gets in my way, and I appreciate that, I really do. It's good for business.'

'So what? You're a boy scout?'

'Now, I've done my fair share of nasty things, I don't deny, but I swear I have never killed another human being.'

'Not directly, at least.' The panic in Adrian had dissipated, he didn't feel threatened any more. He knew Ryan was telling the truth.

'My dad was connected, well connected. He knew a lot of people. Important people. You know what it's like around here. You scratch my back and I'll scratch yours. The rich stick together and they are all into weird shit.' He swigged back the drink and took a deep breath.

Adrian saw a trace of fear in his face, the kind of fear you have when you're about to break a promise or spill a secret. This was a side of Ryan he wasn't used to seeing. 'I'll give you credit, Detective, you really did make my life a living hell.' He poured himself another. 'My father doesn't like ... didn't like people sniffing round his business, he told me he would make the charges against me disappear and then a few days later, BAM! I'm off the hook and you're in deep shit.'

'And you think your dad had someone with that kind of access? Someone on the force?' This was not something that Adrian had even considered before now. Adrian had been so focused on self-recrimination that it never occurred to him that he didn't fuck up.

'Not just one someone, my friend, he had several people.'

'Are you high?'

'This city is tied up tighter than you can imagine. This? This is nothing!'

'Bullshit.'

'How else would that evidence go missing? Think about it.'

'But the knife we found in your place, the pathologist confirmed . . .' Adrian jerked back as Ryan stood up quickly, grabbing his own hair and pulling it, pacing.

'If I did kill my dad, do you honestly think I'm stupid enough to keep that lying around in my own house? Knowing what a hard-on you have for me? Give me a break!'

'So how? Who?'

'Someone on the search team? Someone in evidence?

Hell, even the fucking pathologist for all I know. I have no idea how deep this thing goes. All I know is I didn't do it.' Ryan's voice started to crack. 'They showed me the photos, that shit was sick. I couldn't do something like that.' Ryan stopped pacing and stared into space. 'I hated that man, I mean really hated him, but I didn't kill him, I was too scared of him. You don't know what he was like, and he would have made it his business to haunt me forever or something.'

'I didn't have you pegged as a spiritual man.'

'I am whatever kind of man the situation calls for, I'm a survivor, and my dad never gave me a damn thing that didn't benefit him in some way too. Even that fucking school I had to go to was for him, to continue his stupid family traditions. He went there, his father went there, going back fucking generations. He didn't give a shit about me! I had to get where I am on my own. But I do believe he was the only reason I wasn't in prison. Not for me, you understand, for himself. So that he could keep doing all the dodgy shit he was doing. It was all about the public image, because in private, I can't hold a fucking candle to that man.'

'I saw your hospital reports from when you were a kid, you had it pretty rough.'

'Just how it was back then, it was normal. I remember you back in the day . . . after I got expelled from Churchill's and stuck in your school. I remember your dad, too.' Ryan was pacing again, scratching at his face. Adrian recognised that behaviour, he wanted a fix.

'You don't get to talk about my father,' Adrian snapped.

'You're telling me your father never laid a hand on

you?' Ryan laughed incredulously before grabbing the bottle from the table and drinking straight from it.

'So you've got no reason whatsoever to want your father dead?' Adrian avoided the question, they both knew there was no need to answer.

'I've got about a million. But why now? Why the fuck would I do it now? And why would I do it like THAT? He's out of my life, I see him a couple times a year, tops. I'm telling you he was protecting me. I'm being set up, I don't know why but you KNOW me! You know I didn't do this!' He flung the bottle, it smashed against the door and a honey-coloured blossom of liquor trickled down. The smell of whisky suddenly overpowered the room.

'So who else had a motive to kill your father?' Adrian didn't want to make any sudden moves so he remained calmly in his seat, fully aware that Ryan was on the edge and his son was just upstairs.

'A shorter list would be who didn't.' Ryan sat down next to Adrian before snatching his half-filled glass from the table, he leaned in close. 'Do you know why he came here? To this city? Do you have any idea what kind of sicko he was?'

Adrian got up this time and went to the window, he looked through the blinds. If his colleagues knew Ryan was in his house they would have burst in by now. Adrian should have called it in, he shouldn't even be listening to this, but there was a disturbing ring of truth to the words Ryan was sharing with Adrian.

'He was here in Exeter on business. Your mother told us that much and his colleagues confirmed it.'

'My mother.' Ryan spat the words as though they were sour milk. 'No. He was here to hook up with young men.'

'We have no evidence of that.'

'I'm telling you, he comes down here to cop off with guys, the younger and dumber the better. Picks them up and takes them back to that seedy pad of his, beats the crap out of them and does all kinds of other messed-up stuff to them, has them do the same to him!'

'And how do you know that?' Adrian looked straight at Ryan who refused to meet his gaze, instead pulling out some cigarettes and lighting one, sucking on it until almost a quarter had disappeared in one drag. The atmosphere in the room dropped.

'He likes it rough.' Ryan gulped, Adrian suddenly knew what he meant. Adrian knew that haunted look, he had seen it in victims of sexual abuse before. How had he missed this? He almost felt sorry for the guy.

'The pathologist's report showed no evidence of . . . what you're suggesting.'

'Then he's in on it too!' Ryan's anxiety levels were getting visibly higher, Adrian wondered if the years of substance abuse had made him paranoid or, like so many stoners Adrian knew, he saw the world as it really was. Sitting there Ryan looked like a scared little boy, chewing the inside of his cheek as he spoke. 'Whoever's behind this is framing me, they're not going to let me testify about my dad, what kind of a man he was, he told me he was well protected.'

'How do you know that he wasn't just trying to scare you?'

'Because I remember them, they came to our house, when I was a kid.' The look in Ryan's eyes had transformed to sheer terror and Adrian knew that he wasn't lying. 'They got to him too, that Stone guy, the headmaster of Churchill School who killed himself.'

'Wait, what?'

'He used to be there, at my dad's house. There were times . . . the way he used to look at me . . .' Ryan's eyes were pink with the strain of trying to hold his emotions. 'He was part of this, I know he was.'

'Can you remember anyone else?'

'Not really, I mean, maybe. That guy that got gutted on the news looked familiar, that's what made me really suspicious. Someone's bumping off my dad's mates one by one; that can't be a coincidence, not with the way they died. There was this one guy, I think he might have been a policeman, I'm not sure; it was so long ago. They were at school together, you know how they like to look out for each other.'

'You need to come in and make a statement so that we can corroborate some of this, all I have right now is your word.'

All Adrian could think about was Tom in that school. He clung to the only thing he knew for sure: Ryan was a liar. Still, there was something inside Adrian screaming that he had to get Tom out of that school before the summer holidays ended.

'I can't. If they get hold of me then I won't make it to the end of the week.'

'Then let me take you in?' Everything Ryan was saying made sense. Adrian had to give him the benefit of the doubt.

'You can't guarantee my safety, those same people stitched you up, almost ruined your career. My father was just a small part of it but he was covered, if they want me gone, I'm gone.' Ryan was fidgeting, out of control, he stood up and started to pace again. 'No, no, no, I have to go, I have to disappear, it was a mistake coming here, and they are probably watching your house.'

'Let me help you.'

'You believe me?'

'Yes, I believe you, but you can't run for ever.'

'I have to go. I have to get out of here.'

'Well, just in case, you better make it look convincing, once-in-a-lifetime offer here.' Adrian stood up and held his arms outstretched, poised to take a punch.

'Under different circumstances, I would be enjoying this a lot more.' Ryan threw two punches, one to the gut and one to the face, Adrian doubled over. 'Sorry, Detective.'

'Under different circumstances, I'd be fighting back,' Adrian gasped as the blood oozed from his mouth, grabbing his side. 'Go, you've got five minutes before I make the call.'

Ryan left and Adrian slumped on the sofa, staring at the clock.

Chapter 20

The Oak Tree

Abbey looked over at the sofa, Parker lay there sleeping soundly. He looked so different with his eyes closed. Those eyes dominated his face; it was hard to see anything else about him when they were open. They were so bright, so pale, and so grey, almost like mirrors in the right light, but in the rain they had taken on a green tinge, like recycled glass. Abbey resisted the urge to touch him, to brush his black curls away from his face, instead she took a blanket and covered him. He had been sleeping almost two hours when the phone rang, she lunged for it to make sure it did not wake him, it was her father.

'Dad?' she whispered.

'Abbey, I can't come today, sorry. I had an emergency call-out and I can't afford to turn it down.' Another weekend, another excuse. She wondered why they continued to play this game, but they did. For years now they had invented their own reality, where they were still as close as they always had been, but the truth of it was that nothing had ever been the same since that Saturday night at university. They could not get past the resentment they had for each other, she knew her father resented her for not looking after herself – as if she'd brought on what happened to her herself – he'd brought her up to know better, she did know better, but still the worst had happened. And she resented her father because she knew that he thought she should have fought harder, screamed louder, or at all, he just didn't understand how she had got in that situation and she couldn't find the words to explain. So the wall between them became taller until they could not live in the same house any more. She moved out less than a year later and took a small one-bedroom flat on her own in the city where she was attacked, a move that alienated her father even more. A year later he moved further away, and the year after that even further, until he ended up over a hundred miles away. Abbey was stuck here though, not so far from the University, the place she felt she had left a part of herself in all those years ago.

After she had put the phone down she looked outside, the rain was still hard and heavy, and Parker and Sally were still asleep. She had held him for a while until he drifted off and then she just watched him sleep until she felt she was intruding. Something about the way Parker slept made her think he hadn't slept this deeply in a while. She looked down at herself, suddenly

192

aware of her flannel pyjamas, she ran herself a bath and climbed in. Part of her wanted Parker to walk in on her when she was in there, she was not brave enough to instigate anything with him but she wanted to kiss him again, she had never wanted anything more. If nothing happened after that then that kiss would be enough. She didn't know the story of his scars but she knew they were more than surface deep. She wondered how old he had been when he got them; they looked so faded and stretched. She couldn't imagine the kind of pain you would have to undergo in order to end up so mutilated. She wondered what kind of device could even cause some of the scars he had, like the little stars on his back. Parker was so gentle, so sweet, who would do something like that? She tried not to cry as she thought of the tears that must have sprung from those crystalline eyes as he was evidently relentlessly beaten, tortured.

Clean now from her bath, she slipped on a dress – she wanted to look pretty. When she re-entered the lounge Parker was putting his trousers back on, the rain still pouring outside.

'What are you doing?'

'I should go, I have intruded long enough.' He looked up and saw Abbey. 'You got changed.'

'I got dressed.' She smiled.

'I'll get out of your way before your father comes.'

'He's not coming, I want you to stay,' she blurted it before she even thought about her words, but it was too late, it was out there. 'Let me make you lunch at least, it's still raining, you can't go out in this.'

'I don't want to put you to any trouble.'

'You any good at chopping onions?' She smiled and walked out to the kitchen, hoping he would follow.

They made some food and sat at the table eating together, it was still so dark and cold outside but for the first time it felt like a home in her little flat, she hadn't made many friends in the four years she had lived here, she liked to keep herself to herself. This felt like playing happy families. They smiled and laughed together, talked about the museum.

'I think Gemma likes you,' Abbey said, trying to get a reaction.

'I get the impression Gemma likes everyone.' Parker smiled as he cleaned the final morsels from his plate.

'She doesn't like me much, we don't talk, but I see her watching you sometimes when we are out in the main foyer.'

'You watch me sometimes too.' He smiled and Abbey blushed.

'Sorry, I don't mean to make you uncomfortable, I don't even notice I'm doing it most of the time.' She was flushed.

'Don't apologise, I like it . . . I mean, I don't mind you looking at me.'

'I've never met anyone like you before, Parker.'

'No, I don't suppose you have. Some people are harder to fool than others.' He held her gaze for a moment. She could feel his mood darken and she wanted to distract him from whatever had just taken over his mind.

'What are you writing in those little books of yours?'

she asked, her courage around him growing, this inter-action felt less strained with every passing moment, it almost felt natural.

'Oh, nothing special, just drawing Giacometti men.' He smiled awkwardly and stood up, taking his plate to the sink. He picked up his sodden newspaper which was stiff and cumbersome; Abbey had attempted to rescue the local paper with the radiator. It had all but glued together in parts, he pulled out what he could and looked over it.

'Are you kidding me?' Abbey mumbled to herself as she picked up one of the sheets he had discarded. She read the article, it was a piece about Carl Taylor. A local businessman had paid tribute to his son, Christian, with the construction of a fountain in the centre of town. There was a picture of Christian in the photo with a big vulgar grin, it was the smile she had spotted, the smile had compelled her to pick up the newspaper and read. She hated herself in that moment for her weakness, for allowing him to beat her. He had won, he had won because she had lost the person she used to be. She had let him take everything. She looked up and Parker was looking at her, concerned.

'Who is that?' She detected jealousy in Parker's voice, she wasn't sure if he was threatened, but she hoped not, there was nothing to be jealous of.

'Someone from another life.' She echoed his words from earlier, hoping he would understand the need to tread carefully. She felt him searching her eyes for a clue, she didn't want Parker to know how stupid she had been, how easy to manipulate. She cared what

Parker thought of her. She turned away and faced the window, the large oak situated behind her building bending to the whim of the elements, trying to remain stoic but failing as the wind whipped at its branches. She looked back at Parker and wondered if everything that had happened in her life up to this point had just been a prelude to meeting Parker, if she had continued with her life as she had planned it, there would be no chance of them ever crossing paths. She would never have worked at the museum. Abbey was grateful in that brief moment for all that had happened, and given the choice, going back again, she valued her friendship with Parker more than anything she had lost. In the past few weeks she had found it hard to keep him out, he was unexpected and his presence made her feel again, feel something other than fear or guilt. He was extraordinary; he was special.

She thought of the kiss they had shared and felt her cheeks flushing again, she wished she could recapture that moment in the museum. Parker's eyes were watching the tree too, his gaze was unwavering as she stood in front of him, watching him, his stare so full of empathy and for that instant she wished she could climb inside his mind. Instead she stood on her tiptoes and placed her lips on his, he pulled her in and kissed her as though he had been waiting for this all day, maybe longer.

She kissed his neck and he reached his hands up to hers, cradling her head, he made her feel so light and ethereal. She slid her hands under the robe and ran her fingers across his chest and around to his back, forgetting about the markings as she pulled him closer. She was overtaken with desire, something she thought she was incapable of feeling ever again. He seemed hesitant about touching her, almost as if he knew how fragile she was. He let her take the lead and as she undid his trousers she felt his sharp intake of breath. He stood still but his body was begging her to take control.

She took him to her room and pushed him gently on to her bed. She wondered if he had even been with anyone before. He seemed to keep everyone at arm's length, yet there was something about the way he kissed that said this wasn't his first time. There was also an undeniable innocence about him. She couldn't feel that baseless desire all men appeared to get as soon as the hint of a promise was on the cards. She had tried to get close to men before but as soon as they would kiss her with any kind of intent she felt the bile rising in her stomach and she ran a mile. With Parker it was different; his hunger was born of curiosity and not the need for self-gratification. He touched with hesitation, keeping his attention on her face, looking for a reaction, constantly searching for approval to continue. His lips were parted and she could see he was trying to control his breathing, to suppress his desire. His hand hovered over her breast, slowly edging closer until it was resting there, frozen. She could feel the warmth of his palms through her dress. His uncertainty only made her want him more, she took his hands and kissed them before she turned her attention to her own buttons, she wanted him to know that he was allowed to touch her.

She followed his eyes as he watched her slowly,

deliberately remove her dress. They had changed colour again and were almost white in their clarity now, like diamonds. She wanted to lose herself in that look, she wanted to be that woman. No one had ever looked at her that way before and it was a revelation. She would make him want her more than he had ever wanted anything. For once, the power was hers and he seemed happy for her to have it.

The syncopated sounds of the pounding rain seemed to echo her heartbeat as she climbed on top of him, she could see his chest heaving in anticipation, she kissed his bare white skin and then slowly lowered herself on to him. She kept her eyes on his mouth, breathing in time with him now as they knew what was about to happen. He held his breath as he entered her and then let out a barely audible gasp. It was as though the last five years had been a bad dream, this felt new, she felt new. She realised she wasn't so tainted that no one would ever touch her again. She was here and he wanted her – him, a man so extraordinary, so perfectly flawed. He put his hands on her waist and pulled himself up. They were locked together now, chest to chest, skin to skin. She didn't know where she ended and he began. She didn't want to run away, she just wanted to stay like this with him. He buried his face in her neck, breathing her in. This was the feeling she had been searching for her whole life: belonging. She moved slowly but the heat between them was incredible. Even the smell of Parker's fresh sweat was intoxicating. She wanted him to lose control, she wanted him to give himself to her completely. She could feel the mounting delirium rising from beneath the pit of her stomach, trying to take her over but she suppressed her excitement and waited for him. He wasn't far behind and he dug his fingers into her flesh as he came with her; his face, so intense and full of concentration just moments before, softened as he fell back on the bed. He lay there breathless and glistening. He reached out and took her hand, pulled her on to the bed beside him.

Lying with Parker on top of the covers, she didn't feel the overwhelming urge to get up and put something on, she didn't want to hide any part of herself, she was happy for him to just look at her. Maybe it was because in her room it felt like they were cocooned away from the world, safe in that one place from everything that was outside. She had no fear, no insecurities, she felt like the Abbey of 'before'. The bond between them, although fragile and distended with unanswered questions, was unmistakable. In the past Abbey had always been with men who were settling for her, making do, but with Parker she knew this was not the case. Any ideas about how damaged she was, about dying alone, living her life in a solitary bubble of self-loathing, had vanished. She could see that he had needed her even though he seemed almost embarrassed about it – not embarrassed to be with her but more loath to show that side of himself.

She fell asleep, knowing that when she woke up she would be a different person. She didn't know why or how, but she knew Parker needed her. Parker had made her realise that she could salvage herself, his vulnerability had forced her hand, made her take control again. She had never been the strong one. She had been waiting to be saved, for what seemed like for ever. This was it, it had just happened, this day, this wet miserable day had turned out to be the day her life would change. The day she would finally feel worth something again.

Chapter 21

The Blonde

Then

John waved goodbye to Abbey as she walked towards her building. He wondered if that was where it had happened as he started the car and pulled away, he hadn't asked, he didn't really want to know. She had spent the last week in her room and he had spent it at the bottom of a bottle. There is no manual for being a good parent. Most of the time you just had to wing it. John grew up in a loving home with both parents. They were good parents but they died when Abbey was young. She had no mother, no grandparents, just him.

He put his foot on the pedal and drove as fast as he could without getting pulled over, he cut people off, ignored traffic lights. Part of him hoped to lose control of the car and crash into a tree, ending it all, so he wouldn't have to think any more. His brain hurt from all the thinking, the mess of thoughts that would not form any coherent value, just question after question and the feeling that he had failed to protect her, failed as a father.

He had done his best, he really believed that. She had done all the after-school clubs, school holidays, outings, excursions, holiday clubs, everything. She was smart, sensible and independent. He had been so proud of her. She saw her mother once in a blue moon, but there was no love there. Her mother was toxic. He kept up their meetings because he wanted Abbey to make up her own mind about her mother, so the facts couldn't get twisted in later life. He couldn't help feeling she needed a mother more than ever now, but God only knew where she was. She got in touch when she had time, once a year, twice if they were lucky.

When she'd told him she wanted to go to university and live there he was confident she could handle herself, but at the same time, she was his world, his baby, and he wanted her to be sure. He wished now that he had just kept her at home safe, empathising with the wicked witch who kept Rapunzel hidden from the world in an unreachable tower for all those years.

He'd known when she called that there was something wrong, he thought it would be homesickness or, at worst, a falling out with her room-mate, Dani, an ill-suited friend from the start. He worried that Abbey would hero-worship a girl like Dani, a girl who had everything handed to her, he'd worried that Abbey would wish she was like her, when the truth was Abbey was a far better person, caring, kind, selfless. John was a bit of a snob when it came to precious little princesses, maybe because of his experience with his ex-wife, but he knew that the prettier the packaging, the more emotionally expensive the contents. His marriage had cost him dearly, but he was grateful that she was so selfish that when she breezed out of his life as quickly as she had breezed in she left Abbey behind. From a young age Abbey had always been responsible. While her friends were out getting drunk in the park at school lunch break or sleeping with wannabe drug dealers in the back of their Cortinas, thinking somehow that made them mature, Abbey would be studying or looking after her father. He knew she had missed out on a lot of street smarts and maybe it was his over-protectiveness that had made her such a target. But they looked after each other – always had. Now, when it had mattered the most, he wasn't there.

He had so many questions, questions he didn't want the answers to, and the images that just wouldn't stop, the image of his little girl set on like a scrap of meat by a pair of hyenas. He wondered why she hadn't called for help. Had she screamed? Bit? Fought? Anything. He knew ultimately that his questions came from a different place entirely. Since her mother had left he was supposed to take care of her, it was his job to keep her safe and he knew he hadn't done that and nothing he could do would change it. His head was pounding with the things he could see in his mind. As though his thoughts had become insects and were crawling under his skin, eating him alive. He saw a pub up ahead and indicated, he needed a drink, and he needed it now. As he parked his car he wondered for the hundredth time why pubs had car parks anyway. He was about to break a cardinal rule of his but he was only a couple of miles from home. He could walk home if he needed.

Sitting in the bar alone he stared into his whisky, the reflection of his face looking back at him. He wished the smoking ban had never been put into effect. He had never smoked but he liked the feeling of going to the pub and being surrounded by thoughtless self-indulgence, he missed the smell on his clothes, he missed the smell on the women he used to flirt with as he watched smoke billow from their lips and imagined what else they could do with them. This morning his biggest problem had been an overdue tax form and now that seemed so completely irrelevant.

A woman at the end of the bar smiled at him, she had served him his drink, she was older and worn but had a gentle face that he couldn't help but smile back at. He couldn't remember the last time he was in a pub alone and he wasn't used to women smiling at him. John was a good-looking man but he wasn't out in the world – he worked, he occasionally went to football matches with his mates and he watched documentaries on the History Channel, that was his life. He could tell you anything you needed to know about the bombing of Dresden or the fall of the Roman Empire but ask him about women and he would have no idea. Since Abbey's mother he had had a few short-term relationships but they never worked out because Abbey was the centre of John's world and most women didn't like the competition.

'My name's Carol, haven't seen you here before.' She slid into the seat next to him.

'Hi.' He didn't want to tell her his name.

'You OK? You look a bit lost. I work here. Here all the time, me. I live just upstairs.'

'Oh right, yeah, you served me.'

'Yep. Not working now though, finished for the day.' He wondered why she was telling him and it occurred to him that she was making a pass, strange and unfamiliar, and exactly the right time, exactly the right distraction. She looked into his eyes, her mascara was thick and clogged around her cat-like eyes, eyes of a much younger woman. 'That's a lot of scotch for a Monday afternoon.'

'Can I get you a drink?' John didn't know what else to say, he didn't drink in the day, hadn't for years.

'I've got plenty to drink upstairs.' Like a middle-aged guardian angel she took him by the hand and led him out of the bar and up the stairs. The floral wallpaper and smell of talc pushed her age to a slightly higher value than he had previously assumed. Her brittle blonde hair and harsh pink lipstick were exciting to him. There was a sadness about her that made him feel safe, she wasn't a user, and she was lost too. Two lost souls looking for comfort in the arms of a stranger. He felt he had failed as a father so maybe he could go back to being just a man, a man with desires, needs and wants. A man who talks to women and wants to have sex, a man who brags to his mates about flirtations and conquests.

They lay on the bed, the afternoon sun highlighting every flaw and blemish on their ageing bodies. He wasn't put off by her scars or her puckered skin, he was aroused, it had been so long since he had felt like a man, a man that women wanted. For now he couldn't be a dad, he couldn't think about his daughter, he wanted to pretend he only had his own needs to tend to and this was what he needed right now.

Carol's kind eyes made this unknown exchange so much easier. He lowered his body on to hers and remembered what it felt like to care only for himself, he just wanted that release. She stroked his hair as he ploughed into her. This was not making love, this was just sex, but in many ways it was one of the tenderest moments he had ever experienced.

When they were both satisfied, he climbed off and she lit a cigarette. He watched the smoke rise up and disperse in the sunlight. He wanted to leave now but he didn't want to go back to his life, he wanted to stay this person for ever; nameless, unattached, a mystery. He knew as soon as he left this bedsit he would be John again, he would be Abbey's father again, and he would have to deal with whatever happened next. He left Carol in her room alone. He walked back to his car, he should not have driven but today he was not following the same rules, all the rules had changed.

His house felt cold and unwelcoming, for the first time in years he wanted to speak to Abbey's mother and ask her advice, but he didn't know where she was. He dialled the number he had for her but it was a disconnected mobile; she never stayed reachable for long.

He couldn't help feeling, from what little information Abbey had given him, that maybe she had not been clear with the boys. Maybe they just got carried away and it was all just a big misunderstanding. These thoughts, he hated himself for them. He hated that he didn't just take her word for it and he knew what teenage boys were like, he had been one once. But then this was his Abbey, his little girl he was thinking about, she just wasn't the type of girl that fooled around then made false accusations, was she? She had to be telling the truth and he realised that was what was killing him. He trusted her, she just wouldn't lie, and so it was time for him to face up to it, too. No matter which way he looked at it she had been raped and he had to find a way to make it better.

He searched the kitchen cupboard for a glass and pulled out the pink china pig mug he had bought Abbey once. Tears invaded his eyes and anger welled up inside him, and he threw the mug against the wall, watching the shattered pieces fall to the floor. I'll just drink straight from the bottle, he thought to himself as he unscrewed a bottle of economy German wine and sat in his armchair in the darkness. He could still smell Carol's cheap perfume on his shirt. He wished Carol was there, telling him what to think, feel, say, stroking his hair and whispering security into his ear. He fell asleep bottle in hand, dreaming of his flaxen-haired angel.

Chapter 22

The Newsreader

David Caruthers sat patiently in his chair waiting for his make-up artist Diane to finish. She jabbed him in the eye with the foundation brush.

'For fuck's sake!' he said, saline water streaming down his cheek.

'Sorry.' She scuttled away and he turned to face the camera.

'Where the hell is Bev?' David shouted across the sea of people as he dabbed his eye with a tissue.

'Sorry!' Beverly Windham ran across the newsroom floor and sat down next to David, still tucking her blouse into her skirt. 'Toilet emergency.'

'I don't need to know,' David said and then winced as the light shone in his face. Beverly threw him a quick V sign.

The blinking red light came on the camera and David started to read from the autocue.

'Welcome to the six o'clock news, I'm David Caruthers.'

'And I'm Beverly Windham.'

'Forensic experts have identified the partial remains found in Devon last Tuesday when a German couple who were hiking dialled 999 after finding a body part on their trail. A number of police officers and crime scene investigation officers have been working round the clock to locate the rest of the body. What they discovered has been described by one of the officers at the scene as "something out of a medieval horror movie". The body, which has now been identified as local businessman Ian Markham . . .' David stalled on the name, the words on the autocue blurred for a moment and his voice caught in his throat. He felt Beverly kick him under the counter. 'Um . . . Ian Markham . . . um earlier believed to have fled the country after being implicated in a massive . . . um . . . fraud case that's still under investigation by the Inland Revenue.' David felt his cheeks redden, the anxiety rising. Beverly looked at him, the autocue still rolling but nothing coming out of his mouth. He stared at the glass of water on the news desk; he reached for it and took a throaty gulp.

'David, what the fuck? Read the fucking words!' A voice came through on their earpieces.

'Um . . . what was found of the body was so badly decomposed that he was finally identified through dentist's . . . sorry . . . dental records . . .'

'Beverly, take over, he's fucked it,' David heard in his ear.

'At the scene of the crime,' she jumped in, having missed the first few words, 'Mr Markham had been subject to a brutal ordeal. We're going to hand over to Simon who is on site to give more details.'

'You prick, Dave,' came over the earpiece again.

The red light flicked off and David jumped out of his chair, ripping his earpiece out.

'What the fuck are you doing? We are back on in thirty-five seconds!' Beverly panicked.

'You'll have to finish up, I have to go.'

'What the hell are you playing at, Dave?' Chris the producer barked.

'I don't feel well,' David said as he dashed out of the studio, he didn't have time to explain, he had to get out of there.

He ran into the bathroom and pushed open the stall, the gourmet pizza he had eaten for lunch sprang from his stomach, his mouth awash with the taste of regurgitated hoisin duck and white wine. He went to the sink and looked in the mirror, his eye still streaming, and the foundation was the only thing holding colour in his cheeks. He splashed his face and the door burst open.

'What the fuck was that?' Beverly screeched as the door thumped closed behind her.

'I'm sorry; it just crept up on me. Can we do this later?'

'You made us look like total fucking amateurs, Dave!'

'I'm sorry, if it's any consolation, I just puked my guts up.'

'Maybe.' She softened and smiled a little, came and kissed him on the cheek. 'Lunch went straight through me, too.'

'Sexy.' He grimaced, trying to hold together the illusion that everything was fine apart from the pizza.

'Go home. I'll come over later with some chicken soup, look after you.'

'No, you're OK, let's just leave it tonight. I think I need a good night's sleep or something.' He had things to do, people to talk to, he had to find out what had happened. There was an alarm bell ringing in his mind, there could only be one explanation for what had happened to his old friend Ian. He needed to make a call.

'I'm away tomorrow though, I'm on assignment covering that stupid TV awards thing, have to stand out all night in the sodding rain interviewing a bunch of wannabes and Z-listers.'

'Friday, I'll take you out for dinner, not pizza this time, I promise.' That should give him a couple of days to go and see the others.

She smiled and walked out swinging her hips from side to side, looking back at him seductively as she pushed the door open and left the men's toilets. He wiped his face with a paper towel and left quickly before anyone else cornered him.

He showed the door security guard his pass and swiped his card to open the door. Outside, he gulped for air, his head spinning, he wanted to be sick again, he put his hand out for a taxi and one pulled up immediately. He couldn't be bothered to walk to King's Cross station, he didn't want to be around other people.

He pulled out his phone and searched through his extensive directory. He found the name he was looking for and pressed the green button.

'The number you are trying to reach is no longer in service.'

'Fuck!'

He pressed the green button for another name.

'Hello,' came the woman's voice on the other end.

'Hello, is that Patricia? Patricia Stone?'

'Yes, who is this, please?'

'I'm Jeff's friend David, David Caruthers,' he said in his newsroom voice – he found it impossible to say his name any other way, 'could I speak to him, please? Is he home?'

'Oh, David the newsreader guy? He spoke of you sometimes . . . um, no, sorry, Jeff isn't here, I mean . . . I'm afraid Jeff passed away.'

'When?' David held his breath.

'A few weeks ago. Sorry I didn't send you an invitation to the funeral, I didn't think you were still close.'

'How . . .' He didn't want to know the how, but the word just came out.

'Oh um . . . well . . . there's no easy way to say this, he took his own life.' Her voice was flat and emotionless; a certain type of acceptance in her tone, as though she had always known it was on the cards.

'Thank you, Patricia, sorry for your loss.' The phone clicked and the dial tone sounded, she hung up without saying anything further.

He dialled another number.

'Hello? Who is this?' An older, gruff voice answered the phone, slightly panicked.

'It's David, David Caruthers.' He cringed as he said his own name again.

'You heard, then?'

'Jeff's dead, too.'

'Ian was mutilated, completely, strung up and left to nature.'

'It was him, then?'

'I believe so, and Stephen died on some kind of sex holiday in Paris, I dug around a little and the police said natural causes but I get the feeling there was a cover-up there, can't get any bloody straight answers from those people.'

'I tried Steve, his phone was out of service. I just thought it was an old number. What the hell are we going to do?'

'He wouldn't come after us, I mean, you are practically a celebrity, David, and he would be an idiot to come after me.' David wasn't sure whether the use of his name was added as an affirmation or condescension, he didn't like the tone either way. He hung up.

He paid the cabby and went inside, wary of what he might find, but the flat was empty, untouched, it looked exactly as he had left it. He poured himself a drink of scotch and then filled the glass with ice from the fridge dispenser. He pulled off his tie and then sat down. David flicked the TV on and trawled the channels for the news, he didn't want to know but like a raw nerve in the back of your mouth that you just can't help touching with your tongue, he had to know. All the reports were generic, no details. Inside his mind were all the details he needed to know, and the memories of the things he had done. The boy that got away, the other boys that weren't so lucky, the faces of his friends as they revelled in the suffering of those adolescents. He remembered standing in front of his friends and handing out judgements; David always did like an audience. He drained the last of his drink and switched the TV off. He had to get out, go somewhere, he couldn't just stay here and wait. He stood up but his feet gave way, he smashed violently through the glass coffee table on to the floor, he tried to move his feet but they were heavy, so heavy. David looked up and saw an old 'friend' standing there.

'Oh, please! Please don't hurt me!' David cried as the man dragged him back to the sofa. David tried to grab him but the man punched him in the face. He recoiled from the blow and steadied himself with his hands, his fingers felt strange. Pins and needles crept up into the palms of his hands.

'We don't have long.' The man put a tripod in front of David and set a camera on top, adjusting the settings. He walked over to the stereo and hit play. The familiar sound of Mahler enveloped David, cementing what he had known the second he saw the man standing in front of him. He was going to die.

'Long for what? What's that for?'

'I want a confession.'

'Do you want money? I have money, I can get you money if you want it, I know loads of people; I can get you anything you want.' The words tumbled out of

David's mouth before he had a chance to form them into coherent sentences.

'Well you know I have money, and why on earth would I want anything from you? What is your life worth to you?'

'Just name anything and I'll get it for you!'

'I want a confession.'

'You don't have to do this,' David pleaded.

The man stood behind the camera. David studied his face, it had changed so much, and it was hateful.

'I do have to do this, the years you have had are more than you deserve, you can't have thought you had got away with it.'

David couldn't move his fingers any more. He couldn't move his legs at all. His body felt cold and he could feel saliva building in his mouth.

'What have you done to me?' David slurred.

'Hemlock, do you remember that one? I remember it. Do you remember how it works? First comes the nausea, I believe you already experienced that one. I took a bit of a risk putting it in your water at work but I just couldn't resist.'

'You were at the s-studio?' David's head was pulsing; he felt the spit trickling out of his mouth with every word.

'Drooling!' the killer listed, holding up two fingers. 'Have you got the stomach pains yet? They are pretty special.' He held up yet another finger, he was counting through a list, uncaring, no empathy.

'Please.'

'If you start talking now I can save you, all I have

to do is put a tube in your throat and call an ambulance before your respiratory system shuts down.'

'No, I can't, please, you don't understand, my children will see it.'

'It's going to get painful soon, you know, David, and you might get lucky, the paramedics might make it before you shit yourself.'

'Who . . . is going to see the video?'

'Maybe no one, or I might put in on the internet. Maybe I'll send it to your girlfriend Bev, she might get a kick out of it, or she might prefer reading out the story of how they found what's left of your body, on air.'

'You leave her alone!'

'You're not in a position to tell me what to do, David.'

'OK, OK, I'll do it.'

'State your name and then confess your crimes, along with the names of your fellow perpetrators.'

'You'll never get away with this.'

'Maybe I don't want to.' They looked at each other – a knowing look, a look with history – until the man broke his gaze. 'Now talk!'

The red light of the camera came on, David could feel the dribble pooling in his mouth, he knew when he opened it that it would run down his chin, his neck, funny that with everything that was happening this should be the thing that concerned him the most. Not the fact that his lungs could collapse or that within minutes he could be sitting in a puddle of his own excrement, he worried about the image, what people would think when they saw him labouring with his tongue for words.

'I'm David Caruthers and this is my confession.' David spoke slowly, concentrating on the words as they formed in his mind, and pushing them out of his mouth. 'I have done very bad things, evil things.' His thoughts were becoming cloudy and his stomach reeled with pain. 'I have hurt children, with my own hands. I belonged to a group who believed in personal sacrifice for the greater good. We thought we were doing the right thing! When we took you we were trying to make you better. It was Peter and Kevin . . . they took it too far . . . No one was supposed to die . . . it wasn't supposed to be about that.' Exhausted, he began to cry. 'I can't, I just can't do this.' The camera switched off.

'I guess that will do, for a start – although personal sacrifice makes it sound so noble, you should probably mention that it wasn't your person that was being sacrificed.'

'You'll let me go now?' He hated the sound of his own pathetic voice and he knew, he knew the more pathetic he sounded, the more likely he was to die. David understood the rules, hell, David made the rules.

The man lifted David over his shoulder in a fireman's lift and carried him through to the bedroom, another room with a view – this time the Thames echoed in the full wall of mirrored wardrobes. He threw David on the bed and tied his hands and feet to the posts, David was helpless, too weak to move. 'What are you doing?'

'Don't worry, you're not my type.'

'Please, just let me go.'

'Do you know what Ling Chi is, David?'

'You said you would let me go!'

'Ling Chi is the Chinese execution also known as death of a thousand cuts, or the lingering death.' The man left the room and David looked desperately for a way to escape, there was nothing and even if there had been he was powerless to do anything about it. The man returned with the camera and positioned it at the end of the bed. David began to sob again. 'The scary thing is this was only made illegal around a hundred years ago, but then you know all about that, don't you?'

'If I could take it back, I would!'

'No. You wouldn't.' The man pulled out a knife, a curved knife, already stained with blood. 'Do you like this? Your friend Kevin liked it, too.'

'Kevin?' So that was five of them gone already. How did he not find out about this until now? Why had it been kept from him? Why hadn't it made the national news?

The man stuck the knife into David's sternum. He screamed, he could see it was only about a centimetre deep, the man pulled it, until a thin line of blood appeared on his torso. He pulled out the knife and then put it in again, still shallow, pulling down in uniform formation, then again and again until there was a barcode configuration across his chest. It took a few seconds for the blood to start flowing from the cuts, shallow and short. The knife went in again, all the while David focused on the camera, the red light blinking – this was being filmed, who was going to see it? The feeling was disappearing from his body as the hemlock took effect, he prayed for it to work faster, for death to come quickly. The room was blurring, there was something soothing about the repetitive action of the torture, now that he couldn't feel it, at least. He closed his eyes and waited for the darkness to wash over him.

David woke with a start. His eyes hurt, his throat hurt, he tried to swallow but he couldn't. He tried to turn his head to look at the clock but the pain in his throat was unbearable, he reached up and felt the tube in his neck, he clawed at his mouth and ripped it out, the hard plastic scraping against raw skin. He looked over at the bedside table, the only light in the room was coming from the digital alarm clock. He had been there, lying on the bed, for hours. The room was silent, beyond silent, his laboured breathing the only sound. It seemed he was alone, but he couldn't be sure. Still unable to fully process his surroundings, he tried to move. He fell on to the floor; it was sticky and cold. The lower part of his body was still numb so he couldn't stand. He reached up to the bedside and switched on the lamp.

The first thing David saw was his arm. His eyes took a moment to adjust to the light. His skin hung from his forearm in ribbons, the blood congealed and clotted. From the corner of his eye he saw the wall of mirrors, he closed his eyes, afraid of what he might see, afraid his assailant was still there. He tried to pull himself back up on to the bed but he felt so heavy, there was no leverage, just pure weight. He felt around with his hands, the bed sheets were covered with blood. He grabbed at them and felt the glutinous liquid seeping through his fingers. His blood, no wonder he felt so weak. His fingers brushed something cold and metal, he opened his eyes and saw the strange knife, quickly he picked it up and held it out in front of him, eyes wide, vigilant, ready to fight if need be, forgetting for a moment the mirrors. Then he saw it, saw himself. His feet were gone, holes where his knees used to be, the rest of him covered in deep red lines where the knife had left its mark. The cuts were shallow enough that his bleeding had been mostly superficial, the bigger cuts had been cauterised. The poison had also slowed things down considerably. His eyes wandered up the reflection. He was relieved when he saw his genitals were still in place but then experienced another horror altogether as he saw his face. Cuts spiralled out in a spider-web pattern, and in the centre was nothing but a hole, his nose was gone. He looked over at the phone. He was alone, he was sure of it, he could reach out and call the police, the paramedics would be there soon and they could take him to a hospital, he would survive, but then what? He looked at the knife in his hands and realised why it had been left there; a small act of mercy. It only took one more look in the mirror and he was resolute. He pushed the blade into his chest, just slightly to the left of centre, beneath the ribcage, pushing upwards until his hands fell to his side and he slumped against the bed.

Chapter 23

The Museum

After the gruesome discovery of Ian Markham's body, which was Adrian's case due to him and Grey visiting the aggrieved wife who thought he had fled, he had managed to secure a foothold in the murder investigation team. The obvious connections between the murders meant Adrian was no longer on the sidelines. The search for Ryan Hart was on. The station was buzzing with bodies, all leave had been cancelled, and it was all hands on deck. Adrian was now sharing a desk with Grey to accommodate all the extra personnel that had been brought in from other stations around the county.

'Have you found any connection between Ryan and Ian Markham?' Grey said as she closed another file and threw it on the stack next to the desk.

'Maybe there is no connection,' Adrian said.

'Ryan was just trying to put the wind up you, he knows he's caught, that's all.'

'I wish we could get our hands on the Kevin Hart file, namely the pathologist's report.'

'We're on the Markham case.'

'I know. You can't tell me this has nothing to do with it. I know it's not the same but you have got to admit, it fits.' Adrian sighed. 'We need to find out if he has any connection to Churchill School. Did you speak to his wife yet?'

'Yup, turns out she's getting a huge insurance pay-out now they found a body, well, enough of a body to determine he's dead.'

'She didn't have any idea who did it? Does she have an alibi?'

'None, but to be honest I think she was focusing all of her energy on trying to sound upset. She was at some yoga retreat with her sister for the time of the murder so she is definitely not in the frame.'

'Did you ask her about Stone? About the school?'

'I did, she said she couldn't remember, but she was lying. She just doesn't want to be involved in the investigation any more.'

'Grey!' Morris called across the room. Both Adrian and Grey looked up as Morris signalled her over. 'Here!'

There was a man, an officer from another division, in Morris' office, Grey went in and Morris closed the door behind her. Adrian watched as the men spoke to Grey, she in turn folded her arms and stayed well back looking at her feet like she wanted to get out of there as fast as possible, nodding reluctantly at the DCI.

Grey squeezed a smile out before almost ripping the door off its hinges as she left his office.

'Everything OK?' Adrian asked as she walked straight past and out of the station, it didn't take a detective to figure out she was upset.

Outside, Grey was pacing back and forth smoking a cigarette, running her hands through her hair repeatedly.

'I'm fine,' she said as she saw Adrian approaching.

'What was all that about? Was he from your old station?'

'Don't worry about it, Miley.' She offered him a cigarette, he took it. 'Some people I used to work with are going to be helping out here, they had to run it past me first, although it wasn't really a request.'

'Run it past you?'

'Yeah, I tried to get a restraining order against one of the detectives. Against my old partner, actually.'

'Bloody hell, what for?'

'It's a long story, trust me.' Grey looked around to see if they were alone, she grabbed Adrian by the arm and pulled him round to the side of the station. Adrian watched as she took one last drag of her cigarette and stamped it out, he was waiting for her to speak again but instead she took the bottom of her sweatshirt and pulled it up to just beneath her bra. There was a diagonal scar running from up under the shirt right down across her abdomen and down past the waistline of her jeans. She obviously ran or something, her core was rock solid and he could see the definition of her muscles under the scar.

'Another officer did that?'

'Not exactly.'

'So what exactly?'

'I figured out that he wasn't being completely straight with me about a few things on a fairly big investigation we were working, the one that put me out of commission.'

'You think he was bent?'

'I got a lead that took me to the residence of a well-known criminal and when I got there, some other undesirables were waiting for me.'

'You think he set you up?'

'My partner must have told them I was coming, they knew things about me, things I only told him.'

'What kind of things?'

'Just personal things that you might say to your partner.'

'How did you get that scar? It's pretty nasty.' Adrian didn't know how far to push this. He had noticed her getting anxious a couple of times in the past, he hoped it wasn't something he needed to be concerned about.

'I got pinned down and I was cut, they were fitting up the guy whose house it was for my murder.'

'Pinned down?' he repeated the words that stuck out the most to him.

'I can hold my own, Miley, don't worry.'

'Did they catch them? Why would your partner do that?'

'I wasn't playing the game properly. I think I was being taught a lesson. I spotted him talking to someone he shouldn't have been talking to . . . and no, they haven't caught them. Not yet at least.'

'Wasn't playing how?'

'I had spoken to my DCI confidentially about him, said I didn't trust him. A day after I made the complaint, this happened.'

'That's why you transferred?'

'It was this or a desk job. Anyway, he's here, he's working on the Hart case. Apparently he's a great detective or something, got a promotion and everything.'

'Are you going to be OK?'

'I'm not made of glass, Miley, don't worry. The official line was that I shouldn't have gone without backup. I brought a lot of media attention to the house. Lots of debates about the competency of the brass. No one likes that. Funny thing is I think they put me with you as punishment.'

'Me?'

'You may not know this but you have a bit of a rep with the ladies. I guess I'm lucky I'm not your type.' She smiled. 'Anyway, I think I may have caught us a break.'

'How so?'

'They brought in my old forensics guy too. Markham's crime scene is a complete mess. They needed the extra help.'

'And that's good why?'

'If we can get hold of the knife they found at Ryan's, he will look at it for us.'

'You trust this guy?'

'Absolutely, he was the only one who had my back in Plymouth towards the end, he's a good friend.'

'Let's go see Ryan Hart's mother.'

* * *

Martha Hart answered the door with a big smile. She was wearing a bright red dress; hardly the outfit of a woman in mourning.

'Officers!' She beamed and with a welcoming flurry of her arm she invited them inside. She took them to the first room nearest the entrance and swung the door open to reveal a plethora of boxes. 'This is absolutely everything of my husband's. Feel free to do what you want with it. I have some charity people coming tomorrow, it's what Kevin would have wanted. He was very charitable. But take whatever you need.'

'We don't have a warrant.'

'You don't need one. *Mi casa su casa.*' She smiled.

'Mrs Hart, have you heard from Ryan at all?' Miles asked.

'Sadly, no.' Her smile dropped. 'He no longer trusts me, sees me as the enemy because I always took his father's side. I don't blame him, either.'

'If you knew where he was, would you tell us?' Grey asked.

'Probably not, and no I don't think he is capable of the things they are saying on the news.' Her false smile returned. 'Let me go get you some lemonade.'

She disappeared. They heard the clip clopping of her feet on the parquet flooring as she made her way to the kitchen.

Grey opened a box and started rummaging through the paraphernalia inside. The box Adrian chose was full of watches, cufflinks, aftershave bottles, solid-gold tie pins and other expensive trinkets. Kevin certainly liked the finer things in life. In another box Adrian

226

found paperwork, bills and other business correspondence, a laptop with a smashed screen.

'Whoa!' Grey exclaimed. Adrian looked up to see Grey holding up an S & M porno magazine. 'There's a whole box of these.'

'Ryan did say his dad was into all that.'

'Some of this is pretty hardcore, foreign stuff, illegal over here.'

'Can't imagine what the charity shops are going to do with those,' Adrian mumbled.

Adrian kept looking through the same stack of papers. He didn't know what was ringing the alarm bells. There were some old receipts, a parking ticket, an invitation and some business cards. He put them in a clear plastic bag and put them in his pocket, he would take a look later on back in the station.

Grey discovered four more boxes of pornography, a box full of sex toys and other paraphernalia like restraints, blindfolds and gags. None of which had ever come up in any of Daniels' reports they had seen.

'Here are your drinks.' Martha Hart had reappeared in the doorway.

'Thank you.' Grey smiled, quickly hiding what she had in her hand.

'Oh, don't worry, dear, who do you think packed all those boxes?' Martha's smile was unwavering, she was obviously accustomed to putting on a front for appearances' sake. Adrian knew for a fact that she had taken more than one or two beatings from her husband herself.

'Thank you, Mrs Hart.' Adrian stood up and took a drink from her, she patted him on the arm and watched him drink. He took a gulp and her smile widened. 'Delicious.'

'Old family recipe.'

'Who came and took your statement?'

'Lovely young man, tall, what was his name? Detective Daniels.'

'Did you happen to mention your husband's um . . .'

'Oh yes, I showed him my husband's shed, told him he'd probably find all the answers he was looking for in there.'

'OK, thank you, we'll get out of your hair now.'

'Thanks for the drink.' Grey smiled.

Outside the house Grey gave Adrian a look, she was thinking what he was thinking. They would have to look over any statements Daniels had taken again, he was obviously selective about what was relevant or not. Adrian's phone rang, it was Daniels.

'We found Ryan Hart,' Daniels said.

When Adrian and Grey arrived at the disused petrol station on the A38 just outside the city, Daniels was waiting with a big shit-eating grin on his face.

'Where is he?' Adrian asked. He presumed Daniels was basking in the glory of having found Ryan before Adrian had been able to.

'In there.' Daniels pointed to the large white building at the rear of the station. It had been a café at some point but now it was all boarded up, it was striped with rust where the pipes had leaked on to the unkempt paintwork. 'This place has been shut for thirty-odd years, perfect hiding place for scum like Ryan Hart.'

Adrian walked into the abandoned building noting the smell of stale urine and the metallic aroma of blood. This place was obviously frequented by the city's undesirables and unseen homeless. There were empty bottles and cigarette cartons strewn around the floor. Judging by the volume of discarded hypodermic needles on the surfaces this was a regular hangout for the addicts. Adrian found himself wondering if his father had ever spent time in here. This was a city with money and prestige, no one liked to think about the ones without it, it would impinge on their imagined superiority.

A group of techs huddled around Ryan's body, which lay on a blackened mattress in the corner of the dismal room. His eyes were bulging and a needle was hanging from the pit of his elbow with a constellation of fresh needle marks. He was right, he hadn't even lasted a week.

'How did you find him?'

'Little something I like to call police work.' Daniels smiled.

'And he was just like this?'

'Some junkie phoned it in looking for a reward.'

'What junkie?'

'Didn't leave a name after he heard there was no reward. Public phone box, no CCTV. What's it matter, anyway? Thought you would be glad to see this scumbag dead,' Daniels quickly answered.

They moved Ryan into a body bag when they were done taking photos. Adrian watched Ryan's face disappear as they zipped the bag up. Adrian looked over the scene, Ryan had plenty of friends who would have put him up, failing that plenty of people who wanted to impress him. Alternatively maybe someone saw a kink in the chain of Ryan's command and decided now would be a good time to take him out. Whatever had happened Adrian was certain it was not a clear-cut case of suicide by overdose, or even accidental overdose, for that matter. As far as anyone knew, Ryan had never been known to inject. Yet again Adrian felt Ryan's conspiracy theory taking on even more weight in his mind.

Back in the station Adrian had made his excuses and headed for the toilets. He closed his eyes as he splashed water on his face. His eye was still sore where Ryan had hit him. The familiar pain that came not only from Ryan's fist but from the countless times his father's fist had connected with the exact same spot, the pain felt almost like coming home. He missed that pain sometimes. Sometimes he wanted nothing more than to be broken and bleeding on the ground. He thought about Ryan's body in that disused café, the slender muscular frame looking more like a junkie than ever. He looked at the bruise around his eye in the mirror, it was yellow and green. In a few days it wouldn't be there at all and Adrian's last tangible connection to Ryan would be gone. He pressed the spot to see if it hurt to the touch. When it didn't he just pressed harder.

He couldn't help thinking about his conversation with Ryan. What was he missing? There had to be some connection he wasn't seeing, he just needed to find it. Now more than ever he was convinced that for once Ryan hadn't been lying. As he looked at his reflection he wondered what would happen if he just lunged forward, driving his face into the glass, just to feel the pain. It would be crazy, he knew that, but when you are born into a life of violence and pain, anything else feels wrong. Maybe that's why Ryan had become the man he had. Adrian knew what it felt like to be betrayed by a parent and he also knew that a large proportion of drug addicts were victims of childhood sexual abuse. Ryan was an easy person to frame, his whole life had been a prelude to being set up. Even without the charges sticking in the past. Why hadn't they stuck?

He walked out of the bathroom and over to Grey who was looking through Ryan's crime scene photos. She looked up at him.

'What's going on in that head of yours?' Grey asked, obviously noticing the pained look of confusion on his face.

'Daniels found the knife at Ryan's place.'

'Right.'

'Daniels found Ryan's body.'

'I'm with you.'

'You called Daniels when we found the doctor's body, he got there pretty sharpish, was happy to let us go without taking our statements straight away. Maybe he didn't want us there for the search.'

'What are you getting at?' Grey asked.

'It's always him, always. What if he's part of this big conspiracy Ryan was going on about?'

'Why Daniels? What could he possibly have to gain from framing Ryan Hart? And what do we do if he is? How do we prove it?'

'Nothing to gain, as far as I can see. You need to get

your friend in forensics to look at all the evidence . . .'
Adrian paused for a moment, thinking about what Ryan
had said to him. Something occurred to him. 'Get him
to look at Kevin Hart's pathology report too. I'm pretty
sure the doc was part of it somehow. He might shed
some light on this and then we can figure out what to
do with Daniels.'

'What about Markham?'

'I don't know, I can't figure out where he fits in. I
think we need to assume Ryan was on to something
and take him out of the frame for the murders and
start again. I think it's plausible that he was just a
convenient scapegoat.'

'Are we going to tell the DCI?'

'I don't want to start flinging shit until I'm sure. I'm
going to look at all three murders and see if I can't find
something that ties them together.'

The boards in the incident room were being cleared
and everyone seemed to be pretty happy with themselves. Adrian was putting away the files on his desk,
the box of documents from Ian Markham's place, when
he remembered that the papers he had found at Kevin
Hart's were still in his pocket. He pulled them out and
laid each one on the table, doing the same with
Markham's. There was only one item that appeared in
both piles. A private invitation to a local museum-
restoration fundraiser.

What were the chances of both of these men being
invited to the same party?

He looked at the tickets. They were labelled numbers

004 and 006. He would have bet his left leg that if he had access to the doctor's house he would have found number 005. This was a connection, tenuous maybe, but a connection. There had been nothing anywhere else to link these men, no mutual friends, no mutual hangouts, nothing. From what Ryan had said it was something to do with the school, but so far there was no concrete evidence of that. They would have to get more than a dead addict's word to get a warrant. He wanted to tell Morris, but right now no one wanted to hear it. Everyone was still in the throes of their victory dance. Grey was walking across the room towards him, she checked around her before leaning over his desk.

'I gave the evidence and the autopsy report to my friend.'

'I found a connection.'

'Between Ian Markham and Ryan?'

'No, between Ian Markham and Kevin Hart.' He smiled, Grey leaned in closer.

'What connection? The school?'

'No. The school says none of them attended, but Ryan already told us his father went there so I think we can assume someone is lying, or the records have gone. The connection I found is the museum.' He held out the two invitations.

'Are you actually trying to clear Ryan's name? It's already all over the news. His poor mum.'

'I just don't want the real people responsible to get away with it.'

'Well, I admire that, Miley, I really do.'

'Go home for now, museum's not open until nine-thirty. This party isn't for a couple of days, they would have both been going, maybe we will find out who else got a private invitation.'

'See you in the morning.' She grabbed her coat and left.

Adrian shoved the invitations in his pocket and put the files back on Daniels' desk. There were too many people around the office for him to have a proper look at what Daniels was up to, he would wait and see if Grey's friend came through for them. He wanted to know if the knife found at Ryan's place really was the Kevin Hart murder weapon.

Adrian was surprised to see Grey was sitting in her car smoking as usual when he left the station. Another officer that Adrian recognised as her former partner was sitting next to her, he had seen him before in the DCI's office. Adrian smiled and waved as he walked past the front of her car. She had that look on her face again. The one he had seen at the doctor's house – scared, pale and anxious. Adrian glanced inside the car and saw the man had his hand on her shoulder. He was a small but thickset man with dark hair, combed just right so you couldn't see the receding hairline. Grey was staring at him as he talked quickly at her. Adrian went to the passenger side of the car and opened the door, the man's hand moved immediately.

'Can I help you?' he asked.

'You're in my seat.' Adrian smiled.

'I beg your pardon?'

'I said,' – Adrian grabbed him by the collar and

dragged him out of the car, smacking his head against the door frame on the way out, before shoving him against the car – 'you are in my seat!'

'Who the hell are you?'

'I'm the guy who will fuck you up if you don't take me seriously.'

'Imogen, who is this dipshit?' The man turned his head to look at Grey. Adrian open-palm slapped him across the face, the look he gave him was priceless. Adrian knew that if you wanted to upset a man, you didn't punch him, you slapped him.

'Stay away from Detective Grey.' Adrian got in the car and shut the door. He looked over at Grey who was visibly stunned. 'Drive, then! We need to make a dramatic exit.'

'Yes, sir!' She slammed the car into gear and pulled away, the wheels screeching beneath them.

'You need to drive me home.'

'All right.'

'And pick me up in the morning, no point coming before nine though.' He smiled.

'Anything else?'

'You can bring me a coffee too.'

'All right, don't milk it.' She looked at him and they both erupted with laughter.

Adrian entered his house and looked at the space on the sofa where Ryan had been sitting only a few days ago. He had been scared and now it turns out he had been justified. Ryan had been dealt a crappy hand, Adrian knew all about that.

He fell asleep on the sofa watching some interactive phone-in bingo, longing for the days of low-budget American glam-hair cop dramas that only ever seemed to run at three o'clock in the morning – even that was better than being subjected to this tripe.

As promised, Grey knocked on Adrian's door at nine sharp. She had coffee.

'Come in!' Adrian opened the door and walked through to the kitchen. He had sausages and bacon under the grill. He cracked some eggs in a pan.

'What do you think the connection is, then?' Grey asked as she shoved a piece of buttered toast into her mouth with a satisfied moan. It was like she hadn't eaten in a week.

'I don't know, if only I could get into the doc's place.' Adrian watched her eat in mild disgust as she put the food in faster than she could chew it.

Grey rummaged around in her pockets and pulled out an envelope. Adrian handed her a full English breakfast and in turn she handed him the envelope. He opened it. Inside was the same invitation, this time with the doctor's name. He smiled and looked at the number, he had been wrong, it was 003, and it really couldn't be a coincidence now, could it?

'You'll make someone a lovely wife someday, Miley,' she said between mouthfuls.

Chapter 24

The Dean

Then

When Abbey arrived back at halls over a week after the assault, the room was empty. She figured Dani was at a lecture, which was a relief really. She still felt guilty for kissing Christian. Whatever happened in the moments after she had kissed him, she had still made that decision, still betrayed her friend. Above Dani's bed were several pictures of Dani and Christian together. She recognised some as pictures from the night of the party. She felt sick at the thought of him, seeing his fake smile. She had seen his true face and now this one looked so insincere, so completely counterfeit.

She had to get out of that room. She changed her clothes and walked out of her halls and towards the University green by the plaza, a thin layer of mist made the place seem haunted. The University had relocated to this affluent part of the city near the beginning of the twentieth century. It was previously a private residence and three-hundred-acre country estate owned by one of the founders of the East India Company. Of course, it looked so different now, with the multi-million-pound red-brick and glass structures that had been added one by one over the years nestled in among the registered botanic gardens. The University was highly respected and had several wealthy benefactors, as well as proactive alumni who helped to keep it as one of the most highly regarded universities in the country.

She imagined all the things that had happened at this college, all the boys like Christian, all the naive girls like her. She felt their ghosts around her as she walked. She would have to go and see her lecturer, explain why she had missed her mid-term exam, what could she say? Not the truth, she would have to think of something. She entered the building. Even though the standard day had ended there were still students around, handing in late papers and attending their extra-curricular societies. As she approached her lecturer's office she noticed people looking at her, people she didn't know, some muttering to each other and laughing while keeping one eye in her direction. She had a sinking feeling as she tried to block out the sound of the whispers. What were they talking about? What were they laughing at? She could tell by the looks on their faces that they knew something, she didn't even want to think about what they thought they knew.

The huge open space around her meant there was

nowhere to hide. She couldn't stay here, but she couldn't throw her future away either. She had to go and speak to someone about what had happened.

Helen Lassiter's office was open as always so she just walked in.

'Nice of you to grace us with your presence, Abbey.' Helen's tone was sharper than usual. She had always been nice to her before but now Abbey felt a sting in the air.

'Sorry I wasn't at the test last week, I haven't been well; I spent the week at home.'

'I was surprised when I saw the photos of you on the college student network, you kids forget we have access to that. I was a little disappointed too, if I'm honest.' Abbey remembered the tequila, the short dress, the kiss and cringed inwardly to herself. She had forgotten. She dreaded to think what she looked like, what people must think of her. Helen turned her computer screen to face Abbey and scrolled through the images of the party. There she was, clearly drunk and draped over various people over the course of the evening. The next picture she saw was not of her antics in the living room but of Christian's bedroom, cold and sparse. She was partly covered by the dress, face down on the bed, hanging over the edge. She could see Christian's arm with the tattoo and distinctive custom-made watch, shirtless, with his hand grabbing at her thigh. She felt her stomach churning. She didn't know this picture existed. Anyone who had seen her that night would know it was her, and anyone who knew Christian would know that watch. Dani. Dani must have seen this by now. She expected almost everyone had, if it had already got back to Helen.

She looked up at Helen who was semi disapproving but also slightly smirking. 'I didn't know you had it in you' was written across her face.

'It's not what it looks like. This is what I came to see you about! You gave that talk at the beginning of the year on campus safety.' She saw Helen's face harden as she spoke. 'It was Jamie Woods and Christian Taylor, Christian took me up to his room and then Jamie came in . . .'

'Think carefully about your next words, Abbey,' Helen interrupted. 'You know I have to mark you down for missing your test, don't embarrass yourself by making claims you can't substantiate.'

Abbey was lost for words. What was she saying? Maybe she didn't understand what Abbey was trying to tell her.

'I didn't have a choice; they forced themselves on me, Jamie Woods and Christian Taylor,' she reiterated more adamantly, annoyed at Helen's dismissiveness.

'Abbey, it's pretty obvious from this picture that you're having a good time. If you're worried about your reputation I am sure this will all blow over eventually.' She leaned in to Abbey and lowered her voice. 'These boys have bright futures. Abbey, are you sure you want to sully their reputation to protect your own?'

Abbey was unable to speak, she had never stepped out of line in her life, and she had never even so much as handed in an assignment late. Her reputation? As if she cared about that any more. She thought by being the best person she could be that she would be above reproach, she thought at the very least she would get a fair hearing.

'Helen, it's really not what it looks like.'

'Let me give you a little life advice, Abbey. We've all done embarrassing things, you just have to dust yourself off and keep going.' Helen sat next to Abbey and put her hand on her shoulder, she looked her dead in the eye. 'Think about how you want to proceed with this. You have two choices in this world, you can be a predator or you can be prey. There are no other alternatives. You need to decide which side of that fence you fall on, because once you brand yourself as one, it's almost impossible to become the other.'

Abbey stood up and backed out of the office, unable to continue this conversation, unable to listen, unsure what was offending her most.

As she walked back to her halls she saw people looking at her, pointing her out, this time it felt so much more personal, she felt so violated. She looked up and saw the bedroom light on. Had she left it on? She couldn't remember. Oh God, please don't let Dani be home.

She heard the music through the door as she approached, soft guitar riffs with an anguished male voice accompaniment that Dani so liked to listen to. Abbey wanted to run away but she knew there was no running away any more. Surely it was better to face it now, then she could deal with whatever shit was thrown at her next.

Dani was sitting on the bed, shoulders shaking, head

in hands. Abbey was considering walking straight back out when Dani looked up.

'How could you?'

'It's not what it looks like.'

'Oh, it can't be what it looks like, because it looks like you and Christian . . .' She began to sob slightly more dramatically than before, even with Abbey's guilt she felt like it was an act to some degree.

'I'm so sorry; I kissed him, that's all.'

'That's not all, is it though? I mean, I saw those pictures.' Those pictures, plural. Abbey didn't even want Dani to elaborate on her words, she could imagine, camera phones, the easy way to spread bad news fast.

'I swear that's all I did; I didn't want anything else to happen.'

'How can I believe a word you say? I thought we were friends.'

'He forced himself on me . . .' She saw Dani's look of despair change to one of disbelief, almost mocking, like that was an impossibility.

'You?' Dani spat out. Abbey realised all the words of encouragement Dani had given her over their time together had been empty words, designed to cement their friendship but not actually words she believed. She made clear at that moment, with that one word, that she thought of Abbey as beneath herself and therefore beneath Christian. 'At least have the courage to admit you're a man-stealing slut, Abs.'

'I kissed him, I thought he liked me, I don't know what I was thinking, I was really drunk.'

'But now you're accusing him of rape? Because you were too fucked up to remember?'

'I remember just fine, I know what happened, him and Jamie . . .'

'Him and Jamie? Together? He's not gay, what are you saying?'

'I don't know, I just know it was both of them, they just wouldn't stop.' She realised that Jamie must have been the one taking and sending the photos, probably in a bid to split up Dani and Christian, to weaken their relationship.

'You are so full of shit! I'm going to stay in a hotel; I can't stay here with you.'

'I'm sorry, I didn't want to break you guys up or anything.'

'Oh, we haven't broken up, Abbey.' She stood up and looked down her nose at Abbey with a contemptuous smile. 'I'm not letting a double-crossing bitch like you ruin this for me. He was drunk, he apologised, clearly his judgement was impaired.'

Abbey recalled that Christian wasn't drunk. She started to see how manipulative he really was, or maybe this said more about Dani than him. Over the last few days Abbey's world had fallen apart, she knew her father had struggled with the news, Dani was no longer her friend and even Helen her favourite lecturer had abandoned her. Maybe her father was right to suggest she go to the police, but she just wanted to come back to college. They had been strongly encouraged to deal with these matters 'in-house' and she had heard stories of girls in other universities being ostracised for prosecuting, trial by social media. If she could just get the University to discipline them then no one else had to find out. She just didn't want to be around them, that's all.

She walked out of the room. She couldn't stand being judged, partly because she felt it was deserved – she had played a part in this game, she had kissed him, she couldn't deny that, she knew that would make anything she said subject to scrutiny.

As she was walking through the campus her phone beeped. She pulled it out and looked at it, it was a picture, different to the one she had seen before, more skin, more shadows. The picture was taken from behind Christian as his clothed body lay on top of her. Her head was turned away from the camera but her dress was reduced to a belt around her waist and the inside of her thigh was finger marked and red. She started to hyperventilate as her pace quickened, she found herself walking towards the dean's office in the main building, and she knew she had to say something now, something official; she couldn't take much more of this.

This was the first time Abbey had been to see Dean Talbot. She had seen him just a handful of times on the campus. He was a short, bearded man and his opulent office made him seem like a garden gnome, out of place in this grand oak-panelled surrounding. She had to wait for almost an hour in the receptionist's office before she could get an audience with him. The great and powerful Oz and she was Dorothy, lost with no friends and no way home. By all accounts the dean was friendly but formidable; from what she had heard about him he had a no nonsense approach to governing the University, putting the establishment first and woe betide anyone who tried to besmirch the great name the institute had earned over the last century. She sat on his red leather chesterfield sofa, which she was sure was older than him. She waited for him to speak and thought about her father, wondered what he was doing right now. She wished she hadn't come back, she wished she had stayed with him.

'How can I help you, Miss Lucas?'

'On Saturday night I was at a party on the Beston Road campus and I was raped by two students.' His face did not change, he stood up and walked over to her. Afraid of what he might say, she found herself shrinking backwards, already regretting her forthright outburst. She didn't want to beat around the bush, she wanted it out, gone, done before she talked herself out of it.

'Have you been to the police?' His concern seemed sincere, he sat next to her and looked into her eyes with understanding and she felt like she could trust him. She felt safe, safer than her father had made her feel.

'No, I haven't.' The sympathetic gaze did not waver as he took her hand, gently cocooning it in his own warm hands.

'Have you been examined by a medical practitioner?'

'No.' Abbey thought she saw a glimmer of relief on his face but she couldn't be sure.

'What about your parents?'

'I told my father, yes.' This time it was harder for him to conceal his emotions as anger flickered through his eyes. He stood up and walked back to his desk and picked up a pen.

'If you give me the names of the perpetrators I will launch an investigation.'

'Jamie Woods and Christian Taylor.' He looked up from his pad at the mention of Christian's name. Christian's father, Carl Taylor, was a well-regarded alumnus with a heavy presence on the school committee, his company had funded the refurbishment of the gym and the track fields. She knew the mention of his name had changed the game, it was written all over the dean's face.

'I see.' He put his pad down and picked up his phone. 'Gloria, could you get hold of someone over at Kane and Hall's, please, preferably Jim if he is available. And fetch Miss Lucas a cup of tea, please.' Kane and Hall were solicitors, she knew that much.

'I'd like to have my father here, too,' she said. Of course she didn't want him here at all, but she didn't have anyone else and she knew she couldn't face this alone. Her dad would want to be here; at least that's what he would tell her afterwards if she didn't ask him to come.

'I suppose you should have someone here to make sure it's all done by the book,' he acceded reluctantly. 'Let you tell your side of the story.' Her side of the story? She wondered what the other side would be, would they say she took advantage of them? She wondered if the dean had seen the photographs; she wondered how many photographs there were. Her stomach lurched at the very thought of it.

She sat in that same spot for over an hour while the appropriate factions were gathered and then they sat themselves around her. Eventually she was surrounded by the dean, three solicitors and a paralegal, who had all been introduced to her. Just one seat was empty; they were waiting for her father to arrive. She had told them she wouldn't start without him and he had a fair drive to get there.

After twenty minutes of silence and awkward stares, John walked into the office, baseball cap in hand. Abbey could smell the whisky on him as he planted himself next to her. He barely managed to smile at her. He had been drunk for the last week, she had had to call him in sick to work after she had found him out cold on the bathroom floor. For the first time in years she was embarrassed by her father, but even more embarrassed that she had turned him into this.

'Would you recount the events of Saturday night for us?' No easing, no small talk, straight to business.

'Why are they here?' John pointed at the lawyers.

'It's just standard procedure,' Dean Talbot said dismissively. 'Saves confusion later on. Please, Abbey, go ahead and tell us what happened.'

As she started to speak she noticed the girl with the laptop was typing furiously, it took a moment before Abbey realised the girl was recording Abbey's words verbatim. This made Abbey nervous. No one spoke as she told them of the party and the drinking. No one spoke as she told them of the kiss, ever aware of her father sitting by her side, listening to details about his daughter that no father ever should have to hear. It wasn't until she talked about Jamie entering the room that one of the solicitors finally broke ranks.

'So at that moment you were actually consenting to the relations with Mr Taylor?'

'I consented to kissing him, but I didn't want to do anything else.'

'Did you make that clear to Mr Taylor at any point?'

'When Jamie walked in I tried to leave, but I couldn't.'

'Did they lock the door?'

'No, but I couldn't leave.'

'Did they hold you down?'

'I think so, I don't know, maybe, yes . . .' She was getting flustered.

'And at any point did you tell the boys to stop? Are you sure it wasn't a misunderstanding?'

'A misunderstanding is when you forget whose turn it is to do the washing up! They assaulted me!'

'Listen, it's obvious those boys knew what they were doing!' John piped up aggressively. For the first time Abbey felt like someone was in her corner, and more importantly, that someone was her father. Relief swept over her. John's face was stern, eyes directly on the dean as they had been since Abbey started talking. John reached for Abbey's hand and squeezed it, she felt safe again.

The dean leaned forward and smiled at John.

'We have a lot of experience dealing with allegations of this nature, Mr Lucas, better to just let our guys handle it.'

'Oh, I can see how you are handling it. You don't give a shit about my daughter, you just care about your precious university.' John's venom was new to Abbey, she had never even heard him raise his voice before.

'Mr Lucas, if you could just calm . . .'

'And why so many lawyers, anyway? Maybe I need to call my lawyer too!'

'Please calm down, if you could just continue with your account and then . . .'

'Then what? Let me guess, she signs it then you pick it to pieces making everything look like her fault.' The lawyers looked at each other guiltily, having previously assumed that John and Abbey would be easy to take care of. The dean's smile faded.

'Mr Lucas, we take allegations like this very seriously, I promise you. We just need to decide what the best course of action for everyone is. We don't want to put anyone through any unnecessary ordeals.'

'Unnecessary ordeals?' John said through gritted teeth.

'The fact is that only twenty-eight per cent of rapes in the UK are then referred on to the Crown Prosecution Service. Of those, the actual conviction rate is considerably lower.' The dean spoke with confidence. Abbey wondered how many times he had to wheel these statistics out. 'Unfortunately, with the pictures, the boys' exemplary records and also witness accounts of your daughter's behaviour at the party, going to the police may not be a course of action you want to take . . .'

John stood up, yanking Abbey up with him.

'Where was your goddamned security when this party was going on? Who exactly was watching those kids while they all got wasted on speed and booze? My daughter and I *will* be contacting the police, and if you have anything else you want to ask then put it in writing, I'll get my lawyer to look at it.'

The dean stood up and looked at John with feigned sincerity.

'I would strongly advise against that course of action, Mr Lucas, you wouldn't want this to have any kind of long-term effect on your daughter's education. Or anything else, for that matter.'

'What exactly are you saying?'

'I'm saying there has to be some kind of arrangement we can come to so that this goes no further, this could be quite damaging for everyone involved, including poor Abbey.' The dean looked at Abbey and she found herself withdrawing and edging behind her father.

'So we just let it go? Just like that? Life goes on? You don't seem to understand, I've been at home with my daughter since it happened. She's a mess because of what they did!'

'I'm sure that we could reimburse you for any time missed . . .' The dean leaned forward and spoke softly. Abbey saw the lawyers straining their necks to hear what he was saying.

John lunged forward and grabbed the dean by his collar.

'We don't need your fucking money!'

The lawyers all jumped to their feet and Abbey tried to pull her father back. John pushed the dean and he staggered backwards, one of the men catching him before he fell to the ground.

They stormed out of the office, leaving the rest of

the people in the room stunned. She saw John in a new light. Abbey's father's outburst had both shocked and impressed her. She knew that people often underestimated her father, herself included. They mistook his placid nature and soft-spoken voice to mean that he was somehow a pushover.

She squeezed John's trembling hand as they waited for the lift. She was glad he had come after all. The lift doors opened and Abbey was confronted by both Jamie and Christian, with who she assumed were their parents. She moved out of the way and they stepped out of the lift, as she moved forwards she noticed a slight smirk on Christian's face and for a second she was almost sure he winked at her. She had to get out of there, she wasn't even sure if she was breathing any more and she didn't want her father to realise who they were. She pulled him into the lift and pressed the button manically.

They arrived at her dorm room, John standing in the doorway as she entered. Dani's side of the room was stripped bare but the same could not be said for hers. The world slowed and she wanted to run and shut her father out but it was too late as she turned and saw his face. He was looking at her wall, the words 'watch out, slut' were scrawled in red paint behind her bed, dripping down the wall in a menacing font. Surrounding the message were large printouts of the party, coupled with some imaginatively photoshopped pornographic images, some were real, some were not, but all of it had happened. Only someone who had been in that room would have known what images would have upset her the most. She didn't even want to take her things, she just wanted to leave. She ran out, pushing her father out of the way, running through the hallway, down the stairs and out into the open, gasping for air. It wasn't enough, she needed to be gone, away from this place.

She knew now that there was no way she would be able to get justice for this. She had no evidence, in fact all she had was her word against theirs and she already had a demonstration of how much weight that carried, especially given the circumstances. She couldn't bear to be made to feel like a liar any longer. Her father believed her, she was sure of that now, and that meant more to her than anything else. It was almost enough.

John led her to the car, arm around her shoulder. People looked and smirked. She wanted to scream at them but she just got in the car, happy when the engine started, even happier when the college was in the rear view mirror.

At home she went straight to her room. She couldn't talk, didn't even want to look her father in the eyes after what he had heard, after what he had seen. She wanted to die in that moment, to exist no more, to not have to think, to feel, to hurt. John was the only reason she would not, could not end it. She loved him, she knew how much her mother's betrayal had destroyed him, she couldn't betray him too. She would stay and they would look after each other, just as they always had, just like old times.

She awoke to the sound of the front door closing, she looked at the clock and knew that her father had gone to work. She had slept through the night, knowing her father was there for her had been enough. If today was a work day then things had returned to normal. Maybe they could go back, maybe they could pretend that it had all been a bad dream and they wouldn't have to face the reality of it. Who needs reality, anyway?

Her bowl and spoon were laid out on the table when she walked in the kitchen and she smiled. The phone rang, it was her father. He had probably forgotten something; maybe he wanted her to bring him lunch as she had done so many times before.

'I'm coming home, I've lost my job, Abbey. They fired me.'

Chapter 25

The Sanctum

At the museum the unveiling of the grand old ballroom ready for the big fundraiser had been a triumph. Using the likeness of a picture from the fifties, they had tried to make it as authentic as they could. No one could deny they had done a good job. Abbey and Parker had relocated the animals that had escaped the cull. Abbey was proud of herself, proud of them. She couldn't remember a time before Parker, couldn't remember how lost she had felt, only that she had felt lost. But that was a distant memory. Abbey was now helping to oversee the arrangement of the ballroom for the centenary this evening. It was all hands on deck, she had had to work through lunch. She hadn't seen Parker since before noon, she looked around the museum in his usual haunts but he was nowhere to be found, it was unusual for him to not be near her.

'We're all done now, here's your gear back.' The foreman handed her a stack of photos and old documents with the plans and blueprints of the museum. She struggled to hold on to them as she made her way up to the filing room.

When she got to the cramped office she looked at the intricate drawings of the building. She saw something that didn't make sense, different to the map on display to help tourists to find their way. On the second floor of the museum there was a blank space, as if there was nothing in that location, but knowing the building as she did, she knew there was not actually a gaping hole in the centre. The rooms were identical to the rooms downstairs only a few feet smaller, nothing too noticeable, not unless you knew what you were looking for.

As she walked through the large corridors to the fossil room, she looked at the paintings of the former directors, a tradition that had been carried on through the ages right up to Mr Lowestoft, the most recent addition. His picture was modern and out of place among some of the other faces and grand golden frames. She took a step back and looked at one of the men, it took her a few seconds before she realised why she had been drawn to this particular portrait. She checked the name, Giles Epler, Mr Lowestoft's late predecessor, who had left a great portion of his estate in trust to the museum. He had paid for most of the work that had been undertaken. She had never met the man when he was alive, but there was something about his face that was familiar, something, what was it? Then it hit her, it was his eyes, a sinister version of the ones she adored. Was he connected to Parker? Could he be Parker's father? No, he would have been too old; he must have been his grandfather, someone he trusted. She thought about the room, the secret room on the plans, and her stomach listed. Pieces fell into place in her mind. Did she even want to find it now?

It took her a while but she finally located the part of the wall that was just a few feet too short, she felt a little fantastical looking for a secret lever or revolving bookcase, but there must be a way in. She tried to picture in her head which other rooms would back on to the hidden chamber, then she remembered something that had always seemed out of place to her: a brass hook on the wall in the museum's aviary. It was small and unobtrusive but it was clearly as old as the building. Abbey ran through the museum until she reached the room, she found the hook and pulled, nothing, she then tried to move it and it turned a quarter, she heard a click but could not see anything different about the room. She placed her hands on the wall and felt as she walked along it, then she saw the slither of light down the side of the glass cabinet holding the ravens she had worked on when she had first started at the museum. There were seven of them, in a series of natural poses, but she knew what was under the skin, what went into making them look so natural. Glue and staples, paper and wood, wires and screws. The click sounded again and the slither of light disappeared, she rushed back to the hook which was straight and performed the action again, returning to the cabinet and searching for something out of place, something that should not be there; then she saw the switch. A tiny hole in the fascia, barely noticeable, just large enough for her to slide her finger in. There was a lever on the inside. She flipped it and the cabinet came free from the wall on one side. It was stiff and audible when she tried to move it, she squeezed through the gap and found herself in a room she had never seen before, and wished that even now she had not found it. Her eyes struggled to take in what she was seeing.

The door clicked shut behind her and the first thing that struck her was the stained-glass window, it was almost identical to the one she had kissed Parker in front of the first time. The rest of the room was more formidable. An arrangement of dirty, gilt throne-like chairs fixed to the ground in a circular fashion, all facing the centre. In the centre of the room a large hook hung from the ceiling, dangling over a wrought-iron grate, which appeared to be some kind of drainage system, with a parallel track on the floor and remnants of something else that had been bolted to the ground. She looked at the walls, the large oak panels were similar to the walls in so many of the other rooms, but on them hung various artefacts, obviously old, devices used to torture people in the medieval ages, maybe even earlier. Spiked whips and chains hung from the walls, every size and design you could imagine. Each item was conceived with a sole purpose in mind, to stretch, maim, brand, disfigure or kill. She couldn't quite see into the corners, she didn't want to venture over but curiosity had driven her this far, surely she had seen the worst of it.

In each of the far corners there was a large wooden chest, the bolts that had held them both closed had been cut, what seemed like recently to Abbey. A shiny new pair of bolt cutters lay on the ground next to them. She knew it was Parker who had been here of late. She was terrified but she wanted to look inside the chest. She took a deep breath as she heaved on the unwieldy lid, immediately regretting it as the foul air entered her lungs. More weapons, knives, a mace, a miniature crossbow, she looked at the bolts and saw the five pointed nibs, she recognised the pattern immediately, she had seen those markings on Parker's back, intermingled with the giant asterisk that dominated his body. The bottom of the chest was also a wrought-iron grate; she presumed it was so the base would not become rotten with the blood from the rusty arsenal.

The realisation that this room had been created by the original architect, presumably by instruction from the owner, sent chills coursing through her body. She could never have imagined this, in all of her suppositions about what may have happened to Parker, something she often wondered since she had first seen the scars, this had never entered her mind. She made her way to the other chest, filled with dread as she quickly pulled it open. Like ripping off a plaster, she just wanted to get it over with. This chest was different, it was full of slender leather boxes, slotted carefully next to each other, each one monogrammed on the spine. Some were so old they had warped and buckled. She pulled out one of the boxes and opened it, inside there was a large leather journal, the corresponding monogram on the front. Unsure of how many more revelations she could take, she opened the book to find the first entry was dated 1842. The writing was small and perfectly formed, with even pen strokes that on a first glance looked beautiful until the words became legible. At the top of the page was a list of members present – members of what? The initials of the first name matched the ones on the front of the book, she assumed the name belonged to the curator of that particular time period. *Subject 17 displays signs of improvement, withstanding the rack for almost thirty minutes before any significant tissue damage.* She turned the pages and was faced with drawing after drawing of a nameless young man, in various gruesome situations, limbs stretched and strangely inhuman. Just then she remembered Parker's reference to drawing Giacometti men, the faceless bronze sculptures from the mid-twentieth century. She realised at that moment that Subject 17 was a person. A horrifying thought entered her mind. She looked back into the chest and saw a box with the letters G.E. engraved on it.

Her blood ran cold as she reached for the box. She felt she owed it to Parker to look inside, that even though she couldn't bear the idea of what she may be confronted with, it could not be as bad as anything he had endured. Her suspicions were confirmed when she saw the name Giles Epler at the top of the page. This book was fatter than the previous had been, due to the photographs wedged in between the pages. The first picture was missing; she could see the ridges in the page where the picture had sat, presumably instead of a register. She turned the pages until she came to a picture of the room she was standing in, only it was illuminated with candles, every chair was filled, the occupants were wearing hooded cloaks that shrouded their faces. In the centre was a chair, not an ordinary chair, it was metal, it had bolts, spikes, rods and wires in various locations. The chair was secured to the ground on the tracks. A silver-eyed adolescent boy was strapped to the contraption, his face contorted in pain as he bit into the leather strap between his teeth. She could see the veins in his arms trying to rip their way through his skin as they bulged from the electricity that ran through them. She turned the page again, unable to look at that any longer. The next page was worse: arms shackled behind his back and hung from the hook, his shoulders protruding and inflamed, blood running the length of his shadowy naked body from his wrists. She turned the page again, *Subject 89 shows little reaction to the stimulus*. The picture was of the boy strapped to the chair, a metal restraint holding his head in place, his emotionless face staring forward. She couldn't look any more. She slammed the book shut and threw it on the ground. She ran to the part of the room she had come in by, there was a clear lever for her to pull, she was grateful for that one thing at least in this room of horrors. She looked at the brand name that was engraved on the base of the lever, it had been made by a company called Parker industries. She thought about the desperate boy in the pictures. She was flooded by a feeling of immense sadness. Things she hadn't dared to think about suddenly made sense, but at this moment all she could think about was her Parker, where was he?

She ran down to the foyer and up to Gemma.

'Parker, have you seen him?'

'Oh, he took the afternoon off.' Gemma seemed to be pleased that she had known something about Parker that Abbey had not, her grin smugger than usual. This wasn't like Parker. What did this mean?

'I have to go now.' Abbey's breath was getting more laboured as she felt herself going into a panic.

'What about the party?' Gemma called as Abbey dashed from the building.

Abbey pushed the door to Parker's home, it wasn't locked. Parker stood in the window, his hands in his pockets, staring out over the tennis courts in the square across the road. Sally lay loyally at his feet, a sad look on her face, she barely raised her eyebrow when she saw Abbey come in, just grumbled a bit – she was worried about her master. Abbey felt her voice catching in her throat as she approached him. He turned his head slightly, letting her know he was aware she was there, then he returned his gaze to the vista outside.

She slid her arms around his waist and began to sob into his back. He remained unmoved, his eyes fixed on the amateur couples' tennis match. She felt the muscles beneath his shirt and remembered the angles his body had been contorted into.

'I found the room,' she whispered through trembling lips, she wondered if she needed to elaborate, would he know which room she was talking about? She felt his heavy sigh as he pulled away from her and she knew there was no need, he knew exactly what room she was talking about. She had been afraid this would happen, his shame would drive a wedge between them. He turned to her, his face calm but his eyes screaming. He moved towards her and placed his arms around her, she had so many questions, but she dare not ask them for fear of him answering so she kept quiet and just relished the warmth of his contact. He stroked her hair, soothed her. He had assumed the role of protector and she felt so unworthy of his sympathy. Any unresolved anger or hatred she had towards her own abusers didn't matter any more; nothing mattered but Parker. Thoughts of herself disappeared entirely, now all she wanted was to protect him at any cost. She was filled with a new hate. She wanted to avenge Parker, she wanted to know who perpetrated these horrific acts, who had hurt him like this? With every fibre of her being she wanted them to pay.

'It's OK. Abbey. it will all be OK,' he lied. She felt his hesitations and his chest heave as he placed a hand on her head again, smoothing her hair in comforting strokes.

'When I was ten years old my parents died. My grandfather was my only living relative and so I came to live with him on his estate. He was a wealthy, well-respected man. I had met him maybe once before. My father hated him. He was the history teacher at the private school before he came to work at the museum.' Parker's voice was calm and monotone, as though he were reading a menu; emotionless, cold.

'He was the director, right?'

'He was. I thought he chose to work there because he loved the museum, my father used to talk about it a lot. My grandfather put me in Churchill School for Boys but I struggled. I had been home-schooled up until that point, with my parents' work it had made more sense because they had to travel extensively. I was in a strange country and I didn't fit in with the kids at that place. My grandfather was a disciplinarian. He liked rules and he made it very clear that I was disappointing him. We didn't get on well.' He took a deep breath and turned his shoulder ever so slightly, just enough so that she couldn't see the expression on his face.

'What did you do?' She thought of her father and how lucky she had been. She went to put her arms around Parker but he stepped away even further, she looked at his hands and saw him squeezing his fingers anxiously.

'I started skipping school and I made friends with a boy. His name was Nathan. He had been living on the streets for months. He had run away from home. Sometimes I would let him come over to the house and take a shower or have a hot meal. One day my grandfather had a call from the school saying I had called in sick and he came back to find Nathan in my room in just a towel and he completely lost his mind.'

'What did he think you were doing?'

'He wouldn't listen to me when I tried to explain.' Parker swallowed hard and looked at Abbey; his eyes were brighter and shinier than usual. He was holding back the tears.

'What happened to your friend? What happened to Nathan?'

'I couldn't find him anywhere. He seemed to disappear. I kept asking my grandfather if he knew what had happened to him. I asked him if he could find out if he had gone home to his family, but he just told me to let go of Nathan, that he was gone and that was that.'

'But he wasn't?' Abbey asked gently, seeing that Parker was still fighting to keep his composure. Parker shook his head.

'I didn't let it go and my grandfather became more and more distant from me. I had to go back to school as though nothing had happened. The deputy head there, Jeffrey Stone, took a special interest in me, it was creepy and I knew what it was he wanted. I caught him taking photos of the boys in our class in the changing rooms. I told him I was going to tell my grandfather – they knew each other. He gave me a choice, either I could do what he wanted or he could ruin my life. I had no idea what he meant and I didn't give him what he wanted. He went and told my grandfather that he had caught me and one of the other boys together. So one day soon after my grandfather took me to the museum after it was closed and took me to this room . . . THAT room. Nathan was there, well, what was left of him was. It was a miracle he was still alive. He had been tied up backwards to the central beam. I could see he had been hanging there for days. It had been weeks since I had seen him. He had been starved, beaten and worse.'

'Oh God.' She desperately wanted to reach out to him, to touch him.

'They made me watch as he confessed to having feelings for me and they cut him like he was nothing. One of the men stood over him reading out all the sins he had committed as they did it.'

Tears rolled unreservedly down Parker's cheeks now, but his voice remained as calm as before. 'The doctor guy put weights on Nathan's feet and his shoulders popped right out. He was crying, pleading with them. By the morning, he was dead. I was inconsolable. My grandfather told me that's what happened to people like Nathan. People who wouldn't change.'

'I'm so sorry.'

'For a while I tried to pretend nothing had happened, like I hadn't seen what I had seen. You have to understand, I had no one to turn to. I was being watched at school, at home, everywhere. I was terrified. It was a few months before anyone found Nathan's body. One of the men had taken his organs.'

'Why? What did he do with them?' she asked, shocked.

'The doctor told me he . . .' Parker's voice faltered, cracking slightly. 'He told me they were in the school science refrigerator, ready for the next week's Biology lesson. He said human and pig organs are very similar. Thirteen-year-olds certainly wouldn't be able to tell the difference.'

'Why did they go after you?'

'I was distant, I was failing horribly at school. In all honesty I think it was inevitable, I think my grandfather was in so deep that he couldn't see anything but darkness. I wasn't really family, I was just another teenage boy. When Jeffrey Stone told my grandfather of his suspicions, he didn't even question it. He brought me to the museum again and there was another boy, then another. They tried to make me a part of what they were doing, they tried to make me hurt people, but I just couldn't. When the boys were . . . gone, they started with me.'

'But why did they do it?'

'They thought they were right. They thought it was some kind of calling. They had a misguided sense of religion. The school chaplain was one of them. They would chant and do other strange ritual things before they started. They said these things had been going on for a lot longer than they had been alive. My grandfather had recruited them through their ties to the school, they had all been students there, some had even worked there as teachers. He had been recruited that way too. But they were kidding themselves, it wasn't about making anyone better, it was about feeding the monsters inside them. I saw each one of them for what they are.'

'How long did they have you? How did you get away?'

'I couldn't tell you how long I was there. I can remember everything they did to Nathan. As time went on I only remember fragments of what they did to the other boys and what they did to me. I remember hanging there. I remember being shot in the shoulder with a crossbow. I remember being burned, hit, cut, but most of all I remember pain, so much pain.' He stared at his fist as he clenched and unclenched it.

'Parker I . . .' Abbey could barely stand to listen to any more. She didn't know what to say to him, there

266

were no words that could help him. She was powerless. 'What's your real name?'

'My name is Sebastian . . . you must think I am so weak for not going to the police . . .' He turned away.

'I don't! I swear I don't think that! You were a kid! I can't even imagine . . .' she lied. She knew all too well that feeling of being silenced by fear, of wanting so desperately to scream but not having a voice. She wanted to destroy the people that had hurt him.

'These murders? The ones on the news . . . are those the men that hurt you?'

'Yes.' He looked ashamed but she reached forward and took his hand, cupping her fingers around his to make sure he knew that she didn't want him to feel that way. He looked at her, his eyes burning with a mixture of sadness and anger. She knew she should probably be dismayed by this revelation but she wasn't. She knew what it was to be a victim and she knew what it was to disappear inside the shame, to be eroded by self-loathing. She was glad Parker hadn't let them destroy him completely. She was more than glad; she was proud.

A thought occurred to Abbey.

'The fire in the museum.'

'I had to get away but I had to stop them, too. I had to destroy that place. I couldn't bear the thought of them doing it to anyone else. I thought the police would find the room and they would all be put away.'

'How did you escape?'

'My grandfather, a momentary bout of conscience. He released me and left the room, told me to hide, begged for my forgiveness. As soon as I started the fire I got out of the building and just kept going.'

'Where did you go?'

'I went to a church first of all, I didn't know where else to go. I didn't want anyone to find me, I knew they would be looking. The priest and his housekeeper, Mrs Wilson, took care of me until I was eighteen, then I received the trust my parents left for me.'

'And your grandfather?'

'I spoke to him one more time. He called me and cried and pleaded for absolution, tried to confess to me about all the boys, alleviate his conscience, but I hung up. When he died he left me almost everything. But he still gave money to that godforsaken place.' Parker turned around and put his hands on Abbey's shoulders, his face streaked with the saline liquid. 'I thought I was OK . . . I thought I was over it, but when I heard he had done that . . .'

She pulled him close and hugged him tightly, stroking his hair as he shuddered into her.

'It's OK . . . you're OK now.'

'I had to do it, Abbey . . . but . . . it's not over yet. I'll go to the police, I promise. When it's over I will hand myself in.'

'I don't want you to do that. I want you with me.'

'But the things I have done . . .'

'People can be driven to do bad things . . . it doesn't make them bad people. I've done bad things, too.' She paused for a moment to take a breath, now wasn't the time to share her dark past with him. 'You're good. I know you are . . .'

'When I started this I never intended to meet someone . . . to fall in love . . .' He wiped the tears from his face with the back of his hand and took a deep breath, as if he had resolved to put his feelings in a box and lock them away for ever. 'I didn't think I could.'

Abbey recognised that look in his eye, accepting that people like them could never be happy. That you can't have everything. But that was before, now she knew, she knew that she could.

She took his face in her hands and locked eyes with him.

'Neither did I, but here we are. And I do love you, Parker, this changes nothing. You did what you had to do. Please don't turn yourself in. Stay with me.' She pulled his face towards her and kissed him.

'But how could you ever forgive me?'

'There is nothing to forgive.'

Chapter 26

The Accident

Then

The kettle clicked and steam billowed from the spout as Abbey stared at the brown-speckled tiles on the kitchen wall. John sat on the sofa watching television, a relentless supply of repeated make-over programmes. Explaining why what you have isn't good enough, why you should have more. An endless cycle of reasons to feel like you are failing. Buy, buy, buy.

'Cup of tea, Dad?' Abbey asked, with what had become the usual fake cheery optimism. John's last mug of tea was still untouched on the coffee table, stone cold. She picked it up and replaced it with a steaming hot alternative.

'Thanks, Abs.'

'Going out today?' Abbey looked at her father, his

eyes were glazed and drooping at the corners, it made him look so sad, so hopeless. He responded by turning the volume on the TV up.

'I got a phone call from the museum,' she said. John continued to stare forward. 'I have a trial run at the job, I start tomorrow.'

'What?' He looked up.

'I got the job at the museum.'

'Doing what?'

'I think they want me to help them fix up all the animals, some admin as well, maybe, I don't know. It was a pretty loose job description.'

'But they're dead?'

'I know, but we did study anatomy and we also did some animal autopsies at uni. I can handle dead animals.'

'You don't want to go back and finish your degree? You've wanted to be a vet ever since you were knee high.'

'I need to work, Dad.' She looked down, not wanting to make him feel bad. 'The bills . . .' She saw him switch off from her and back to the orange-skinned presenter. Losing his job had been the final straw for John, he had sunk into depression and Abbey had to hold it together, for both of their sakes. She was embarrassed that she didn't have the strength it would take to go back to study. University was ruined for her, even if she went to a different place, it wouldn't make any difference; she didn't want that any more.

'You never used to lie to me, now you lie all the time.'

'What do you want me to say? That I was an idiot? That it was all my fault? I can't talk about it any more, Dad. I can't let it take over my life!'

'If you let it take away what you want then they've won, you can't let them win!'

'You don't get it though, there is no winning or losing, not any more. It's already happened, it's over. They won!'

'Did I raise you this way? Is this how you think you should deal with it? By running away . . . Maybe this is all my fault . . .'

'Don't you dare say that!' she shouted. He turned back to the television, indicating the conversation was over.

'Call me when you finish, I'll pick you up,' he muttered.

'Don't worry, I'll get the train.'

Abbey had not visited the museum for a long time but it looked the same as she remembered it from trips with her father when she was younger. The same damp smell filled her nostrils and caught at her throat. She was greeted by the director and led through the expansive corridors to his office, occasionally passing cordoned-off areas that were waiting to be re-plastered. Most of them looked like exhibits themselves, un-touched. The walls were grey and the dimmed light made it hard to make out shapes, only shadows. There was more shadow than light.

'So you've never worked in a museum before?'

'No, but I am a fast learner and a hard worker.'

'I see you have some good references.' Abbey smiled, embarrassed that the references had been the only price for her silence. The dean and her favourite lecturer oozing about her wonderful character and her dedication on paper even though they had made it more than clear in person exactly what they thought of her.

'And why did you stop your studies, if you don't mind me asking? It sounds like you were good at it.'

'My father isn't well. I need to focus on looking after him. I am the only family he has.' She gripped her bag, ringing the canvas instead of showing the anxiety in her face.

'Well, let's start on something simple and we can see how you get on. If you need any help I am sure one of the custodians will help you out, they are usually lurking around somewhere.'

'Thank you, sir.' Abbey stood up and reached across the desk to shake Mr Lowestoft's hand.

'Have a look around if you like, and you can start formally on Monday, there's no hurry.'

'I would be happy to start now, sir, I just want to work.'

'I like your enthusiasm, Abbey, and your family values. I can already feel you will be an asset to our little family here at the museum.'

'I hope so, sir.' She smiled. Finally she had direction again, she felt relieved that they had accepted her even with her limited experience.

Mr Lowestoft led Abbey back through to a room full of birds, it was one of the closed rooms due to the mould and fire damage to the glass cabinets that housed the creatures.

'Do you think you could do anything with this? It hasn't been touched in years. Unfortunately after the

fire we had no choice but to just close the rooms
until we had the funds to restore those that were the
most affected. We didn't remove any of the creatures
as the casing seemed to keep them intact and we
didn't have the funds to hire someone who knew how
to handle them properly. Some of the animals are
very old.'

'How long ago was the fire?'

'A little over fifteen years,' he said as she moved closer
to the box.

The thick layer of dust and soot obscured the contents
of the box, she could see very little of the black birds
that were displayed inside.

'Are they crows?'

'Ravens, but as you can see the cabinet is ruined and
the birds inside didn't fare much better. If you could
fix them up for us that would be wonderful, we have
a new display case for them arriving soon.'

'I will be happy to try, sir.'

'You are welcome to take the animals home, or to
work here if you have trouble transporting them, but
I must warn you, we hire out the function room for
parties and this weekend we have two, so the place will
be a touch out of sorts. We are still trying to raise funds
to fix the old girl up. She's seen better days.'

'No problem.'

'Here,' he reached into his pocket and pulled out a
small brass key, 'this is a skeleton key that fits all of
the cabinets. This is yours now. Your predecessor left
a tool kit here, too, until you get one of your own.
We'll see if we can't organise a proper space for you

274

to work in as well.' He smiled warmly and walked away.

'Thank you,' she said as he disappeared out of the tiny room.

She wiped her hands across the glass and a thick coating of black appeared on her fingertips. The tools were meticulously placed in a worn leather pouch; they had been much loved and taken care of. She ran her finger along the various blades, all blunt now, but there was a sharpening flint inside, she could make them work for her. She put the key in the lock to the cabinet but it was jammed, with a little force she managed to open the case. Inside the case smelled even worse than it looked. She carefully removed the birds and placed them in an empty crate. She would be able to use the parts of one bird to help fix the others that were damaged and missing feathers.

She was still lost in her own world when the curator returned.

'Gosh, you really got stuck in there.' He smiled his warm, friendly smile again. Abbey stood up, her clothes covered in grey chalky patches and wayward feathers from inside the glass case. She dusted herself down. 'I just came to tell you that the museum will be closing soon, half day today.'

'Oh.' She looked down at her unfinished work; she didn't like to leave things unfinished. 'Would it be OK if I took some of these home?'

'There really is no rush, and no shortage of work for you to undertake. We have thousands of items for you to be getting on with. You may be here for the rest of your life.' He chuckled.

'I'm looking forward to it,' she reassured him. She wasn't lying either. For weeks, months now she had been sitting at home watching her father deteriorate in front of her eyes. He had claimed her pain as his own and now she felt duty-bound to take care of him. If it hadn't have been for what happened to her their lives would still be on track. If only she had not trusted so blindly. A warm smile and a few kind words from someone out of her league had made her vulnerable when every moment in her life before that had been confirmation of her place on the food chain. She blamed the movies she had loved to watch, where the plain girl gets the prince and the pretty rich girls end up crying into their Jimmy Choos. Life didn't work like that.

She clambered through the front door with her menagerie in a large basket-weaved bag she had borrowed from the museum. Her father was still in the spot where she had left him, the hair on his face visibly longer. She left him to the evening's soap operas and nature programmes. He didn't want her around anyway.

She placed the birds on her desk and pulled out her surgical kit, the only thing she had kept from university. It felt strange to hold it in her hands again. She picked up the first raven and dusted him off with an old make-up brush so as not to damage the plumage that remained. She didn't wear make-up any more; she was never very good at it anyway.

She worked through the night. It was all very simple

really, and the information she didn't have she researched on the internet. The weekend seemed longer than forty-eight hours but she worked diligently to bring these birds back to their former glory at the expense of the most damaged of the bunch. She wrapped each bird in tissue and placed them back in the bag.

The following Monday she returned to the museum where she was presented with a brand new glass cabinet that the carpenter had delivered that morning, an exact replica of the one that had been keeping the birds safe until they found a new home, right down to the faux landscape that was painted on the backboard. She had been given carte blanche to arrange the birds as she saw fit, before they were re-displayed in the room known as the Aviary.

She felt like herself again in the halls of that museum, the shadows of the past fading and being replaced with a passion for learning again. Night after night she would borrow the books from the museum library and read thirstily. The magnitude of the task she had to undertake was not lost on her. But instead of feeling intimidated by the vast storage rooms, she knew that as long as she did her job well she would be here for many years to come.

'Abbey, I have something to show you,' Mr Lowestoft exclaimed one morning, many weeks after she had started there. He took her back to the room where they had first stood and discussed her job and he showed her the results of her hard work. The room was finished.

It was a small room but it was immaculate, with the ravens in the centre. Mr Lowestoft had overseen the restoration of this room personally. He said it was his favourite in the museum. She couldn't understand why; it was small and slightly claustrophobic. 'I will leave you to admire your work.'

'Thank you.' She felt a sense of accomplishment, something she had not realised was missing from her life. In the few short weeks at the museum she had turned this dingy little corner of the building into a tiny paradise of dead things. She identified with the birds, trapped for ever in the one moment that had rendered them as nothing, but that moment was for ever frozen in time. They had crossed paths with the wrong person, as had she, like the hundreds of other animals in this place. All the little beasts had probably been completely unaware of their impending fate. She thought about the moment of their death as she looked at the creatures. Each one was a victim, each one represented misplaced trust. Trust in your surroundings, trust in the ones you care for to protect you, trust in your own survival instinct. Most of the birds had been killed with a slingshot, silent and stealthy, requiring some level of intimacy. She thought of the moments before the death occurred and the mind of the hunter, watching the prey with patience, waiting for the perfect opportunity. Waiting for that moment when the world blinked simultaneously and no one was looking except him. Well, these animals were hers now, she would protect them, and she would never close her eyes, not even to blink.

*   *   *

John waited for Abbey to leave the house. She was happier now, she had moved on. She wasn't the Abbey he had raised any more; in the six months since the attack she had become a different version, a quieter version, less confident. She didn't have the same lack of self-assurance that all teenage girls had, this ran deeper. She was no longer holding on to the unconfirmed questions that he had noticed in her before. Am I pretty? What does life hold for me? Who will I become? No, those days were over, the timidity he saw in her now was steadfast. She had been shown her position in this world and he hated the world for that. Now at least she had found something just for her. It was a solitary job but he did not care as long as she was smiling. She really was all he had left. The job he had worked in for decades was gone, his drinking had seen to that. If he could be bothered he would sometimes fix friends' cars for cash. But he had never been one for pity.

He could not stand this place any more. Truth be told, he could barely stand Abbey, or himself for that matter. He didn't understand how she could go back to the city, knowing that they were there, after what they had done. He didn't want to admit it but a little part of him blamed her for what had happened, he couldn't deny it, thank God no one asked.

He walked into the local benefits office and waited on the stain-ridden couch to go and sign on, surrounded by the apathetic, the angry and the ignorant. He looked at the face of the girl sitting directly opposite him, all hair and nails, a pregnant swelling and a defensive glare, she was entitled to this, this was hers to take. John hated it; he hated having to depend on anyone else. He hated that he had worked his whole life, never colouring outside the lines, always doing what he was supposed to, always doing the right thing, and obeying the rules. He played the game the way they wanted him to.

His name was called and he went and sat with the advisor. A young man who had barely left school, sitting in judgement over him, it made him sick to his stomach. He gave the boy the list of jobs he thought he might be in with a chance of getting.

'Sir, I'm afraid these positions are only available to people in the eighteen to twenty-four age bracket.'

'And why is that?'

'To keep youth unemployment down.'

'And what about those of us with families to support?'

'Come and see us again on Friday, that's when the majority of new opportunities come in.'

'When do I get my first cheque?'

'I should be able to tell you that on Friday, too.' The boy smiled but John just wanted to smack him in his smug little face.

John smiled and stood up. The advisor shoved his papers into a large folder and then turned to his computer, indicating he was done talking to John.

John didn't have the energy to feel humiliated; as usual the only emotion that consumed him was anger. He again found himself heading in the direction of the University halls of residence where Abbey had been living. Since Abbey had started work he found himself venturing up here time and time again. He stood outside the halls and waited, he didn't even know what he was waiting for. Within the hour he saw Danielle emerge from the building. She walked over to a red convertible Porsche Boxster and kissed the boy in the driving seat. John suddenly knew who the occupants of the car were. It hadn't clicked with him immediately but they were the boys he had seen outside the dean's office at the University. As soon as the lift doors had closed that day he had realised who they were; as soon as Abbey had started breathing again. This time he could only see the back of their heads and for that he was grateful. He wanted to go over, he wanted to cause a scene. Instead he walked away. He needed to go home, he needed to sleep off some of this anger. He needed to think.

The next day John woke up and he knew what he had to do. He waited for Abbey to catch her morning train and he drove back to the city, to the University. If she was going to be there he would make sure she was safe. This time he went to each campus and looked for the red car, eventually finding it parked outside one of the University bars.

Abbey returned home from yet another day at the museum to find her father sitting and watching the local news. He still had not found a job and he barely ever looked her in the face, maybe it was time to find a place of her own. Her wage at the museum would afford her a small flat somewhere in the city. She sat next to her father on the sofa and put her hand on his, he pulled away immediately and she heard him trying not to breathe, splintered intakes of breath as though he were holding back tears. He wiped his eyes and sniffed, she didn't want to look at his face, didn't want to see him cry. She couldn't bear that. Instead she looked at the screen, it was the news. For a moment there was a picture of a mangled car and then the screen switched back to the newsreader. In the corner of the screen under the headlines she saw the familiar faces of Danielle and Jamie.

They were dead, killed in a car crash.

'Oh my God, Danielle.' Her hand involuntarily sprang to cover her mouth. A closer look at her father's face and she saw the tears.

'Dad, what's the matter?'

'I'm sorry. I'm so sorry.'

'It's OK, Dad, it's not like we were friends any more; it's horrible but . . .'

'No, it wasn't meant to be her, it was supposed to be them!'

Abbey felt a chill up her spine as she looked harder at her father's face. She saw behind the tears; she saw his guilt.

'Dad, what are you talking about?' A thought, the whisper of a revelation, came into her mind, she tried to shoo the idea away before it took hold, not wanting to listen to what her instinct was trying to tell her.

'I tried to fix it, I'm sorry. It was supposed to be them, the ones who hurt you.'

'What did you do?' She could feel the thought clutching at her, holding on; not letting her dismiss it.

'I just wanted to make things right. I couldn't stand the thought of them walking around like nothing had happened.'

'Jesus Christ! Please tell me you didn't!' She felt the tears rising in her own throat, the enormity of what her father had done finally taking hold. 'What if they catch you? You can't go to prison, Dad!'

'You think I don't know how to make it look like an accident?'

Christian's face appeared on the screen, he seemed to be distraught. Abbey picked up the remote to turn the TV off; she couldn't bear to look at his face. She knew he didn't give a crap about Dani or Jamie, it was just an excuse for him to get on camera. Then it occurred to her that he was being put into a police car, so she turned the volume up instead. He was being arrested. It was his car which he never let anyone drive except for that afternoon when he let Jamie drive Dani back to the halls of residence. He and Dani had fought publicly in the uni bar, everyone had seen them threaten each other, and apparently Christian didn't come off looking like the good guy for once. He had met his match in Dani for crowd-manipulation. The police believed he had tampered with the steering on his car before going home with another girl from his course. An alibi, they supposed.

She clicked the TV off and looked at her father. Was he really capable of this? Yes, she supposed he was, if anyone hurt him she would do anything, she guessed it was only fair to expect he would do the same.

'Did anyone see you?'

'I don't know, I don't think so.' He reached for her hand but she stepped away and folded her arms.

'Why, Dad? Why did you do it? We were all right,

weren't we?' She tried not to sound angry, part of her was touched, but the other part of her was scared of losing him, of him being caught.

'We're not all right, Abbey. I'm not all right! I can't sleep at night thinking about what happened, what they did. I couldn't stand the idea of you running into them again, of them being on the same planet as you.'

'What if you get caught?'

'Why would I? There is no record anywhere of what happened to you, they all saw to that. The police won't make the connection, why would they? Those bastards made sure there were no connections!'

Abbey walked out of the lounge and took her bag before heading out on to the street. She couldn't believe this. Her father was the kindest man she had ever known, it broke her heart to think of him like this, driven to taking a life, two lives. She knew that even though he probably had no regrets about what happened to Jamie, eventually the weight of Danielle's death would catch up to him, and would probably destroy him.

After an hour of roaming the streets, Abbey returned home and John was in bed, she looked into his room and he was sleeping on top of the sheets, fully clothed, a bottle at his bedside. If he were caught she would be an accessory. She contemplated phoning the police and handing him in herself, for his sake as much as hers, but the thought was fleeting. All things considered she was a little proud of him for taking a stand, for taking the power back. She knew what it was to be helpless and she admired him for having the courage to do something about it.

The next day in the museum she went to her corner and buried herself in the work. Mr Lowestoft had entrusted the keys to her and asked her to lock up when she left, her current task was to restore artefacts for the Asia Room. The best ones would be displayed inside the modest museum as there wasn't room for all of it. The day drew to an end and she stopped working the leather on the samurai warrior's armour. Each piece was laid out ready for the next day when she would reassemble the complicated leather piece mail and encase the wire-structured dummy. She had her own work room now, it was a small nook that she had been allowed to set up her tools and workstation in.

She stepped outside the museum, the dusky sky turning cobalt blue, ready for the night ahead. She inserted the key in the lock and the hairs on the back of her neck stood on end, she turned her head slightly and saw a figure standing behind her. She didn't need to look; she recognised his aftershave. She quickly pushed the door open and dashed back inside, trying to slam it in Christian's face. He put his boot in the way and with one swift movement knocked her on her backside. He came in and locked the door behind him, putting the key in his pocket.

'We need to talk!' He stared down at her.

She looked around the lobby helplessly, there was nowhere to go. She was trapped.

Chapter 27

The Director

Ted lowered his feet from the bed on to the floor, searching for his slippers with them. He reached over to the bedside table and felt for his glasses. He could smell the warm, sweet smell of waffles in the air. He walked slowly out of the bedroom, his slippers shuffling across the luxurious pile.

The bathroom always seemed too white at the start of the day. The sun rose behind the house and the light would flood in the most the first thing in the morning. He felt the burning in his groin as he expelled the toxins from his bladder. All the pills he had taken before bed had worked their way through his system. His urine was a deep yellow, and against the fine white ceramic bowl it looked every bit as dirty as it was. Back at the sink he washed his hands and then looked at himself in the mirror. He was old. He was always surprised at how old he looked, inside he felt twenty-five.

Downstairs now, sitting in the day room, his plate ready for the delicious treat his wife had specially prepared for this special day. Today Ted was sixty-five years and four months old, not a birthday but an age worth noting. Tomorrow though, tomorrow night at the museum he would feel young again, before he formally announced his retirement, before he and his wife left for warmer climes.

He put on his favourite suit, it was blue wool, warm with a herringbone weave, it had been tailor-made just for him several years ago. This suit hadn't fitted him for a long time but since he received the cancer diagnosis he had lost weight. He was unsure whether it was psychosomatic or a result of the disease gradually working its way through his body. Either way he was grateful for a chance to wear this suit again.

Ted brushed what was left of his hair in the usual side parting, aware that he wasn't fooling anyone but he didn't care. He was going to enjoy this day. Since he had heard about the deaths of the others he didn't care much to listen to the radio in the car; scared of what he might hear next. The first of the disconnected reports came when he heard Jeff Stone had killed himself. He assumed that he just couldn't live with himself any more; it was not as though the thought hadn't crossed Ted's mind once or twice over the years. Then came a small report in the newspaper about the disappearance of his friend Ian Markham, which drew his attention. He had contacted Harry immediately after that, who had then informed him that Stephen Collins had passed in Paris. That's when it clicked into place. It was too much to be a coincidence, despite Harry's assurances. Then came the huge news of David Caruthers' demise. As yet no one had connected them together. Ted knew he was one of the few who were left. He hoped he would be dead before the truth came out. One way or another, his time was coming.

He had almost laughed when the specialist had told him the news. He had been waiting for a sign that maybe there was a God. How was he allowed to live this life unpunished for what he had done? For years he had been happy, his life was good, his kids loved him and he had never especially wanted for anything. It just didn't seem right.

It's true that once you have tasted the darkness it is hard to turn away and make a normal life for yourself, but he had managed to do just that. He missed the time he had spent with his brothers-in-arms but he did not miss the fear of discovery. Just as he had been told of his illness, more good news had befallen – his prede-cessor, the director Giles Epler, had passed away and left a great deal of his considerable fortune in trust to the museum. The money was to conclude the restora-tions and renovations that were taking an eternity; at least the entirety of Ted's time there. He could not believe it had been eighteen years since the fire. Painstakingly they returned each room to its former glory. Well, almost every room.

At the museum, Gemma informed him that the police had been to visit, wanted to know the names of all the employees at the museum. She had given them. He was slightly disappointed that they had never arrested him; he waited for it almost daily.

Ted ran his fingers along the familiar grain of his mahogany desk. He would miss the old girl. She had been with him through thick and thin. She was well over a hundred years old and had been the stalwart of eight curators. Bespoke, commissioned for this very museum, this very room. She had survived countless atrocities, including the fire that would have ravaged her given half the chance. Nothing burns like old wood. She was accompanied by the tall-backed green leather chair, they stood together, majestic against the Georgian grey backdrop. He looked around at the bookshelves full of priceless books, the walls covered in framed awards and certificates of excellence. He wondered if he would have been allowed this life if anyone had known. That's the thing though, people did know. He had waited all this time for someone to go to the police and take the life that he didn't feel he deserved away from him. It didn't even occur to him to go to the police himself; that he could be the whistle blower, that he could put an end to this feeling, the endless feeling that something terrible was coming.

Walking through the rooms he smiled at the patrons, all marvelling at the improvements that had been made. It had been a long time since he had made the rounds like this. He remembered a time when he had walked the corridors with the same wonder and amazement as the children he could see today. It was a lifetime ago.

Ted's father was a Nazi sympathiser and had told

Ted many stories of how they were just misunderstood and misinterpreted by the closed-minded 'bloody do-good liberals', how the world would be a better place if they had been successful in cleansing the gene pool of impurity and imperfection. After the war, Ted's father had become director of this very museum and shown Ted all of its secrets before introducing him to Giles Epler, the man who would succeed him and precede Ted. Ted's part in this had been inevitable. Lowestoft's father and Epler had both been students at Churchill School for Boys themselves, in fact, they all had. When the boy had escaped Jeff Stone had gone through the records and altered them. There was nothing like a boys' school for identifying who the sadists were, the bullies and the brutes; you just had to know what you were looking for. For eighteen years they had been anticipating some kind of retribution, they just hadn't imagined it would be so brutal and completely inhuman.

Ted walked towards the Aviary and waited for the people to leave. He turned the hook and released the door that led to the secret chamber.

Inside the room was lifeless now, but he remembered it how it had been when he and his brothers had restarted the old traditions of directors past, under the tutelage of Giles Epler, the overseer of the whole operation. Ted instinctively went to his own seat and looked around the room, the perspective increasing the unwanted feeling of nostalgia. He remembered the boy, he remembered telling him just to cooperate and everything would be OK, just to do what they wanted and he could go. The boy had been different from the start.

Epler had recruited him even though he clearly had no inclination to cause harm. It was the first mistake of many from the old man.

Ted knew the room had been disturbed and he knew by whom, he wondered what the boy looked like now, he wondered if he would recognise him. The fire and water damage had destroyed their sanctum sanctorum and they had been forced to give up the room. In the beginning it had all started as a harmless supper conversation up at the school, jokes about the way things were dealt with in the past. Epler had told them about the local history regarding the treatment of homosexuality. It was easy to discern which men were responsive to the notion; they were the ones who didn't raise protest at the barbarian nature of the practice, the ones who looked almost excited at the prospect. Then he had told the selected few of a darker secret history, one hidden from the mainstay of record, passed down to true believers only, people who believed in a cure. In the past where no cure could be administered, the boys were afforded the mercy of death, but they were not operating in the past, things had changed. He wondered, if the boy had never escaped would they still be doing their duty today? Would they have succeeded? He rather imagined they would be in prison. Already the power trip had pushed things too far, mistakes were being made, starting with the homeless boy. He was not supposed to die, it had not been agreed. Egos were taking over and the cause was lost. Peter, Kevin, Harry and Jeff had taken it upon themselves to take action alone. The boy's disappearance appeared in the news and then the eventual discovery of his body on the floor of a derelict building, discovered by some solvent abusers. The only loose end after the boy died was Sebastian Epler, Giles' grandson. Epler had gone soft at the last moment and helped his grandson to escape.

Ted wandered back to the lobby. Gemma chirped away at Shane, flirtatiously ordering him around.

'Mr Lowestoft!' She composed herself and stood to attention. He half expected her to salute.

'Sir.' Shane nodded, a smirk on his face, and he turned and winked at Gemma.

'Carry on, I'm just going to go look at our lovely ballroom again.' He plodded past them, his legs hurting with every step. Part of him wondered when he would be relieved of this burden, when his time would come, he knew it must be soon, there weren't many of them left.

'Oh, the police are in your office, sir,' Gemma offered. 'I tried to tell them you were busy with the preparations for tomorrow but they wouldn't listen.'

'Thank you, Gemma.' Ted smiled, they could wait for him. It didn't make any difference now.

The ballroom was looking grand again, back to how it was before the fire, back in the glory days. He hated himself for looking back on those days with fondness but the truth was if he could go back, he would. He knew when he received the call about Giles Epler's death that there would be a reckoning. He assumed the old man was the only reason the boy had not come back sooner to exact his revenge. Part of him wondered if Epler hadn't left them the money to enable them to start again. To reignite the flame that had once burned so brightly in all of them.

'Officers,' Ted said as he opened the door. The female was looking through the books on his shelf, he cringed as she thumbed through the first editions with much less care than they deserved.

'Hello, sir.' The male detective stood up and offered his hand, Ted took it. 'I'm DS Miles, and this is DS Grey.'

'How can I help you? I'm a little busy today, as you can see. We have a big do tomorrow.'

'Yes, it's the fundraiser we wanted to talk to you about.'

'Fire away.' He smiled and smoothed his suit before sitting in the trusty green leather chair.

'Three victims from recent murders have all had private invitations to your party tomorrow. We need to know what your connection to these victims is.'

'Over a hundred of those invitations were sent out to various important people in the community, it's a fundraiser.'

Three? So they didn't know about David Caruthers or Stephen. David's murder had been all over the news, mainly because he *was* the news, but it was almost two hundred miles away. It didn't seem like they had put anything together yet. Ted hoped he was gone before they did, before they looked into the most sordid corners of his past. The truth never stays buried, Ted had learned that over the years, and the longer it takes to come out the more vile and foetid when it eventually does, and God knows he didn't want to be here when it did. If it came to it he would follow Jeffrey's lead and do the Spandau ballet. Part of him was curious as to how the public outcry would go down. He wondered if there would be people out there who understood. After all, he had been brought together with a handful of like-minded people by the former director Giles Epler all those years ago.

'Are you personally acquainted with Mr Markham?' DS Grey asked.

'Yes,' Ted replied.

'How do you know Ian Markham, sir?'

'His company has been very generous to the museum over the years.'

'What are the names of the other people who received private invitations for tonight?'

Ted tried to think of a way to stall the inevitable, he had lied about the private invitations, they had been for his comrades alone, they would take one look at the list and everything would fall into place. Ted cursed the risk he had taken in inviting them this way, but it had been almost twenty years, no one remembered the boy who had died. No one except the one that got away. It wasn't until Ted heard about the other deaths that he realised the invitations were a stupid idea. Eighteen years is a long enough time to convince yourself that you are home free, safe. It seemed inevitable now that the blinkers would be removed and the connections would be made.

'I'm afraid I don't have that to hand. I sent that information over to the printers. If you have a warrant you can look through my emails.'

The female looked up and straight at Ted, he had obviously said the magic word, her indifference turned into mistrust.

'We can get a warrant if you like, Mr Lowestoft.' She smiled and sat in the chair opposite him. He could tell he had said the wrong thing, suspicion was all over her face where it hadn't been before. 'Do we need one?'

'I'd like to protect the information on our contributors as much as possible. You understand that, don't you, Officer?'

'We could always just come to the party tomorrow.' She smiled. 'I could do with a good night out.'

DS Miles smiled at him.

'Please do what you have to do, Officers, and I will do what I have to do.' He smiled but Ted never had a very good poker face. DS Grey was walking out the door, almost halfway down the corridor, when DS Miles finally broke his gaze and followed her, closing the door behind him. Ted picked up the phone and dialled a well-rehearsed number, he didn't even have to look it up.

'Harry! You need to do something and do it now! I just had two police officers in here asking questions about Ian. They are going to get a warrant and find out about the others, about you!'

'I'll fix it,' Harry said. 'Stop panicking.'

The phone went dead. Ted sat at his computer and clicked open the control panel, he clicked the button to restore factory settings. They wouldn't find anything on here without a fight. He looked up and caught a glimpse of something nailed to the back of the door. It was a pendant, an ankh symbol, the Christian sign for eternal life. It was the symbol that had been painted in gold on the back of Ted's chair, not this chair – the chair in the room. The chair he had occupied in the covert meetings. They each had their own symbol; eternal life had been Ted's. Ironic really as his body had other ideas. Inoperable is a word no one wants to hear, it carries the same weight as the words malignant and terminal; so completely final. His thoughts were interrupted by the familiar sound of his black Bakelite telephone. He didn't want to answer it, didn't want to talk to anyone, but he lifted the receiver.

'Hello?' Ted asked tentatively.

'Come to the Aviary, Mr Lowestoft, it's time,' a deep, muffled voice came over the line, he had obviously covered the mouthpiece.

'Very well.' So this was it, the end he presumed.

He looked around the room before pulling the door closed. He would not give the boy the satisfaction of the chase, although he could hear in his voice that he wasn't a boy any more. He would come to him and take his punishment like a man, whatever it may be.

The Aviary was far too generous a name for the mausoleum that contained all of the bird carcasses, killed unsuspectingly and without compassion. The birds had all been arranged as though they were in the wild, either nesting or in flight, with great care and attention to detail. Yes, this was his favourite room. It certainly was a beautiful sight to Ted, seeing the fantastic array of colour that seemed to have no place in nature.

Ted walked into the room and saw the back of the man. He had a black hood over his head.

'Do you know what the collective noun for crows is?' the voice asked.

'A murder,' Ted answered. 'A murder of crows.'

'Very good, Mr Lowestoft.' The man turned around and Ted was confronted with the familiar sight of Parker, the PhD student who had been helping Abbey.

'Parker, I thought you were someone else,' he said, an unintentional sigh of relief escaping his lips. Had Parker scared his executioner away? Parker smiled a lopsided smile and shrugged. He was staring straight at Ted.

It took a few moments before the clouds of confusion dissipated and Ted finally understood what was going on. Ted realised he had never really paid much attention to Parker before. Then he saw it. The questions had finally been answered. What had happened to the boy? Would Ted even recognise him if he saw him again? In Ted's mind Parker had been burned as an image of adolescence and youth, as if time would stand still just for that one person. He had forgotten that people grow, people change.

'I was almost sure you would recognise me. But you didn't. I was a little disappointed when you didn't, I have to admit. But to be honest, that's the only reason you're still alive.'

'I suppose it's no use me telling you I'm sorry for what we did,' Ted said as he stared at the cabinet and not Parker, he couldn't look into his eyes and see the hate that he so much deserved. Parker walked across to the beautiful big glass case that stood in front of the secret entrance to their special room. Several black birds with a blue and green tinge to their leather-look plumage. It was as though they had been dipped in petroleum and the slick feathers looked wet to the touch.

'An unkindness of ravens.'

'Excuse me?'

'That's what you call a group of ravens, an unkindness. They were called that because they would push the young from the nest and leave them to die.'

Ted's heartbeat was thumping in his ears, steady and regular, the anxiety medication keeping the rhythm for him because his body no longer could. His collar was getting tighter, it was getting harder to breathe. To live a life of pretence you have to ignore many things about yourself. They become harder to ignore when the product of them is standing in front of you, threatening to end it all. Parker looked at him.

'What did you do?' he asked.

'I took my pills, all of them, everything I could find,' Ted admitted.

'Good for you, Mr Lowestoft.' Parker smiled and patted Ted on the shoulder. Ted would have flinched if he weren't so numb from the medication. 'Are you scared?'

'Of you? Probably not as much as I deserve to be.'

'I don't believe you to be capable of remorse so don't play that card with me.'

'I'm surprised you believe in anything after everything you went through.'

'Spare me your coffee-table psychology, there's nothing

you can tell me that will erase the memory of who I know you to be. Have you forgotten who you were?'

'I know who I was, who I am.'

'Then you know I have no choice. It was always going to end this way.'

'Yes. I know.'

'I have grown fonder of you these last few months, there's almost no trace of the monster I once knew. But then I come to this room and I see the ravens, I remember what's behind them.' He paused for a moment and looked at Ted, who was clutching at his collar, feeling weaker by the second. 'Your chair was the closest to mine.'

'Please.' Ted felt his knees weaken. Parker rushed to him and held him up, he was gentle; it was almost as though he cared.

'I remember in the beginning, when I was first brought to the room, I had hoped you would free me, you were the only one who brought me water. Not even my grandfather showed me that compassion.'

'If I could take it back . . .' Ted sputtered.

'You can't. We have to go now.'

'Go?' Ted's vision was inconsistent, his gut swirling, words stuck to his tongue that felt too heavy to move. Ted leaned on Parker who led him through the museum, it was empty and Parker was cautiously looking around each corner before moving forward. Ted was struggling to focus on what Parker was saying.

'It was worse, you know. With the others I expected it, but with you I had hope. You know the only thing left in Pandora's Box was hope, some people believed that's because hope is the most evil emotion of all. When hope fails all that follows is complete and utter despair. Without hope there is no despair.'

Through his blurred vision Ted could see they were approaching the ballroom. Parker opened the door and they both went through, closing the doors behind them.

Chapter 28

The Rat

'This all feels very surreptitious.' Gary Tunney, the digital forensic analyst and general supernerd, shovelled spaghetti into his mouth. 'Sorry, I'm starving. I've been stuck in a bloody seminar all morning, part of the new terror training stuff. Had to learn how to get shot well. As if you get a choice where to get shot.'

Adrian and Grey just watched him, they didn't have any food.

'You said you had something,' Adrian said, just to stop the sound of Gary eating, it was not pleasant.

'Oh boy do I have something!' Gary said, polishing off the rest of his dinner, oblivious to the contorted grimace of disgust on Grey's face. He shoved the bowl to one side and reached into his messenger bag, pulling out a wad of files. Gary was mid-twenties with auburn curly hair poking out from beneath his beanie. The hat

301

was thick black wool, completely out of place in this weather, grey and shiny in the creases where the dead skin and sweat had settled; it didn't look like he ever took it off.

'What's all that?' Grey reached across the table to take the files. Gary pulled them back, a wicked smile on his face.

'No way, you have to wait for the big reveal.'

'You're so lame.' Grey smiled.

'You look cute without the glasses, DS Grey,' he said. She raised her eyebrows at him and he hurriedly turned his attention back to the files. 'OK, so the knife they found at Ryan Hart's place was not the knife that was used on either the pathologist or Kevin Hart, although it does seem likely that the same knife was used on both of those unfortunate fellas – it's just not this one.'

'We kind of guessed that,' Adrian said.

'Fair enough, but did you know that a similar knife was used in another high-profile murder-slash-suicide recently? Not only that but the knife was left at the scene.' Gary Tunney's eyebrows were raised; he was excited, waiting for a prompt.

'Whose?' Adrian moved forwards, leaning on the table.

'David Caruthers, the news guy,' he whispered like he was gossiping.

'You mean that horrible scene up in London?'

'That's right. They didn't find any DNA other than Caruthers' on the knife, it was a kukri, the kind used originally by the Nepalese army, it's pretty old school. Big and shiny.'

'Do you have the notes on that crime scene?'

'Oh yeah, it was majorly messed up. Ancient Chinese torture method, he had hundreds of lacerations on his body, or what was left of it. Be warned, dude, it's one of the most gruesome things I have ever seen.' Gary handed one of his files over to Adrian. Adrian looked through the photos. It was unreal, in the same way that Kevin Hart's scene was unreal, not to mention the coroner's.

'You think it was done by the same person?' Adrian asked, even though he knew the answer, there was no way this was done by anyone else.

'No doubt about it; and it certainly wasn't done by Ryan freakin' Hart.'

'And no one's made the connection between the Caruthers murder and our ones down here?' Adrian asked.

'Not officially. You might want to kick that information upstairs though; probably get you some brownie points.'

'OK, is that all?' Grey asked.

'Well, no, funny you should ask that, that is definitely not all. I had a look at the crime scene notes for Kevin Hart, and the autopsy report, and then I kind of managed to blag a look at the remains.'

'And?'

'None of it makes sense. I mean, it makes sense, but it doesn't make any sense.'

'Now you're the one who isn't making any sense.' Grey smiled impatiently.

'Well, this crime scene report does not fit with the

autopsy report, and neither one of them fits with what I managed to deduce from looking at the remains.'

'Go on.'

'That pathologist was either suffering from some kind of illness that affected his ability to carry out his job to any kind of satisfactory degree. I could do better than he did and I don't have anywhere near the kind of experience he had. I specialise in computers!'

'Or?'

'Or the more likely explanation is that he was well bent. He hid a bunch of stuff, or misreported it. It was so far out of whack there was no way it was unintentional. He was covering something up.'

'Why?'

'Well, isn't that the golden question?'

'You think the pathologist was in on it?'

'I don't know! You're the detective. I would say that was a fair assumption though.' Gary held up his hand to the waitress, she walked over. 'Can I get a double espresso and a banana split, please?'

'Right away, sir.' She scuttled off again.

'A banana split? What are you, five?' Grey asked.

'I like them, sue me!' He still had tomato sauce from his Italian lunch on his chin, entangled in with his gingery beard.

'Is there anything else?' Adrian couldn't watch Gary Tunney's ham-fisted attempts at coming on to Grey so he diverted the conversation back to business.

'Well, the lovely Detective Grey informed me that something was bugging you about the Hart crime scene, senior, not junior. Although I have a few things to say about junior's as well. Anyway, I had a look at the pics and you're right, there was definitely something familiar there. So I spent a while looking online for stuff.'

'Online where?'

'There are plenty of websites on serial killers, horrific murders, theories on things that have happened, unsolved cases and shit like that. People are fascinated with the macabre. Don't ask me why.'

'You found something then?'

'About twenty years ago there was a body found right here in this city in a warehouse along the riverbank – well, parts of a body – inside a suitcase. Down past the old mill. Really horrible case, I mean really horrible murder, I don't know what the suitcase was like.' He half giggled.

'It was a kid, wasn't it?' Adrian remembered.

'They aged the body at around thirteen years old, there was no way to identify the body, although the marks indicated extreme neglect and malnutrition, torture, some really, *really* sick shit.'

'You think all of this has something to do with that?'

'Well, coming back to that pathologist. He was on that case; it was one of the first autopsies he was on. I had to find the original paperwork on it though because he's not listed on any of the copies.' The waitress placed a tower of ice cream, jelly and bananas in front of him, she glanced down at the pictures on the table, blood and guts everywhere. She looked at them in shock. Adrian opened his wallet and flashed his badge at her; in return she flashed him a smile. Grey groaned and shook her head. Adrian winked at Grey.

'That's some great work, Tunney.' Grey smiled, grabbing the cherry from the top of his dessert.

'You don't have to steal my cherry, Grey, all you have to do is ask.' He licked his spoon in what Adrian imagined was supposed to be a flirtatious way but Gary Tunney was clearly not used to flirting.

'So what did this website say about the case of the boy in the suitcase?' Grey asked.

'Quite a few boys went missing around that time; it was not a good time to be a young man round here.'

'Did they have a theory about it?'

'These sites are all well and good but I wouldn't look to them for actual insight, basically they talked about some evil satanic cult making human sacrifices, which is pretty much the go-to reason for things that have little or no reason behind them. They try to find a rational explanation for an irrational act. There's very little evidence that satanic cults have ever actually existed. There was also some speculation that it might be a gay thing, I don't know. It wasn't long after Dennis Nilsen, the Muswell Hill murderer who killed a bunch of men and boys back in the seventies and eighties. He would meet guys in gay bars or lure homeless boys back to his place in north London. There was a real public interest in his case, like there is with most serial killers. After that point though, of course, every man or boy who went missing was assumed to have been taken by some deviant serial killer. Back then people weren't very forthcoming in their reports. It wasn't the same murderer though, the boy and the pathologist, it was a copycat, very similar MO but different strength,

306

different angles, just different. Pretty good copy, though. Whoever did it knew some pretty specific details that were not in the press, either a copper or someone who was actually there. The organs were missing for a start, never found. His fingertips had been removed, sliced right off post-mortem, presumably to prevent identification. His teeth weren't intact either, but that seemed more likely to be a part of the systematic torture he endured.'

'That's great, Tunney, thank you.' Adrian slammed the folder shut, unable to look at any more pictures of Caruthers. He didn't understand how Gary Tunney could sit and eat that banana split with its oozing strawberry sauce. Some people just have a stomach for that stuff.

'There are a couple of other things you might be interested to know.'

'Jesus, why don't you do our job for us, Gary?' Grey flashed him a winning smile, throwing the dog a bone.

'You know me, Grey, I'm meticulous.' He winked.

'Nosy, you mean.'

'Ryan Hart had some really shocking drug cocktail injected into him, there is no way a man with his contacts would be putting that crap in his body. He would be looking for a primo high. Do you remember those OD's last year, the ones you worked on in Plymouth? It was a pretty close approximation of that mix, same chemist, I reckon. Each chemist has their own signature when you get down to the raw formula. It was crystal meth mixed in with a few low-grade narcotic substitutes, generic household cleaners.

Anyway, he had like ten times the recommended dosage, at best it was suicide. But the scene looked staged to me. Also an experienced user like Hart wouldn't take four goes to find the vein, whoever injected him hadn't done it before. There's more . . .'

'OK, lay it on me, what else is there?' Grey asked.

'Three of the boys that went missing in the seventies were from the Churchill School for Boys. Ryan Hart's old school, way before he got kicked out for dealing.'

Adrian's face paled. That was Tom's school. Then he remembered what Ryan had said about 'that teacher' and Jeffrey Stone's suicide. Something else was going on here, something bigger and he needed to find out what.

'Is there something else?'

'Yeah, there's one other name that keeps popping up wherever I look.' His banana split was almost gone, Adrian could see Gary Tunney contemplating licking the banana boat.

'Who?'

'Your Detective Daniels.'

Grey looked at Adrian. She had some experience of working with scumbags, he saw her breathing become slightly more laboured, as though she were conscious of trying to control it, she pulled her eyes away and looked straight ahead. Last time she had a run-in with one of her colleagues she had ended up with a scar running the length of her torso. Adrian wanted to stop the train of thought he could see written all over her face.

'So where is it, then?' Adrian asked loudly, snapping Grey out of her own head.

'Where's what?' Gary wiped his mouth.

'The best place to get shot.'

'Well, it's complicated,' Gary said excitedly, apparently unfazed by a question from left field. 'Assuming you can't actually point your backside at the shooter . . . the fattier the area the better apparently. But if it's a torso shot then avoid bone and major organs. So either a very particular spot on the left side of your stomach about an inch under your ribs – you'll bleed and it will hurt like hell but it's not going to kill you – or the soft bit under your collarbone facing out away from your spine. Interesting fact: eighty-eight per cent of people who are shot recover fully.'

'You're a good man, Gary. Let me buy your lunch.' Adrian reached into his pocked and pulled out a twenty pound note, putting it on the table. Grey stood up with him and patted Gary on the back.

'Cheers, Gary, I owe you one.'

Outside the café Grey gave Adrian a foreboding look. This was a lot of information, a can of worms.

'What do you think?' he asked her.

'I think Gary's information is solid. He is a puzzle solver, he loves putting crap like this together until everything makes sense, he wouldn't have told us if he wasn't sure.'

'Do we go to Morris?'

'I don't see how we can. I know Daniels is a creep but I just can't see him being bent. He's much younger than these other victims, too. A different generation. We need to get some solid evidence that we can use before we go to Morris.'

'What Ryan told me about the men coming to his

house when he was a kid, him recognising that teacher? He was my Tom's headmaster. If this is about what it seems to be about then . . .'

'Don't think about that. Granted, they all seemed a little perverted but we need to be careful before we start throwing those kinds of accusations around,' Grey said. 'We just need to find out if any allegations have been made against the school before. It could be about something entirely different. Markham's perversion was gambling with other people's money, not messing with kids. There's no evidence to say that's what's going on here.'

'There haven't been any allegations like that against the school, at least none on record. I looked into it before Tom went there. I just have a bad feeling, Grey. I feel like everyone is lying to me, to us. We need to find someone who can tell us what happened, someone who was there. Whoever is involved, they got rid of the paper trail. I can feel myself getting sucked into this one, in a bad way. It's going to be one of those cases where there are no winners.'

'That's usually what happens with murders, Miley.'

'So what do we do now?' Adrian asked, knowing full well that he intended to call Andrea and tell her that Tom wasn't going back to that school.

'I think we need to go back to the station and sound Daniels out.'

Imogen pulled into the car park at the station, making sure to park as far away from her former colleagues, whose cars were all nestled together in a big metal lump, as possible. So insecure that they all had to park together, in their little clique. She walked past 'his' car, in her mind she didn't even want to acknowledge his name. She cursed the fact that there were cameras facing the forecourt, she would love to let his tyres down, key his car, stab him in the eye.

'Grey,' she heard from behind her. The hairs on the back of her neck stood on end. She knew it was her former partner, Detective Samuel Brown.

'What do you want this time? How many times do I have to tell you to leave me alone?' She turned around, hand on her hip, trying to give the impression she was calm and collected, it couldn't be further from the truth. Her heart was racing, and not in a good way.

'I was hoping we could put all that business behind us, Grey. You got a promotion.'

'So did you!' she interrupted.

'I'm just saying, can't we go back to being friends?' He stroked her arm, she was grateful she had three layers of cloth between his hand and her skin, which was crawling. She backed away from him but he walked with her.

'Friends don't try and have their friends killed. Friends don't stalk each other!'

'That is not what went down, you're overreacting as usual. You don't have all the facts.' His hand was still on her arm. She thought about shrugging it away, or cutting it off. She couldn't move though, she was frozen.

'I have to get inside. Don't talk to me again. We are done.'

'You're making a mistake, Imogen.'

'The only mistake I made was trusting you, Sam.'

She stared at his hand. He didn't move it, instead he held on with more conviction, leaning forward and staring into her eyes.

'Let me give you a little friendly advice.'

'What's that?'

'Just watch your back, OK?'

'Are you threatening me?'

'You know what? If it gets you to step back, then yeah, I am! You've been told to back off by your boss already, maybe you should listen to him.'

'There's nothing you can do to me that you haven't already done!' she shouted; he put his hands up and stepped back. She really wanted to punch him in the face, instead she just spat on him, somehow that seemed appropriate.

She shook off the anger and walked into the station and saw the familiar sight of Denise the desk sergeant looking wistfully across the squad room at her partner. Miles, of course, was oblivious to it. He didn't seem to be very aware of other people's feelings. Imogen was fine with his introspective nature, he never pushed her for details about herself, he wasn't overly chatty or even friendly, he seemed driven in his work and that was about it. So far she hadn't felt the overwhelming urge to manipulate him, something people often brought out in her.

'Did you bring any food?' Miles asked her, reminding her that she was starving. She always forgot to eat at work, and thank God she kept a massive stash of emergency chocolate in her glove box.

'Never mind that, what are we doing now that the old duffer at the museum stonewalled us? We can't get a warrant without Daniels finding out, we need to maintain a low profile, we don't know who is involved.'

'I figured we have a couple of invitations right here.' He waved the invites of the dead men in the air with a smile on his face. 'We don't need a warrant to use them, and we can see who is at the party in person, you never know, we might get lucky.'

'Lucky how?' She frowned at him, half joking, knowing his propensity to charm the pants quite literally off of almost every woman he had contact with.

'I mean, the killer might be there.' They looked at each other, well aware the pretence of the conversation they were having was for everyone else's benefit.

'Are we running this past the DCI?' She looked around to check if anyone was in earshot. She knew full well the answer to that question.

'Come on, Grey, what do you say? Wanna go on a date with me? I'll pick you up at seven.'

Curiosity would always win out, it was why she became a police officer in the first place, so she could legally stick her nose in other people's business. It's how she got into most of the messes she got into – she just wanted to know first-hand. She wanted to see what was going to go down at this party, not just interview people in the aftermath. She had a feeling something bad was going to happen there. There's no such thing as coincidence.

'OK, I'll do it, but I'll drive myself there, I have some things to do tomorrow. I can't meet you until eight.'

His excited face forced her to smile a little, he was goofy all right.

'There's a small catch.'

'What's that?'

'You have to dress up . . . you know . . . like a girl.' He put his coffee to his mouth and raised his eyebrows in an apprehensive manner. Obviously waiting for her to back out or tell him off.

'You mean pigtails and a gingham dress, Miley?' She twiddled her hair and batted her eyelashes at him, he almost choked on said coffee.

'Woman, you need to dress like a woman, it's black tie,' he stuttered as he wiped the coffee spatters off of his shirt.

'That might be a problem.'

'I'm sure you'll think of something.' He continued to rub the shirt, mumbling something as he sloped off to the toilets to clean the big brown splodge off.

Imogen huffed and looked down at her clothes, pretty much everything she had looked like some variation of this. When she had left Plymouth she had gotten rid of any trace of who she used to be. After the attack she donated all of her clothes to a charity shop and went out and bought clothes a little more reminiscent of her youth, from when she hung around with skater boys and listened to alternative rock music in the park until all hours of the morning. She was never particularly into pretty dresses or high-heeled shoes but it would have been useful to have some around, for situations like this one. She hated shopping, so that was out. She scanned the room until her eyes rested on Denise, the doll-faced desk sergeant. They were roughly the same size. She walked over to her, noting that every so often her eyes would glance in the direction of the toilets, clearly waiting for Miles to come out.

'Denise, I need your help.' Imogen realised this was one of the three times she had engaged in conversation with Denise, apart from the hellos and goodbyes before and after shift. She rested on the desk and leaned over, a slight look of fear on Denise's face. 'You're about a size ten, right?'

Adrian put his phone down again, Andrea wasn't answering and he needed to talk to her about Tom. He hated leaving her a voicemail, besides, this was more of an 'in person' kind of discussion. He wanted to talk about the possibility of enrolling Tom into a new school before the new term started. He wasn't looking forward to the conversation, he knew she wouldn't be reasonable about it. He walked into DCI Morris' office. Daniels was standing in there on his phone. He quickly hung up.

'You could knock first!'

'Where's the DCI?' Adrian asked.

'He's out, left me holding the fort.' Daniels put his phone back into his pocket and walked over to the door to leave. Before he could get to the door Grey walked in and closed the door behind her, leaning on it.

'Are you out of your mind? You need to let me go.'

'We have some questions, Mike,' Grey said, crossing her arms, determined.

'What's going on?' Daniels looked concerned.

'You have to admit things have been pretty weird around here lately,' Adrian said, moving closer to Daniels.

'I don't know what you're talking about.'

'I feel like I've been running around in circles, where I am allowed to. Like every move I make is being watched.'

'I don't know what you're talking about,' Daniels said again, flustered.

'You said that already.' Grey half smiled at him.

'You and I both know Ryan Hart didn't kill himself. Did you do that? Did you kill him?' Adrian asked directly, no point beating around the bush at this late stage in the game. There were going to be more murders, he knew that much, he just didn't know when or how many. He needed to get to a version of truth that made sense to him.

'Miles, you need to leave this alone, trust me.'

'Or what?'

'You don't know what you are dealing with, best just let it go, it's all under control.'

'Does this look under control to you?' Adrian threw Caruthers' crime scene photos at Daniels; they landed on the floor, red upon red. Daniels looked down and shook his head, he fought back tears.

'He promised me it was all under control.'

'Did someone get to you, Mike, is that it?' Grey put a comforting hand on his shoulder, he shrugged it off. She walked behind him and leaned on the desk.

'First it was just a little favour here and there. Then it got bigger, until it was out of control.' He let out a sigh of relief as he spilled the secret that had obviously been playing on his mind for quite some time, he looked instantly relieved.

'Like what?'

'That evidence that got you suspended, I had to frame you up for that, they needed you out of the station. I got rid of the most incriminating paperwork and the gun and made it look like you had fucked it up.'

'They? Who is they? Kevin Hart's people?' Adrian's heart was pounding, had he really been set up? He had never questioned his guilt, knowing that he was out of his mind at the time when the evidence went missing.

'When I was asked to get rid of Ryan, I really had no choice. There is so much dirt on me now, there's no walking away from it.' He wiped the tears from his eyes and took a deep breath. No one in the squad room was even looking at them, they didn't have a clue. 'It started years ago. I would help get Ryan out of trouble, until he got too big and started getting noticed. Then of course there was you. They tried to keep you off him but you were like a dog with a fucking bone.'

'What did Kevin Hart have on you?'

'Kevin Hart? This goes beyond him, Ade. I was stuck! I would have lost my job. I got caught drink driving, bloke got run over and almost died, they wrote it off as a hit and run. They sorted it for me, as long as I helped them out.'

'So who else?'

'Stone, Markham, Hart, some vicar who died over in Paris. Respected people, people who could crush someone like me.'

'Adrian,' Grey said solemnly. He looked up at her,

she never called him Adrian; she was holding something out to him. He took it from her and felt the blood drain from his body as he read it. It was an invitation to the museum fundraiser, number 001, and the name on it read Harold Morris. The DCI.

'I'll deal with you later, Mike, go home for now! Don't talk to anyone. I'll help you get out of this, I promise.'

Adrian walked out of the office dialling the DCI's number on his phone, straight to answer phone.

'There's an explanation for this, I am sure.'

'I know. Of course there is.' Grey tried to reassure him.

'He's got nothing to do with this.' Adrian was trying not to hyperventilate; trust once broken can never be repaired. He didn't want to lose all faith in Morris until he had a chance to speak to him. If the director was telling the truth and over a hundred of those invites were sent out, then it made sense that Harry's name would be on it. Didn't it? He wasn't sure how much sense it made that Morris would be number one, though.

'You're right, of course he hasn't.'

'I can't get hold of the DCI. I need you to keep this to yourself, Grey. Don't tell anyone.'

'No, I won't. Of course I won't!'

'We act as if nothing is different.' He managed to calm himself with a deep breath, trying to stop his thoughts from spinning out of control. 'You want to grab some lunch?'

'I'd love to but I can't. I kind of have somewhere to be and I'm off tomorrow. I'll meet you at eight tomorrow night, yeah?' She put her hand on his shoulder. He knew he could trust Grey, she wasn't a part of whatever was happening, he was sure of it.

Adrian left her standing in the station. He had to get out of there. His world was turning upside down. Again.

Chapter 29

The Shop

The pub was near the train station in the centre of town. It's where the young marine wannabes would come before getting the train back to the training centre. It was renowned for being the chosen hangout for the testosterone-filled angst-ridden late teens. A short train ride away from the Lympstone Commando stop. They got drunk in the city to get away from the watchful eyes of the COs. Adrian pushed through to the bar. He was pretty sure that the girls who came here weren't eighteen yet, you could usually tell because of the excessive make-up. Just for tonight Adrian wasn't a police officer. Just for tonight? Who was he kidding? He let them finish their alcopops and display their bare midriffs, cleavage and thighs all in an effort to pull the most obnoxious of the boys, as if their volume and bravado was an indicator of their importance in the group, it was like watching Animal Planet. Adrian wasn't fucked up like that, he appreciated how easy it would be to be interested in these eager young women and he thanked the stars that he wasn't. Everyone has a secret behaviour they are ashamed of, something they try to suppress, something inside that constantly tries to force its way out. We all have something that will not be denied.

He watched the teenage girls being mauled by the overenthusiastic hyenas. He saw the boys indiscreetly slipping their hands between the girls' thighs and pressing up against them. He remembered Andrea and how they had made out like this when he was younger, not too long before Tom had come along. They had been younger than this and they would cling to each other like no force on earth could tear them apart.

Adrian ordered his third drink from the bar, already knowing how he was going to end his evening. It's easy to start a fight in a place like this without even throwing a punch. He took a deep breath and turned away from the bar, scanning the close proximity for a female, apologising to his body before committing this act of treason on himself.

'Can I buy you a drink?' Adrian walked a few steps towards a plainer girl that appeared to be alone. She was standing next to her friend who was in the throes of a rather unbecoming embrace with one of the men.

'No, thanks.' She half smiled, uncomfortable but still cocky. Sucking her vodka pop through a straw until the final drops rattled in the bottle.

'You sure? You're getting low there.'

'Hey, old man, she said no thanks, are you deaf?'

Adrian felt a hand on his shoulder.

'I'm just being friendly.'

'Well, go be friendly someplace else, she's with me.' A freckle-faced nineteen-year-old stood behind Adrian with his arms folded, presumably in an effort to make his biceps look bigger.

'Really?' Adrian scoffed. 'With you? She's well out of your league, mate.'

'Just leave it out, "mate". You've been told nicely.' He was holding his head high, making sure that everyone around knew who had the upper hand.

'By you?' Adrian turned to the girl. 'I bet this guy wasn't your first choice. Got stuck with the runt of the litter, did you?'

She was enjoying the attention, her female companion even seemed a little jealous that two men were fighting over her plain little friend. The pub had quietened and people were starting to watch. It wouldn't be long now; the young man would have to save some face somehow.

'What are you saying, old man?' he said. Adrian saw his knuckles getting whiter around the base of his pint glass. He hadn't quite decided if he was being insulted or not.

'I'm saying, I'm surprised you didn't have to roofie her to get her to let you touch her.'

Adrian thought he might have to bait the boy some more by cracking some insults about his mother as he saw him obviously trying to quell his anger. Apparently not. Adrian saw the clammy fist quickly approaching his face. Adrian could take a punch. He barely even recoiled, which seemed to anger the young man even more. The marine was holding back though, he was still so cocksure of himself that he didn't want to lose it completely in front of the young woman in hooker shoes. He saw the foam gathering in the corner of the marine's mouth.

'Is that all you've got? My dead grandma hits harder.'

There it was, the uppercut. Harder to pull off if your opponent is fighting back, but Adrian had no intention of fighting back. It was better than his right hook anyway. His ears were ringing but he still heard the rest of the pub laughing. Within moments he felt fist upon fist until he was on the ground shielding all the important bits. The shrill sound of the girls screaming mixed with some encouraging chanting and the occasional giggle.

'Shit, he's a fucking copper!' Adrian heard someone exclaim and the beating stopped. His wallet had made its way out of his pocket on to the floor in a bid to save him, traitor. He was mildly annoyed that he had even brought it out at all. There was a neurochemical imbalance in Adrian that could only be diminished by pain or humiliation. He had accepted this a long time ago. He was addicted to the rush he got from being beaten. It triggered the same stress reactions as intense arousal, only without the intimacy or the feeling of want. It was a way to forget himself. He attributed this to both his addictive personality and his fucked-up family. As someone who had always been in control, had taken hold of his own life at a young age, forced to assume the role of parent both literally and figuratively,

Adrian needed to be out of control once in a while. He couldn't bear the thought of putting anything stronger than alcohol in his body and on the occasions when he had done that the self-reproach lasted a lot longer than any bruise. He thought back to the times when he saw his father wasted and high, wielding a knife, hurting others, hurting Adrian. At least this way he knew the only person getting hurt was himself. This was a fix, nothing more. Adrian's dad had always maintained that he was like a cockroach, indestructible. He didn't feel that way when the owner of the pub helped him to his feet and showed him the door.

Adrian staggered towards his house. He looked for the dark spot in the street where the street lamp outside his house was broken. He could make out shapes, he could just about see the pavement. His eye was so swollen he could feel the pressure of his eyelids being forced together by the blood that was pooling under the surface of his skin. His eyelashes were beginning to matt together. He should have had a couple more drinks before instigating the fight. Usually in this situation he couldn't tell if he was concussed or just very drunk. He was in fact just sober enough to realise that he needed to sit down. He saw the step outside Uncle Mac's corner shop and headed for it, it was a little closer than the ground and he could use the door to steady himself on the way down. He slumped against the door, even with the wall for leverage it was a long way down. The blood had stopped seeping from his nose but his ribs still hurt, they weren't broken, he knew what broken ribs felt like, but it still hurt every time he drew breath. Adrian felt the door behind him give way and he found himself lying flat on his back looking up at the shop girl.

'Are you OK?' she asked him, she was kneeling on all fours looking straight into his eyes, all the lights were off and there was no one else there.

Adrian struggled to take in a breath before heaving himself upright again. She sat on her heels watching him as he laboured to his feet.

'I didn't mean to disturb you, I'm sorry.'

'No, please, come in, let me help you.' She smiled and took his arm. He followed her inside, he was still curious as to why she was in there at all.

She led him to the back of the shop and opened the big green door that led to the storage cellar. She helped him down the stairs and he saw there was a fold-out bed in the corner of the room. It occurred to him that whenever he saw her she was wearing the same clothes. She lived here. There was a small toilet cubicle behind a curtain with a sink and there was a counter top with a kettle. She turned the kettle on. He leaned against the wall and watched as she gathered a hand towel and some bandages. She poured some boiling hot water into a bowl and brought all of the items over on a tray which she placed on the floor. Adrian had never really looked at this girl before. She was young, he wasn't sure how young though, and her eyes were so brown they were almost black.

'You don't have to do this, I can make it home.'

'Please, let me.' She smiled as she dipped the towel into the boiling hot water.

He flinched as the steaming towel touched his skin. She mopped away the blood from under his nose and his lip. She went to the sink and rinsed the towel out with cold water before giving it to Adrian to put on his eye. He winced as he leaned forward, instinctively putting his hand to his side. She slowly reached up to his collar button and undid it, she continued to undo his shirt buttons and he watched through his one good eye.

'Why are you helping me?'

'You are always nice to me.' She smiled.

Adrian felt kind of bad at this point because he could only remember seeing her on one or two occasions in the past, she had not registered with him as someone he was either nice to or not. Obviously the brief encounters they had had before had meant something to her at least. Which in turn begged the question, was no one else nice to her? As her fingers brushed against his bare, bruised skin he couldn't help but look at her in a different way. She was very pretty and he had never seen her hair down before, it was always swept up in a bun, but at this moment it was trailing down her body and resting in her lap. He hated himself for always boiling everything down to this feeling of desire, as though he had no control over it, as though it were an involuntary reaction. It was still sore to breathe and he held his breath as she pulled his shirt further open, the bruises were really starting to come up now, so was the swelling. She pressed on his rib and he flinched again.

'It's not broken,' he whispered through the pain.

'I will wrap it anyway, give it some support. I think

'it is still deciding whether it is broken or not.' She looked up at him.

'Your English is very good.'

'Thank you.' She looked away. 'Stand up, please.'

Adrian stood, it got harder to move every time. She slid his shirt off of his shoulders and threw it on the bed, it was still caked in his blood and a mixture of alcohol from when he lay on the floor and people poured their drinks on him. What a waste. She started to wrap the bandage around him, getting really close as she passed the bandage from hand to hand behind his back. Adrian couldn't help himself, as usual, he leaned forward and kissed her. She pulled back surprised, shocked in fact.

'I'm sorry, I don't know why I did that. Well, I do know, you're beautiful and I'm an idiot.'

She tucked the bandage into itself and walked over to the sink to wash her hands. 'You looked like you needed help, I hope I didn't give you the wrong idea.'

'It won't happen again, I'm sorry. You didn't do anything wrong.'

'You think I'm beautiful?' She smiled.

'Yes, I do.'

She turned back to him and pulled her T-shirt over her head, she stood there in nothing but her skirt.

'What are you doing?'

'I like you, you're kind to me.'

Adrian couldn't ignore his surroundings. He also couldn't ignore the pain he was in. He picked the crochet blanket up from the bed and walked over to the girl, wrapping the blanket around her.

'You don't need to do that, I shouldn't have kissed you like that. I'm sorry.' He put his hand under her chin and kissed her again, this time on the forehead. Her eyes were glistening, threatening to cry. He hoped to God she didn't cry, then he would feel like a complete arsehole. He pulled her to him and hugged her, she buried her face in his bare chest. 'I don't even know your name.'

'My name is Eva.'

He stood there holding her against his broken body, but feeling as though he were the least damaged person in the room.

Chapter 30

The Daughter

Laughter. She could 'cope' with laughter. Imogen slipped the key into the lock and pushed the door open. She stepped over the bundles of old newspapers and wine bottles, making sure she didn't accidentally step on one of her mother's many cats. The laughter seemed to be coming from the living room. Part of her wanted to walk out and leave, like she did every time she visited her mother, which was most days.

'Immie! Immie, is that you?' an excited voice came from inside. Imogen's palm rested on the door for a moment while she composed herself, she put on her best carefree smile and pushed the door.

Imogen's mother, Irene, was sitting on the sofa next to another lady around the same age as her. The lady had her arms full of Irene's belongings, the good stuff, what little was left of it anyway.

'Hi, Mum, who is your friend here?' Imogen looked straight at the lady who was desperately trying to avoid eye contact.

'This is Wendy-Julia, we met in the library.'

'Let me show you out, Wendy-Julia.' Imogen held the door open and Wendy-Julia walked out carrying her plunder. At the front door Imogen stood in her way. 'You can leave the stuff on the sideboard there.'

'She offered, said I would be helping her out.'

'Well, you will be helping me out if you leave it behind.' Imogen pulled her badge out and showed it to the lady who huffed and put the stuff down. Same old story, Imogen thought as she shut the door behind the woman. Her mother would pick up waifs and strays and give them all of her things. One day Imogen came home from school to find her mother had allowed a homeless man to move into her bedroom. Imogen often saw women in the neighbourhood wearing scarves or jewellery that she had bought her mother for Christmas. This was the reason why she stopped buying her anything worth anything. Her mother was ill, but not the kind of ill you can see, not the kind of ill you can put a plaster on or diagnose definitively. Every few years the diagnosis would change. This was also the reason why Imogen hated labels, she knew they only meant something until the terms of your illness were redefined and then you got a whole new crazy badge altogether.

'You staying for dinner, Immie?' Her mother's face was alight with fondness as she walked back into the room. It was nice to see her smile, in the brief moments when it occurred Imogen treasured it, never knowing what the next moment would bring.

'No, I can't tonight, Mum, I have to work.'

'Well, that's just fucking typical, isn't it? You don't give a shit about me! I know you wish I was dead.'

'Why would I want that, Mum?'

'Because I'm a fucking boulder round your neck, you don't even want to spend time with me.' She began to sob.

'Of course I do, Mum,' she half lied, sitting next to her and smoothing her hair. Irene blinked a few times, obviously trying her hardest to be normal. 'How long have you known Wendy-Julia?'

'We just met today. She's such a sweetie, offered to come round and clean for me once a week. Apparently when she was in the womb she ate her twin, can you believe that? That's why she's got that funny name. Her mum gave her both names!' Irene said excitedly, forgetting about her recent outburst.

'Sorry to do this, Mum, but I really have to get back to work after lunch.'

'I wish you'd get married and give up that silly job.'

'Even if I did get married, I wouldn't give up my job.'

'It's not decent, a woman in that profession.'

'I'm not a prostitute, Mum, I'm a police officer.'

'Same difference,' she huffed.

'Come on, I'll make you some dinner before I go.'

Two hours later, Imogen followed Denise into her flat. She was struck by the whiteness of everything. It was so clean and uncluttered. A stark contrast to her mother's place. She couldn't imagine living like this.

'Do you want short or long?' Denise called from the bedroom as Imogen loitered in the hall, unsure what to do with herself. 'Come in here, Grey.'

'You can call me Imogen, if you want.' Imogen walked into the bedroom and saw Denise scooping handfuls of dresses off the rack in her wardrobe and throwing them on the bed. The room was lined from wall to wall with a built-in set-up. Imogen felt a little sad for her modest chest of drawers at home.

'What size shoes do you wear?'

'I'm a six.'

'Perfect!' Denise slung open a door to reveal an obscene amount of shoes. 'Who knew we had so much in common.'

'Not me, that's for sure.' Imogen concentrated really hard on not rolling her eyes. This was very sweet of Denise, even if Imogen didn't 'get it'.

'Well, if it's black tie you should probably go with a long dress. Who are you going with?' she asked. Imogen noticed a slight inflection in her voice, as though she were trying not to sound interested.

'Detective Miles.'

'Oh.'

'It's a work thing, there's nothing going on between us.'

'I've heard that one before, that's like . . . his shtick, isn't it?'

'Is it? I mean seriously nothing. I'm totally not his type. Why? Have you got a thing with him?' Imogen wasn't sure if she wanted to know the answer to the question, it felt like a betrayal of Miles' trust to ask any questions about him when he wasn't present.

'It's funny that you think he has a type. And anyway "thing" is a strong word for what we have.' Denise picked up a navy blue satin dress and held it up against Imogen before screwing her face up in disapproval. It obviously wasn't right. She looked up at Imogen. 'We fuck five times a year.'

Next she held up a white evening gown and smiled excitedly.

'I'm not wearing a white dress, a little too bridal for my taste. Besides, Miley might freak out.'

'Oh, I have the perfect dress, here.' She pulled out a deep emerald-green corseted mermaid dress. 'Trust me, it will look amazing. Take your stuff off and I'll help you get into it.'

What the hell, Imogen thought as she pulled her sweatshirt over her head and stepped out of her jeans, glad that she had shaved her armpits and worn a vaguely matching under set for a change. She knew that Denise's underwear would match. Why was she even worried about this? She could see Denise's fleeting look of curiosity at her scar, but she ignored it as she stepped into the gown. Denise laced her up and spun her around.

'Oh, you're his type, honey, underneath those big ugly clothes of yours.' Denise beamed and thrust Imogen in the direction of the mirror.

'Wow, thank you,' she managed to say after realising it was her own reflection in the mirror. Imogen looked good, she had to admit it.

'Now for the hair, sit on the bed.'

'I'm not sure if I can sit, it's pretty tight.' She waddled to the bed and perched on the edge. Denise rifled through one of the drawers and pulled out a strange hair contraption. In one scoop, twist and click Imogen's hair was in a French roll, wispy tendrils hanging down at the front.

'To be honest, Grey, I think you will get away with just a little lipstick, you look so lovely.'

Imogen didn't have female friends; she had been friends with her male colleagues at her old precinct and they had all shown her exactly how much she meant to them when the shit came down. So there it was, she didn't really have any friends, so this was weird. She felt the urge to hug Denise, which was out of character for her, but she stood up and did it anyway.

'Thanks, Denise, I really appreciate this. I mean that.'

'Here try these on.' Denise handed her a pair of six-inch black suede heels.

Imogen parked her car round the back of the museum, it was still light out and she didn't like the idea of walking through the city centre in this dress, she didn't like people looking at her at the best of times. But here, in this dress, she felt like even more of a spectacle. She took a deep breath and held the sides of the car door frame, hoisting herself forward with momentum. This dress was not built for comfort. She left the black suede shoes on the passenger seat; no one would be able to see her black leather boots under the dress. She told herself that she needed to be able to run if the situation called for it, she was on the job after all. Of course, that was a lie. She had been a nervous wreck since she left Plymouth and even this, dressing like this, made her feel vulnerable, exposed. They had no idea what they were walking in to, she needed to know she could escape without getting a stiletto stuck in one of the fancy iron grates in the museum floor. She needed to know she could get away.

Chapter 31

The Warrior

Then

Abbey lay on the floor looking up at Christian. His face was white with fury, or maybe it was fear. Whatever it was it made a change to see some emotion in him, part of her wondered if he was faking it to get her to react. There was no one else in the museum. It had been stupid of her to think that she would be safe here. The security cameras were just for show, Mr Lowestoft had told her that it was enough of a deterrent them just being there. She had convinced herself the past was behind her but now here it was, literally staring her in the face.

'I saw him . . . I saw your dad that day. I saw him a couple of other times, too. I figured he was going to make a scene or something, embarrass himself. I didn't think he would do something like that!'

'I don't know what you're talking about.' She crawled backwards on her hands, eyes fixed on him.

'I'm not here to hurt you, Abbey.' He held his hand out to help her up. 'I just want you to talk to your dad, get him to admit what he did.'

She ignored his hand and stood up of her own volition, still backing away from him. He kept moving forwards, slowly, hands outstretched with a beseeching look on his face. If she hadn't known him the way she had, she might even think he was sincere. For a moment she wished her father had succeeded in his plan to get rid of Christian, he wouldn't be standing here now; she would be walking home for the first time in months without looking over her shoulder. She wouldn't search the faces of every person on the street in case he was approaching her, or standing somewhere in among the crowds. But he had failed and now she had to deal with him. Again she found herself frozen in fear, unsure of what to do next.

'They arrested me, questioned me like a criminal . . . They think I killed Jamie . . . they think I killed Dani . . .'

'You are a criminal.'

'Oh come on, that was just a misunderstanding.'

'Misunderstanding, that's one way of putting it.' She looked either side and behind her, frantic, searching for something she could use as a weapon. 'I can think of another way to put it too.'

'We didn't hurt you though, did we? You were up for it, Abbey, you were so wasted and you were all over me. I don't want to hurt you now either, I want you to talk to your dad for me.' Christian kept walking forwards, she knew she couldn't outrun him, but she had an advantage, she knew the museum. She made a break for it, bolted, running up the mahogany staircase towards her little makeshift workshop, there was a lock on the door, and she could keep him out of there.

She got halfway up the stairs and looked behind her to see he was gaining ground, if she even slowed a little he would be able to grab her. She wasn't built for this. She ran to the far corridor, his smell was getting stronger but she didn't want to check how close he was this time, she felt a tug on her cardigan and she shook it from her, he could have it.

'Abbey just wait, I don't want to hurt you!'

She made it past the threshold of her work room, she grabbed the door to push it shut but he was already there. He grabbed her by the shoulders and slammed her against the wall.

'Let go of me! Let go of me!' she shrieked and thrashed. He looked genuinely upset that she would not indulge him; as though it never occurred to him before that anyone might refuse him anything, that anyone might dislike him.

'Please, I can't go to prison for this! You know it's wrong!'

'I don't know what you want from me! Even if what you were saying was true, why the hell would I help you?' She felt his grip loosening, he moved his hands away and rubbed them through his hair in frustration.

'You're a good person, you know it's not right!'

'I'm not putting my dad in prison for you, Christian. You took everything from us! My dad's been going crazy because of what you did, he lost his job!'

'You're the one who told him!' He pulled at his hair some more.

She sidestepped across the room. He was too preoccupied to see what she was doing. She reached her fingers across to the desk, making sure not to make any sudden movements. She could see he was on the edge and she already knew what he was capable of. She managed to get her fingers on the handle of her scalpel. She pulled it gently towards her and slipped it off the table and behind her back. She was still finding it hard to breathe around him. Why didn't she go for her phone instead? She knew the answer of course, she couldn't call the police, he would tell on her father, something he hadn't done until now. Why hadn't he?

'Why haven't you told the police about my dad?'

'The lawyer told me not to say anything about any of it. I don't want to come off as crazy or desperate, apparently. I wouldn't have made bail if I was considered a flight risk.'

'Are you a flight risk?'

'My dad wants me to leave the country, said he doesn't care about bail money as long as I am safe. He's made arrangements with a private company to smuggle me out.' He laughed nervously. 'I think he thinks I did it!'

'So you get to be all squeaky clean someplace else?'

'You don't know the kind of pressure my dad puts me under, he has all these expectations and sometimes I just need to blow off a little steam.'

'By assaulting people?' She gulped as she said the

words, unable to be any more specific about what exactly he had done.

'That's not what happened and you know it. You wanted it, Abbey! You wanted me!' he shouted, he was so loud, the words echoed and rattled around inside her skull. He was right, she had wanted him. She almost found herself seeing the reason in his argument but then she remembered Jamie. She remembered the hands over her mouth, she remembered the smell of their alcohol-ridden breath as they took it in turns to violate her. She remembered the sound of their laughter and she remembered the photos she had seen posted on social media, the things people had called her. No, she hadn't wanted any of that.

Before she even had time to think she saw the blood, pumping rhythmically from Christian's neck. She wasn't even sure if he had noticed yet, he looked confused and pale, so pale. She looked down at the bloody blade in her hand, she dropped it instantly. She could see his eyes losing focus, his pupils getting bigger and smaller, even his body was confused. He swayed a little and looked down, his hands were red, his shirt was red, so bright, so utterly single minded in its redness. One hand reached for his neck, he had finally realised what had happened. His other hand reached for her, she couldn't move back, there was nowhere to go, but he wasn't moving forwards, he was gradually falling away from her, an incredulous look on his face. He fell on to his back and she stepped forwards, standing over him, still staring at his eyes. Blood was seeping from the corner of his mouth, he was still looking at her but the brightness of his eyes was fading, his hand fell away from his neck and for a fraction of a second she saw him pleading with her, but then there was nothing. He was gone.

There was no panic, no crying, and no thought to calling her father or the police. The system wasn't fair; she knew his father would go after her. There would be no calling it self-defence. The law had proved already that regardless of the truth it was not always on the side of justice. The pumping had stopped and now just a steady stream of blood oozed from his neck. His skin was already beginning to lose its human appearance, becoming translucent. The blackened red circle beneath him grew steadily, she had to do something.

She grabbed some dust sheets and placed them around him, hopeful that they would absorb the majority of the blood, she knew she needed to let him bleed out. She grabbed the scalpel and made nicks in his wrists and ankles, so he could bleed more. The blood was slowing, the heart had stopped so there was nothing to force it out of his body.

She was going to embalm him and then she was going to hide him; she had known it from the second she had stuck the blade into his neck. It was instinct. He could never be found. She looked across her modest work space and saw the samurai warrior's armour lying polished and ready, as though the universe was giving her an out, reimbursing her for all it had taken; restoring the balance. She began the process by gathering as much formaldehyde as she could, there were large plastic bottles of it in her store cupboard, she didn't have enough and so she looked for something to mix it with. She saw the large sacks of plaster sitting in the corner, she used them to make casts of the animals where the carcass needed to be replaced and re-skinned. She mixed the plaster and the formaldehyde in a bucket and then attached the pumping mechanism that the museum kept in case of flooding. She grabbed the rubber tubes and connected them to the body, putting them in the major veins for the noxious liquid to be pushed around the body, replacing whatever blood was left and pushing it out of the arteries. The smell of the formaldehyde was making her giddy, she had to go and find more dust sheets. The ones she had laid down already were saturated.

When the liquid coming out of Christian's corpse finally ran pale pink she turned off the pump. It was approaching ten o'clock at night; she would have to phone home and lie to her father. She had learned the importance of lying since the attack, she knew the truth was not always what people wanted to hear; sometimes it was better to keep the burden of truth to yourself.

She worked determinedly. She had put the large sodden red canvas sheets into bags, the smell of them was sweet and sticky, the unmistakable stench of death. She wrapped the body in wire to help her pose him and then tied ropes around his wrists, placing him on a clean sheet. It had been three hours since he had died, and she knew that rigor mortis would start to be an issue soon, between two and six hours. She hoped the embalming process would interfere with it long enough for her to finish. She dragged him across the hall and into the Asia Room as though she were a horse and he were the carriage, the rope cutting across her stomach. The glass cabinet was ready for the samurai warrior. She could do this. She ignored the aching in her bones as she tried to lift Christian. With the plaster and formaldehyde running through his body he was even heavier than before, he must have weighed more than twice what she did. But she persisted, there was a way, there had to be. She threw the rope over the beam and pulled it so that Christian was upright. His eyes were still open, part of her wanted him to see everything that was happening, just like they had made her watch. She had to work fast to pose him before the glutinous concoction set inside him. With the help of some props she managed to get him to stay in place, she had used a nail gun to secure him to the large wooden brace inside the space that would now be his resting place. She used bandages soaked in plaster to encase his skin so he would just look like a plaster cast of a man under the armour, not that this box would be opened again for a long time. She started to dress him, she had her needle and thread and sewed him into the position she wanted. She sewed his eyelids shut and wrapped a black gauze blindfold over them, so there was no chance of him being seen through the bronze mask that would eventually cover his face. Finally the leather plates were positioned correctly and laced together. The sun was fully up. It was only a matter of a few hours before the museum staff would show up.

She was exhausted but there was no evidence that the samurai was not just her finest piece of work to date, there was also no evidence that he was real. She dragged the bags full of stiff and bloodied sheets down into the basement where the furnace that heated the museum was kept. She turned the heat up and started to throw in anything that could connect Christian to the museum. She found a day-rider bus ticket in his pocket and was relieved that she didn't have to move his car. She scrubbed the floors and locked the office when she was done, she didn't want to look at it again for a while. She would call in sick today. She could barely move her arms or legs through fatigue. She could not wait to get home, to lie in her bed, to sleep, to dream. She closed the door to the museum and locked it, sneaking away before any of the other staff arrived.

She slept like she had been awake for a thousand years, a sweet blissful sleep. Her father was right, the world was a better place now that Christian and Jamie were no longer in it. This was her chance, she had a place in the world and this time no one was going to take it from her.

Chapter 32

The Chair

Adrian waited on the steps to the museum looking at his watch. It was ten past eight, Grey was late. Various faces from the community had already arrived but there was no sign of DCI Morris.

'You look good in a tux, Miley. Even with a black eye.'

If it weren't for the familiar turn of phrase Adrian would not have placed the woman, but it was Grey, she was the only person who called him that. He posed his lips to give Grey a compliment but the look in her eyes made him think better of it.

'You're late,' he finally said, unable to verbalise or even form a thought about the way she looked. Of course she looked good, but he wasn't going there, not with her.

'Took me about twenty minutes to get out of the car! This dress was not made for driving!'

'Certainly not in a Mini.' He smiled. *Keep your eyes on her face*, he repeated to himself over and over.

'What happened to you?' She pointed at her own eye.

'I walked into a door,' he said indifferently before turning and walking up the steps.

'Where do we start?' She shuffled after him, accepting the blatant lie.

'I say we split up and have a look around, I'll see if I can get into the old guy's office again, you try and keep him out of there.' He paused at the top and leaned in. 'If you see the boss, come and find me, don't talk to him on your own, not until we know what's what. I've got a really bad feeling about this.'

'Don't worry about me, Miley, I can look after myself.' She smiled uneasily and he thought about the last time she had said those words to him, he thought about the scar that ran the length of her torso and he patted her on the shoulder. He knew she was nervous.

They walked in and showed their invitations. They didn't even bother to check the names, just invited them inside.

There was no sign of Lowestoft or in fact anyone else that would fit the bill of the other murder victims. So far the victims had all been a similar age, but everyone at this party was somewhat younger. Miles managed to slip past the security guard who was fawning all over the receptionist, getting angry if she even spoke to any of the well-turned-out men who had come alone. Adrian recognised that type of anger, jealous anger. His father had been a similar type when he was alive. If Adrian had had time he would have stopped to pay her some attention, just because men like that wound him up. But there were more important things to be getting on with.

Adrian walked the length of the corridor that led to the director's office, it was dark in that part of the museum, eerie. He put his hand on the door knob and suddenly a flash of the doctor's conservatory came into his mind, the blood, the cat. The horror of that scene had stayed with him, what if something like that was behind this door? *Brace yourself.* He turned the knob slowly and waited for the click, he pushed the door open a slither and peered inside. The room was dark and empty, the cold twilight pouring through the window and casting its greyish glow across the desk. He crept inside, closing the door quietly behind him. He walked around to the desk, it was tidy and when he tried the drawers they were locked. He pulled out a pocket torch and shone it on the back wall. He could see certificates of excellence and various awards from professional bodies that Adrian had never heard of. There was nothing of any use to be found here without leaving a mess, and without a search warrant that kind of stuff got tricky to explain. He walked back out and straight into a girl. He fumbled with his mind to think of an excuse as to why he would be in the room.

'Are you a police officer?' she said. The question was unexpected.

'Yes, I was just looking for Mr Lowestoft. Do you know where he is? I'm Detective Miles.' He held out his hand but she ignored it.

'What do you know about Mr Lowestoft?' He could

hear tremors in her voice, she was nervous. What did she know?

'Do you work here?'

'I do. My name is Abbey Lucas.'

'Why wasn't your name on the staff manifest?'

'This place is full of liars, Detective. There are a lot of things that aren't what they seem.' She tried to smile but all that came out was a twisted imitation. Adrian wondered what her part in this story was.

'What things?' He stopped and looked at her.

'There's something I want to show you, would you come with me?' She turned and started walking away.

'OK.' He shrugged and followed. There was something ghostly about her, she was a strange girl with her soft-spoken voice and her dark eyes, not dark as in brown but dark as in haunted. He kept to her side as she walked through the crowds of people, he saw Grey looking at him and he shrugged but continued to follow the girl through to one of the exhibition rooms on the other side of the museum. She stopped in a room full of dead birds, resting her fingers on the glass cabinet that housed the ravens; she stared inside and Adrian could see tears in the corners of her eyes.

'Are you OK?' he asked. Stupid question, this girl was clearly not OK.

'I want you to promise me something.' She turned to him, her eyes imploring. It was like looking at an orphaned puppy or something equally as helpless. She put her hands on his and stared up at him. 'Promise me!'

'What is it?' He wanted to be able to promise but he knew better than to make a promise to this girl, not when he knew he couldn't control what was to come next.

'I'm showing you this so that you understand, so that you know what he went through. What they did to him. Why he became who he is now.'

'What they did to who?'

'He was just a child, they made him like this, but if you knew him like I know him then you would understand that this was the only way it could end. I know that better than anyone.'

'What did you want to show me?' He pulled his hands away. She knew, she knew who the murderer was.

She pulled at the display case after clicking a switch and it moved right away from the wall to reveal a secret space behind. It was dark inside, he could see the full moon behind the stained-glass window but it offered no illumination. Adrian didn't want to step inside, seeing the image of the pathologist yet again – it came to him in fleeting visions when he felt threatened. Right now he certainly felt threatened. What was he walking into?

'Do you have a torch?' She smiled and stepped in before him.

Adrian flicked on his torch and shone it in front of him. He remembered what Gary Tunney had said about satanic cults as he looked around the room. There was something very evil about the arrangement, chairs facing a central point, almost like a stage. The floor was stained and Adrian didn't need to use his imagination to figure out what transpired inside this room. The girl walked over to the corner and seemed to disappear into the blackness, but he could still hear her. Something clanked and he heard the sound of iron scraping against more iron. Was she going to kill him?

'Hello?' he whispered.

She returned with a book and handed it to him, he pulled some latex gloves from his pocket and put them on before taking the book.

'This is what they did, those men that died, this is what they did to him. They cut him and burned him; they broke every part of him. They made him hurt others.'

He opened the book and glanced at the pictures, he saw images that were reminiscent of the crime scenes except the same person was in every single one. He could see the faces of some of the perpetrators. He saw the pathologist, the director and he also saw the familiar face of his boss, a much younger DCI Harold Morris. His stomach lurched at each image. These people were respected members of the community, these people were in positions of trust. He saw his son's former headmaster, Jeff Stone, wielding a brand and pushing it into the flesh of the boy, the smoke in the picture demonstrating the heat of the instrument, the damage it was inflicting.

'Why did they do this?'

'Is there any reason that would be good enough? They did it because they were sick inside; they did it because they wanted to do it. Because some people believe that they have a God-given right to subjugate others, to reign supreme over us and we are nothing but their playthings.' The tears lingered on her eyelashes, threatening to fall at any given second, but he could see she would not let them.

350

'Where is he now? Your friend . . .'

'I don't know. I swear I don't. I was with him earlier but when I woke up he was gone. That's why I am showing you this. I saw you here earlier and wanted to make sure you had all the pieces to put together before he got hurt. I know you're going to catch him, I think he wants to be caught. He wants to be punished for this.'

'You asked me to promise you something?'

'Yes, I just wanted to make sure you heard him out. Promise me you will do that one thing. He's not a bad person.'

Under normal circumstances there was no question what Adrian would do next. He would arrest the girl and take her back for questioning. Somehow that felt like the wrong play here. He felt sick that he didn't know who to trust back at the station, that he couldn't guarantee this woman's safety. She had come to him, she had shown herself where she could have stayed off his radar; he made the only decision he felt he could under this unique set of conditions.

'I'm going to need to talk to you later, will you be here?'

He glanced around once more before leaving, chills coursing through his body. This room had been here for centuries, he was sure it could wait a little longer, at least until they knew who else within their department was involved. Tipping them off now, before they had questioned Morris, could be a huge mistake. Adrian was running purely on gut instinct at the moment. When he came out of the room the girl was gone, he pushed the door shut and then went back to find Grey.

*   *   *

351

Imogen chose the orange juice from the trays that were being handed around, wishing she could choose the champagne instead. She grabbed a handful of vol au vents from the accompanying tray, the server trying to keep the look of disgust from his face as she took every single one from the platter and nestled them against her breasts in a napkin one handed while she tried to down her drink, in order to pick up another flute before he walked away. She was a nervous eater and she hadn't eaten anything today. She was aware that when she took this dress off she would have imprints where the seams had been pressed into her skin; it had been a while since she had worn anything so tight. Immediately she could feel the orange juice had made its way to her bladder, this should be interesting.

She walked down to the ladies' toilet, she noticed an air of impending doom when she was alone in these corridors, something wasn't right. As she walked through she became increasingly aware of the shadows from the corner of her eye. She thought there was movement but when she turned her head to check, everything was still. The low tone of the continual monotonous narration in the Roman Exhibit Room sounded like sinister instructions here in the dark.

In the bathroom it took all of her skills as an aficionado of yoga to negotiate her way to her underwear without undoing the dress. She was well aware that if she unbuttoned it she would never get it back on again and would be forced to either spend the rest of her life in the museum toilets or she would have to walk out in just her knickers, because in her wisdom, Denise had made her take off her beige T-shirt bra. Moving around in a tightly fitted evening gown was remarkably more difficult when the space you had to move around in was less than two feet square. Eventually she had to break out of the stall just to get the dress back on right without also pulling her pants down again at the same time. One of the impossibly elegant patrons watched as Imogen wrestled with the dress.

'Can I help you?' Imogen snapped at the woman and she went back to reapplying her lipstick.

As she was walking back towards the party the security guard walked up to her with a glass of champagne in his hand.

'Having a good time?' he asked. He had a sleazy smile on his face. She may not have shown it but on the inside she was rolling her eyes.

'Should you be drinking that? Aren't you on duty or something?'

'It's free. There aren't many perks to this job, as you can imagine. Although right now this definitely feels like one.' His eyes moved down and up her body. She suppressed the urge to groan. He swallowed the contents of his champagne flute in one gulp.

'I need to get back to the party now,' she said impatiently, she didn't have time for this.

'How about a private party? Just you and me?' He moved in a little closer, putting his hands on her hips and sliding them around to her backside. That was not the first drink he had had today, she could see he was drunk, he might have even been high too, his eyes were practically swirling.

353

'Wow, as enticing as that offer is,' – one-handed she reached into her bag and pulled out her wallet, flipping it open and holding the badge in front of his face – 'I think I'll pass.'

He held his hands up, a broad smile on his face, staggering backwards a little and chuckling.

'I wouldn't mind some of your police brutality, gorgeous.'

'Fair enough.' She smiled and looked around to check no one else was there. She slid her dress up her thighs a little to give herself some mobility before thrusting her knee into his groin. Still smiling he crumpled on the floor and whimpered. She straightened herself up and walked back to the party.

'If I could have everyone's attention, please!' the blonde receptionist called out. 'Could you follow me to the ballroom, we are going to formally announce the reopening of the museum, as well as some exciting news about upcoming events and exhibitions.'

The people followed the girl and waited outside the double doors. A thick purple ribbon stretched across the door and the receptionist held the scissors. Imogen guessed there was a little over a hundred people there, she recognised a few of the faces as people she had seen in the newspapers at one time or another. She also recognised the designer labels, dresses that probably cost more than a month's rent. Not to mention the shoes, generally too tight and restrictive but so elegant, she watched some of the women slip their feet out when they thought no one was looking, flexing and stretching before cramming them back in again. She smiled to herself as she thought about her boots under her dress. She checked her watch. The blonde nodded to a man in a bespoke suit amongst the affluent crowd, he walked over with a smile on his face, taking the scissors from her. She whispered something in his ear and he continued to smile although Imogen noticed it was a little more strained.

'Well, Mr Lowestoft asked me to say a few words after him, but apparently he's been taken ill and is unable to be with us tonight. My name is Matthew Holder and I will be taking over from Ted, Mr Lowestoft, when he retires.' After a few 'aww's and some clapping, the man raised his hands to calm the crowds, the same nervous smile plastered across his face. 'Let's have a look at this room then, I've heard it really is a remarkable spectacle. Please feel free to take pictures, but no flash photography.'

Some people pulled their camera phones out to record the moment for posterity. Holder lifted the scissors and cut through the ribbon, more clapping ensued. The girl grabbed the handles to the double doors and pushed them both wide open. Holder still faced the crowds and smiled.

Imogen took a few moments to register what she was seeing.

A few gasps from the crowd and then suddenly a bloodcurdling scream. She pushed through the people.

'Police! Let me through!' Imogen called out, she could see the phones still up in the air recording the sight of a naked Theodore Lowestoft, strapped to an iron chair and open from groin to sternum, his face completely mutilated, cut from ear to ear, his tongue gone and just a clear view of the hollow where it should have rested.

She immediately regretted eating all of the canapés and took a deep breath. 'Turn your phones off, please, this is a crime scene. Close those doors!' Matthew Holder turned and looked inside the ballroom and immediately doubled over, retching. Imogen rushed past him and grabbed the door, pulling one side closed as the receptionist pulled the other side. Shutting Lowestoft inside, preserving the crime scene.

Imogen reached into her bag and pulled out her mobile, she dialled Miles but she heard his phone before she saw him.

'What's going on?' he called across the people, pushing his way to her.

'We got our next victim, Miley.' She tried to make light of it but she could tell she was failing. He put his hand on her shoulder to steady her, he was considerate like that.

'Everyone just go and wait in the lobby, please. Nobody leaves!' Miles shouted. He pulled out his phone and dialled 999, although the emergency was clearly over. Lowestoft was beyond dead.

Imogen walked over to the security guard who was still nursing his ego, but if nothing else her little 'intervention' had sobered him up.

'I need you to make sure no one leaves. Do you think you can do that?'

'Yes, ma'am.'

'It's Detective, I'm not some shrivelled-up old spinster asking you for a favour.'

'Sorry, Detective, whatever you say!' he sneered before walking over to the main doors and shutting them. The guests began complaining. 'Sorry, people. You'll just have to sit tight.'

'How bad is it?' Miles came over and asked her.

'As bad as anything I've ever seen.'

'I'm not so sure about that.' He held up a big leather-bound book with an ominous glare. 'I don't know if you even want to look at that, I wish I could un-see it, kind of like a lot of things about this case.'

'Show me,' she said. He already had gloves on, there was no point in both of them handling it.

'Your decision.'

He opened the book and showed her what was inside.

'I think we might have found our motive,' she managed to say as he turned the pages. The breath was knocked out of her and she could feel the panic rising again. He closed the book; she couldn't deal with that right now. First they had to deal with Lowestoft.

'I'll call the station.' Miles still had his phone in his hand.

Imogen walked over to one of the many servers who still stood dutifully dotted around the room. She grabbed two glasses of champagne and drank them fast. Fuck it. Miles walked back over to her.

'Any news on the boss?'

'No, but they got a call out to Mike's place. He's dead . . . He hanged himself.'

'Jesus! Daniels?' Imogen knew he was on the edge, she had seen it in his eyes after he had told them his

357

part in all of this but she hadn't expected this. 'I don't know who to trust any more, this is so messed up.'

'Well, you can trust me.' He smiled. Yeah she could, she knew that much. Like him she had been on the periphery from the start, from before they had even met. Now the facts were coming out every turn seemed to wield new horrors. The end must be in sight soon, how much longer could this go on? It seemed to be getting more and more public, which was usually a good indicator that things were about to come to a head. Were they the only people looking for the truth? It occurred to her after looking in the book that they might even be on the side of the killer, whoever he was.

'Where did you get this book?'

'A girl who works here, she gave it to me. She showed me the room in these pictures, it was bloody horrible. I've never seen anything like it.'

'Where the hell is she now? Aren't we going to bring her in?'

'She came to me, Grey, just like Ryan came to me, and now he's dead. I don't know who to trust either and I can't have someone else's death on my conscience. We don't know that Daniels was the only one involved. For all we know someone killed him because they saw him talking to us at the station.'

'OK, maybe you have a point. So who was she? Why did she show you?'

'So I could understand, apparently, and the most worrying part of it is that I think I do.'

'Still, you can't just go round killing people.'

'No, you can't. Although I'm starting to think maybe this case is the exception to the rule.'

They could hear the sirens outside. She nodded to the security guard who opened the door. Imogen breathed deeply and looked at the faces of the uniforms and detectives, wondering how many of them had been a part of this, wondering who else was under Morris' thumb. Thank God she wore flats, this was going to be a long night.

Chapter 33

The Son

Another morning, another shower that wasn't quite cutting it. Adrian wanted to wash his brain clean. He had seen a few messed-up things in his time on the force but never anything like this. Some people spent their whole careers looking for a case like this, something big and juicy, something that gets you medals and accolades. Something that gets your face splashed all over the news. All he wanted was a night's sleep without the gruesome images making cameos in all of his dreams. Grey had been right. The sight of Lowestoft was as bad as anything he had ever seen. The sheer hate was written all over the crime scene, this wasn't just about killing Lowestoft, it was about humiliating him, defiling his beloved museum, showing the world his secrets. The truth would come out now, it had enough momentum to get through the fog and reach daylight. Adrian had

360

told the police that arrived on the scene about the secret room and right now they were pulling it apart, taking photos, logging all of the evidence. He could only imagine the DNA samples; he knew that room had seen some things. He had logged the book and given it directly to Gary Tunney to see what he could ascertain – dates, times, anything. He needed to find out as much as he could about this. The boy in the pictures had been bent to the point of breaking, why? Abbey Lucas had been right too, there was only one reason anyone would do something like that. Because they got off on it.

Adrian stood in front of the bathroom mirror and wiped away the steam, looking at his body in a whole new light. He appreciated the fragility of life, knowing there was less than an inch of skin and flesh between the outside and his insides, one sharp cut could change all of that. He looked at his scars and thought about subject 89; suddenly they didn't seem so bad. From the other books in the room, that spanned back to the early part of the nineteenth century, he ascertained that the other eighty-eight 'subjects' were well documented, and also met their demise in that foul room. He thought about growing up with his father, the systematic violence, watching his mother cowering in a corner for most of his youth, followed by unexplained bruises and unconvincing excuses. He knew that seeing those things had changed him. The beatings had made him different to the other kids. Most of the people who went through what he did ended up like Ryan Hart, fighting their way through the world. But one day on a domestic call to the Miles household a Detective Morris had taken Adrian to one side and reassured him. Morris had given him a few comforting words and a phone number, a direct line in case he ever needed anything. Morris was the reason Adrian had joined the police force. He found it hard to reconcile what he had known of that man and the man who was at least partially responsible for the horrific images of torture that occupied the big leather book. Morris had been his mentor, his rock, the one person he had always thought of as family when his own family had been such a disappointment to him. His father the junkie and his mother who just put up with the drugs, the beatings and turned a blind eye when he turned his fists on Adrian.

Adrian's phone rang and snapped him out of his unwelcome nostalgia. He looked at the screen, it was Andrea again. He couldn't deal with her today. She always did this; always called at exactly the wrong time. He would let it go to voicemail. No doubt she was returning his calls about Tom's school, but that conversation would have to wait for now.

Adrian walked into the police station. Denise was blotting her eyes with tissue. The news about Daniels had spread like wildfire. She looked up at Adrian and looked away quickly. He thought he should say something comforting but that was not within the parameters of their friendship so he carried on walking. Grey shook her head as Adrian walked into the incident room, there was still no sign of Morris. No one knew why Daniels had killed himself except Adrian and

Grey, he suspected Morris probably knew why too, wherever he was.

'Do you think he's still alive?' Grey asked quietly.

'I think we would know if he wasn't. The man who did this isn't hiding any more; he wants the truth to come out.'

'I agree.'

'I think Morris is the encore, Lowestoft was the main event. The museum is being investigated now, evil room and all. Lowestoft's connection to the other bodies will come out. Luckily those sickos kept good records.'

'Do we know any more about the killer?'

'The girl at the museum knows who he is. We could have brought her in but I don't feel like we can guarantee her safety.'

'It's a horrible feeling, isn't it?'

'Must be déjà vu for you?'

'Well, yeah, especially seeing as most of those d-bags are here. I know I don't trust any of them. I wonder now if Morris brought them here to mess me up. He knows the history; my old DCI was his golf buddy. I bet they had a good laugh about what happened to me.'

'What did happen to you?' Adrian asked, knowing full well that she had left out some of the details.

'It's not even worth talking about, Miley. All you need to know is that they didn't get what they were after. Not really. The last case I worked on, the drugs case back home, I wasn't quite supposed to make it out of there alive.'

'Was anyone arrested?'

'Yes, a couple of people. Our main suspect died in custody though. Naturally that was my fault, too.'

'Shit. Kind of puts my mishandling of evidence into perspective,' Adrian said.

'Yes, doesn't it just?' She smiled reluctantly. 'Come on. Let's focus on this case. One disaster at a time, huh?'

Adrian felt the vibration of his phone against his backside. He pulled his phone out, Andrea again.

'What is it? I'm working!' he snapped.

'You were supposed to have Tom back by ten this morning, Adrian. Why are you at work? Where's Tom?'

'I don't have Tom, what are you talking about?'

'He told me he called for you to pick him up, we had a disagreement. Where is he, Adrian?' she spat out, he could hear her anger dissipating into worry.

'He never called me yesterday. I don't have any missed calls from him.'

'No, the day before. He must have called the station, then.' The words rang out in Adrian's ears. He ran over to Denise's desk, all calls went through her.

'Denise!' Adrian called out, she looked up. 'Did Tommy call here Friday?'

'Yeah, you guys had left already though.'

'Did anyone speak to him? Who spoke to him?'

'Daniels, he was standing right here when the phone call came in, took it straight off me.' As she said the words Adrian lost his focus entirely. Daniels was dead, where the hell was Tom? He looked down at his phone, it was still connected, he held the receiver up to his mouth.

'Listen, Andrea, I don't know where Tom is.'

'What the hell do you mean?'

'I never spoke to him Friday, I swear.'

'He wouldn't just go off on his own.'

'I know. You need to trust me; I'm going to find him.'

'Trust you? How am I supposed to trust you, you lost my son!'

'Well, no, if we're going to point fingers then it's you that lost him, but that doesn't help anyone.'

'You bastard!'

'This is what I do, Andrea. I will find him, I promise.'

'Let me speak to Harry.' She was breathing heavily, her voice was raised and he could feel the anger but the only thing he noticed was the word Harry.

'Look, call around his mates, he might have just pulled a fast one. It's probably nothing. He's a teenager.' He hung up the phone.

Grey was standing next to him, staring at him with a concerned look on her face. He didn't want to say anything in front of Denise, he didn't know if she was on his side or not.

'Denise, if anyone calls for me, I called in sick today, OK? I mean anyone! I'm taking a personal day.'

Adrian could barely feel the ground as he ran towards his car.

'I'll drive, Adrian, get in my car,' Grey called out to him. He didn't want to argue and he couldn't even see straight so he jumped into her car. Grey drove like a maniac at the best of times, he knew she wouldn't hold back. No sooner was his backside on the seat than the car started moving, the momentum slamming his door shut for him. She raced out of the car park as he punched Morris' address in the navigational computer.

'What do you think about Denise?' he asked Grey as he switched on the sirens and lights; she looked puzzled at the question.

'You want relationship advice right now?!' Grey didn't take her eyes off the road.

'No! I mean, do you think she knows where Tom is?'

'Definitely not. No way.'

'You don't think she's in on it, then? You don't think she was working with Daniels and Morris?'

'There's no way, Miley, trust me. That woman is batshit crazy over you, if she knew anything she would have told you. Trust me, she would never deliberately do anything to hurt you, especially not something like this,' Grey said. He had never even considered that Denise might have genuine feelings for him, he felt momentarily bad for their relationship but he didn't have time to worry about that right now.

Grey zipped through the traffic and ran every single red light, the sat-nav barely keeping up with her. She screeched to a halt outside the house and Adrian was out the door before she even had the handbrake on.

'Call Denise, tell her what's up, Fraser too. I trust him,' he called to Grey, and he ran towards the house. 'We don't know how wide this goes so I think at this point less is more.'

The front door to the house was ajar, Adrian burst through it more than a little scared of what he might find. There were myriad possibilities and very few of them were favourable situations. More than once over

366

the last few weeks they had stumbled across the aftermath of an incident that was unfathomable. He couldn't allow himself to think of what might have happened to Tom. Until he definitively knew any different there was still time to save him. He ran through the house thrusting doors open. There was a strange emptiness about the place, as though it had been deserted. Adrian heard a noise upstairs and ran as fast as he could, pushing open the bedroom door. Adrian balked at the sight of Morris' shirt, it was covered in blood. Harry was folding his clothes and putting them into a suitcase, he was unusually calm given the circumstances.

'Damn, I thought I might make it out of here,' Morris said as he carried on packing.

'Where is he?'

'He's safe, don't worry.'

'If you've hurt him!' Adrian screamed.

'Don't worry, Detective, he's got some pretty good moves, look what the little fucker did to me!' Harry turned his head and pointed at his ear, it had been torn away from his head slightly; it was where the blood was coming from. *Atta boy, Tom.*

Grey burst into the room behind Adrian, she was out of breath.

'There's nowhere to go, boss, just hand over the kid before you get into any more trouble,' Grey panted.

'My two favourite fuck-ups, let's not forget poor old Mike, too. The fucking dream team you lot were.' Harry chuckled. 'Obviously handing Tommy over got the better of him and he decided life wasn't worth living any more.'

'Where is my son, Harry? Where's Tom? You're like

family! You've known him since he was a baby. What have you done to him?' He had to stay angry, it was the only way, anything other than anger and Adrian couldn't handle this, anything other than anger and he would have to accept the distinct possibility that Tom was dead.

'Here's the deal. Tom is somewhere safe, for now. I don't know how long he will last where I have left him, though. You're going to let me go and then when I am where I need to be, I will call you and tell you where he is.'

'There's only one problem with that plan,' Adrian said, feeling sick with every word he uttered. 'I don't trust you.'

'That's unfortunate, but what choice do you have?' The sound of Harry's voice was gloating. He knew he held all the cards, the only card that mattered. 'I don't know if you know this, but a lot of my friends have been dropping like proverbial flies, I need to get out of here, I need to disappear.'

'I know what you and your friends did. A book has come into my possession; I saw what you did to those boys. You people deserve every bit of pain that is coming your way.'

'I wouldn't expect you to understand what we were trying to achieve.'

'I don't think you were trying to achieve anything. You were just a bunch of perverts.'

'Hey!' Harry shouted defensively. 'We were God's soldiers! We were fighting for the human race. To rid the world of the scourge that is homosexuality.'

'You're kidding, right? Do you even know what Kevin Hart was doing on the weekends?' Grey said.

'He knew he was sick, he knew he needed help.'

'Sick is right.'

'And you, you stupid bitch! What do you know about honour or loyalty? Look at what you did at your old force, tore the place apart.'

'Sounds like an excuse for a lot of angry young men to spend a lot of time together all cosy in a darkened little room, if you ask me. God's soldiers my arse.' Grey smiled. What was she doing? Miles had seen her act before; she antagonised people to get them to make mistakes. Adrian didn't know what her play was but he was glad that at least she had one, he couldn't even think straight.

'Shut your filthy mouth.'

'You don't like women much, do you, boss? I mean, look at you, you're still single, why is that? Maybe you just can't face what's inside you.' She was slowly moving forward and Harry was too angry to notice. She was getting to him.

'It was a mistake putting you two together, I hoped you would bring each other down.' He looked at Adrian. 'I can't believe you fell for her shit.'

'All I want is Tom. Then you can go wherever the hell you want.'

'I had my eye on you, you know, Miles? When I first met you, you had all the signs, troubled background, daddy issues, the whole deal. I even told my friends about you. We were going to teach you the right way after we had finished helping Sebastian. Then there was the fire so we had to put a hold on things. Then you got Andrea pregnant and there was no need.'

'You're fucking crazy! You didn't help anyone!' Adrian remembered the pictures of the boy, Sebastian must have been his name. He was nauseated that Harry had considered him for 'treatment'. He thought about the pictures again and felt sick at the idea of Tom being alone with Harry, even though he had been many times before in the past.

'Hello Harry.' A voice came from the doorway. Adrian turned to see a man dressed in black. The man turned to Adrian and smiled, almost embarrassed. 'Detective.'

Harry's demeanour changed again, he was afraid.

'Sebastian, you've grown.' Harry backed away as the man moved forward.

'My name is Parker now.'

'I can't let you hurt him . . . Parker, he has my son.'

Harry lurched forwards and grabbed Grey, he had a gun in his hand. He pressed it hard against her throat. Adrian recognised it instantly as the gun that he had supposedly lost in the evidence against Ryan Hart.

'Up to your old tricks again, Harry?' Parker said.

'You leave me alone or none of you will ever find the boy!' Harry shouted desperately.

Adrian looked at Parker, the man who had apparently perpetrated all of the hideous acts he had seen over the last few months, then he looked at Harry. If Tom's life weren't at stake then he might let Parker have his way with Harry, it scared him that he felt that way.

'Harry, if I let you go then I'll never see Tom again, just take me to him, you and me, no one else.'

'You can't make that promise!' Harry screamed back.

'Fine then, me and Grey, we leave now, we go and look for Tom and you and Parker here can have a good old catch-up.'

'You won't find him without me.'

'Grey, are you OK?' Adrian asked, noticing the colour had drained from her cheeks.

'I'm fine, don't you worry about me,' she gasped, Adrian could see she was anything but fine.

Morris grabbed her by the hair and yanked her backwards forcefully, edging closer to the exit. He slid the barrel of the gun into the gap in her blouse and yanked it downwards, the buttons flew off and her shirt flew open. Adrian could see her chest heaving, she was struggling to breathe; he knew a panic attack when he saw one. He saw her scar again. It ran from under her breasts to way down past her waist, he wondered how she had survived a cut like that. Morris pulled her back to look at it.

'I heard all about this, at least I finally get a chance to see it.'

'Fuck off!' she spat at him. He pressed the gun against the remodelled skin.

'It's harder to cut through skin that's already healed, isn't it, Parker? I bet a bullet would do it though.' Morris stroked the scar with the back of his hand. Adrian's eyes stayed on Morris' finger, checking he didn't put any more pressure on the trigger. 'Do you know the story behind this, Miles? Or haven't you had your hands all over it yet?'

'Shut up, Harry.' Adrian found himself clenching his

fists, wishing to God he didn't have to hold back, wishing he could paint the walls with one good punch.

'Grey here was lucky enough to be spared the inconvenience of motherhood. Apparently it didn't suit her professional aspirations.' He pulled her close to him, the gun thumping against her waist. 'She's going to be coming with me now. I'll take her to Tom and then . . .'

'You're not taking her anywhere!' Adrian said. The panic was evident on Grey's face. 'Take me if you have to take anyone!'

Adrian looked at Parker, still focused on Harry but his eyes were glistening. Just then Grey grabbed hold of the gun and pushed her finger hard down on Morris' causing the gun to fire through her shoulder. Just under her collarbone. Morris recoiled back grabbing his arm, the bullet had gone straight through the fleshy part of his bicep. Imogen slumped to the ground, doubled over and covered in blood. She had one knee raised to her chest in an effort to slow the bleeding or control the pain, Adrian wasn't sure which. She needed a hospital but Miles couldn't let Harry out of his sight. Morris pointed the gun at Parker and fired, Parker dived on to the ground. Morris moved around the room, firing until the clip was empty, then he ran out of the room. The sound of his car starting followed just moments later. Adrian rushed to Grey's side and grabbed hold of her hand.

'What the hell did you do that for?'

'Don't worry about me, Miley,' she barely managed to say.

'You can look after yourself, I know.'

'I had a plan.'

'It was a terrible plan, Grey.' He stroked her forehead and her smile turned to a sob.

'I couldn't let him take me!' she said through clenched teeth, tears rolling down her cheeks. 'I'm so sorry . . . oh my God . . . Tom.'

'I will look after her.' Parker put his hand on Adrian's shoulder. 'Don't let him get away. Go and get your son.'

Adrian looked at Parker, he had a decision to make only it didn't feel like a decision at all, he had no choice. He had to go after Harry. He looked down at Grey again and she was so completely white, like porcelain, he couldn't see the freckles across her nose any more.

'I should arrest you,' Adrian said to Parker.

'I know,' Parker said, he ripped the sleeve from his jacket and pressed it against Grey's wound.

'If I see you again I will arrest you. That's a promise.'

'I know.'

'I'm sorry, Grey.' Adrian took the keys from her pocket and rushed out of the room; leaving her in the hands of the perpetrator of the most violent and horrific acts he had ever seen.

Chapter 34

The End

Adrian couldn't think about Grey as he followed Harry, he was a fair distance behind him but he knew where he was heading – the airport. Harry had a friend on the airlines; in fact, Adrian didn't doubt that he had friends everywhere. He had seen the face of the killer and it was not what he expected. He expected a monster but instead all he saw was a lost boy. He saw someone who had been unravelled, someone who had been unmade. It's a terrible thing to have your mind played with, for someone to fundamentally change you from the inside out. Of course every person you meet in life has an impact on who you become, no matter how small the interaction, everything matters. Like finger-prints on a sheet of paper that is being passed down a line. Some fingers are dirtier than others; some leave a more permanent stain. He thought about Andrea and how she would be beside herself, for all of her numerous faults her adoration of Tom was not on the list. She was a genuine and warm mother, a damn sight more than Adrian had ever had. He couldn't think about what Andrea was going through right now, and if he told her what he knew she would be even more distraught, so he just centred all of his thoughts on one thing, getting Tom back.

It was hard to maintain the focus on the task at hand when the task at hand was so utterly horrifying to contemplate. Adrian had to disassociate his feelings or he wouldn't be able to do this. He was doing this for Andrea. If he actually thought about where Tom might be or what he was going through he could feel his heart tie in knots, he would be no use to anyone, so for now it was someone else's problem. It couldn't be his.

The turn off for the airport was next, Adrian put his foot down, knowing that Harry's adrenaline would surge now, the idea that he was almost away, almost home free. Adrian pulled into the taxi bay at the front of the airport and ran out of the car, into the airport and up to the security personnel on the door. They reached for their batons as they saw him approaching, he realised he was still covered in Grey's blood so he held his badge up for them to see.

'I need you to secure this airport, there's a very dangerous man here.'

'I'm sorry, sir, we would actually need some kind of official documentation to put anything like that in motion.'

'I could just stand in the middle there and scream

bomb if you want? Help me out guys, come on!' Adrian pleaded with the guards.

'About five minutes before you arrived another guy went running through, he had some blood on him, too . . . and a badge. We asked but he said he had an accident with his clippers, showed us his ear so we let him through.'

'Thank you!' Adrian shouted as he ran towards the gate. Exeter airport wasn't very big and it didn't take Adrian long to reach the gate. He scanned the crowds but he couldn't see Harry anywhere. He saw a bloody handprint on the bathroom door. He couldn't imagine anyone getting away with this at Heathrow. He went in and Harry was standing at the sink scrubbing his hands. Harry's coat was on the counter and he had duct tape holding a tissue in place over the bullet wound in his arm.

'Where's the gun?'

'Airports, even the little ones, don't allow guns.' Morris shrugged. 'Frisk me if you want.'

'I'll pass, if it's all the same to you.'

'I had to try, you know?'

'I'm not letting you go.'

'You'll never see Tom again.'

'When you left I knew there was no chance I would ever see him again if I didn't catch up to you.'

'So what now?'

'You're going to take me to him.'

'Or what?'

'Or I just let your old friend find you. You saw what

he did to those other bodies. You should have seen what he did to Lowestoft.'

'They were all soft, he would never have got to me like that.'

'I will make sure he does, if you don't give me Tom I swear to God I will hold you down while he slices you open.'

'You don't have it in you, Miles.' Harry smirked, grabbing a paper towel and drying his hands.

'Try me.'

'You can't touch me, Adrian, I have people who will take you down.'

'What people? Daniels killed himself.'

'Mike Daniels was a stand-up bloke but no, I don't mean him, I mean people who matter, other people on the force, higher up than me.'

'What the hell were you lot up to? Why would you do those terrible things?'

'It was a different time back then.'

'Not that fucking different. Torturing kids? Jesus, Harry, you're Tom's godfather!' Adrian could hardly believe what he was hearing.

'We had a purpose, we had a mission! There's evidence to prove that you can change that kind of behaviour in people. You can make them normal.'

'What do you know about normal? Look at what you've done. You created a killer of the likes I have never seen before.'

'He was different. He had protection on the inside, his grandfather wouldn't let us do what we needed to do, he pussied out at the last minute. That's why we couldn't help him.'

'He didn't need your help! None of them did! There was nothing wrong with them!'

'Don't give me that liberal bullshit.'

'What about the boy, the homeless kid? He was one of your . . . victims.'

'Now that wasn't me. Pete took it too far. Made the other kid, Sebastian, watch while they cut his friend to pieces, that's what sent him over the edge, not what we did.'

'You think what you were doing wasn't too far?'

'You need to leave this alone, Miles, for your own sake. You have no idea how high this goes.'

'I'm not afraid of heights, sir. Whoever this person is, I'm not afraid of them.'

'You should be afraid. It's not one person, Miles, it's any person. These people are everywhere.'

'Were you getting kids from the school? Is that how you got them? Why did no one miss them?'

'The school had a deal with some of the foster homes in the area, they would take on the brightest and the best. All part of an outreach programme. Jeff Stone was in charge of that operation. The paperwork is never that tight on kids in the system, even now, but back then it was virtually non-existent.'

'The way you talk about it, it makes me sick. Can you hear yourself? You actually believe in that shit?'

'I thought you might understand. What we were doing was just our own little indulgence; our experiment. You rounded up all the players in that game, I'm the last one. But the thing is it's much bigger than that. There are people in this city who have a lot to lose if this ever comes to light. You wait. There are things going on that you just don't see. You're not even looking. Those people just let us do our thing as long as it didn't interfere with their operation. No one talks about them because you never know who is listening.'

'You're bluffing. Stop with this conspiracy nonsense, you sound even more nuts, if that's even possible. There is no "they".'

'I wish that were true. This conversation here has put me in more danger than I was ever in from that boy. They aren't interested in making things better, your case is going to disappear and maybe your career with it. I'm telling you, if you keep digging on this, Adrian, you're going to dig yourself into an early grave.'

'I think you're trying to give me a reason not to hurt you, but . . . I still really want to hurt you. More than that though I want my son back, Harry. If you really want to save your neck you'll give him to me right now.' Adrian grabbed his arm.

'OK, I'll take you to him.' Harry looked down at Adrian's hand. Adrian's fingers were white his grip was so tight.

Adrian marched Harry back to the car. He nodded at the security guard who had helped him before. If this panned out he would come back and thank him properly. Adrian cable tied Harry's hands together before throwing him in the passenger side. He got into the driver's side and they pulled out of the airport.

It was still light but the sky was grey, rain clouds

threatened as they drove along the dual carriageway towards the coast.

'Take the next slip road on the left,' Harry finally said. Adrian did as he was told. He wanted with every fibre of his being for this not to be a ruse, but there was a niggling feeling in the back of his mind, poking at him. If there was anything that Adrian knew about Harry it was that he knew nothing about Harry. Each revelation today had been more shocking than the last to the point where there was no familiarity any more. Harry was not a human being, Adrian could see that now. The veil was lifted and he could see the monster underneath.

They drove through a forest road lined with trees, like a tunnel of green, what little sun there was poked through the trees with a cold white glow. On the other side they were faced with the staggering beauty of the countryside. The patchwork quilt of greens and yellow, soft and billowing, like a blanket covering the vale. Tiny dots of rain appeared on the window, just a light shower. As Adrian turned on the wipers he heard a click, he looked over to Harry to see he had undone his seatbelt. Why? Quickly, Harry un-clicked Adrian's seatbelt too before grabbing the wheel and thrusting it to the right. Adrian heard the crunch as his car broke through the barrier, he saw the drop, quickly he grabbed at his seatbelt and plugged it back in. Then the force of the speed of the car versus the chunks of wood and rock that stood in its path meant the only thing left to do was pray this wasn't the end. Adrian had never been very good at praying.

*   *   *

Imogen couldn't feel anything any more, she could still hear and she could still talk, although she didn't understand the words she was saying. She was cold, she knew that much. She was grateful for the adrenaline, it was the only thing keeping her conscious at the moment. The man stroking her hair, he was this cold-hearted killer they had been chasing. She was propped up in his lap and he was holding her hand. He stroked her hair and he talked to her, soothed her, keeping her in the present. The last time she had been attacked there had been no one with her until the police finally came, she didn't even know if anyone would come. This felt so much better than that.

'The ambulance is on its way.'

'Thank you,' she heard herself say. She was somewhere between lucidity and a dream. She couldn't move towards the dream, the dream was the end.

'Keep talking to me. If you go into shock you will almost definitely die, stay with me even though it hurts. Your name is Imogen, right?'

'Yes, Imogen.'

She thought about her mother, how her mother would take her death as a personal affront. She could just imagine her telling all her friends, 'I told her it would end like this' as they comforted her at the funeral.

'Did you know that before Shakespeare, that name didn't exist?'

'No, I didn't know that,' she managed to say. She concentrated hard on his soft voice, concentrated even harder on what she was saying back to him.

'It was a mistake at the printers, they were supposed to type the name Innogen instead.'

'How do you know that?'

'I love to read. For a long time books were my only friends.'

'How did you get away?'

'I'll tell you if you tell me why you shot yourself.'

'A friend told me this was a good place to shoot myself. He forgot to mention how much it would bloody hurt.' She made a mental note to punch Tunney really hard in the shoulder if she ever got out of this.

'That's not what I meant.'

'Before I transferred here . . . I was on a case . . . I was held against my will and assaulted, stabbed and left for dead . . . I thought I was going to die . . .' The burning sensation in her shoulder was getting worse, she focused harder on what she was trying to say. 'I couldn't go through that again . . . I promised myself I would never . . . oh God . . . I don't know how you got through what you did.' She started to cry. 'I haven't slept since it happened, not properly, and it was nothing compared to what they put you through.'

She remembered the pictures from the museum and wished she could comfort him back. If he had been her son she would have taken care of him. When she had found out she was pregnant she had been shocked, unhappy, but when they stuck the knife in her she would have done anything in that moment to protect the life that had just begun growing inside her.

'I can hardly remember getting away, my mind has blocked out so many details. My grandfather gave me the key to the shackles I was in and some money to run away with,' said Sebastian. 'I started a fire. They

left me alone for a few hours, thought I was uncon-
scious, but I was just pretending; my body had stopped
responding to anything and so it was easy enough to
pretend to be out cold. So yes, I started a fire. There
are a lot of dry old things in a museum. I grabbed the
lighter from my grandfather's desk and set fire to a
diorama largely made out of husks, it went up so quick.
The official word was electrical fire, but that wasn't
true. My grandfather paid off the man investigating the
cause of the fire and no one was any the wiser.'

'Did you know the boy they killed?'

'He was my friend, he was the reason I was there, I
was the reason he was there.'

'You saw them kill him?' she whispered, finding it
harder and harder to talk. She felt as though she were
falling, she was waiting for the crash but it never came,
just this endless feeling of falling. *Is this what dying
feels like?*

'You can get through this, just stay awake, trust me.
It was a good shot, straight through, most of the danger
from shooting comes from infection if the bullet stays
in, we know it didn't do that. Come on, you can do this.'

'I can't.' She began to cry.

'Just focus on staying awake, I won't let you die.'

'OK,' she sobbed. She could hear the ambulance
coming, along with police cars. 'You need to go, if they
catch you . . .'

'I won't leave you.'

'Please, I promise not to die, I really promise.' She
couldn't save the baby that had been inside her,
she couldn't save the boys that had been tortured at

the hands of those animals, but she could at least give this man a way out, she would not be the reason he ended up in prison. She felt him gently moving from underneath her and slowly resting her head on the ground. He squeezed her hand affectionately and then she could have sworn she felt him kiss her forehead. She heard the window open and then she was alone.

'Can you hear me, darling? What's your name?' said the paramedic leaning over her.

'Imogen, like Shakespeare.' She laughed, at least inside her head she laughed.

The steering column pressed against Adrian's bladder, he didn't have the will to stop himself from urinating; when all was said and done that was the least of his problems. His mouth was both dry and wet at the same time and there was a crunchy feeling that he first assumed to be his teeth but soon realised was in fact the windshield, which had shattered on impact with the tree. The metallic wetness he could taste must have been blood from the tiny incisions the reinforced glass had made as it rolled around in his mouth.

He was still disoriented, the memory of the last few moments was trying to claw its way to the conscious part of his brain. A branch loomed near his face; he could smell the wet bark as it hovered under his nose. He could see Harry's body protruding from beyond the windshield. His body was stretched across the bonnet of Grey's car. There was no movement. He was dead.

Adrian gasped involuntarily, a desperate cry escaping his mouth. He was no longer able to subvert his feelings.

He knew he would never find Tom now. There had been a distinct possibility since he went missing that there was no Tom any more, that Harry had lied and Tom was already dead. If Tom was still alive then Adrian had no idea how he would find him, he had no idea if he would even make it out of this car. The salty taste of tears mixed with the metallic taste of blood made him queasy, his head was pounding. He reached down and unclipped his seatbelt. He couldn't feel his legs. He could see the light of his phone in the foot well of the car as it rang. He knew it was Andrea; even if he could have reached it he had no idea what he would say. He had no idea if he could even talk. He gathered just enough energy to spit the glass from his mouth. He pushed his arms against the wheel to no avail. Dizziness returned and the fog came down on him again.

Adrian could feel hands on him. He could hear a drill of some description followed by an unholy mechanical moan, the car cracking as the Jaws of Life spread it apart to make a safe passage for him. His whole body jarred as they moved him on to the rescue board, his muscles tensing against the movement, resisting liberation. Adrian's subconscious didn't want him to survive, neither did the fragment of consciousness he was trying to ignore. He knew that when he woke up the reality of losing Tom would be unavoidable so he tried to stay in this limbo as long as he could. He was somewhere between life and death, where time was both eternal and unmoving. He heard the voice of the paramedic trying to lure him back to the now but still he resisted. He wanted to scream at the man. *Leave me alone, leave me to die.* With every laboured breath Adrian was being sucked back into the present. No longer able to hide inside the safety of his own injured body and broken mind.

'Detective Miles, can you hear me?' The paramedic's voice was getting clearer. Adrian groaned, it was too late, he was waking up.

'Detective Miles, you have some fractured ribs and a nasty cut to your head, but you are fine.'

Fine. Now there's a word that means nothing, a word that people throw around. Adrian wondered if he would ever be 'fine' again. He ached inside and out.

'Harry,' he finally managed to utter through the oxygen mask. The paramedic leaned in and pulled the mask away slightly. 'Harry?'

'I'm afraid he didn't make it,' the paramedic said in a consoling voice.

Adrian closed his eyes, he was so tired, the oxygen made him feel lighter; he wanted to drift past the pain and into sleep. He was crying, he couldn't swallow, and he felt as though the weight of the world were gathered in his throat. Tom.

The next time Adrian opened his eyes he saw the blurred image of Andrea sitting by his hospital bed, her hair was down, no make-up on. She had been crying. He wondered if he should continue being asleep to avoid this inevitable interaction. He could hear the beeping of the heart monitor; the rhythm must have changed slightly because Andrea looked over. She came into focus and his heart broke yet again.

'Did he say anything about where Tom was before he died?' she asked. He could see that glimmer of hope in her eyes, hear it in her voice. He had no choice but to shake his head. She erupted into tears, he reached his hand over to hers and held it; she pulled away.

'How long have I been here?'

'A few hours. The police got a call when your car went off the side of the road last night. It was on the news, too. It's almost six a.m. now.' Her voice was monotone, there wasn't even any hate in there.

He struggled to sit up. He pulled the drip from his arm and ripped the wires off that were taped to his chest. He swung his legs out of the bed, instantly wishing he hadn't moved so fast. His ribs burned as he placed his feet on the ground, a jolt of pain surged through him like lightning. He steadied himself on the bed with his one bandaged arm.

'I need some clothes.'

'What are you doing?'

'I need to look for Tom.'

'You can hardly move.'

Adrian heard the familiar sound of Denise's voice arguing with the lady at the nurses' station. He turned back to Andrea and squeezed her hand.

'I promised you I would get him back.'

Walking was a new level of pain, his bruises had bruises. Denise caught sight of him and rushed to help him, he put his arm around her and she took some of his weight.

'Oh my God, Adrian, what the hell is going on?'

'I'm still pretty fuzzy on those details myself.'

'Morris is dead, Mike's dead and Imogen's just got out of intensive care.'

'She's here?'

'Yeah, I have been here most of the night, they wouldn't let me see you though because I wasn't family or something. Not until you woke up properly anyway. I can take you to see her, if you want?'

Denise found a wheelchair and helped Adrian into it. She pushed him through the hospital to the room where Grey was. As he looked at her body covered in wires and tubes he remembered the deathly shade of white she had been. He remembered leaving her there to die.

'Back again?' Grey smiled at Denise.

'Yeah, I brought you a visitor.' Denise went over and smoothed the hair away from Grey's forehead. 'I'm gonna go and get myself a coffee.'

Grey's lips were trembling; her eyes were full of tears. Adrian couldn't bear the weight of the guilt he was under but he had brought this on himself. He had allowed himself to be manipulated, he had been too trusting – not something he ever thought himself capable of. The goalposts had moved, the definition of evil that he had been labouring under had changed. It happens in other places, not in Adrian's world.

Grey held her hand up, reaching for his, he moved forwards and took it, she squeezed his hand tight.

'I'm so sorry, I let you down.'

'What are you talking about, Grey? You have nothing to apologise for. I'm the one who should be sorry. I didn't want to leave you there alone.'

'You didn't leave me alone.' She smiled.

'I left you with a psychopathic serial killer.'

'The doctors said he saved my life, he tied off the bleed and packed my wound. He called the ambulance and held my hand until he heard the sirens.'

'That should have been me. I should have been there for you.'

'Did you find Tom?'

'No.' Adrian shook his head, fighting back the tears. 'I'm going to go look for him now.'

'Good luck.'

Denise reappeared with two coffees and handed one to Adrian.

'Got anything stronger?'

'Sorry, Imogen, you are still nil by mouth.'

'You're lucky, this coffee tastes like shit.' Adrian forced a smile.

'I hope my car looks better than you, Miley.'

'About that . . .'

'It's my fault for insisting I drive, I could have done you a favour and let you drive that rusty old lemon of yours into a fricken ravine instead.'

'I should go. I'll come back and see you later though.'

'You better.'

Adrian walked into his house. It felt lonelier than ever. But it wasn't loneliness that he was feeling, it was loss, a loss he refused to accept. He thought of all the parents out there he had spoken to in the past whose children had gone missing, how he had felt bad for them and tried to comfort them. He realised now how empty his words must have been. Empty like his promise to find Tom. He had no idea how. He thought he knew Harry, he thought he was one of the few people in the world he could trust. He made his way upstairs into the bedroom and sat on the edge of the bed. He was still wearing his hospital gown, he looked at his arm and pulled at the bandage, exposing the stitched cut. He dug his fingers into the wound, ripping the stitches from the skin. He couldn't cry. He wanted to invoke a physical response that would make him cry; he needed to expel this knotted ball of anger, fear and sadness from his body. As a kid he was taught that crying was weakness and so he fought against it on a level below consciousness, it was out of his control. The blood came out but still no tears, always threatening but never delivering. Instead the saline clung to his eyeballs until they stung, but never venturing out. He watched the blood fall on to the carpet. He didn't care. He wanted to get dressed, to get up and fight some more, but he was just so tired. He fought against the urge to crawl inside a bottle and went to the cupboard, pulling out jeans and a shirt. He ripped the hospital gown off and threw it on the floor.

He looked down at the bandages across his ribs, red seeping through. He had an overwhelming urge to remove the bandages and put his fingers inside, to find the source of the bleed and make it bigger, until it swallowed him whole. He ignored the feeling and put his clothes on. The shirt immediately became saturated with the blood that was seeping from his arm. Walking down the stairs was every bit as painful as walking up them.

He thought his ears deceived him but as he approached the lounge he heard the television. Had he failed to notice it was on before? He picked up speed and saw Tom. Was he hallucinating? Had he passed out on the bedroom floor? Tom lay down and stared ahead. Yet again Adrian found himself wondering what the hell was going on. He rushed to Tom's side and finally the tears came, he put his arm around Tom, not noticing the sharpness of his jagged ribs any more.

'I thought I'd lost you!' Adrian sobbed.

'I didn't know where I was, I tried to get out. It was so dark,' Tom mumbled in between sniffs.

'Are you really here? How are you here, Tom?'

'A man helped me. I'm so tired, Dad.'

'OK, shhh, you go to sleep. It's OK, you're safe now.' Adrian stroked his hair and pulled out his phone ready to dial Andrea, God only knows what she was going through.

As he stood up he turned and saw Parker standing in the doorway.

'I'm sorry,' he said.

'Sorry? Why are you sorry? Where did you find him?'

'I have been following Harry Morris for a while, I know all of his secrets. He rents a single lock-up garage in that little village Pinhoe, just outside the city. This is all my fault. I'm sorry that I didn't kill them all a long time ago. If I had this never would have happened.'

'Who are you? Are you the boy in the pictures?'

'I was once, not any more.'

'How long ago was that?'

'Eighteen years ago now. I managed to get away from them.'

'The police are going to want to talk to you. Why did you come back? I told you I would have to arrest you if I saw you again.'

'I know. But I wanted to bring him home. It was important.'

Adrian looked over at Tom laying on the sofa. A part of him thought Tom was dead, he could still feel that ache in him. He had to keep checking Tom was real.

'Well, it's a good job I never saw you again, then,' Adrian said after some consideration.

'You don't need to do that, Detective. I knew when I started this that the possibility of me even surviving was slim. I am ready for my punishment.'

'I know it's not my call, but you have been punished enough, in my opinion, anyway.'

'Abbey told me she gave you the book. You can give that to the authorities if you want. They need to know what happened.'

'She's your girl? She cares about you a lot, I can tell.'

'She had nothing to do with any of this, she didn't know a thing.' He paused. 'There's another boy in that book, his name was Nathan Cole. I don't know the other boys' names but I knew him. His body was never identified. His family never knew what happened to him.'

'The boy in the case?'

'We were good friends once, apparently our friendship was cause for concern and my grandfather in his wisdom took me to see his friends.'

'Your grandfather?'

'He was a bitter, twisted old man. I was the only reminder of his dead son. In the end he did help me, it's the only reason I am still alive. Nathan wasn't so lucky. I watched them kill him, they made me watch.'

'Are you done now? Why did you wait so long?'

'I had promised the old man I would disappear. He provided me with a new identity and I was to stay hidden. I would not retaliate, but when he died there was no one to protect them any more. He left me the majority of his estate. I had more than enough money to finally put things right, for Nathan. In answer to your question though, yes, I am done now.'

'Grey and I are the only ones who know who you are, we won't be on the case any more and we only found you because you let us.' Adrian knew he couldn't take Parker in.

'How is she?'

'Alive, thanks to you.'

'I understand the burden of keeping secrets, Detective. I am not asking you to do this for me.'

'I know. I've done plenty of things I can beat myself up over, I have a feeling letting you go won't be one of them.'

'Then I am indebted to you.'

'You already gave me more than I can ever repay.' Adrian looked over at the sofa.

'Go be with your son, Detective. He isn't hurt, just a little confused. He was drugged I think, but he's OK. Take him with you when you go back to the hospital.'

'Thank you.' Adrian reached out and put his hand on Parker's shoulder. 'What will you do now?'

'I'm going to take Abbey to some of the places I've told her about. There's nothing to stop us any more.'

Adrian saw the beginnings of a smile on Parker's face. He knew this was the right thing to do. He didn't think he could live with himself any other way.

'Good luck, Parker.'

Adrian watched Parker leave. He couldn't believe that in his mind it was OK to let this man go, after the things he had seen, but it was, it was justified, he shouldn't be in prison. He walked over to the sofa and sat next to Tom, he could see he was still groggy. Adrian watched the beautiful sight of Tom breathing heavily as he slept off whatever Harry had given him. He should call an ambulance, but first he had to figure out how the hell he was going to explain any of it. He knew the shit storm that was about to hit was going to be incredible. He was ready for it. He had his son back and that feeling of hopeless emptiness was gone, he never wanted to feel that way again. There were now less than a handful of people in the world that Adrian trusted and that's how it was going to stay. He picked up the phone and dialled Andrea's number.

'Andi, I have him, I have our boy.' He barely believed the words as he said them but they were true. He heard Andrea sobbing and burying her face in her husband and him consoling her. He hung up and lay back on the sofa, finally allowing himself some rest.

He couldn't imagine the full story of what had happened coming to light, not if Harry was right about the magnitude of the corruption. There would be cover-ups and there would be lies. Adrian knew that his whole perspective had now changed and life would be more complicated than ever, but it's still better than living your life blind. All things told, he would rather know the truth, no matter how ugly it was. With his hand on Tom's head he waited for the circus.